W9-CJE-910

SECOND *wind*

SECOND *wind*

Neil Shulman, M.D. and P.K. Beville

authorHOUSE®

What happens when you grow old? Some folks stop working, some folks stop living, but others get
. . . a Second Wind

Stop the next time you go by a nursing home and check it out.

Ida will open the door for you and welcome you inside, the same way she did for customers at Best Mart for years. The man sitting at the checker board in the recreation room—the one with the hearing aid that only works when he wants it to—that's George. There's Beatrice Wellington, an elderly woman of regal stature and blue hair . . . her wheelchair is amazingly similar to the shiny black stretch limousine parked outside. And then there's Hank and Ethyl, both in their eighties; they have discovered love in the later years of life and live for conjugal visits each week.

Check out the dining room on your tour through the nursing home. You may see George's 'edible mural' of creamed spinach and squash on the wall. He finally got so offended at being fed soft old people's food that he created a lovely design in protest. You may see Dr. Price in the recreation room. The house physician can usually be found playing chess or checkers with the residents when he's not picking teams for wheelchair races.

Be sure to speak to the staff on your way out and tell them what a nice time you had. Tommy won't care too much—he's the juvenile delinquent who was ordered to perform community service at the nursing home in lieu of juvenile detention—but Patti, the director of nurses, will enjoy hearing about your visit. Michelle, the activities director, might even talk you into joining in a song with the Blue Bird Singers (they're always a sure bet on clearing the room).

So, the next time you drive past a nursing home . . . don't. Visit for a while. You'll be surprised at what you'll find. People participating in activities such as beauty pageants, raucous fishing expeditions, bingo and sex. Maybe, like these folks, you'll find a *Second Wind*.

AuthorHouse™ LLC
1663 Liberty Drive
Bloomington, IN 47403
www.authorhouse.com
Phone: 1-800-839-8640

© 2014 Neil Shulman, M.D. and P.K. Beville. All rights reserved.

No part of this book may be reproduced, stored in a retrieval system, or
transmitted by any means without the written permission of the author.

Published by AuthorHouse   12/23/2013

ISBN: 978-1-4918-4694-0 (sc)
ISBN: 978-1-4918-4693-3 (e)

Any people depicted in stock imagery provided by Thinkstock are models,
and such images are being used for illustrative purposes only.
Certain stock imagery © Thinkstock.

This book is printed on acid-free paper.

Because of the dynamic nature of the Internet, any web addresses or links contained in
this book may have changed since publication and may no longer be valid. The views
expressed in this work are solely those of the author and do not necessarily reflect the
views of the publisher, and the publisher hereby disclaims any responsibility for them.

Third edition, 2013, Rx HUMOR

For further information:
Rx Humor
2272 Vistamont Drive
Decatur, Georgia 30033
Tel: 404-321-0126
Fax: 404-633-9198

Soon to be a Motion Picture

*Dedicated to everyone
who has gotten a second wind.*

We also wish to dedicate this book to our parents, whose
insight and sense of humor has inspired us.

Mary Shulman
Herschel Stalvey
Gwyn and Judy Voss
And in memory of Dr. Israel Shulman and Katherine Stalvey

Acknowledgments

Thanks to Robin Voss for collaboration on this novel.

All names and characters in this tale are either invented or used fictitiously. The episodes are fictional although often inspired by real experiences.

A special thanks to John Beville, Evelyn Hershatter, Nancy Pender, Sandra Glass, and to all the residents and staff who are part of the eldercare family.

CHAPTER 1

S MOKE billowed from the back of the bright orange moving truck as it chugged up the hill, gears grinding with the strain of the engine. The three burly men sitting in the cab of the truck bounced along on the broken pavement of the rural Georgia highway.

"Don't think I've ever hauled furniture that big before," Larry said, stroking his beefy arms, "or that expensive—made me nervous."

"That butler is as big as the furniture. He spooked me," Carl said, leaning across Larry to spit tobacco juice out of the side window. He wiped the drool from his mouth with the back of his hand. "I thought if he warned me one more time, 'Please refrain from scarring any of Ms. Wellingtons possessions or I shall have to hold you completely responsible,' that I was gonna have to pop him one."

"Pop him one?" Charlie hooted. He slapped the steering wheel of the truck. "Pop him one? I saw the look on your face. You didn't look like you were gonna pop anybody."

"That dude was a long, tall drink of vinegar, wasn't he?" Carl laughed. "Sorta made me shrivel up inside when he locked those steely grays on me." The truck hit a pot hole, throwing the three men to the left of the truck cab. "Charlie, you better quit gabbin and start watching the road. You know that butler guy is gonna be wherever it is we're going, and he ain't gonna be pleased if you've scarred Ms. Wellington's possessions.'" He said the final four words with the affected air of a snooty butler.

"Where are we going, anyway?" Larry asked. "I can't say I've ever been in this part of Georgia before."

"Pull out those directions, Carl. I think we're getting close," Charlie instructed. "Stalvey, Georgia. There's something there about turning near a flea and antique market." Carl pulled a wrinkled piece of paper out of the glove compartment and turned it around and around in a 360 degree vertical radius. There was a puzzled expression on his face.

"Which way's up, man? I don't get it," Larry said, leaning over Carl's shoulder and gazing at the paper. Tobacco juice drooled onto the map from Carl's bulging cheek. Larry wiped the dark liquid away with a laugh. "You covered up the whole town, man." "Just give it here," Charlie growled, snatching the piece of paper from Carl's grip, which still held a severed corner. "Now look what you done, idiot," he snapped, glaring at the map. "Y all are so stupid, if you could read a map you'd see that we're supposed to turn right up ahead there. I knew y'all had problems with words, but this here's a picture."

Within the next mile, the flea and antique market announced itself in bright yellow colors and signs that alerted approaching motorists from one thousand feet on up to the front entrance: "Slow up or you'll pass it," warned one poorly lettered sign. "Whoaaaa!!!" the next one read, followed by "Boiled P-Nuts 4-Sale" and on and on they went. Carl down-shifted the rig before turning left by the bright yellow barn, the image of the large, looming butler in his mind. The winding, rural Georgia road took the trio through peach orchards and old farms, whose neglected out-buildings had long ago fallen in roof first. Soon, however, the road led to a fair-sized town bustling with activity. "Welcome to Stalvey—Home of Bucky Roach."

"Who the hell is Bucky Roach?" Larry asked. "I ain't never heard of him before."

The other two shrugged their shoulders.

"Wait a minute," Carl said in sudden recognition, "isn't he one of those wrestlers on TV? The one that runs around screaming all the time and dresses like a big cockroach?"

"Yep, you're right," Larry agreed, "that's Bucky Roach all right. Those big antennas he wears on his head are pretty funny." The truck cut an orange path through town, aggravating drivers who had to watch out for wide right turns and projectile tobacco juice, until it approached the opposite out skirting.

"Take that left up there by the 'Sea O' Suds' and we should be there," Charlie said, muttering more to himself than the other two. "The road ends right here at this 'X'—that must be her new place. Wonder if it's as big as the one she just moved out of?" he mused aloud.

"You know them rich folk. They don't down-size if they can help it," Larry said. "The other one was probably too small," he laughed, a touch of jealousy in his cackle. "She's such a little old prune; she probably needs that butler just to keep her from getting lost in that big old house."

"Yeah, that mean old dog could just sniff her out with a honker like the one he's got," Larry laughed heartily, then choked on his chewing tobacco.

"Milly's Merry Roost . . . what kinda name is that for a house anyway?" Carl asked. "That's what the butler said it was called. Wasn't the old one called Kensington Place, or something uppity like that?"

"Yeah, this one sounds like a 'ho house," Larry said, with the winking facial expression of a man who's been to a 'ho house before. The dead end was just ahead, but there was no sign of a house in sight. Instead, a dilapidated wooden sign that read, "Milly's Merry Roost—just ahead" was followed by an arrow pointing down what looked to be a long driveway. Charlie worried briefly about the top of the moving van taking down pine boughs along the tree-lined driveway, but forgot it when he saw The Roost.

"Well, I'll be damned." Larry whistled softly. "They're moving the old girl to a nursing home!" The three burly men were all quiet, caught off-guard by the appearance of an old one story nursing home instead of a sprawling Georgian mansion.

"Wonder if she knows that? She seemed awfully frisky for someone who's losing her castle and getting moved into a dormitory," Carl said. "Bet that sorry old butler didn't even tell her. You know her family didn't tell her—they spent all morning dancing around the old lady, talking to her like she was retarded or something. But now that I think about it, she was whisked away before we ever started loading anything. I'm not even sure she knew who we were," Carl said, his voice trailing away. He thought of his own mother who had spent the final four years of her life in a rundown nursing home. He'd hated to take her there, but he hated to visit her there even worse.

Charlie maneuvered the big truck to the front of the nursing home. "Go on inside and ask where her room is," he instructed Larry. "And wipe that spit off your face." After Larry had tumbled out of the truck and headed into the building, Charlie said, "Don't know how were gonna get all this stuff in her room. I've seen nursing home rooms before, and even the big ones ain't very big." Charlie pointed to the banner that hung over the front porch: Come See Our New Wing! the sign proclaimed. "Let's hope she at least got on the new wing."

Larry came ambling back to the truck, a wide, mischievous grin on his face. He stood outside Charlie's open window and beat on the side of the truck. "Yall ain't gonna believe this shit," he said.

"What?" both Carl and Charlie asked together.

"Unh uh, y'all see for yourselves. Come on, now, open the back of the truck." He slapped the truck door again. The two movers stepped out of the truck, stiff from the journey. Charlie unlocked the back door and with a snap it rolled upward, revealing the full-sized moving van's cargo of furniture. The musty smell of old furniture that hadn't seen sunlight in decades wafted from the assortment of heavy oak, dark material, and oriental rugs.

"So which two pieces of furniture are we going to try to fit in her room?" Carl joked.

"You'll see," Larry said, the wide smile returning to his face. "You'll see."

Charlie and Carl grabbed one of the end tables from the rear of the truck and Larry followed with a fringed table lamp. Charlie rested the table on his hip and held one corner with his left hand while he opened one of the home's front doors with his right. He turned around quickly, letting the door rest on his shoulder as he backed into the foyer.

"Good morning!" a bright cheery woman's voice screeched, causing Charlie to drop one corner of the table. "Welcome! And will you be needing a shopping cart today?"

"What the . . ." Charlie said, not able to see this audibly perky woman behind him. He quickly grasped the piece of furniture before it hit the floor.

"Ohmigod." Carl said, giggling, and he kept walking forward with the table so that Charlie could get a look at the woman. She was about five feet call, slightly rounded in shape, and was smiling as though someone had just handed her the winning lottery ticket. She wore an apron with tiny blue flowers all over it and tied behind the neck. A large plastic name tag that read: "Hello! I'm Ida!" was fastened to the front of the dress.

Charlie choked back a laugh and said, "Hi, Ida. You must work here. Can you tell me where this goes?"

Ida eyed the piece of furniture, her lips pursed and her fist cupped around her chin and a finger pointing outward. "Yes. Yes indeed I can," she proclaimed, as though she'd been giving directions to errant shoppers for years. "That's furniture, so it belongs in house wares. House wares are on aisle nine."

Charlie's mouth fell open. He was speechless. This woman couldn't be for real.

"If you need assistance finding aisle nine, I can have one of the boys take you back," Ida said sympathetically, as though she encountered direction-deficient shoppers every day. "You know, though, they generally bring the merchandise in from the loading dock, not through the front of the store." With that proclamation, she turned and shuffled away from them, down a hallway. Carl supposed she was going to get security to throw them out.

"Just keep going, guys," Larry laughed from the doorway. "I got directions from someone else." The three men made their way down the left hallway, tracking dirt on the dingy linoleum from the deep treading of their steel-toed boots. They glanced through doorways as they moved through the building, catching glimpses of old people in various positions of living: some watching television, some sitting, some rolling around in wheelchairs, some visiting with family or friends, some visiting with each other, others just staring vacantly. Though no origin was in sight, the sound of a poorly tuned piano accompanied by tinny voices reverberated softly throughout the halls. Larry recognized the song—"Farther Along"—as one his daddy used to sing all the time.

The smell of food was strong in the hallways, though dinner was still a couple of hours away. As an old man with a shuffling gait passed by, his nose tilted up in the air, he muttered, "The only thing they know how to cook around here are turnip greens."

The place looked as though it had been a long time since money had poured in—maybe since it was built. The vinyl couches in the TV room had been patched and repatched until they resembled furniture collages. There were worn down tracks in the hallways, signifying the high traffic areas, but the polish on it shone like glass. The dark blue carpet in the lounge had pale blue spots. Despite all that, the rest home was immaculate and sunny, warm and inviting. The staff of Millys Merry Roost had done the best they could with what they had. On the hallway walls hung bulletin boards of various activities. One held pictures of a recent party—one elderly man in a wheelchair sported a lamp shade on his head while dancing with a woman whose expression showed delight in his antics. Another bulletin board held a calendar of events for the week, with signup sheets below each announcement. All the signup sheets were full of signatures.

Still another bulletin board listed the meals that would be served that week. An elderly graffiti artist had drawn an angry slash through Thursday's "liver and onions" and had written, "Again? How about hot dogs?" As the three movers watched, the old man with the shuffling gait approached the bulletin board, tracing the day's menu with his finger. As his finger rested by the dinner menu, he wordlessly mouthed each food item for the evening, shaking his head. He shuffled away with a scowl, muttering to himself as his corduroy bedroom slippers flap-flapped down the hallway.

Carl was struck by one thing: the sizes of the rooms. They were not the smallest rooms he'd ever seen by far, but none were roomy enough to house the truckload of furniture that was waiting outside. He estimated that Kensington had been at least 20,000 square feet in size—big enough to house a bowling alley. By this time Larry had passed, going on ahead to lead the way. Larry stopped in front of a closed door. To the side of this door, just like all the others they'd seen so far, there was a small white index card with the name of the room's occupant penned on it: Ms. Beatrice Wellington. Another sign was taped on the door. It was a paper plate with the word WELCOME on it, made entirely out of dry macaroni and glue.

"Looks like she's already got a friend here somewhere," Charlie said. "That ought to make her feel better about moving into this tiny little . . ." he stopped in mid-sentence as Larry swung Mrs. Wellington's door open with a flourish.

"Welcome to the new wing," Larry said, laughing at the surprised look on his buddies' faces. The room was huge, about the size of the cafeteria they had passed earlier. The ceiling of the room was twice the height of any they had seen so far, including the hallway. Three of the room's four walls had windows, which soared to a height of nearly ten feet and were covered in heavy drapery. A crystal chandelier hung from the center of the room, and oak flooring glowed richly across the wide expanse. Carl knew where the furniture was going to go.

A commotion was beginning in the parking lot outside Milly's Merry Roost. Several of the patients had gathered on the front porch to survey the big black limousine idling beside the moving van. An elderly woman appeared to be sitting calmly in the back while a frantic young man ran from one side of the car to the other pounding on the window.

"Granmummy, open up, please. We were going to tell you once you got here," the young man yelled at the glass. The woman must have been deaf because she didn't even turn toward the commotion beside her head. The grandson was a weasel shaped man, probably in his late twenties, wearing an expensive suit and very shiny shoes. A red silk handkerchief peeked out of his breast pocket.

He turned to an imposing man dressed in a black suit who stood staunchly beside the limo. "Niles, why the hell did you teach her to work the power window lock?" he yelled, rubbing his hand through an already disappearing hairline. He looked pinched turning to the window again. "Granmummy, you know I love you so much, I would never do anything to upset you. Kensington was much too big for you—and I got a really good offer for it, too. A businessman from Arabia bought it. He was very proper." The elderly woman was having no part of her grandson's act. "I brought all of your favorite things," he yelled at the window, exasperated. "They're in that big orange truck right there. I've even had a nice large room built for you, Granmummy. I've donated a lot of money so I'm sure they'll look after you. Please open this door!" The young man, tie askew, started to kick the back tire of the limousine, but then seemed to think better of it and slowly lowered his foot to the ground. He turned back to Niles and rolled his eyes. "You've spoiled her," he groused, walking toward the front door of the nursing home.

The residents who had gathered to watch the ruckus scattered like nesting guineas under threat of an approaching dog.

Once the young man disappeared through the double doors of the home, Niles approached the back window of the car. "He's gone, Madame," Niles said to the glass. Ms. Wellington lowered the window with a touch of the power button on the door.

"Niles, how could you let them do this to me?" she whispered pitifully, a wild look in her eyes. "You are my butler, my friend. One minute we're out for a country drive, the next, all my possessions have been shoved into an orange truck and deposited here, at this hell hole." She looked around with disdain. The grass looked as though it hadn't been cut in a couple of weeks. Most of the cars in the parking lot were domestic family cars and the nosey old people on the front porch wouldn't know a Christian Dior original if it bit them on the nose.

"Madame, I assure you, I had no idea. I was told to take you for a drive and keep you occupied for at least five hours. Master Tipper said he would have a surprise for you at this address. I mistook the movers for furniture restoration movers. You see, Madame, I, too, have been duped."

Beatrice Wellington seemed to consider this piece of news, rolling the information over as though it were a marble in her mouth. Finally she spoke.

"I believe you, Niles. Only because I know you would never lie to me. What are we going to do?" The elderly woman looked lost and frail.

"I don't know. According to Master Tipper, Kensington has been sold to an Arab and he's moving in this afternoon. Apparently, you have no home to speak of." The elderly woman once again seemed to let the words of her butler soak in.

"Will you be coming with me if I stay here?" she asked.

"No, Madame. I'm afraid not. Master Tipper has informed me that as of this afternoon I will be relieved of my duties."

She seemed not to hear the butler's words. "Master Tipper is a poor excuse for a grandson. I'm thinking about changing my will—leaving my fortune to the manatees in Florida. What do you think about that, Niles?"

"They seem to be a nice enough family, Madame. I'm sure whatever you decide will be best."

"Niles, would you do something for me?"

"Anything, Madame."

"Would you shoot Tipper when he comes back outside? I know you keep that handgun in the glove compartment." Niles' eyes grew wide with horror. "That gun is for your protection. No, Madame, I cannot commit such a crime for you." "I don't mean kill him. Just aim for his leg or arm or something to keep him in the hospital for a few days while I figure out what to do. I will not stay here."

"Of course not, Madame."

"What would my friends say?"

"Precisely, Madame."

"I can just see the social column in the newspaper: Lady Wellington Admitted to Rest Home. All the gossip columnists will have a ball with that one."

"I understand, Madame."

The two fell quiet for a moment—the elderly woman sitting on the edge of her plush leather car seat and her butler kneeling painfully on the gravel driveway with his right hand resting on the door handle. Niles didn't even try to turn the handle, he knew it would remain locked until Madame Wellington either agreed to stay or decided to leave. Years of service had taught the old butler that much.

Suddenly the crowd on the front porch parted, allowing the passage of a woman dressed in multi-colored surgical scrubs. The woman marched right up to the limousine. Beatrice had, by the time she arrived at the car, rolled up the window. The woman's brunette hair was swept on top of her head, held in place by a silver clasp. A pencil was tucked behind one ear. She had a plastic I.D. tag that read "Patti McLeod, Director of Nurses."

Niles stood up quickly, brushing the gravel from his knees. "May I help you?" he asked, glancing at the name tag. "Ms. McLeod?"

"Is that Mrs. Wellington?" she asked, pointing to the woman sitting in the limousine.

"May I help you?" he asked again.

"I would like to speak to Mrs. Wellington, please," she said, placing her hands on her hips. The woman definitely had a no-nonsense air about her.

"Now is not a good time, Ms. McLeod."

"It won't take a moment—I just wanted to express our appreciation. We all thought bankruptcy was imminent, but it looks like we've got a second lease on life now, what with Mrs. Wellington and all."

Niles heard a soft whirring noise and turned slightly, seeing the window being lowered a few inches. Mrs. Wellington was intrigued. The windows, he knew, were soundproof, so Mrs. Wellington had not heard anything yet.

"Excuse me, Ms. McLeod, but could we continue this conversation inside? I don't like to trouble Madame Wellington with details.

"But I thought I could just . . . ." Patti floundered, wondering why this butler wanted to keep her from complimenting and thanking Mrs. Wellington.

Niles took her arm and turned toward the open crack in the window. "I shall return momentarily, Madame Wellington," he said. "I need to impress upon the staff your desire not to reside here."

"Very good, Niles. Make it quick so we can start looking for a new home."

"Yes, Madame." With that, the butler turned on his heel and walked with Patti across the parking lot and up the steps into Milly's Merry Roost.

Tipper had been watching the limousine from his perch on the hood of the moving truck the whole time. Seeing an opportunity, Tipper dashed across the parking lot toward the limo's open window as Beatrice hit the power window button.

"I love mechanical devices," Beatrice sighed as she watched her grandson slam into the door. "Sound-proof glass wasn't such a bad idea, either."

Niles eyed the welcome lady warily. "Do I need a what?" he asked, incredulously.

"A cart, sir. For your shopping pleasure."

"But ma'am, this is a nursing home for the elderly, not a shopping market for the infirm."

"Just say okay," said Larry, maneuvering his way around the butler, a lamp in each hand. "It doesn't do any good to argue she'll just call security and have you arrested as a shoplifter."

Patti, visibly upset over Mrs. Wellington's refusal to stay, had left Niles in the lobby while she went to get the appropriate documents for Mrs. Wellington to sign.

Niles was impatient; a plan was unfolding in his mind.

"I need to find Mrs. Wellington's residence," Niles said to the mover.

"Follow me, I'm heading that way right now," the burly man said. The tall butler fell in behind, picking up one of the electrical cords dangling behind Larry.

"Oh, thanks," Larry said to Niles.

"You're quite welcome Mr . . . . Mr . . . ."

"Larry, the name's Larry."

"You're quite welcome Mr. Larry."

About thirty minutes later, Niles reappeared in the parking lot, talking animatedly with the mover.

Hey, that's a great idea, Niles old boy," Larry said, slapping the butler on the back. The familiarity made Niles uncomfortable.

"Anything to help Madame Wellington," Niles said.

"But having everyone agree to act like this is her house, like they're her servants and all, that was pretty cool. How'd you get 'em to do that?"

"It's all a matter of simple economics," Niles said, heading toward the limousine. Tipper was sitting on the ground, his back up against the door of the limousine.

"She says she's having me cut out of her will, and then she's going to commit suicide," he said dramatically. "I think I'll join her. Say, Niles old boy, do you think you could rig up a dual garden hose to run out of the exhaust pipe here? We might as well both end it all. Hey, you could join us if you want—you don't have a job now anyway."

"Might I have a word with you, Master Tipper?" Niles asked. The young man looked up miserably at the old butler and nodded.

"Sure, why not? It only suits for the butler to be ordering me around right now, too. After all, I'm just the only surviving heir to the Wellington fortune. After Granmummy dies, I'll have to beg the damn manatees to hire me on as a personal valet or something. Since when did she start caring about endangered species anyway?"

"She actually thinks the manatees are some poor family who lives on the coast of Florida." Niles held out his hand and helped Tipper to his feet.

"Please make yourself more presentable," Niles said, indicating Tipper's untucked shirt, messy hair and the amount of parking lot gravel attached to the back of his wool trousers. Tipper obliged, tucking in his shirt and smoothing back his hair. "I shall return, Madame Wellington," Niles said to the woman in the car. She nodded. Niles and Tipper walked toward the end of the parking lot, Niles choosing his words carefully before speaking.

"You would like for Mrs. Wellington to reside here, would you not, Master Tipper?"

"Yes, Niles. I would. I mean, sure it's a nursing home, but they're nice people and I've donated a lot of money to make sure she's well taken care of."

"A lot of her money, don't you mean?"

"Well, yes, her money. But it was my idea to have the wing built for her. It's rather spacious, don't you think?"

"Not as big as Kensington. However, I think I know how to get her to stay here," Niles said.

"Yes?" Tipper leaned into Niles conspiratorially.

"I must stay here as well," Niles said simply.

"That's it? You want to be her butler at Milly's Merry Roost? Are you bored with your life or something? Sure, that's a deal." "It will require a raise."

"Absolutely—you deserve one."

"I would like my own home built nearby." Tipper thought about this, but only momentarily.

"Okay, your own house. I'll call the architect tomorrow." "And," Niles added, pausing for effect.

"Yes?" asked Tipper.

"You must visit every Sunday afternoon, send cards for every holiday and occasion, and you must not act like a spoiled rotten brat every time you come here."

"Well, okay. Is that it?"

"Not quite. You must also tell your grandmother that this is her new home."

"But it is her new home."

"No, I mean hers—all of it. Which means the building, the grounds, and the people here."

"You mean like she owns these old folks?"

"Not exactly. She must think that the people who work here are under her employ, and those who live here are simply reaping from the generosity of Madame Wellington."

"Well, your little game is fine with me, but what about everyone else?"

"I've already spoken to several of them and it's taken care of. It seems as though your bringing Mrs. Wellington here, along with the sizeable donation, has saved the facility from bankruptcy. They're willing to do anything to make sure she's happy and remains here. The nurses want their jobs, the residents want their home. It's really quite simple. And, I've taken the liberty of implementing a cash reward system which will be bestowed on those who give exemplary performances."

"That's very generous of you, Niles."

"You will be providing the cash, sir."

"Oh, of course. Yes, very good." The two men stood facing each other, each staring off into space as though considering the ramifications of this ploy.

"So, Niles, is that the gist of my penance?" Tipper finally asked, looking the butler in the eye.

"Yes, I should say so, sir. I shall take care of the rest. You may leave now." The butler dismissed the grandson of his employer as though he were no more than a bothersome fly. Tipper nearly ran to his car in his haste to leave.

He turned to wave. "Oh, bye Granmummy! I shall be back to visit— every Sunday afternoon," he added, with a look toward Niles.

"Where is he going?" Beatrice asked, seeing her grandson skip through the parking lot. "Is he leaving me here?"

"Madame, Master Tipper has just told me your plans and I dare say you are the most generous, benevolent woman I have ever known."

"What are you driveling about, Niles?"

"Tipper told me your plans to save Milly's Merry Roost," Niles said, pronouncing the name of the rest home with disdain. "My plans?" Beatrice asked. "What plans?"

"That you instructed Tipper to purchase this rest home because you heard it was on the verge of bankruptcy. That you were going to oversee the business end of it."

"I don't remember . . ." Beatrice trailed off, wheels spinning in her head. "You mean this is my business?"

"Yes, Madame, according to your employees inside and according to your grandson. That was quite a generous move on your part, considering this place was a step away from closing down for good. You must have thought about the families of the employees when you made your decision."

"Well, yes, the poor families—how would the children eat?" Beatrice said, gaining speed on the situation.

"Exactly, and the poor residents. They would be turned out on the street if this place closed down."

"Poor old people," Beatrice cried out, leaning forward in her seat, the window now rolled fully down. "I couldn't bear to think of them wheeling around in the city, holding out tin cups and selling pencils— wearing those awful gloves with the fingers cut out. I had to help them, don't you see, Niles? Don't you see they need me?" Beatrice said, shaking and breathless from exertion.

"I do now, Madame. At first I thought it was an overly generous thing to do—even for someone with your history of philanthropy. But now, I see what a truly selfless thing you have done. You have agreed to live and work here in order to better take care of Millys Merry Roost."

"Enough, Miles. You know how modest I am," Beatrice said, leaning back against the plush of the limousine seat. "It was just an idea I had, that's all."

Niles held up his hand. "But Madame, surely you do not wish to reside here."

Beatrice looked through the smoky glass of the limousine at her new business venture. The home was fairly run down, but 'she could see so much potential! There was nothing that a little attention, love, and a whole lot of money couldn't fix. It could work, she thought.

"Yes, I shall stay. I think I should be here to keep a close eye on the operations, don't you think1" And then, as though the thought suddenly occurred to her she asked, "Niles, you will stay with me, won't you?"

The butler straightened up from his crouched position at her window. "Madame, I would stay with you even without a salary." "Don't be silly, Niles."

The butler exhaled loudly with relief. "Shall we go inside, Madame?" Niles asked, reaching for the door handle.

"We shall," said the new benefactor of Milly's Merry Roost as she reached to press the button to unlock the door.

CHAPTER 2

"**B**INGO!!" screeched a woman in the back of the recreation room, causing all the players who weren't hard of hearing to jump in their seats.

"Damn it, Gladys, you don't have to yell so loud," grouched one old man, pulling a hearing aid out of his ear and adjusting the volume. Gladys, who appeared not to hear his lament, stood beside her bingo card and wailed, "Yes, thank you Jesus!" and began to make her way up front, shaking and wiggling her hips with her arms held high in the air.

"Gladys, this is not one of your Southern Baptist tent revival meetings," the man with the hearing aid said with irritation.

Gladys stopped in mid-celebration to face George. Her hands dropped to her side. "But George, I won," she said, her face crumpling. "I've never won before."

"There's nothing to be excited about, Gladys. The women win leftover Mary Kay cosmetics from the last makeover session and the men win either a fishing lure or a deck of cards. Whoopee," George said, throwing his hands up in the air in mock celebration.

"George, must you rain on everyone's parade?" Michelle Peterson asked, setting a numbered ping pong ball down on the table and placing both hands on her ample hips. Michelle was the activities director and social worker for the nursing home. "Why do you have to be such a grouch all the time?" All the other bingo players turned expectantly towards George, who sat in the back corner.

George took out his hearing aid and shook it. "Sorry, I can't hear a word. My hearing thing is on the blink." With that, he turned and shuffled out the door without a backward glance. George's oversized trousers hung low in the rear and his brown corduroy slippers scuffed the floor lightly as he exited the room.

Gladys had stopped in the middle of the aisle, unsure as to what she should do. "You come right on up here and get your prize," Michelle said, gesturing toward her. The elderly woman took the pink plastic compact case from Michelle's outstretched hand and returned to her seat. A smug expression played around Gladys' lips.

"Told you it was just makeup," George's voice bellowed from the hall.

"George can't take losing," Michelle said toward the doorway. She waited to hear the retreat of his slippers along the corridor before addressing the rest of the group.

"We have a nice surprise in the day room. There's another special activity waiting there for you!" Michelle sang out with excitement. The group made their way slowly along the hall. Those who had no problem waited patiently for the others, some shuffling with walkers, and others in wheelchairs. The group soon passed George, who was shuffling slowly down the hallway from the opposite direction.

"It's the Blue Bird Singers, everyone! There's still time to turn back!" he growled, never slowing his pace. "Run before it's too late!"

"George, that's not nice. Everyone else loves the Blue Bird Singers, right?" she asked, turning to address the others. Much to her dismay, several members of the activity group were sneaking along the hallway—in the opposite direction.

"Hold on just a minute!" Michelle shrilled, causing the escapees to stop in their tracks. "The Blue Bird Singers are a wonderful bunch of women who take time out from their busy schedules to entertain us," she said. "The least we can do is listen." No one moved. "All right," Michelle said, defeated, "everyone who goes gets extra refreshments, and we're having ice cream." All but two of the defectors turned back around and joined the others headed to the day room.

"You will all be polite, and you will all sing with the Blue Birds and you will all enjoy it," Michelle concluded, not noticing three of her charges dropping back out behind her.

On the way to the day room, Michelle tried to coax others from their rooms. "Mrs. Coates, come join us for ice cream in the day room," Michelle cooed into one room.

"No, thank you. George told me the Blue Birds are going to be there," Mrs. Coates said, turning back to her soap opera.

"I'd rather have an enema," said the next man she asked, who was beginning a game of checkers with George in the lobby. Michelle had all but given up before she remembered Mr. Tyler.

"Gladys, has Mr. Tyler come out of his room yet?"

"Not since he's been here," the aide said with concern. "We've tried everything to get him out, but nothing seems to work. He's a very bitter man."

"Let's stop by his room and have a try," Michelle said, the eternal optimist. Though the door was open, Michelle knocked lightly on his doorframe.

"Good afternoon, Mr. Tyler," she said brightly.

"What do you all want?" he asked, noticing all the others gathered around behind the activity director. A game of solitaire was laid out on the table.

"We were just on our way to have some ice cream and thought we'd see if you would like to join us," Michelle said.

"No."

"Has George been by here?" Michelle asked suspiciously.

"No."

"Mr. Tyler, have you left your room in all the weeks you've been here?"

"I don't recall."

"According to the nurses, you haven't."

"They ought to know. They make it their business to know everything about me—even when I go to the bathroom," Mr. Tyler said. "By the way, I did number one just a few minutes ago—you might want to jot that down."

"Can we bring you some ice cream by on the way back?" Michelle asked sweetly, undaunted by Mr. Tyler's gruff demeanor.

"No, you cannot. And now I'd like for you all to remove yourselves from my doorway."

"If you change your mind, Mr. Tyler, we'll all be in the day room. Please come," Michelle said as they left. By this time, only five people followed Michelle towards the day room. Passing back through the lobby, Michelle told Ida to make an announcement. Ida scurried happily towards the PA equipment and within minutes, the scratchy, whining sound of a microphone being turned on was heard all over Milly's Merry Roost.

"Attention shoppers!" Ida said cheerily. "There's a blue light special in the day room—a blue light special in the day room. Don't be late!" The microphone clicked off.

Those who hadn't been forewarned about the Blue Birds joined Michelle's group in the day room and politely sat through an hour of singing before the refreshments were served.

Afterward, Michelle made a point of locating George. She found him watching bowling in the television room.

"Oh, George? I thought you'd like to know that the Blue Bird Singers did something different today. We played poker, drank beer, and ate potato chips instead of singing around the piano. We had a great time. Gladys ran the table and won about twenty dollars. Too bad you weren't there."

George stared after Michelle, open mouthed as she left the room. He slammed his fist against his thigh once she was out of ear shot.

The next morning Michelle approached several staff members to talk about Mr. Tyler. She found Dr. Price in the recreation room, playing checkers with George.

"Dr. Price? Are you familiar with Mr. Tyler? One of the new residents on the East Hall?"

Dr. Price looked up thoughtfully from the checker game and pursed his lips. "If you were me, would you jump the red checker on the right, or the one to the left?"

"Dr. Price, I'm asking you about a resident. Do you know Mr. Tyler?"

"Is he the one who won't leave his room?" the doctor asked, not raising his eyes from the checker board.

"Yes, that's the one."

"He won't play checkers with us, either. Even when we offered to bring the board to his room," Dr. Price said, picking up one of his black checkers and jumping quickly over two of George's red checkers. Dr. Price picked up the two red checkers and set them to the side of the board.

"Dr. Price, don't you think that this is odd behavior?" Michelle asked, growing impatient.

"No, he's relatively new here, so it will take time to adjust," Dr. Price said, watching with dismay as George jumped three of his men. "Now look what you've done, Michelle. You've distracted me. Leave the man alone for now and we'll see what happens later on."

Michelle got more attention from the director of nurses.

"I asked Dr. Price, but he's too busy playing checkers to care about the residents," Michelle said with a sniff.

"It's not that Dr. Price doesn't care," Patti said, carefully choosing her words, "he's just got a lot of things on his mind." Patti wondered if that explanation sounded as hokey as it was. In truth, Patti felt Dr. Price had been more interested lately in playing games with his patients than treating them. He had come to Milly's Merry Roost to work until his retirement, which was a little over a year away. It was Patti's opinion that the doctor was so close to retirement that he was practicing for the time he actually entered a nursing home. Patti felt that she was in more of a doctor's role than the actual doctor.

"I just want someone to be aware that Mr. Tyler is totally antisocial. He won't participate in any activities and won't have anything to do with anyone," Michelle said.

"I know. The nurses flip a coin to see who has to deal with him each day," Patti said glumly. "They try to coax him out—they even try to trick him into leaving the room—but it doesn't work. What's weird is that I called his family and they say we must be mistaken because their father is the nicest man in the world."

"I beg to differ," Michelle said quickly.

"I know, I know. I just don't know what else to do. There's no rule that says he has to leave his room. He's paying the bill, so I suppose he can stay in his room as long as he likes. Eventually, he's gonna have to come out for a real bath . . . I dread the day."

"What about the fishing club?" Patti asked.

"I tried. He says he hates to fish."

"What about television?"

"He's got his own set in his room."

"Could we make it malfunction?" Patti asked sincerely.

"Not without him knowing about it. He's always in his room and the television's always on."

"Keep trying to include him in all your activities, and we'll see where we go from there," Patti said.

A few days later, Beatrice Wellington was gazing at the activities calendar. She looked up from her wheelchair—not the traditional metal wheelchair, but the wooden kind with the high back and caned seat—to Niles.

"Niles, that doesn't say Pet Parade does it?" she asked fearfully.

Niles followed the direction of her finger and read silently. "Yes, Madame, there does appear to be a Pet Parade scheduled for this Thursday afternoon."

"We'll see about that," she said haughtily. "Niles, drive me over to Nurse McLeod's office." She sat up primly as Niles pushed her chair over to the administrative offices. Once there, Beatrice rapped authoritatively on the door several times with the cane she kept at her side.

Patti opened the door, revealing an ongoing meeting inside. Beatrice grabbed the side of the door and pulled herself through. "Good, you're all here," she said. "I have an issue to bring before the board."

"Hello, Beatrice," Patti said, stepping out of the way of her wheelchair. Seated around the conference table were Dr. Price, Michelle, and several staff nurses.

"Hello, Beatrice," Michelle said a little over zealously. No one was quite sure how to deal with Beatrice since Niles had them agree to "the deal."

Beatrice ignored their greetings. "I want to know why I wasn't consulted about this Pet Parade thing. I don't allow pets in my own home, so why in the world would 1 allow them here?" she asked the group.

"I know what she's talking about," Michelle said. "The humane society is bringing some pets over this Thursday for the residents to pet. We did it a couple of months ago and everyone loved it."

"I don't care. Pets are nasty and infested with disease," Beatrice said, "and I will not tolerate them here."

"But Beatrice . . ." Michelle said.

Beatrice interrupted. "Are you all forgetting who runs this place now?" she asked imperiously.

"No," they all answered quietly.

"May I suggest something on Michelle's behalf?" Patti asked Beatrice.

Beatrice nodded.

"Michelle works very hard at lining up various activities for the residents here. The Pet Parade has been one that all the residents truly seem to love." Beatrice raised her hand to interrupt, but Patti held up her own hand. "No, Beatrice. Please allow me to finish." Beatrice nodded.

"What if we have a compromise? Beatrice, you think pets are filthy and shouldn't be allowed indoors. So why not have the Pet Parade outdoors in the courtyard?" Patti looked around and noticed that all the others were nodding.

"That's fine as long as you make sure that everyone who handles a pet washes their hands when they come back inside," Beatrice said. She didn't want to be completely disagreeable. After all, this was still her first week as the new owner of the nursing home and she wanted to make a relatively good impression.

"Thank you, Mrs. Wellington," Michelle said humbly, with the hint of a curtsy.

"She's not the queen," Patti whispered to her as Beatrice left the room.

"She might as well be with the leverage she's got now," Dr. Price said, getting up from the table. "Now, are we through? I've got to help run a checkers tournament this afternoon and I need to draw the brackets."

Milly's Merry Roost was abuzz Thursday morning in anticipation of the Pet Parade. Even the most disagreeable old codgers softened when handling a puppy or kitten. The courtyard was entirely enclosed with beautiful ornate fences, making it impossible for the animals to escape. Beatrice, propelled by Niles, patrolled the area on a regular basis to make sure none of the rules were broken. The other residents had discovered the real reason that the Pet Parade would be held outdoors and made a few off color remarks about Beatrice when her back was turned.

"Ought to trade that cane of hers in for a scepter," said one.

"Or a broomstick," said another.

"She probably doesn't want pets inside because Niles might get confused as to who his master is," said one woman, not attempting to disguise her disgust. The others snickered at her blatant irreverence. Beatrice was quickly becoming known as "Queen Wellington" throughout the nursing home.

The volunteers of the county animal shelter arrived at two o'clock in the afternoon, unloaded the animal cages from the van and set them in the courtyard. The program director for the animal shelter was concerned that the animals might be able to escape the confines of the courtyard.

"Why in the world are we having the Pet Parade outdoors?" she demanded, looking around at all the expectant residents waiting in the courtyard. The volunteers were busy taking the animals out of their cages and handing them out. Dogs on leashes trotted right up to the residents and began licking their hands.

"Queen Wellington thinks pets are nasty and won't have them inside," offered one elderly man gently stroking a mixed breed puppy.

"Who is Queen Wellington?" the director asked, confused. She didn't realize they had royalty here at the Roost.

"She's the old biddy who's saved The Roost from bankruptcy," said a tiny wrinkled woman with a rabbit.

"We should be grateful to her instead of bad-mouthing her," a nurse said, shaking her finger at the group gathered in the courtyard. "You should all be ashamed of yourselves."

George snorted loudly. "What? Has she got you on her payroll too, Lucy?" he asked.

"No, I'm just grateful to have my job and it seems like you all would be grateful to keep your home," Lucy said, her hands firmly on her hips. "George, you especially should know better."

"What? I can't hear you," George said loudly, taking out his hearing aid and tapping it with his finger. "Damn thing won't work."

The rest of the Pet Parade went by quietly, with no more mention of Madame Wellington. Adult dogs milled around the courtyard, eager for the petting and dog biscuits offered by the residents. The smaller puppies and kittens were held, not allowed to wander off in the paths of wheelchairs. Everyone was enjoying the warmth of the sun and the quiet of the courtyard.

"Oh, my rabbit! I've lost my rabbit!" cried the wrinkled old woman who had spoken so sarcastically about Mrs. Wellington. She sat up in her wheelchair and looked around frantically. "The bunny must have jumped out of my lap when I fell asleep."

"You couldn't have been sleeping long, Ms. Racine," Lucy said.

"Long enough to lose my bunny," the old woman snapped. She leaned forward on the arms of her wheelchair and craned her neck to look for the missing rabbit.

The volunteers began going in different directions around the courtyard searching for the rabbit.

"Let's not worry about Homer," the volunteer director said. "That bunny has gotten a taste of the outdoors and is probably in some farmer's garden right now having the time of his life."

Mr. Tyler restlessly channel surfed with the television remote control. The afternoons were the worst time to try and find something to watch. It was either soap operas, talk shows, or really bad movies. Ball games didn't usually start up until early evening and his favorite fishing shows were shown on the weekend. The nurses here bugged him and the old folks were just intolerable, he reminded himself. Jack was lonely, and had been ever since his daughter left him at The Roost a couple of weeks ago. He didn't blame her, he couldn't take care of himself very well any more since Vivian had passed on. Vivian had spoiled him without shame, doing all the cooking, cleaning and virtually everything else. All he'd had to do was go to work and bring home a paycheck while she took care of their home. He missed Vivian. He glanced at the calendar tacked up behind his bed and calculated she'd been gone seven weeks and three days. Jack tried to make it on his own after she died. His only child, his daughter, had offered to take Jack into her home, but she already had four children and a lousy good-for-nothing husband that didn't raise one hand to help with anything. Everyone said Jack was the same way, but he didn't believe them. Even so, it seemed he missed almost everything these days—his own bed, his own food and Blue. Blue, a dog of questionable lineage, had kept Jack company for eight years up to the time he'd come to this miserable place. Blue had been a gift from Vivian.

"You need someone to putter around with," Vivian had said, handing him the wriggling spotted puppy.

"I don't need no damn dog," Jack had said irritably, taking the pup from Vivian and setting it on the ground. The puppy immediately started chewing on Jack's shoe strings. He reached down, popped the puppy lightly on the rear end and pushed it away. The first couple of days had been a love-hate relationship between Jack and the dog. Jack hated the dog, the dog loved Jack and followed him wherever he went. Soon, Jack was won over by the dog and gruffly allowed it to follow him around.

"Jack, do my ears deceive me or are you actually calling for Blue?" she asked with a twinkle in her eye.

"No, I just haven't seen him all day and I know for a fact that mutt's too stupid to fend for himself," Jack had said, not willing to give in to his affection for the dog. "Now," Jack told himself! "I'm too stupid to fend for myself."

Jack had given away everything from the house—furniture, tools, even the car. Blue had been another matter. Jack's daughter didn't have a fenced in yard, and really didn't need another warm body to take care of. He'd called everyone he knew who might take a dog and each one gently declined. Jack didn't blame them. After all, Blue was getting on in years and was an ugly dog to boot. After failing to locate a home for him, he turned the matter over to his daughter, who said she'd handle it. Jack didn't want to know what happened to Blue, and shuddered to think his old pal might be in a dog pound somewhere waiting for Jack to come get him and take him home. The dog had been nothing but faithful to Jack all these years.

Jack pulled a dog-eared pack of playing cards out of the top drawer of his night stand and half-heartedly began playing solitaire. He knew several different ways to play solitaire and played them all, losing each time. Jack's heart just wasn't in the game. He felt something pulling on one of his shoes and looked down. A white and black spotted rabbit was chewing earnestly on one of his dangling shoe strings. Jack instinctively pulled his foot away and the rabbit, rather than being frightened by the sudden movement, stood up on its hind legs and looked at Jack curiously, its pink triangle nose twitching furiously.

"Well, who are you?" Jack asked, grinning at the rabbit. He reached down and picked up the rabbit, placing it on the bed. The rabbit snatched up one of the playing cards in his teeth and began chewing busily.

"Whoa!" Jack said, taking the card out of the rabbit's mouth. "How am I going to play cards without the jack of diamonds?" He stroked the rabbit gently, thinking about how different the rabbit's silky soft coat was from Blue's coarse hair. Leaving the rabbit on the bed, Jack walked over and shut the door to his room. "These folks around here are too nosey," he said to the rabbit as he approached the bed. The rabbit's nose twitched in response.

Soon there was a tentative knock at his door. "Mr. Tyler? Are you okay in there?"

"Of course I'm okay, I just wanted a little privacy is all," Jack said testily in the direction of the door.

"You haven't seen a rabbit, have you? We seem to have lost one," the voice said from the other side of the door.

Jack protectively pulled the rabbit onto his lap as he sat next to the bed. "A rabbit? What in the world would I want with a rabbit?" he asked a little too loudly.

"Sorry to bother you, Mr. Tyler," the voice said. Jack heard footsteps retreating down the hallway.

"I knew this would happen," Beatrice said angrily, shaking her fist in the air. "Niles, didn't I tell you something like this would happen?" she asked the butler standing beside her wheelchair.

"Yes, Madame, I believe you did," Niles answered stiffly. "The rabbits probably not even indoors," Lucy said. "Were just looking everywhere and wanted to check your room."

"If that rodent is found in my room, I want the whole place fumigated. Niles, take me to the day room," Beatrice sniffed.

The rabbit still hadn't been found by dinner time and residents of The Roost were abuzz with updates of the disappearance.

"I heard he was last seen down by the road," said one. "It's probably long gone by now."

George pointed to the unidentifiable piece of meat on his sectioned plate. "Hey, maybe we're having rabbit for dinner!" "If the pet department personnel had been on their toes, this would have never happened," Ida said, pursing her lips together primly.

While all the others dined in the cafeteria, Beatrice and Niles were conducting their own search for the rabbit. "I just know that rabbit is here on the premises and I won't have it. There's no way it could have gotten out any other way," she said. They checked each room thoroughly. It was interesting to see how each person had added his or her own personal touch. "Look at this, Niles. Such small rooms. I don't know how they do it." Niles simply listened. As they entered one room, pictures of years gone by were everywhere. In one, a young woman was holding a new baby with her young husband beaming behind her. "Niles," Beatrice pointed in amazement at the picture, "I bet that's Gladys right there. Her husband is certainly dapper." "She looks very proud, Madame," Niles agreed.

Finally they came to the closed door of Mr. Tyler.

Beatrice read the name off of the name plate on the door. "Mr. Jack Tyler," she said, turning to Niles. "Isn't he the one that always stays in his room and won't have anything to do with anyone?"

"I don't know, Madame," Niles said.

Beatrice rapped on the door with her cane. "Mr. Tyler? Open up," she commanded.

"Leave me alone," Jack yelled out angrily. "I told you I don't want any dinner."

"I am not delivering your dinner, Mr. Tyler," she said huffily. "We're conducting a search and your room is next."

"They've already been by looking for that rabbit. What makes you think you can do a better job?" he asked, looking around for a place to hide the rabbit.

Beatrice didn't give him a chance. She flung the door wide and rolled her chair inside. His room was in sharp contrast to the other people's rooms. There were no personal belongings or pictures, just the nursing home furnishings and there was Jack, sitting on the edge of his bed with the spotted rabbit in his arms. "Aha!" Beatrice cried. "So you are protecting a known felon!" "No, I'm just petting a bunny," Jack said, his voice dripping with sarcasm. "Is that a crime?"

"Niles, remove that mite-infested rodent from Mr. Tyler," Beatrice instructed her butler. Niles took a step towards Jack.

Jack pulled back instinctively. "Why do you have to take him away?" he asked. "It's not like I brought the rabbit in here. I was playing cards and looked down and saw him chewing on my shoe laces. Just like Blue . . ." Jack trailed off.

"Who is Blue?" Beatrice demanded. "Do you have another animal in here?"

Jack looked at her sharply. "No, I do not have another animal here. Blue is . . . was my dog. The rabbit here just reminded me . . . oh, never mind." Beatrice saw tears glisten in the corners of the old man's eyes as he quickly looked away. She suddenly understood his bitterness.

"Mr. Tyler, you are aware that the rabbit must be returned to the animal shelter, are you not?" she asked gently.

"Yes, I know. Can we wait until the morning? I just called the nurse to bring me some salad for dinner and I sure would like to feed him before he goes."

"I'm sorry, Mr. Tyler, but we'll have to take him. Animals are not allowed in the home."

Jack looked at her coldly. "It's true what they say about you, then, isn't it?" he said. "You're just a heartless old woman who likes to hear herself talk and wants everyone else to jump when you say jump." Jack set the rabbit down gently on the floor. "Here, take the damn rabbit. I don't have any use for him anyway."

Beatrice stared at Jack in silence. Jack thought he saw a softness in her eyes, as though she were getting teary-eyed. Niles walked over and picked up the rabbit.

"At least go by the kitchen and get the rabbit some salad greens," Jack said gruffly. "He hasn't eaten all day." Niles pulled Beatrice's chair backwards through the door. "Close the door behind you," Jack yelled. "I don't want anyone bothering me."

Beatrice was quiet as they moved along the hallway. The Roost was quiet since all the residents were having dinner in the cafeteria.

"Am I a mean old woman?" Beatrice asked Niles.

"Of course not, Madame," Niles replied.

"I'll double your pay this week if you tell me the truth," Beatrice said sternly.

Niles considered this and then answered. "Madame, you are irreproachable when it comes to behavior; however, there are times when your sense of responsibility overrides your compassion."

"Niles, I think you just called me a mean old woman."

"Not at all, Madame," Niles said simply.

"Take me to the administrator's office," Beatrice commanded her manservant. When they got there, the light was off to the set of inner offices. Loraine, the secretary, usually went home around six o'clock each evening. Niles opened the door and pushed Beatrice over to the filing cabinet. She read the contents which were written on the outside of each drawer and selected "Medical Records." Beatrice pulled open the drawer and rolled her wheelchair alongside it.

"Hmmm, here it is," she said, pulling out a file marked "Tyler, Jack A." Beatrice flipped through the file until she found his admission sheet. "His next living relative is Donna Benson from Athens, Georgia. I think a talk with her is warranted."

The next morning Jack awoke and decided not to get out of bed. The first nurse to come by tried to get Jack to get up.

"Why should I get up?" he asked. "All I do is sit around in my room, play cards by myself and watch television. I don't even need to change out of my pajamas for that."

"But you don't have to be alone," the nurse persisted.

"Look, I hate everything here, so why not be alone? I hate the food, I hate the activities, I hate the residents, and," he said, glaring at the nurse, "I hate the nurses most of all." The nurse left in a huff and Jack rolled over on his side facing the window. He didn't even want to watch television although a bowling tournament was scheduled to start at ten o'clock.

"Dad?" a voice called from the hallway.

Jack rolled over quickly, recognizing the sound of his daughter. She stood half in the doorway, her head cocked to the side. "Donna? What are you doing here? Who's keeping the kids?" "Whoa, Dad. One question at a time. I'm here because I got a telephone call last night from someone who said you were being a royal pain in the ass around here. As for your second question, the kids are with Bill. Now, is it true what they say?" "They just don't like me because I don't play well with others. I'm fine by myself and I intend to stay that way as long as I'm here. So you can just go back home. And, if you don't mind, tell me who called you so I can have a little chat with them." Donna was still standing in the doorway, not making a motion to come closer. "You're such a Mr. Tough Guy, Dad. For once can't you let down your guard a little? It's not so hard to admit you're lonely, you know."

"I'm not lonely. I'm alone and I prefer to be alone."

"Then I'll just take Blue back home," Donna said, backing out of the doorway.

"Blue? You've got Blue here?" Jack asked excitedly, sitting up. Donna pulled her hand into the doorway, which had been hidden the whole time. In her hand was a leash—the same leather leash Jack had used to walk Blue every day. Donna tugged gently and said, "Call him, Dad."

"Here, Blue," Jack said, clapping his hands together. At this point he was standing beside the bed. Jack heard the excited clatter of Blue's nails on the linoleum in the hallway just before he darted through the door and into Jack's arms. The old dog was whining and wiggling in his excitement. Jack laughed happily as Blue licked his face. The two wrestled together for a moment before Jack looked up with concern.

"Donna, he's not supposed to be here. Animals aren't allowed here." Jack stood up and sadly handed the leash back to Donna. "You'd better take him on, I can't have him here."

"You don't understand, Dad. I've brought him for you to keep here. The person who called told me it would be all right, that they would bend the rules for you."

Jack looked at his daughter in disbelief. "Who called you?" "Some woman named Wellington," Donna said with a shrug. "Evidently, she's already talked with the staff here because they let me come in with Blue."

"Mrs. Wellington told you to bring Blue? Well how about that," Jack wondered aloud. "Just yesterday she was threatening me because I had a rabbit in here."

After Donna left, Jack took Blue for a walk down the hallway to Beatrice's room. He grasped the brass knocker and rapped three times. Niles pulled open the door, glanced at Jack, and then stood to the side announcing, "A Mr. Tyler to see Madame Wellington," he said loudly.

"Let him in," Beatrice said from the back.

Jack had never been in the monstrous wing built especially for Beatrice. If he didn't know better he'd swear he had stepped into a museum, what with all the fancy furniture and art pieces scattered throughout. Niles signaled for Jack to follow him inside.

Jack shook his head. "I'd better not, Niles," he said, nodding towards Blue. "I don't think she'd appreciate my dog here."

"Oh, bring the dog, too," Beatrice called out, having heard their conversation.

Jack walked into the back sitting room where Mrs. Wellington sat in a huge brocade antique chair. He hung his head slightly. "I suppose I said some ugly things about you yesterday and I've come to apologize. I've also come to thank you for what you did for me and Blue."

Beatrice waved him off. "It's nothing. I made the rules, so I can change them if I wish."

"Well, thank you anyway. It means a lot to me to have him here."

"You just hold up your end of the bargain and keep him clean and keep your room clean. I don't want everything smelling like a dog around here," Beatrice said. She waved him off as though to dismiss him.

"I don't care what the rest of them say, Mrs. Wellington," Jack said, backing towards the door, "you're all right by me."

"Just make sure you keep him clean," she warned.

Jack nodded happily. "He'll be the cleanest dog you've ever seen. He'll be so clean, why Blue could even sleep in your bed with you."

Beatrice's face clouded over. "No, I don't think that will ever happen."

"No, I suppose not," Jack agreed with a laugh. He stopped by the recreation room to show off his dog and talk to some of the residents before he took Blue outside for a walk. He even invited George to come along.

CHAPTER 3

"PLEASE, your honor, you got to let my baby go," the large, overly made-up woman cried. She was on her knees in front of the judge's bench, twisting a sodden handkerchief in her hands. Mascara ran down her pudgy cheeks. Beside her stood a tall, thin teenage boy whose hair hung long and stringy over his left eye. He wore tattered blue jeans, a white tee shirt, and a blue jean jacket with the sleeves torn out at the shoulder. His head was cocked to the side and his expression was one of exasperation.

"Get up, mama," he said, firmly grasping one of her ample forearms. She shrugged him off and raised her arms toward the judge in supplication.

"Your honor, he's a good boy. It's his friends that are bad," she said. She picked up the beaded purse that lay beside her and in one smooth motion, she hit her son's legs.

"Ow, mama, what's that for?" the boy asked, rubbing his leg.

"Because you know better, Tommy. I tol' you and tol' you to stay at home, but every night you go out." She swatted him again with the purse, glancing toward the judge occasionally to make sure he was witnessing her disciplinary action.

"Mama, don't call me Tommy. Everybody calls me Skeeter now," Tommy said, pulling a cigarette out from a pack in the front pocket of his jacket. He looked up at the glaring eyes of the judge and returned it to the pack.

"Skeeter? What's wrong, you don't like the name we gave you?" she said, standing up. "Those filthy boys you hang out with call you 'Skeeter' to make fun of you and you're too stupid to know it," she said, swatting the tall skinny boy on the shoulder with her purse. Tommy took the hit, looking bored with the whole process.

The judge was watching the mother and son with amusement. "Excuse me," he said, clearing his throat.

The big woman stopped her purse in mid-swing and dropped back down on her knees, her hands in the prayer position. "Yes, your honor. My son is so rude to have interrupted you." She swatted her son forcefully.

"Stop it, mama," Tommy said, grabbing his leg.

The judge cleared his throat. "Tommy, this isn't the first time you've been in my courtroom." The judge flinched as the mother's purse made solid contact with her son's shin. He continued, "For that reason, I can't let you go with a slap on the wrist like I did the other times."

"See, Tommy? I tol' you," Tommy's mother said, striking him again.

"Ma'am, please stop striking your son until I'm finished," the judge said, beginning to feel sorry for the juvenile delinquent in front of him.

"See? You get me in trouble," the mother said, swinging her purse at Tommy.

"What I have decided," the judge said loudly, trying to regain control of his courtroom, "is that you need to be punished this time." Both mother and son stared expectantly at the judge.

"This time I'll give you a choice," the judge said to Tommy. "I can send you to the Youth Detention Center, or, you can perform three months of community service at the nursing home. What's your choice?"

The young boy shrugged his shoulders indifferently as though he didn't care what he did with his life in the immediate future. "YDC," he said.

His mother swung her purse forcefully, causing Tommy to stumble backward.

"Stupid," she yelled. "'You pick jail instead of working with old folks?"

"Yeah, so what?" Tommy said, flinching in anticipation of the next blow. It came.

The judge tried again. "Son, I'm willing to give you one more chance by allowing you to serve time doing volunteer work at the rest home. If you complete the three months without a problem, this incident will never be recorded. If, however, you don't behave, you will leave me no alternative but to send you to YDC for a period of not less than one year."

Tommy's dark eyes grew wide with the prospect of a year behind bars. That meant no cars, no chicks, no freedom, nothing. But he remained silent, not wanting to bend to the authority.

"Tommy, I've already spoken to the administrator of Milly's Merry Roost, who has graciously agreed to let you work there every day after school and weekends for three months. He will send me weekly reports on your progress. Let me warn you, though, if you fail to show up for work or if you cause trouble there, the police will pick you up and take you to YDC so fast it'll make your head spin. Do you understand?"

Tommy rolled his eyes in answer.

"Don't you care what happens to you?" the judge asked. "No. Why should I? No one cares about me," he said simply. The judge started to point out how much Tommy's mother cared about him, but saw that he was too busy getting slugged by her to listen, so he let it drop.

"The next time I see you, at the end of the three months, I hope to see you've learned to care about someone other than yourself. You can go."

The judge watched sadly as Tommy walked out of the courtroom, his mother beating him constantly with her purse along the way. "God bless you," he whispered. Back in his chambers, he dialed a number on the telephone.

"Steve? Hi, it's Andrew Brooks. Looks like you've got a new volunteer."

That afternoon, Steve Tallison, administrative director of the Roost, called a meeting to prepare the staff.

"From what the judge says, Tommy's basically a good kid, he's just fallen in with a bad crowd. While he's here, you can have him do anything you want, short of hard manual labor or medical functions. We want the community to see that we are willing to help the judicial system by working with one of its transgressors.

"But can we trust him?" Patti asked. "I'm not insensitive to the situation, but I think that's an important question. I mean, he's a criminal, not a candy striper."

"Judge Brooks says we would be doing ourselves a disfavor if we didn't keep close tabs on Tommy," Steve said.

"In other words, we can't trust him," Patti said. "That's just great."

"I can't believe I'm actually going to have to do time in this death trap," Tommy thought as he flipped his cigarette into the bushes before walking into Milly's Merry Roost. Through the window beside the door, Ida saw the flagrant act.

"Excuse me young man, but you will go out to that bush and retrieve that cigarette," she said, meeting him at the door.

"Bullshit," Tommy said under his breath.

Ida stood in front of him with her hands on her hips. "What would we do if all our shoppers decided to throw their cigarettes in the front yard?" Ida asked. "I don't think you're being very considerate."

"Who cares," Tommy said, walking around Ida. "I'm supposed to find somebody named Steve," he said to the receptionist.

"You must be Tommy," the receptionist said. "Wait right here, but don't touch anything while I'm gone."

Ida was suddenly at his side, holding his cigarette, which was still burning.

"You will take this cigarette and dispose of it properly," she commanded.

"Get lost, lady," Tommy said. This woman might be more of a pain in the ass than his purse-swinging mother ever thought about being.

Ida pulled open the top pocket on Tommy's jean jacket and dropped the cigarette inside. "See how you like having cigarettes deposited on your property," she said smugly, walking away. The cigarette burned a small brown hole in his pocket before he could take it out. Tommy dropped the cigarette on the carpeted flooring and stepped on it with his high top tennis shoe. He made sure Ida's back was turned before he kicked it across the room.

"Tommy!" Steve said, approaching with his hand held out. "Welcome to the Roost."

Tommy grunted in response.

"Let's go into my office so I can explain your duties to you."

Tommy followed the administrator into his office, eyeing him suspiciously as he closed the door behind them.

"So, Tommy," Steve said, "I suppose you're wondering what you will be doing here at the Roost."

Tommy grunted again as he slumped into a plastic covered chair. The chair squeaked as he sat. Tommy thought to himself, "Oh, yeah, I was up all night worrying about it." Surprisingly, the office looked like any other office he would have pictured. Your typical diplomas on the wall, of course, the picture of the little wife posed sweetly in her upper middle class wedding dress sitting on his desk for all the world to see. He ought to be proud, Tommy thought, she's not half bad compared to the stuffed shirt Stevie-boy seemed to be.

Steve Tallison interrupted Tommy's thoughts. "Actually, we're not exactly sure how to classify your position because you're not medically trained, nor are you a volunteer, but that's what we're going to call you. Is that okay?" Steve asked cheerfully.

Tommy grunted in response.

Steve grew serious. "Tommy, the judge was doing you a favor by allowing you to work community service here instead of sending you to juvenile detention. I hope you realize that," he said, searching Tommy's face for signs of understanding. There was none. Tommy was suddenly interested in the condition of his fingernails and was no longer paying any attention to Steve.

"Tommy, you will come here every day after school promptly at three thirty. Thirty minutes is enough time for you to get here. Don't get sick, because that's not an excuse that I will accept. Even if you don't feel well we will give you an assignment in the laundry for the day that will keep you away from the residents in case you're contagious. You will report here Saturday and Sunday mornings at eight o'clock sharp and will work until five o'clock in the afternoon. You will do this for three months, at the end of which I will give my opinion to the judge concerning your rehabilitation. If you show up every day on time and do your work properly, I'll give you a good recommendation. If not, you'll go to juvenile detention to serve out your sentence. Do you understand?"

Tommy felt like responding, "Yes, Massa Steve, I be's good," but he held his tongue. There was one thing Tommy understood, and that was detention. Might as well call it jail from what his friends told him. He nodded without looking at Steve.

"So, what am I gonna be doing here?" Tommy asked apathetically.

"Whatever the staff members tell you to do, basically," Steve said. "You may have to deliver the mail, push someone around in a wheelchair, feed a resident, clean up after a resident, help organize activities—the list could be endless. I've instructed the staff to use your services at their discretion—within reason, of course," Steve added with a smile. Tommy did not return the smile.

Steve stood up and rubbed his hands together. "You can begin working today. As a matter of fact, you're needed over in the activity room." He told Tommy how to find the activity room and watched the sullen young man leave, closing the door behind him. Steve shook his head, wondering what in the world the judge could have been thinking when he decided to send Tommy to the Roost. "I'm going to keep a close eye on you," Steve said to the closed door. "A real close eye."

Tommy sauntered through the open door of the activity room which was occupied by several ancient people sitting at tables working on what seemed to be the same kind of crafts Tommy did in the second grade. "Just terrific," he thought, as he leaned into the door frame. "I'm going to be helping take care of a garden full of vegetables."

Activities Director, Michelle Peterson, was the first to spot his entrance.

"Excuse me, young man, but how did you get in here?" she asked shrilly. To her, the boy looked like some kind of escaped axe murderer she'd read about in the National Enquirer.

"I walked down the hall," Tommy said sarcastically.

"Well, you can just turn back around and leave," Michelle said, her finger poised above the intercom button on the telephone that would bring help if she pushed it.

"Fine with me," Tommy said. "Steve told me to come down here, so I'll just leave."

"Wait a minute. Steve Tallison told you to come here?" Michelle asked suspiciously.

"Yeah, I'm the new community service volunteer," Tommy said with a sneer.

"Oh, you're Tommy," she said with dismay. Michelle quickly regained composure. "We're finger-painting today, so your duties are to make sure everyone has enough water and paint. Also, keep an eye out for spills and clean them up if they occur."

Tommy rolled his eyes, walked to a table in the back of the activity room and sat down in a metal folding chair. He put his head down on the table in front of him and prepared to take a nap.

Michelle marched to the back of the room and grabbed Tommy's collar. The large woman, usually bubbly, and upbeat, had a stem look on her face. She pulled Tommy's face so close to her own that their noses touched.

"Look, you," she said, speaking softly so the residents wouldn't hear. "You're working with me today. Do you have a problem with that?"

Tommy's eyes were wide. He didn't answer. All he could think about was whether she had a large beaded purse to hit him with nearby.

"Tommy, if you do right by me, I can be your best friend here. Otherwise, I can be the biggest bitch you've ever seen. Understand?"

Tommy swallowed hard and nodded. This woman was not to be fooled with, but at least I don't have to actually talk to the fossils, Tommy thought. He refilled water cups and paint trays the rest of the afternoon without any further incidents.

A spoonful of creamed spinach splattered on the cafeteria wall, leaving a dark green splatter.

"That's all it's good for—modern art," George groused, his spoon still pointing toward the wall. He held up his thumb and looked at it, the way an artist would contemplate a painting. "Nope, it still needs something," George said, spooning up the yellow creamed squash. He turned the spoon upright, pointed it toward the wall, pulled the top end back with his finger, and let it fly. The aim was perfect, the yellow mush exploding beside the green pulpy stain on the wall.

"That's better," George said, admiring his art work. There was a smattering of applause from several others in the cafeteria.

"George, don't do that," Patti said, frustrated, as she approached the table. She'd been eating her own lunch a few tables away and witnessed the creation of the edible mural. "I assume you plan on cleaning it up," she said.

"Not," George said. "Look, I pay good money to stay here, so I think it's only fair that the cafeteria serves decent food. Not everyone likes to eat this mush," he said, gesturing toward his sectioned plate. "I've still got my own teeth." George smiled broadly, showing two rows of beautiful white teeth.

"I like mush," Gladys said from the adjoining table. She put a big spoonful of spinach in her mouth as proof. "I don't even have to chew it," she said with delight after swallowing.

"Shut up, Gladys. Go play bingo or something." Gladys, easily wounded, continued eating her creamed vegetables in silence.

"George, we aren't a five-star restaurant, but we do the best we can, so we go with what the majority wants. You know we would love to serve you things you request but lobster bisque and cherries jubilee just aren't in the budget," Patti said matter-of-factly. George's culinary-induced tirades had become a daily occurrence. She started to tell him to order takeout food if the cafeteria food was so bad, but bit her tongue. George didn't have any money. The government had been taking care of him for years. Patti suspected financial dependency had something to do with George's bitterness, but the social history they had on file for him was sketchy.

"I'll get you some rags so you can clean up the wall," Patti said.

"What? I can't hear you—this damn thing's on the blink again," George said, shaking his hearing aid and replacing it in his ear. "Can't hear a thing. I'll see you later, Patti," he said, shuffling out of the room and leaving his culinary mess behind.

Patti shook her head and followed George out of the cafeteria. She'd just tell the janitor to clean it up. Because of George's frequent demonstrative outbursts, the janitor hated George nearly as much as George hated the cuisine. She dreaded hearing the string of expletives that the old janitor—a retired sailor—would hurl in George's direction.

Then Patti had a better idea. She walked down to the activity room and got Tommy.

"I'm not going to clean food off of the wall," Tommy said angrily when Patti explained his next task.

"Oh, pardon me," Patti said. "I thought you were here to help us. I'll just call Steve and inform him you've decided not to honor your service commitment anymore." She turned to walk out of the activity room.

"Where's the cafeteria?" Tommy sighed as he called after her. Patti gave him directions over her shoulder as she walked away.

"You missed some over there," George said, pointing out a glob of spinach still on the wall.

Tommy stopped scrubbing to turn and look at the old man. The teenager was torn between being falsely polite and blatantly disrespectful. He chose the latter.

"Look, old man, I wouldn't be scrubbing this crap if you hadn't thrown your food. What's your problem—you got a problem hitting your mouth?"

"I'm a culinary artist," George said.

"Why don't you eat it instead of throwing it?" Tommy asked.

"You eat it," George said bluntly.

Tommy considered the yellow and green mush on the wall. "I ain't eating that—that's gross."

"How do you think I feel about it?" George demanded. "I think it's gross, too."

"Well, why not just go call the pizza place or something?" Tommy asked. "I mean, they can't stop you from ordering out, can they?"

George's face turned cloudy. "Just clean the wall," he snapped, shuffling out of the cafeteria.

Late that night, hours after he was released from his first day's work at the Roost, Tommy came back. He slipped between the cars in the parking lot, careful not to wake the sleeping security guard on the front porch. In less than five minutes, he was inside.

During the day Tommy had noticed that a certain back door always stayed open for the residents who went outside to smoke in the courtyard. A half mile down the road, parked in the woods, five of Tommy's friends were waiting in an old Chevy van for his return.

His biggest problem would be slipping past the nurses' station, Tommy knew. It was midnight and all the residents were asleep. He had worn his soft soled shoes, not wanting to make any noise. Unfortunately, it had rained that afternoon. The wet soft soled shoes squeaked on the linoleum as he tip-toed through the hallways. Tommy ducked into a patient's darkened room to gather his wits. He was sweating with nervousness. He didn't want to be here, but knew it could be his ticket back into the gang. After his arrest, the gang he ran around with had dropped him like a hot potato, afraid he would point his finger in their direction. He had not. In fact, he accepted all the blame without regret. That's what gang brothers did, Tommy thought. At first they had laughed at his community service with the rest home, and told him they didn't want any candy stripers in the gang, but Tommy made a convincing case for how the new job could benefit the gang.

Most of the gang came from broken homes and all were poor as dirt. Tommy wasn't quite as poor as the others, which wasn't saying much, but it made it that much more difficult to be accepted in the gang. They were constantly demanding that he prove himself worthy. For tonight's re-initiation, Tommy had to steal food from the cafeteria to take to a party the gang was throwing down at the dam.

"It's not good food," Tommy had told Deek, the self-appointed leader of the rag-tag band of teenagers.

"You don't want back in the gang?" Deek had asked loudly, so the others would hear. "Food's food. Just grab all you can."

"No, no, I just don't know if you'll like the food," Tommy had said, remembering the mess on the wall.

"You know us, Skeeter, we'll eat anything," Deek had said. The other members laughed.

"Especially if it's free," said another.

Tommy slipped into the cafeteria, surprised to find it unlocked. He'd had no problem getting past the gabbing night nurses. Tommy had dropped below the level of the counter and scooted along the wall. His shoes remained mercifully silent. He found the supply closet in the back of the kitchen and opened the door slowly. He flipped on the light switch, removed the empty backpack from his back and began filling it with cans and boxes of food. The backpack was almost filled.

"Who goes there?" a gruff voice asked from the darkness beyond the doorway.

Tommy instinctively threw his hands up in the air and turned with his back toward his captor. "I'm not armed," he said.

"Sure you are," the voice cackled. "That can of creamed peas in your left hand could be considered a lethal weapon."

Tommy dropped the can as the body that went with the voice moved into view. It was George.

"What's the matter, you didn't get enough of that garbage today?" George asked, indicating the nearly full backpack.

Tommy's face turned flush. "No, I . . . uh . . ." he stammered.

"Look, I'm not going to rat on you, so just tell me what you're doing," George said.

"My buddies are throwing a party and they told me I had to bring the food.

"You're going to feed them this stuff?" George asked incredulously.

"I tried to tell them, but they said they wanted it any way."

"Let me ask you something, kid. How long have you been breaking the law?" George asked.

"Since I was about six or seven," Tommy lied. Fourteen was more like it, but he didn't like others knowing he'd been a late bloomer.

"For someone who's been in the business that many years, you're lousy at it."

"What do you mean, lousy?" Tommy said defensively.

"That's what I said, lousy. You're wearing a white sweatshirt, tennis shoes and you turned the light on," George said as a way of explanation.

"So?" Tommy asked.

"So? It's night time, Tommy, you don't wear white. Don't you watch cops and robbers movies? The bad guys wear black. If that security guard hadn't been asleep on the porch, he could have seen your white sweatshirt weaving and bobbing through the parking lot with no problem." George was clearly enjoying his role as mentor.

"Secondly, your tennis shoes were wet, so they squeaked through the hallway. You should always carry a pair of dry shoes with you—that'll add a little more baggage, but it may save your life." Tommy was nodding slowly, realizing the old man had some good ideas.

"And never, never turn on a light switch. You'd be surprised how far away that little beam of light under the door can be seen. Carry a little flashlight with you, but use it only if you have to," George finished, pleased with himself.

"How do you know all this?" Tommy asked.

"I used to be a bit of a crook myself," George said proudly.

"You?" Tommy said, surprised. He studied the withered old man.

"It was years ago, but I was one of the best," he said, a faraway look in his eyes. "One night I slipped from a fire escape and landed in a dumpster. They kept me in jail for years until they figured I couldn't hurt anybody and sent me here to the Roost."

Tommy was amazed by the old man's story. "Did you ever do any big hits?" he asked.

George waved him off. "Of course I did, but we'll talk about those later. Right now, we've got to figure out what to do."

"What do you mean, what to do?" Tommy asked. "I thought you weren't going to turn me in."

"I'm not. We've got to figure out how to sneak out of here." "We?" Tommy asked, alarmed. "You're not going with me." "I beg to differ. Either you take me to your party, or I turn you in and you go to jail. You choose."

Tommy knew he'd been defeated. He shouldered the backpack and followed George out of the cafeteria. George grabbed one of the dark green table cloths on the way out of the kitchen and told Tommy to wrap it around his shoulders, covering up the white sweatshirt. He also instructed Tommy to dry the soles of his shoes before they stepped out into the hallway.

Halfway through the parking lot, halfway to freedom, George stopped.

"Hey, Tommy, you want to really impress your friends?" "Sure," Tommy said aloud. To himself, he thought, "I'd better because I'll have a hell of a time explaining you."

"Then follow me."

Tommy followed George through the parking lot, stopping in front of a long shiny limousine.

"I think we'll take Beatrice's car," George said with a smile. "Cool. Do you have the keys with you?" Tommy asked. "Don't need keys, kid. Haven't you ever hot-wired a car before?"

"Sure," Tommy lied.

"Then go to it, boy," George instructed.

"Okay, I haven't."

"What kind of street kid are you? Well, come on, I'll teach you a new trick that'll amaze and impress your family and friends. Well, maybe just your friends."

Carefully, without scratching the paint or molding of the black limousine, George jimmied the lock. He instructed Tommy to sit in the driver's seat and took him step by step through the procedure of hot wiring the car. The limo was an old antique, and was easy to hot wire. Within minutes the old car was purring.

"Okay, Tommy, help me into the passenger's seat and we'll be off."

"Um, I haven't driven a whole lot," Tommy said, suddenly losing his cool-guy attitude.

George stared at his young charge. "I need a new sidekick," he said glumly. "All right, get in and let's see how you do. But whatever you do, don't turn the headlights on until we get out of sight."

The old limousine bucked along the dirt driveway. At the end, George allowed Tommy to turn on the headlights. Tommy pulled the limousine alongside the Chevy van and rolled his window down.

Deek rolled down the driver's window and stared at Tommy with mouth wide open.

"Wanta ride?" Tommy asked. The five boys didn't need to be asked again. They jumped out of the van and into the limousine.

"Who's the old guy?" Deek asked when they piled in back.

"This is George," Tommy said. "He's cool."

"This George's car?"

"Nah, I wired it," Tommy answered coolly.

The silence that followed indicated the new level of respect Tommy had acquired. For the next several miles, the boys became acquainted with Beatrice's limousine, playing with the power windows and locks and stretching out in the large seats.

"Whose lake house are we going to?" George asked the group.

"We don't know. We just break in and use one whenever we feel like it," Deek said toughly. "The guys are waiting for us in the one we broke into an hour ago before we went to get the food."

George simply looked out the window savoring the freedom and excitement he hadn't felt in years. Within twenty minutes they had reached the lake house. The guys who had arrived earlier came outside to check out the limousine. Deek began taking all the credit and Tommy started to chime in but George tapped him on the leg and whispered, "That's the way it's done. The leader always gets the credit."

Everyone accepted George easily. He taught the guys how to play five card stud. Perhaps a more valuable lesson, he taught them how to cheat effectively at poker. After taking one look at the food Tommy brought, the boys declined to indulge.

"That's pretty bad food if these guys won't eat it," Tommy said to George.

The group drank cheap wane and played cards until about four in the morning, at which time George thought it wise to return.

"Go home?" Tommy said. "The party's just getting good."

"I realize that, but we've still got a few more chores to do before the morning," George said. Tommy already knew George well enough not to argue. They made sure the others could get a ride back to their van and left.

"Congratulations, kid, looks like you're back in the gang," George said.

"You didn't do so bad yourself, old man. I think you're the first honorary member we have ever had."

They drove back in companionable silence. A couple of miles from the Roost, George instructed Tommy to pull into a self service car wash.

"What for?" Tommy asked in surprise.

"Were going to clean up Beatrice's car."

"Why? If no one saw us take it, why should be bother to clean it up?"

"Because we did take it, and we don't want to arouse suspicions. So we can at least be sure it's exactly like it was when we borrowed it."

Tommy was bemused by his new friend's attitude and cleaned the car inside and out. There was a great deal of mud along the sides where the limo had bogged down on one of the dirt roads that led back to the lake house. Next, George instructed Tommy to top off the gas tank. Afterward, they drove the limousine back to the Roost, careful to avoid mud puddles. They parked the car in the same position they found it.

George inspected the limo carefully. "No one will ever know we took it," he said triumphantly.

"Who cares?" Tommy said.

"I do. Why get caught for something when you can avoid it?" George asked. He also made Tommy carry all the canned food back to the cafeteria and restock the shelves. "Thanks for the ride," George said, telling Tommy goodbye at the back door. "You sure you want to walk home?"

"I may be able to sleep in the van until the guys get back," Tommy said. "See you tomorrow.

George looked at his watch. "It's been tomorrow for about six hours now."

Niles came storming through the front doors of the Roost and went directly to the administrator's office. He knocked loudly.

"Come in," Steve called from behind the door.

Niles didn't have time for salutations. "Someone has stolen Madame Wellington's limousine," he announced.

Steve ran to the window of his office and looked into the parking lot. "No, Niles, it's right there," he said, pointing at the black limousine.

"Yes, I realize that. What I mean is that the car has been stolen and returned during the evening."

Steve stared at the butler. "How do you know that?"

"The odometer has eighty extra miles on it this morning."

"When's the last time you checked the odometer, Niles?"

"Yesterday evening, sir."

"You check the odometer in that car twice a day?" Steve asked in surprise.

"Three times, actually. I check it at mid day as well."

"Well, has the car been damaged?"

"No, sir. It doesn't appear to have been damaged. In fact, it appears to have been washed and cleaned thoroughly."

"You think someone stole your car so they could wash and clean it?" Steve asked. This guy's been a butler too long, Steve thought to himself.

"So what's the problem, Niles?"

"The eighty miles, sir."

"What would you like to do about it?"

"Call the police, sir."

Steve decided to call the police and let them talk some sense into the old butler. He was getting nowhere. The police showed up later that afternoon and spoke privately with Niles. Beatrice, fortunately, had spent the entire day in her private wing and had no idea what had happened to her precious limousine. Niles thought it best not to upset her until it was absolutely necessary.

The rest home had been abuzz with the excitement of the police investigation all morning, everyone having their own theory about what had transpired. Gladys had been whispering all day that Niles was being arrested for embezzling Mrs. Wellington's money.

"That old butler's just crazy," some declared.

"Beatrice probably took a joy ride last night and didn't want him along," said others.

But the most common story throughout the Roost involved Tommy.

"That new boy, the juvenile delinquent. He took it," the majority agreed, and word got back to the police. When Tommy came into work that afternoon, he was promptly escorted into Steve's office, where the police officers began questioning him.

"Where were you last night, Tommy?" they asked.

"Did you drive that black limousine last night?" they asked.

Tommy refused to answer any of their questions, which infuriated the officers. "If you don't answer, we've got no choice but to take you downtown and question you," they threatened. They also threatened to send him to YDC. Still Tommy did not answer. He was used to getting in trouble. Occasionally, he looked around for George but did not see him, which wasn't surprising. Everyone seemed to scatter whenever the heat was on.

Exasperated, the officers put handcuffs on Tommy and led him to the lobby.

"Whoa, wait a minute!" George yelled out from down the hall. He covered the distance quickly. The officers stopped and looked expectantly at George.

"Where are you taking that boy?" George asked.

"To the station for questioning," one officer replied.

"What for?" George demanded.

"He's being questioned in regards to a stolen car."

"What stolen car?" George persisted.

"The black limousine out there."

"But it's not stolen, it's in the parking lot," George said angrily.

"Yes sir, but we have reason to believe it was stolen and returned during the night."

"But I cleaned that car up when I brought it back," George said, looking directly into the eyes of one of the officers.

"Excuse me, sir, but did you say you brought it back?"

"Yup, sure did. I took it out for a joy ride and brought it back this morning. Didn't think I'd be hurting anything if I took real good care of it. Now, I think you should let that boy go. He didn't have anything to do with it."

The officers complied, removing the handcuffs from Tommy's wrists. Tommy rubbed his wrists gently, all the while staring at George.

"What are you staring at, boy?" George barked at him. "You never seen an old man before?" Tommy left the room quickly, surprised and hurt at George's angry tone.

"Where did you go last night?" one of the officers asked George.

"None of your business," George snapped.

"I'm afraid it is our business, sir, because that limousine was not yours for the taking. Now, where were you?"

"Can't hear you," George said, tapping his hearing aid. "Damn thing's broke."

"You have to answer our questions," the officer yelled loudly. George grabbed his hearing aid and quickly turned the volume down.

"You don't have to yell," he said with a pained expression. George looked around at all the residents and staff who had gathered in the lobby. "Would you mind if we discussed this where there weren't so many busybodies?" George asked. "It's kind of personal."

The policemen followed George into the administrator's office and closed the door. "Now, where were you last night in Ms. Beatrice Wellington's limousine?"

George hung his head sheepishly. "Well, you guys know how it is when you haven't . . . . What I'm trying to say is that sometimes a man gets lonely and . . . . Well, the truth of the matter is, I got me a woman on the other side of town that I wanted to see. I don't have a car of my own and they frown on conjugal visits here." The part about the conjugal visits was a lie, but George didn't think the officers would take time to find that out for themselves.

The officers were clearly embarrassed but understanding about George's plight. They promised to try and smooth the waters with Niles since they couldn't see as George had done any real harm to the limousine, and no one actually saw him driving the limousine.

One of the officers leaned down and whispered in George's ear, "George, the next time you need a ride to see your friend, give one of us a call, okay? Don't take somebody else's car." "That's awfully nice of you fellows and I may take you up on it," George said with a lecherous grin.

Tommy came to George's room later that afternoon. He threw a brown paper sack on the bed. George smelled the hamburger without opening the bag.

"Mmmm, a hamburger with chili and onions," George said dreamily, his eyes closed and nostrils flared.

"You're not bad for an old guy," Tommy said. He turned to leave George alone with his food.

"Hey, Tommy—you're not so bad yourself. Do me a favor and tell those old folks in the cafeteria that I won't be having my mush today."

CHAPTER 4

WITH great determination and strength for a woman in her seventies, Johnnie pushed up the heavy window and unlatched the screen, watching it fell into the rose bushes below. Satisfied, she picked up the telephone beside her bed and dialed. After several rings the operator picked up.

"What city, ma'am?"

"Well I'm in Stalvey, Georgia," Johnnie answered, her adrenaline was building up for the heady rush she knew would follow.

"No, ma'am. What city do you want?" the operator persisted.

"I don't want a city, I need help," Johnnie said, perplexed by the operator's question.

"Ma'am," the operator asked, exasperated, "what number do you need?"

"I don't need a number, I need an ambulance," Johnnie cried out. This was not going as planned.

"You need to dial 911, ma'am."

"I thought I did."

"No, ma'am, you dialed 411. This is Information."

"Oh." Silence ensued. "Well, thank you, operator."

Johnnie hung up the phone and dialed again quickly, determined not to lose her nerve. She was careful to punch in the number "9" first.

An operator picked up on the first ring. "What's your emergency?"

"I'm going to jump out of this window," Johnnie said, indicating the open window with a sweep of her hand.

"Okay, now. Just calm down, ma'am, and tell me why you want to jump out of the window," the operator said with patient concern, she was waiting for the 911 system to trace the caller's location. There it was—the nursing home out on Old Ebenezer Road. She punched a button to notify the ambulance.

"I'm just tired of living," Johnnie said dramatically, with a heavy sigh.

"What's your name?" the operator asked in a friendly tone. "Johnnie. Why do you want to know?"

"Well, Johnnie, I just wanted to be able to call you by your first name. Now I suggest you just take a couple of deep breaths and get away from the window." The operator would have been surprised to know that Johnnie was picking through a box of chocolates instead of standing precariously on a window ledge.

"I can't do that—I hate it here and I want to end it all," Johnnie said, careful not to rustle the candy papers as she spoke. "Why are you so miserable, Johnnie?"

"I hate being here at this nursing home. My family dumped me here because I got old and the nurses here beat me because I'm too old to defend myself. I'm just old," Johnnie said, scraping the chocolate from under her fingernails with a metal nail file.

"There are some people on the way right now who are coming to help you, Johnnie," the operator said.

"What?" Johnnie asked in surprise. She had planned on drawing out the telephone conversation for a least a good half hour of begging and pleading. "Where are they?"

"They should be approaching Old Ebenezer Road right now. I'll check." The operator heard Johnnie's line go dead. The operator picked up the CB radio. "Unit Two, the subject has disconnected communications. Suggest speedy arrival."

One of the town's eight police officers, a mile away from The Roost, stamped down on the accelerator, skidding on the driveway of the nursing home. The front right tire spun wildly on road scrapple and nearly sent the squad car into a nearby drainage ditch. He picked up his own radio. "Dispatch, I'm pulling out of the Dunk and Dine right now—has an ambulance been sent?"

"That's affirmative, they're about a mile behind you."

In less than a minute, the cruiser screeched to a stop in front of The Roost, lights flashing and siren wailing. Residents gathered on the front porch as Officer Radburn searched in his trunk for his megaphone.

Patti emerged from the porch crowd as the policeman approached. "What's going on, Hank?" she asked worriedly.

"You don't know?" he asked, stopping in his tracks. "Somebody named Johnnie is taking a dive from her window."

"That's the first I've heard about it," Patti said worriedly. Johnnie was a new resident at the Roost and had been quite a handful since she had arrived.

Meanwhile, inside the Roost, Johnnie was preparing to jump. She pulled all ninety three pounds onto the window ledge and sat with her back to the outdoors. Johnnie had removed the terry cloth belt from her bathrobe and tied two pillows to her back. Like a deep sea diver she caught her breath, held her nose, closed her eyes, and fell back . . .

The ambulance pulled up behind the squad car and the two paramedics scrambled out. "Has she jumped?" the driver asked.

"We don't know yet—they didn't even know they had a problem here," Officer Radburn said.

Patti was puzzled. Worried and concerned, but puzzled. "It's a one story building," she said. "How far can she jump?"

The paramedics were instructed to run around the back side of the building while Patti and the policeman went through the inside to Johnnie's room. Her door was closed but the twosome busted in, prepared to stop the old woman. No one was in the room, but the window was open, the curtains blowing easily in the spring breeze.

"Oh, no," Patti exclaimed, her hands flying to cover her mouth.

The heads of the two paramedics appeared at the window. "We've got her. She doesn't appear to be hurt too badly—just has some thorns in her . . . . lower torso," the driver laughed.

Patti rushed to the window, and saw that Johnnie was being held in the strong arms of the paramedics. Johnnie's eyes were closed, but her eyelids were twitching. The threesome stood in the middle of what used to be one of the Garden Club's prized rosebush.

"I think," the driver said with a conspiratorial wink, "that Johnnie here is unconscious. We're going to take her back inside to remove the thorns. Actually, it's probably best that she's unconscious because we can save money on pain killer—it's gotten fairly expensive."

Johnnie stirred then, her eyes popping open and flashing with anger. The wiry old woman began struggling in the beefy arms of the well-built paramedic. "Put me down. I'll teach you how to save money—what are you trying to do, kill me?"

"Why, no ma'am. That's your job," the other paramedic said, and received a swift kick from the driver for his crack.

Patti left the paramedics working on thorn removal from Johnnie's rear-end and returned to the lobby. It looked like the reception room of a funeral home. Women were wailing and consoling each other, and tissues were being handed out by the box.

"What's going on?" Patti asked loudly, trying to be heard above the mournful din. "Johnnie's going to be just fine. She's only got a few thorns in her backside, that's all."

"Oh, but Ruby Alexander is dead and gone," one of the women wailed. "She was so beautiful . . . so majestic . . . so pure."

"She brought us such joy," lamented another, wringing her hands in agony.

Patti was confused. The name "Ruby Alexander" didn't ring a bell with her. Patti knew all of the residents' names by heart—even the names of their immediate families. But "Ruby Alexander" escaped her memory. "What happened to her?" Patti ventured fearfully.

"Crushed, just as she was beginning to bloom."

"Halted, in the budding spring of her life."

This must be a young girl, Patti realized. Perhaps the granddaughter of one of the residents. She sat down heavily in one of the vinyl covered lobby chairs. "Whose granddaughter was she?" The ten or twelve women gathered in the lobby stopped sniffling long enough to stare at Patti with distaste.

"Granddaughter? Whatever are you talking about? Ruby Alexander was that divinely beautiful rose bush that grew outside of Johnnie's window."

Gladys said the name "Johnnie" as though the very letters of her name smelled bad, causing her nose to wrinkle.

"It was our only burgundy rose bush," another informed Patti with a sorrowful shake of her head. "We were grooming that particular bush for a reason. We wanted to use the cuttings for the beauty pageant."

The paramedics were having a hard time getting Johnnie to cooperate with them. "Okay, Miss Johnnie," tried one. "We need you to lie still so we can remove these thorns."

"Aren't you going to give me a pain killer?" she inquired. "Now, Miss Johnnie, we were just teasing about that. You don't really need a pain killer for this. If you'll just lie still . . ." "Help!" Johnnie yelled suddenly, causing the two paramedics to jump. "They're killing me in here. Somebody help!"

"Shhhh, okay, all right. Bobby, let's give her a shot for pain," said the driver.

"No shot, I want pills," Johnnie said.

"Pills won't work quickly enough," said Bobby, trying to reason with the elderly woman.

"Well, give me a bottle of them and I'll use 'em later," Johnnie said, already making plans for her next "suicide" attempt.

"I can't believe that they are going to allow these women to parade themselves shamelessly around a stage for the sake of vanity," Beatrice exclaimed to Niles, seeing the notice:

ATTENTION LADIES!!!
IT'S TIME TO SHOW YOUR STUFF!!

The Eighth Annual Ms. Milly's Merry Roost Beauty Pageant will be held this Friday evening at 7 p.m. in the dining hall. Events will include

Evening Gown and Talent competition, as well as a question and answer competition. All contestants should sign up with the activities director, Michelle Peterson.

Hair dressing will be donated by the talented beautician of this year's sponsor, Gillooly and Sons Funeral Home, who will be available all day Friday prior to the competition.

NOTE: Any acts involving Jell-O will not be allowed in the talent competition due to the injury suffered last year.

"I, for one, shall not be present for this tasteless event," Beatrice sniffed.

Niles didn't comment.

Patti stormed into the recreation room. "Dr. Price, we need to have a serious talk."

Dr. Price looked up from his chess game briefly to glance at Patti. "What's wrong, Nurse McLeod?" he asked with little interest. He held a black knight between his middle finger and thumb, weighing the options and consequences of placement.

"It's about Johnnie—she's done it again," Patti said, irritated by the resident doctor's lack of interest in his patients' well-being.

"What's she up to this time?" he asked, placing the knight a few paces beside George's king. "Check," he said. George groaned.

"I just found her lying in the parking lot, dressed all in yellow, parallel with one of the speed bumps, yelling at cars to hit her," Patti said worriedly. "I'm at my wits end with her—this is the fifth attempt in two weeks."

"She's really getting creative," Dr. Price said approvingly. "This may top last Wednesday when she handcuffed herself to the dumpster. It was a good thing the driver of the garbage truck noticed before they had it too far off the ground."

Dr. Price watched as George moved his king safely out of danger. He tapped his chin in concentration.

"Dr. Price," Patti pleaded. "Don't you think we should do something about Johnnie?"

"What, tie her up? Over-medicate her so she doesn't have either the strength or the creativity to come up with these interesting plans? She's not going to hurt herself, Nurse McLeod. All she wants is some good old fashioned attention." He looked at Patti closely. "And it looks like she's got that from you." Dr. Price turned back to the chessboard, moved his rook and proclaimed, "Checkmate, George. It was a pleasure." Patti was gone when he turned back. He rubbed his hands together with pleasure. "All right, George. Set the board up again."

"I'm not sure what color rinse I should get," Gladys said, contemplating her reflection in the mirror.

"Ask the beautician when she gets here," Mona said. "You did make an appointment, didn't you?"

"Oh, sure, it's for noon on Friday. I just wanted to have an idea so I can pick out a dress to match."

"Have you decided on your talent, yet?" Mona asked. "That's going to be my secret," Gladys said, pursing her lips. "If I tell you, everyone will know and it won't be a surprise." Mona pouted. "I'll tell you what I'm going to do if you'll tell me what you're going to do," she said.

"Oh, Mona, everyone knows you're going to play that little plastic ukulele and sing 'Tiptoe Through the Tulips' like you do every year," Gladys said, rolling her eyes.

"Hmmmph," Mona said, turning back to her macramé, "Maybe so, but you don't know what I'm going to wear."

"As a matter of fact, I do. You'll wear that tired old grass skirt with little plastic fish glued to it. You'll also wear those rubber sandals and some sort of tube top that no respectable Hawaiian would be caught dead in." Gladys looked at her friend and laughed. Mona joined in good naturedly; the two women had been good friends for years and teased each other relentlessly.

"Okay, so it's no surprise to you. But there are a few new men here since the last pageant, and it doesn't hurt to show off my wares."

"Mona, I hate to be the one to break this to you, but our wares are worn out," Gladys said. The two women broke into laughter.

Patti walked into Johnnie's room Friday morning with trepidation. She was a little uneasy because days had passed since Johnnie had made another attempt. She had been nearly complacent since the speed bump incident, eating all her food, not complaining, and seemingly happy in her surroundings. Johnnie had even participated in some of the group craft classes without disruption. A couple of weeks ago, the activities director had reported a good deal of macramé twine missing from a session. Patti had later discovered Johnnie in her room, trying to fashion a hangman's noose. Johnnie had protested that it was nothing more than a decorative plant hanger, but Patti knew better and asked Michelle to retrieve the "decorative" plant hanger for use only in the activity room. She was becoming wise to the old woman's attempts. Wise, but not callous like Dr. Price. The old doctor was beginning to fray Patti's nerves with his apathetic attitude toward the patients. All he seemed to want was to be left in peace with his stupid board games.

"Good morning, Johnnie," Patti said cheerily, looking in on the old woman.

"Morning, Patti. How are you today? Isn't it a beautiful day outside?" Johnnie asked, looking out her window onto the grounds outside. Safety bars had been placed on the window since Johnnie's last jump, but she acted as though she never noticed. "I feel bad about the rose bushes— the Garden Club may never forgive me for that one," Johnnie said with surprising sincerity. "What a silly old fool I've been lately." The elderly woman tucked her shawl under her legs and looked at Patti with a cherubic expression. "Can you forgive an old woman?"

"Why, of course, Johnnie." Patti felt guilty for harboring ill will towards her. After all, it must be difficult to live here away from family and old friends. "Are you feeling well today?" "Oh, I'm feeling just fine. In fact, I couldn't be happier." "Are you entering the pageant this evening?" Patti asked. "No, no. An old woman like me? No, I thought I'd stay in my room tonight and write some letters. I think my daughter's coming to see me." Johnnie turned back to the window, rocking slowly in her chair.

Maybe she's finally coming around, Patti thought.

I thought she'd never leave, thought Johnnie. The nursing director was a threat to her plans—always checking on her to make sure she wasn't going to pull "the big one." She pulled the scrap of paper from underneath her shawl and ran through her list again, licking the tip of her pen as she checked off the tasks she had already accomplished. Everything looked in order . . . now, to steal a wheelchair . . .

Gladys arrived in the day room promptly at noon for her hair appointment. She'd watched all morning as the various pageant contestants filed in and out, all sporting a new "do" upon their exit. She had to admit, the beautician—even though she was employed by a funeral home—did good work. She made everyone look quite natural, but then, that was the goal of funeral homes, wasn't it?

"Are you next, dear?" a voice called out to Gladys from across the room. The beautician motioned for Gladys to take a seat in the barber's chair in front of a sink. "Sit here, dear, and tell me what you want me to do with your hair." Gladys couldn't venture a guess on the age of the beautician—she was so heavily made-up and her hair was pulled up into some sort of a bun.

"My name is Margie, dear, and let me tell you, I'm a whiz at hair-do's," the beautician said, waving her long red fingernails in the air. "What'll it be?"

"Well, I'm not sure," Gladys said. "I can't decide exactly what I want—I'd sort of like to try something different, if you have any ideas."

Margie's eyes grew bright with excitement, and she began circling the barber's chair, eying Gladys' hair the way an artist would eye a blank canvas. "Oh, yes, something special for the evening. Hmmm, perhaps a rinse?" she asked suggestively.

"What color rinse would you suggest?" Gladys asked. She wanted the evening to be special and trusted the keen eye of a beautician rather than her own sense of style. She would simply die if anyone knew—especially Mona—but she wanted to catch George's attention. She had recently discovered a certain softness for the old codger.

"Everyone will expect blue or lilac," Margie said thoughtfully, her index finger wrapped around her chin in thought. "How about something soft and light . . . pink?"

"Pink." Gladys seemed to roll the idea around on her tongue, testing the way it sounded as though it would indicate how it would look on her head. "Pink," she said again, then more decisively, "I'll take it." In fact, she said boldly, "make it hot pink."

Margie clapped her hands in approval and delight. It was rare she had a customer so . . . so alive. "Hot pink it is," she cried triumphantly, and set about mixing chemicals. "How about a different style?" she asked Gladys hopefully.

"Why not?" Gladys said gamely. Wait'll George sees this, she thought to herself. Let him choke on his Metamucil.

The florist delivery truck arrived promptly at four o'clock—plenty of time for the Garden Club to decorate for the pageant. Ida met the delivery man at the back door of his van, ready to direct him to the Garden Section. Mae Sellers, president of the Garden Club, intercepted.

"I've got this one, Ida, it's not going to the Garden Section," Mae explained. "These are going to the dining hall for the pageant tonight."

Ida was disappointed that her role had been usurped and slunk back inside the lobby.

Soon, the other eight members of the Garden Club had gathered around the back of the van to inspect its contents. There were several arrangements of red roses.

"They're so breathtakingly beautiful," exclaimed one.

"I still think the Ruby Alexander was much more beautiful than these," said Mae. "But I guess we were left with no choice."

"I've never heard of a Garden Club having to order flowers for an event—it's quite embarrassing," said another.

"Yes, but how many Garden Clubs have to put up with the likes of Johnnie?" said Mae imperiously. They all nodded in agreement, clucking their tongues over the senseless tragedy.

"I had just put fresh peat moss around it, too," said one, barely able to contain her grief.

"And after overcoming that awful battle with aphids, too," said another with a faraway look in her eyes.

Mae couldn't bear much more. She clapped her hands loudly. "All right, girls, we've just got to go on from here—no use crying over spilt milk—or crushed roses, should I say. Now everyone grab an arrangement and take it to the dining room. Chop chop!"

Johnnie crept along the hallway, ready with an alibi in case anyone asked what she was doing wandering around. The bad thing about crying wolf all the time, she realized, was that no one trusted her any more, but she had to do everything she could to get people to pay attention to her. There was a time she was always the center of attention but now it seemed no one in her family noticed how lonely and upset she was. "They've just put me in this hell hole and completely forgotten me," she thought. "But the joke's on them—they'll have to notice me now."

If this one didn't work, Johnnie was quite sure she'd never have another chance. She was constantly quizzed as to her intentions when walking about the home now. If she failed this time, they'd probably strap her to the bed, or send her to some kind of old folk's detention home. Was there such a place? she wondered.

"I'm going to check the bulletin board, I'm going to check the activity board," she repeated to herself softly as she crept along the hall. At the end of the hallway, she made a right turn, toward the new wing. Toward Beatrice's room. Beatrice had the fastest wheelchair in the home and Johnnie wanted it. Everyone knew that Beatrice took a nap between three and five o'clock every single day—at least as long as she'd been at The Roost. It was also common knowledge that Niles usually slipped out to the courtyard for a respite and a tumbler of brandy to sip with his afternoon tea. This would be Johnnie's only chance.

Johnnie reached out for the handle of Beatrice's door and heard a noise coming from down the hall. She immediately bent down to tie her shoe laces before she noticed she was wearing her slippers. So she kicked the slipper off of her foot several feet away and made a big production of retrieving it.

"Well, Miss Johnnie, how in the world did you lose your slipper?" It was Lucy. Everything was all right. Lucy was one of the few nurses who didn't bother her.

"I was just practicing my cartwheels and my slipper went flying," Johnnie joked.

Lucy laughed along with her, then pointed toward Beatrice's door. "We'd better hush up. Miss Beatrice gets awful irate whenever she gets woke up," she said, a finger pressed to her lips.

Johnnie nodded with a smile and pretended to zip her lips. "I'm quiet as a mouse," she whispered. Lucy continued down the hallway. Johnnie waited for her pulse to slow before reaching out for the door handle again. Thank goodness it opened easily. Johnnie opened the door slowly, bracing herself for any ensuing squeaks or scrapes. There were none. She held her breath as though it made her invisible and entered the room. There it was—gleaming right beside the door. A horrible noise made her jump in her slippers, until she realized what it was.

"The old bag sure can snore," Johnnie laughed to herself. She glanced toward the bed and saw Beatrice with one of those blindfolds on and plugs poking out of her ears. Her mouth was wide open and the snores came deep, rough and regular. Johnnie's late husband used to have a chainsaw that made noises like that. Johnnie crept around to the back of the wheelchair, flipped off the brakes, and pushed it toward the door.

"She hardly uses this thing anymore anyway," Johnnie reasoned to herself. "She'll probably never notice it's gone." The wheelchair was beautiful and moved smoothly—just like Beatrice's limousine outside. In fact, the wheelchair was custom made and sort of resembled the limousine parked outside. Johnnie turned around and backed the chair out of the door. She half ran the distance to her room; miraculously, no one spied her. Closing the door behind her, she hugged herself with glee, pleased with her craftiness. She parked the wheelchair in her bathroom, closed the door, and returned to her list to make the final check mark.

"Good evening, ladies and gentlemen. My name is Morty Gillooly and I'll be the master of ceremonies for the evening," said the fortyish, balding man with a gut that poked over and under his tight lavender cummerbund. "As you all probably know, I am the son of Gillooly and Sons Funeral Home, who just happens to be the sponsor of the 8th Annual Beauty Pageant here at Milly's Merry Roost. I just want to let you know . . . when you need us, we'll be there for you."

"What a comforting thought," George said with a shiver. "I don't think I want that man to have my body after I'm gone. He'll probably give me a goofy haircut or something."

"Wonder when he's going to break into 'Feelings.'" said Tommy, under his breath.

"He's definitely lounge-singer material," Dr. Price agreed. "All he needs is a big heavy gold chain to rest on that nappy chest of his." Indeed, Morty fancied himself the consummate showman. His hair was slicked back, his moustache waxed, and the silk shirt he wore was open three buttons down from his hairy neck to reveal an even hairier chest. He even held the microphone as though it were a familiar appendage to his arm.

"It's showtime!" Morty said, doing a little jig over to the side of the stage where the master of ceremony podium stood. The dining hall had been transformed. Gone were the institutional cafeteria tables and serving trays. Gone were the huge black plastic trashcans. Chairs were lined up in rows for the audience members, facing the 'stage' which was where the serving line usually was. White sheets covered the food bar, and in front of the sheets were dozens of beautiful yellow roses arranged ingeniously by the Garden Club. The lights were cut off and replaced by a myriad of candles, which cast a soft yellow glow.

Across the wall behind the stage was a huge banner which read: "Eighth Annual Ms. Milly's Merry Roost Pageant." Pictures of all the past winners were taken from their normal place of prominence in the hall and hung in a row below the banner. The three judges sat behind a table to the left of the stage, looking serious with pens poised over paper, ready to take notes which would help them make the big decision. A red carpet had been run down the center aisle to serve as a "runway" for the newly-crowned winner to stroll down.

"I swear," an elderly man said, looking around the room in amazement, "if I didn't know any better, I'd never guess I ate strained spinach in here just two hours ago."

"I love the candle light," said Ida. "Everyone looks ten years younger. I think we should do this all the time. And the roses—the Garden Department looks marvelous. The employees really outdid themselves this time."

"They're afraid we'd bum the place down if we had candles all the time," George groused; but even his sarcasm seemed softened by the ambience. "It is sort of nice," he relented, "for a nursing home."

"I'm going outside to catch a smoke," Tommy said, rising from his chair. "You want to go?" he asked George.

"You're staying put," George commanded. "If I'm staying, you're staying." Tommy sat down heavily.

"And our first contestant comes all the way from the Green Wing . . . Ms. Frances Donaldson!" Morty announced, sweeping his arm toward the stage. Somewhere offstage, a cassette player was turned on and the marching sounds of "Hooked on Classics" began as Frances made her way to the front of the stage. She was a portly woman who walked with the grace of a model—taking her time reaching the microphone before turning slowly, so as to display her flowing evening gown to the crowd. Approximately 50 people had gathered in the dining room to watch the pageant, a combination of residents and relatives.

As Frances turned, George, Tommy, Jack Tyler and Blue, and two other cronies began whistling and cat-calling. "Take it off, Frances! Take it off!" Frances, caught off guard by the unexpected attention, blushed and walked quickly off the stage—this time, with the blind charge of a stampeding bull rather than the easy grace displayed earlier. George and his friends collapsed in laughter.

"I'm going to have to ask audience members to please remain quiet throughout the pageant," Morty warned the men.

"What?" George yelled out, holding up his hand. In it was his hearing aid. "Damn thing's broke—can't hear a word you said." A crash was heard backstage.

"Frances, are you all right?" Morty asked. The men laughed even harder.

After it was determined that Frances was fine and the four men were escorted to the back of the dining hall, the pageant continued. In all, seven contestants paraded around the stage, each distinctly beautiful in their gowns and dresses. Years were shed from their age-lined faces in the glow of the candles and the excitement of the moment.

Gladys was the last contestant to come out. The breath of the audience seemed to be sucked up into a vacuum as her pink hair came clearly into view. To say it was pink would be an understatement. It was hot pink. In fact, it was so hot that the men on the back row were completely dumbstruck. The color wasn't the only shock—the style was brazen as well-crafted into a punk look with pink spikes sticking out in every direction. When discussed later, no one could remember the outfit she wore, so outstanding was her hair.

Breaths were released and excited murmurings, along with the applause of all the contestants, began as Gladys walked off the stage through the door that led to the kitchen pantry.

"Okay, everyone. Settle down," Morty said, as though he were an emergency director in the thick of a crisis. "The next event will be Talent."

One by one, contestants came forward and performed their talents. Frances regained her composure enough to present a dramatic monologue from Shakespeare's Macbeth, as Lady Macbeth. She was good. She had obviously received extensive theatrical training during her life.

Next, Mona, dressed in her hula skirt and tube top, played "Tiptoe Through The Tulips" on a little plastic ukulele. She received polite, but bored applause as the majority had seen the act many times before. Mona's act was followed by a rousing rendition of "You Are My Sunshine" on the kazoo, an impressive hambone performance, and two tap dance routines. Only Gladys remained and the audience awaited her pink appearance with palpable anticipation.

Suddenly, from the back of the dining hall, there came a shout that was later to be described by a resident/retired zoologist as an almost exact imitation of the primal mating call of an African she-gorilla fully in "season." Instinctively, everyone ducked, leaving master of ceremony Morty a clear view of the aisle. There, at the top of the gently sloping passageway, at the back of the dining hall, was Johnnie. Of course Morty didn't know Johnnie personally; what he saw was a wild-eyed gray-haired woman strapped with the sleeves of a posey vest into a wheelchair. The tips of her slippers, barely reaching the ground, pushed back and forth building up momentum.

With another banshee-like cry, she propelled herself forward down the ramp. "Goodbye, cruel world!" she yelled on her descent. Everyone was stunned. No one moved to stop her, derail her, or even attempt to slow her down in the least. They watched as the shiny metal wheelchair and its cargo picked up speed and headed straight for the stage. The old woman's hair caught wind and blew back from her face in fine gray wisps. On her face was a look of excitement and pleasure—she was reveling in the moment. This was her last chance.

Morty dove out of the way right before the wheelchair reached the stage, his toupee flew off in the opposite direction and landed in the lap of a female pageant judge, who screamed and flung it over her head, much to the dismay of those seated behind her. Meanwhile, Johnnie and her chair hurdled onto the stage, ran over the microphone—which shrieked ear piercing feed-back—and crashed . . . into the dozens of arrangements of yellow roses provided by the Garden Club.

"Oooh," said the crowd collectively, more for the sake of the yellow roses than for Johnnie. Johnnie, they all knew to be indestructible. But then Johnnie had never crossed the Garden Club two times before. The wheelchair lay on its side, the exposed wheel spinning wildly. Johnnie was still strapped in the chair, somewhere, underneath all the yellow roses that covered her.

"Get these damn flowers off of me," Johnnie yelled from under her thorny yellow blanket. "What are y'all trying to do, kill me?" she sputtered. "Untie this straight jacket!"

Patti was the first to rush to her side. With the help of a nurse, they easily righted the wheelchair. The nurse began untying Johnnie while Patti began a physical assessment. "Johnnie, are you all right?" She began feeling the woman's bones for any breaks.

"What do you think? I'm still alive, ain't I?" Johnnie said with disgust. She stood up and brushed yellow petals out of her lap. "I'm feeling just . . ." Johnnie started to say, then saw the contingency of Garden Clubbers heading her way. Out of the corner of her eye, Johnnie spied Niles marching toward the stage as well. Oh, gosh, the wheelchair, she thought. Since she was still alive, she hoped the chair hadn't suffered any great damage.

"Actually," Johnnie said, feeling behind her for the wheelchair and lowering herself into it, "everything is turning black. I may pass out." The Garden Club reached her just as her head was lolling lifelessly onto her shoulder.

Patti stopped them with an upraised hand. "Ladies, I know you're upset about the roses, but Johnnie's not feeling well. Let's all back up and give her some air."

"Just let me take a swing at her," said Mae, rolling up the sleeves of her floral blouse.

A couple of hours later, Patti called Dr. Price at home. She had remained at The Roost long after the completion of the pageant, dealing with Johnnie, Beatrice, and the Garden Club. The Club wanted to get an injunction against Johnnie that would prohibit her from coming within fifty feet of their roses. Beatrice wanted to have Johnnie arrested for grand theft wheelchair. And Gladys was irate over the fact that the pageant had been disrupted and postponed until a later date. Now she was stuck with all that hot pink hair with no one to appreciate it. Johnnie kept coming in and out of 'consciousness', unable to participate in the heated conversations.

"Dr. Price . . ." Patti began when he answered the telephone.

"I know, I know . . . I've already been told about what happened tonight," he said with a sigh. "It makes me sick I had to leave early and miss all the fun."

"Are you going to do anything about it this time?" Patti snapped. "Or are you just going to set up another chess board when you come in. Or maybe checkers. Or whatever it may be that's so much more attractive than doing your job." There, Patti had said it. She held her breath in anticipation of his explosion.

"Look, I still say she's only looking for attention, but you're right, it's getting to the point where she may hurt herself. I'll take care of it."

"Excuse me? What do you plan on doing?" Patti asked suspiciously.

"I don't have it all planned out yet, but I guarantee that as of Monday, Johnnies going to be doing everything in her power to stay around a few more years."

William Price hung up the phone and punched in eleven numbers. He got an answering machine. "Hello, Jack? This is Bill Price. I need a big favor from you—call me back anytime this weekend."

Johnnie awoke Monday morning in a state of depression. She made feces at the surveillance camera they had installed in her room. After breakfast, she took her spoon and ran it along the safety bars on her window, picket-fence style, until Lucy came and took the spoon away from her. When Tommy came in to collect her dirty linens, she tried to bribe him into stealing drugs for her out of the medicine closet. He declined, still smarting from his near brush with jail during the limousine incident. He'd also been verbally disciplined for having participated in the heckling at the beauty pageant the other night. Lately George had been getting him into a lot of trouble.

"Anything," Johnnie had asked Tommy. "Any kind of drug, I don't care. I guess even enough laxatives ought to take care of it," she said.

"No," Tommy said firmly. "Are you kidding? Do you think they'd let me anywhere near the medicine closet?"

"You've got a point," Johnnie cackled.

After Tommy left, Lucy poked her head into Johnnie's room. "Oh, Johnnie, you have a visitor. Somebody named Jack," she said.

"I don't know any Jack," Johnnie said. "He must want someone else."

"Nope, it's you he wants. He's a doctor."

"Well, send him on in," Johnnie said. Probably another one of those interns that loved to poke and prod the old folks at the nursing home.

The doctor looked to be in his sixties, and pushed a funny looking cart in front of him as he entered the room. His face looked familiar to Johnnie, but she couldn't quite place where she'd seen it before.

"Hello, Johnnie, how are you?" he asked pleasantly. "Dr. Price wanted me to come over and help you out."

"Help me out? What do you mean, help me out?"

"Well, I've heard that you keep trying to commit suicide, but aren't having very good luck at it. So, I've brought my machine with me to help you out. My name is Jack Kevorkian—maybe you've heard of me." He began untying the tubes from around the machine and turning dials and flipping switches.

"Now hold on here," Johnnie said, backing up against the wall, "what are you trying to do, kill me?"

"Well . . .," Kevorkian trailed off, glancing up to look at Johnnie from the other side of his machine.

Word of Kevorkian's presence and the attempt at forcing Johnnies hand spread through The Roost quickly. Residents and staff members gathered down the hall from Johnnie's room, waiting to witness her flight from the room. The Garden Club members had front row seats and had brought along popcorn to munch on during the wait.

"It would serve her right to get a good scare," Mae said righteously. The other ladies nodded vigorously. Dr. Price wandered up behind the spectators, munching on popcorn. Patti hadn't been advised of the plan—he thought she'd appreciate it much more afterward than before. And, who knows? she might have warned Johnnie of the plan.

Almost an hour passed before Kevorkian exited Johnnie's room. The group gathered in the hall and watched as he solemnly pushed the cart toward them.

"She's resting now," he said simply. "You won't have to worry about her little shenanigans any more—I've cured her. You might want to notify her family."

"No, you didn't . . ." Dr. Price said, dropping the popcorn from his hand and staring open-mouthed at Kevorkian. Dr. Price rushed to Johnnie's room and burst in through the door, followed closely by the Garden Club. They looked at the bed in dismay. The figure lay quiet and motionless beneath the sheet that had been pulled up over her head. Dr. Price reached to pull back the sheet. The Garden Club gathered around, each one cluck-clucking over the tragedy.

As the sheet came back, they saw Johnnie in a way they'd never seen her before . . . quiet. And, there was a single yellow rose clenched between her teeth.

"Wait a minute," Dr. Price said, a split second before Johnnie's eyes flashed open.

"Thought you'd play a mean trick on an old girl like me, didn't you?" she said, laughing loudly. Mae swooned, but was supported by Dr. Prices arm. "Well, see who's tricked now. Looks like you're stuck with me." Everyone was staring at her in shock, not speaking. "Okay, I have to admit, I'm cured. Your little stunt with Doctor Death worked—scared the bejeesus out of me actually. I just wanted to have the last laugh."

Still no one spoke.

"Can we call a truce?" Johnnie ventured. "I promise not to get near your roses or try to 'check out' if you guys will promise to keep Dr. Death out of my room. Deal?"

"Okay by me," said Dr. Price. "How about you girls?" he asked the Garden Club. They all nodded their approval, still in shock from the incident.

CHAPTER 5

THEY never saw who released the catch, but the door closed anyway, softly, like all institutional doors built for silence. Though the sound was much softer than the ongoing conversation, Gladys and Mona stopped talking and looked at each other wide-eyed.

"Not again," Mona said, closing her eyes and rocking back in her rocking chair. She shook her head slowly. "I wonder who it was this time?"

"I don't want to know, really. I'd just as soon not hear about it," Gladys said, picking up the knitting needles from her lap as though the door had never closed. She, too, shook her head slowly.

"The tables are open for betting," George called out as the door to the recreation room slipped shut. The others gathered there looked around the room, taking inventory, before calling out names.

"Josiah in the Blue Wing," called out one. "He's had pneumonia all week."

Claudia in the Yellow Wing," said another. "Her dialysis hasn't been going so well."

"I don't want to hear any names until I see some cash," George said. Several men and one woman began ambling toward George, pulling dollars out of their pockets.

"Hurry up, you know once someone spills the beans all bets are off," George warned. He pulled out a sheet of paper from his pocket and checked it carefully. "Looks like I won the other bet as to how long it would be until the next one went. Only missed it by two days," George said proudly.

When the door to the Goldberg's room shut, Shirley got up from her chair, walked over to her dresser, and pulled out a black cloth from the bottom drawer. She handed the cloth to her husband, Saul, who took it by the comer, shook it open, and hung it over the mirror that hung in the center of the wall. Saul then went to the grandfather clock that tocked in the corner of the room, pulled open the glass door, and stilled the pendulum. They both then uttered a prayer and returned to the rummy game scattered on the table.

"What the hell is going on?" Tommy asked out loud to no one in particular. He'd just arrived at the Roost from school and noticed all of the doors closed along the main hallway. The effect was spooky. The halls were normally crowded with wheelchairs, walkers, and pedestrians. Today there was no one, no sounds, no travelling devices, nothing. Tommy, normally a garrulous teenager, was hushed into silence. With trepidation, he pushed open the door to the recreation room. "George?" he called out softly.

"Come in here, boy," George said loudly. "You want to place a bet?"

Tommy ignored the invitation. "George, what's going on around here—why are all the doors closed?"

George's face became somber as he realized the teenager wasn't aware of the procedure around the Roost. "The nurses go around closing the door whenever someone dies," George said gently.

"Someone died?" Tommy asked incredulously. "Who? I mean . . . when . . ." He struggled to maintain his "tough guy" image despite the blow of George's words.

George was touched to see the tough young boy so affected by death. It used to affect him the same way . . . years ago. "Come here, boy," he said to Tommy. "Go find something better to do," he barked to the man sitting in the chair across the checker table from him. The man got up quickly and went over to the card table. George motioned Tommy into the chair.

"Now, look here. Death is something that goes on all the time here—it's something that's hard to get used to, but everyone here knows its coming and most of us are ready. Sometimes we even laugh at it or make fun of it. That's how we deal with it. Oh, by the way," George said to the others at the card table, "somebody should go tell Ida there's a check-out on aisle nine." Those at the table cackled at George's black humor.

George turned back to Tommy, who was looking around the room, amazed at the way the residents were going about their business as though nothing had happened. "You've just got to remember that everyone here has already had a long, full life and knows that check out time is right around the corner. Mine, too," he said, looking Tommy in the eye. Tommy looked away.

"I'm gonna go cop a smoke," Tommy said, walking toward the door. George grabbed his arm.

"No you're not, you're going to stay right here with us," George said. "I wonder who it was," he mused aloud. It was the main concern on everyone's mind at the Roost.

"Are all the doors closed?" Patti asked Lucy.

"All closed. And the coroner and the hearse just pulled up," she said. "Should I signal them in?"

"Yes, bring them through the main hallway—that seems to be the shortest route. And if anybody asks . . ." Patti warned.

"I know, I know, don't tell them," Lucy said with a shake of her head. White people amazed her, especially when it came to death. Everything was kept hush hush and hidden away for as long as possible—protecting the living, she supposed. Then, like kudzu after a warm rain, the news would spread quickly and thickly, choking off all the living things to make room for sadness and despair.

Sadie exited The Roost the same way she came in—on a stretcher. Only this time the stretcher was provided by Gillooly and Sons Funeral Home instead of the hospital, and her face was covered, and instead of curious faces peering at her from the hallway she was saluted by heavy closed doors.

"Sadie? Who's Sadie?" George asked, when he discovered the identity of the deceased. "I don't remember any Sadie."

"She was the little old lady on the Yellow Wing," said Gladys, eager to offer George any information she could. She had changed her hair color from pink back to gray once she discovered that George found it unattractive, but it still bore a pinkish tint. "Last time I saw her was when we went door-to-door Christmas caroling last year. I don't think she even knew we were there. She used to be real active until last winter. Remember—she's the one who used to always find a broom and go to the front porch and sweep 'til there wasn't a speck of dirt anywhere. I heard everybody had the worst time trying to convince her she didn't work here, especially when they wanted her to stay off her foot. Poor thing, I guess she's off her feet for good now. She never had any visitors I know of—don't think there's much family to speak of."

"Well, damn. It looks like no one wins the pot—all the money will go into the kitty for the next one," George said in disgust. He'd been pretty sure of his own bet.

"George, that's awful to bet on who dies," Gladys said, trying not to sound too preachy.

"Oh, Gladys, were not hurting anybody. I mean, the person that it might offend ain't even around to get offended," he said with a mischievous grin.

That same afternoon, long after the doors had been reopened and a new resident from the waiting list had been notified that a room was available, Patti asked Ida to call a meeting of the entire Roost—staff and residents alike.

"All personnel and shoppers please report to the deli for a short meeting," Ida's voice boomed over the loud speaker. Everyone gathered in the dining room prior to the evening meal.

"Damn, were having collard greens again," George said, sniffing the air. "I bet they're pureed, too," he groused. "I'm bound to lose my teeth—not from old age or disease, but from lack of use."

"You should just have the dentist pull 'em all out and get false ones," said the man beside him, his lips curved inward from lack of teeth. He pulled his dentures from the top pocket of his pajama jacket and held them up for George to see. "They're a lot easier to keep clean this way."

The administrator, Steve Tallison, walked to the front of the serving line and addressed the crowd. The cafeteria workers were busily filling the food bins behind him. There was still a dent in the stainless steel food cart where Johnnie had plowed into it during the beauty pageant. Beside the dent, someone had scrawled "Johnnie wuz here" with a black magic marker. The insurance company had declared Beatrice's wheelchair as totaled.

The administrator held up one hand to signal for quiet, while the other hand nervously swept several strands of errant hair over the top of his shiny skull, hiding the bald spot. "If I may have your attention," he called out. The dining hall quieted down after a few moments.

"As some of you may know, there was a passing this morning," he began. Several of the residents tittered at his use of the word "passing" and at the fact they all knew about the "passing." "Ms. Sadie died of natural causes—it was peaceful—she went in her sleep. But that's not what we're here to talk about Ms. Sadie lived here at Milly's Merry Roost for nearly 15 years and considered this place home, and we were all her family."

"Did you know her?" George asked Jack. Jack shook his head. "Did anybody know her?" George wondered aloud.

"Not many people knew her because she was confined to her bed the last few years and didn't get out much," Steve said, as though he'd heard George's comment. "But that didn't stop her from feeling close to everyone here." He paused for effect. "So, the reason we're here is because she left specific instructions for her funeral and wants everyone from the Roost to be there."

There was silence. The faces of many residents registered confusion over an invitation to a funeral of a person that few people had even encountered.

"We've all discussed this situation," Steve said, looking to Patti, Dr. Price and the nursing staff, "and we've decided to leave the decision up to you. You can go if you want to." The staff had met an hour earlier and couldn't reach an agreement on whether or not the residents should go. Patti's opinion was that the trip would be too risky for several of the residents. Steve had to admit, he wasn't crazy about the thought of all his residents taking a twenty-minute journey to the other side of the county. The rest of the staff thought the gesture would mean a great deal to Sadie and those who knew her.

"This isn't mandatory?" George asked suspiciously.

"No, George, it's not mandatory, but we think it would be a nice gesture for Sadie," he said, looking toward the ceiling as though he could see through the chipped spackling straight into the heavens.

George thought only momentarily before responding, "No, I don't think I want to go—I get to go to enough funerals as it is."

"I thought you of all people might help to rally the troops for this occasion," Steve said to George.

George's hand flew up to his left ear and fiddled with his hearing aid. "What? I can't hear you, Steve—the damn thing's gone out again."

Steve Tallison ignored George's actions and addressed the others. "Let me see a show of hands—who all wants to go to Miss Sadie's funeral?" There was a great deal of mumbling going on among the residents, but no show of hands.

"No one?" Steve asked in surprise. A wizened old woman stood up in the back of the room. It was Fannie, the roommate of the deceased.

"I can't believe that not one of you will go to Sadie's funeral. I realize you all didn't know her very well, not like I did, but she was a resident here all the same. She spent most of her time by herself in her room these past couple of years and I'd hate to see her go out of this world by herself. Tell you what I'll do—Miss Sadie left me a little bit of money—for everyone who goes to her funeral I'll treat them to a meal at Piccadilly Cafeteria one day next week." The room started buzzing then. Piccadilly Cafeteria was a favorite restaurant with many of the residents.

Steve took over from there. "That's a generous gift, Fannie, but not necessary I'm sure," he said, eyeing the others. "We'll take another vote. The funeral will be tomorrow at noon. Can I see a show of hands from everyone who plans to attend?" he asked.

"Before I make a decision, let me ask a question," George said. "What does that Piccadilly meal include?"

"A meat and three vegetables," Fannie said.

"Dessert too?" George persisted.

"Yes, but that's it, George," Fannie said scolding. "She didn't leave me that much money."

"Okay, then, we can take a vote now," George said, his fears quelled.

Hands shot up all over the room. "Okay," Steve said, "maybe just give me a show of hands from those who don't want to attend." No one raised a hand.

The rest of the day the Roost was abuzz with talk of the funeral. "The way some of the women are carrying on about what to wear, you'd think that the beauty pageant had been rescheduled," Mona said to Gladys. Gladys was busily looking through her closet, pulling out dress after dress and holding them up to her in front of the full length mirror on the door.

"I'm sorry, I didn't hear you," Gladys said, her head stuck deep into the back of the closet and her voice muffled by the yards of polyester that hung there. "I'm trying to find a dress for tomorrow's occasion," she said. She pulled herself out of the closet and said, "What did you say?"

"Oh, nothing. Just mumbling incoherently about old women and vanity," Mona said.

"You don't understand, Mona. This is a special occasion," Gladys said.

"Sure it is, Sadie died and we've got to go see her off," Mona said simply. "She wanted us to, and personally, I feel honored to be invited."

"I mean really special," Gladys said, trying to build curiosity out of her old friend. It worked.

"Whatever do you have up your sleeve?" Mona asked in exasperation. "Ever since that beauty pageant prank . . ."

"I'm going to ask George to be my date."

"A date to a funeral? Gladys, that's morbid and downright tacky," Mona said in disgust. She thought the pink hair was awful, but this time her friend had gone over the edge.

"Well, it's not like we're gonna make out in the back pew of the church," Gladys said defensively. "Besides, he might not even want to take me."

"Sure he will—just promise him food. You two deserve each other," Mona said, feeling a little jealous that her friend wouldn't be going with her.

"I don't know why you have to poor-mouth everything, Mona. Just because you have no desire to rekindle your . . . passion, is no reason for you to be so negative," Gladys said. She took a compact off of her dresser and powdered her nose. "Besides, if I want to get George to go out with me, I can do it on my own. I surely don't need to bribe anyone with food."

"So," George said slowly, "let me get this straight. If I sit with you during the funeral, the next time your little brother comes to visit he's going to bring me a rack of baby back ribs?" He was practically drooling in anticipation of the food.

"That's right, George. But you don't have to act like you're only doing it for the food," Gladys said with a frown.

"But I am."

"What time will you pick me up?" Gladys asked primly.

"Pick you up? You gotta be kidding. We both live . . ."

"Be at my door no later than eleven," Gladys said. "Or, no ribs for you."

Late the next morning, two church buses and the nursing home van were idling in the parking lot of the Roost, the drivers idling by their buses. Niles pulled the limousine behind the busses to pull up the rear of the caravan. Ida watched them from the window.

"When do we go?" she asked as Patti walked by.

"The buses pull out at eleven fifteen, so we need to be ready by then," Patti said. She still wasn't so sure this was a great idea—approximately 70 old people going to a funeral in the backwoods of Georgia. That was the stuff that geriatric horror movies were made of, she feared. Patti had handpicked the bus drivers—only the ones with clean driving records and honest, dependable feces were chosen.

Everyone, except for a few bed-ridden patients, was making the journey to the far reaches of White County. One of the drivers assured her the trip shouldn't take longer than forty minutes. The funeral was scheduled for noon.

At precisely eleven o'clock there was a knock on Gladys door.

"Yes? Come in," she called out.

George could hear the two women giggling behind the door and nearly backed out of the agreement. But then he could practically smell the smoky aroma of the barbecued ribs.

"I'm here, Gladys. Get out here," he called out.

"That's no way to talk to your date," she chastened him as she opened the door. Then her face softened as she saw the corsage clutched in his hand.

"Oh, George—is that for me?"

"You're the only one standing there, aren't you?"

"Sweet talker," Mona mumbled as she walked between the two on her way out the door. "You have her back right after the funeral. And I'd better not see any hickeys," she teased.

Gladys placed her hand on George's arm and proudly walked out of the Roost to the waiting busses. She occasionally turned her head to the side to make sure others had noticed their promenade onto the first bus. They had—the place was buzzing behind the pair—the woman who had the man of her dreams in her clutches, and the man who passionately wanted a rack of baby back ribs.

The ride to Sadie's church took a little longer than expected, the busses arriving a little after twelve. The church was tiny, wooden and white— but the place was vibrating on its cement block foundation.

"What the heck's going on here?" Jack asked as he stepped off of the bus. It sounded like a concert was going on inside. "Did you bring us to the wrong place?" he asked the driver accusingly.

The driver shook his head. "Nope, this is the place. Says here on the directions, The First Tabernacle of the Saints, and right there it is," he said, pointing to the sign in the front yard.

"Never heard of a church called that before," Mona said. "Must be Southern Baptist or something."

"I see people dancing inside, so it can't be Southern Baptist," George said.

"Dancing? At a funeral? I have never . . ." Gladys said, putting on her most pious look.

Everyone filed off of the buses and into the church, George and Gladys at the lead. Not by George's choice, however, but by Gladys' insistence. Every time he tried to hang back or dislodge his arm from her grasp, she would bribe him with stories of her brother's recipe for baby back ribs.

Inside the church, the place was rocking. People were dancing in the aisles, a choir of at least twenty purple-robed people sang and swayed in the front, and everyone, save for the newcomers from Milly's Merry Roost, was African American.

"Sadie was a black woman?" George asked Gladys incredulously.

"Well, of course she was. I suppose I forgot to tell you that," Gladys said.

"Isn't this . . . ethnic," Mona said happily, and was already swaying her hips to the gospel music.

The first ten rows on both sides of the tiny church had been reserved for the residents of the Roost. A yellow ribbon stretched across the expanse of pews was lifted to let them into their seats. The seventy people sat down quietly, only to look around in wonder, seeing that no one else was sitting and no one else was quiet. Not by a long shot.

"Brothers and sisters, we are here today to celebrate sister Sadie," the preacher said in a sing-song baritone. The crowd exploded into choruses of "hallelujahs" and "amen's." The preacher was dressed in a deep purple robe that flowed around his ankles. He exuded energy, going from one side of the stage to the other, with the purple sea of choir robes dipping and bending to the beat of the music. The music was a mystery to the white people gathered on the front ten rows, because besides an overworked tambourine, there were no instruments. All the beautiful musical notes were coming from the lips of the crowd and the chorus. They were humming and singing. The richness of the vocal blend sounded like a musical band.

"Sister Sadie left this earth yesterday," sang the preacher, "to go to a better place."

"Amen," responded the crowd.

"Where she won't be sick anymore," he cried.

"Hallelujah," was the response.

"Where she won't be old anymore."

"Thank you, Jesus!"

"Where she can walk hand in hand with all the family members who have travelled to heaven before her!" the preacher yelled above the din, throwing one arm straight up in the air and the other waving madly about.

The crowd erupted into song. They were all singing the same song, but without the aid of hymnals.

"Where are the song books?" Ida asked, looking all around and under the pews for the staple of her own Presbyterian upbringing. "I can't find the song books."

A woman from the back row, resplendent in a dress of vivid colors and a hat to match, leaned forward.

"We don't need hymn books here, honey," she said joyously. "Just let your heart sing."

"Yeah, but my heart doesn't know those words," George said to Gladys, who smiled at his witticism and squeezed his arm tighter.

Sadie's open casket at the front of the alter was nearly camouflaged by the party-like atmosphere. "There she is," whispered Beatrice to Niles. She nodded her head in the direction of the simple pine casket.

Sadie had been small in stature, but rich in facial features, Beatrice noticed. The woman's upper body was visible from where she sat. Sadie's face was small and wrinkled but with the angular quality of royalty. She looked proud.

"She's very striking," Beatrice said to Niles admiringly.

He nodded. "Yes, Madame, a beautiful woman."

For someone who didn't have any family and considered the residents of the Roost as her closest friends, she sure had a lot of special acquaintances, Gladys noted. She mentally began counting how many people would show up at her own funeral and ran out of faces quickly. She grabbed George's hand. He didn't take it away.

Mae and the other members of the Garden Club eyed the flower arrangements hungrily. Never had they seen so many bright arrangements of flowers at a funeral. She couldn't wait for the funeral home to bring all the flower arrangements to the nursing home like they always did when one of its residents died. If all went well though, maybe they could even offer to save them the trouble and take a few after the service.

"I know just where to put that lovely spray of carnations," Mae said, pointing discreetly in the direction of the arrangement at the foot of the casket. "Right beside the coffee table in the foyer." The other eleven Garden Club members nodded with enthusiasm.

"Look at that arrangement," said another, pointing to the focal arrangement in the center. It was a rectangular piece of styrofoam with flowers outlining the outer edges. A pink plastic toy telephone had been stuck in the center, its coiled cord attached to the receiver. Beside the rectangle, written in bright blue glitter were the words, "God called Sadie home."

"Well, I never . . ." said Mae.

The song continued for several minutes, with various people from the choir singing solos and the congregation responding at certain times in perfect unison. Several of the Roosters, as they liked to call themselves from the nursing home, even joined in, tentatively at first, more boisterously later on. One man came over and took Ida by the hand, leading her out to dance in the aisle. She blushed but followed the man and soon began gyrating her hips and rocking back and forth to the music.

"Not bad for an old lady," Jack said with approval, poking George in the ribs. George ignored his friend; he was deep into conversation with Gladys, whose eyes glittered in the reflection of his attention.

Suddenly, as though a signal were given to all and noticed by all, the church snapped quiet. A large black woman stepped from the myriad of purple robes and took a deep breath. She nodded almost imperceptibly and the choir behind her began humming with a sound that filled the church. The men laid the foundation of the sound with thick, deep bass hums. After that, layer upon layer of vocal sounds joined in, creating a harmony that seemed too large for the tiny wooden church.

The soloist took a deep breath and began to sing in rich alto . . . ."Amazing grace, how sweet the sound . . ." Her ample chest heaved with the effort of song, her eyes closed and her hands clasped together.

Gooseflesh popped up on Patti's arms as the black woman sang. It never ceased to amaze her how old people cope with death. Everyone from the Roost truly seemed . . . happy. As though Sadie was the lucky one. She crossed her arms and hugged herself as she listened to the rest of the song.

"Through many dangers, toils and snares . . ." The whole congregation was swaying as one, Roosters included, some held their hands up in the air in supplication, others closed their eyes in prayer, and still others mouthed the words along with the soloist. When she finished, she stepped back and was swallowed up by the sea of purple, leaving an obvious vacancy on the stage.

The preacher filled the spot immediately, anxious not to lose the attentive crowd. He charged up the congregation, sending it into a swirling spiral of hallelujahs and amen's. The aisles filled with dancers, the choir began dancing and singing, and the windows shook with the energy of it all.

"I wouldn't be surprised if even old Sadie wasn't moved enough to join the party," said George, tapping his foot.

As Beatrice was clapping and tapping her toes along with the music, a woman leaned up from behind her and said, "Now you know why black folks don't need psychiatrists."

Beatrice laughed and agreed.

The burial site was located just behind the church, under an old oak tree. The funeral home employees had taken all of the flower arrangements and placed them around Sadie's casket, which the pallbearers had placed beside the gaping hole in the ground. Not once did the singing ever stop. The choir continued its vocal celebration all the way from the church to the grave site, followed by the other congregation members.

"I'd rather listen to them than the Blue Birds, but don't they ever quit singing?" George asked no one in particular. Gladys beamed up at him, and shyly took his hand. He didn't pull his hand away.

Everyone gathered around the pine coffin. The lid had been closed. Sadie's roommate decided to come so she could tell her friend goodbye. She stood as near the coffin as she could and reached out to touch it. "I'll miss you, old friend," she whispered.

Members of the Garden Club placed themselves strategically beside the arrangements of their choice, quietly selecting which ones they would take back to the nursing home after the service.

Jack pointed to the rectangular flower arrangement that bore the words "God has called Sadie home . . ."

"I think Sadie and the good Lord must have been disconnected," Jack said. The telephone receiver had become dislodged during its relocation and was dangling inches from the ground, still attached by the telephone cord.

CHAPTER 6

"I THINK mother's going to absolutely love this one," Janice said, showing the paint-by-number kit to Ida as she walked into the Roost.

Ida looked at the clown's face on the front of the box and said, "Hobbies and crafts are on aisle three. If you're bringing that in for a return or a refund, we'll have to see your receipt," she said, pointing to the receptionist behind the counter.

The receptionist smiled benignly, familiar with Ida's self-appointed job. "That's right," she said. "No receipt, no refund."

Janice made her way down the main aisle of the Green Wing, where her mother had lived for three months now. Ethyl, her mother, had fought and scratched the whole time, not willing or too happy about going into a nursing home. The decision to put Ethyl in the Roost had been Janice's well-meant gesture. Ethyl's husband had died a few years ago, and ever since, she had gone downhill. Janice felt it best for Ethyl to live somewhere that people could look after her twenty four hours a day.

The transition had taken a toll on the entire family, Janice's family was racked with guilt and Ethyl was wrought with sorrow and pity for herself. The clash of emotions brought on frequent trips by Janice to the nursing home of at least five times a week, sometimes more, depending on her mother's attitude. "She can make me feel like I'm the worst person God ever put breath in with one look," she thought to herself.

Usually Janice called to let her mother know that she was coming to visit, but she had been at the flea market off of Ebenezer Road when she found this paint-by-number kit. She was so close to the Roost that she decided to make a pop-call on her mother and present her with the craft.

Janice looked at the paint-by-number set as she made her way down the hall. She thought that perhaps her mother just needed a distraction like a hobby or something to keep her happy, so each time she visited she brought a new craft. Ethyl always accepted the gift, but Janice had yet to see any of the finished products. When Janice asked to see some of them, Ethyl said she gave the crafts away to the "less fortunate" at the nursing home. That was a mighty Christian thing to do, Janice thought warmly, turning the last corner to her mother's room at the far end of the hall. She felt sure that her mother, though sad a lot of the times when Janice came to call, would get used to living at the Roost before long.

The door to her mother's room was closed when Janice approached.

"That's odd," she said aloud, reaching out for the door handle. The door to her mother's room was always open, mainly because Ethyl's roommate, Suzy, was somewhat of a social butterfly and loved to have visitors at all times of the day. A "Do Not Disturb" sign that looked as though it had been filched from the nearby Dew Drop Inn was hanging from the door knob.

"I declare, what on earth is going on around here?" Janice said, twisting the handle and opening the door. Her mother's bed, at the far end of the room by the window, was completely encircled by the blue privacy curtain. Suzy's bed, located directly to Janice's left, was empty.

"Oh, my God," Janice said, her voice rising in whisper, "Mother's dead." All sorts of visions started flying through her head—the way her mother looked when Janice was a child, how energetic and funny she had been—especially in the company of Janice's father, God rest his soul. She couldn't bear the thought of her mother's death. There were so many things Janice still needed to tell her, so many preparations to make . . . when was the last time she told her mother how much she loved her?

"Oh, Hank, you big brute, you're driving me crazy," a voice said from behind the bed curtain, causing Janice to jump in surprise. Wait a minute, Janice thought, that voice was her mother's. As she watched, the curtains around the bed started moving from side to side, as though a wind were brewing inside.

"Oh, Ethyl," came a man's voice.

"What is going on?" Janice asked loudly.

"Who is that?" her mother said from behind the curtain.

"Mother, its Janice. Are you all right? What's going on in there?" Janice asked worriedly. She reached to pull back the curtain but was stopped by her mother's voice.

"Don't you open that curtain, Janice. Why don't you wait outside and give us a few minutes to collect ourselves. Better yet, could you come back tomorrow? We've only got the room for another half hour and I'd hate for it to go to waste."

All of a sudden it hit Janice what exactly was going on behind the curtain.

"Mother!" Janice yelled. She pulled back the curtain quickly, finding her mother and an elderly man lying side by side beneath the sheets. "Mother, you've been violated!"

"Now, Janice, I have not . . ." Ethyl began, but was interrupted by her daughter's excitement.

"Get out of my mother's bed right now," Janice instructed the man. The man looked at Ethyl, then back to Janice, then back to Ethyl. Ethyl nodded.

"Janice, I'd like for you to meet Hank." Janice made no move to look at the man who was sharing her mother's bed. Ethyl turned to Hank and said, "It looks as though Janice and I need to have a talk about the birds and bees."

Janice marched toward the telephone that sat beside her mother's bed. She dialed a number quickly.

"Police? Yes, I'd like to report a rape at Milly's Merry Roost. Yes, it just happened—I walked in on it so I saw the whole sordid thing. Please get out here immediately, the perpetrator is still here."

Behind her, the man's eyes grew wide. "Wait a minute, I wasn't . . . we weren't . . . . Ethyl, tell her," he pleaded. He had pulled the sheet up to his chest and was clenching it tightly.

"Don't be silly, Janice. I'm not being violated. As a matter of fact, you rudely interrupted us before I could be violated. Now, if you'll just leave us alone for about twenty minutes, we'll call you when were through." Ethyl turned back to Hank and grasped both sides of his face in her hands. "Now, where were we?"

Janice was stunned. She had never heard her mother talk this way before. In fact, she had never even thought about her mother having sex before. Children just don't think about their parents that way. And now, her mother was acting like some kind of teenager who just discovered the mysteries of sex. Janice backed away from the bed, dropping the curtain in her retreat. She headed for the door.

"I thought she'd never leave," she heard her mother say.

That was it! Janice snapped her fingers with the thought. Her mother had finally lost her senses and was simply not responsible for her actions any more. Janice nodded her head vigorously as she headed down the hall. Of course—that's why her mother has been so despondent lately. This Hank person has probably been having his brutal way with her for weeks now, and her mother was simply too weak and feeble minded to fend him off. That explained everything. Janice broke into a trot—which looked more like an agitated shuffle for a woman of her weight—and headed down the hallway. She needed to save her mother, she thought excitedly. Her mother needed her!

"Rape!" she called out, charging down the hall, revitalized by the sense of urgency. "My mother's been raped!" Residents began poking their heads out of doors along the hallway, trying to see what all the excitement was about. Janice barged into the recreation room and marched up to the checkers table. "Dr. Price, my mother has been raped and I need you to conduct a physical."

Dr. Price jumped up from the table, scattering checkers in his wake. "Raped? Did you say raped? Oh, my. Where is she now?"

"She's still in her room with that man," Janice said. She was pleased to hear the concern in the doctor's voice.

"You left her there alone with him?" Dr. Price asked, taking Janice by the arm and leading her out of the recreation room. "We've got to hurry."

"I didn't know what else to do," Janice said, flustered. "I did call the police, so they're on the way."

"Good, good. Now, let's just hope your mother is all right." Dr. Price, anxious to get to Ethyl's room, was half-leading, half-dragging the overweight woman along the corridor. "Look, why don't I run ahead and meet you there?" he offered.

"That's a good idea, you go ahead and I'll be there directly," Janice called out. She hated to miss all the action, but Dr. Price was right in this instance. "Please, save my mother!" she called out to the doctor as he hurried along the hall. Janice stopped and rested for a moment, leaning heavily on the arm railing. As she was trying to catch her breath, an elderly woman in a floral print housecoat approached her. The woman stood directly in front of Janice, her eyes searching both ends of the hallway before speaking.

"They sell drugs here, you know," the woman said with a knowing expression. "Right under our noses they're selling drugs."

Janice leaned more heavily on the arm railing, which creaked under her weight. What kind of place had she brought her mother to? she wondered. First, her mother gets raped, next, she finds out drugs are being sold here. Janice pressed the back of her hand to her forehead. "What are you talking about? Who sells drugs?" As long as she was waiting to catch her breath, she could find out the scoop on this new development. Who knows? Maybe she could uncover one of the biggest scandals in Georgia history.

The woman looked at her carefully before answering, as though she were sizing up Janice's character. "The staff," she said matter-of-factly. "Not the whole staff, but quite a few of them."

Despite her horror, Janice was intrigued by the news. "Really?"

"Yep, they can get you anything you want, if you've a mind to want some drugs," she said. "They deliver it right to your room, too."

A police siren was heard in the distance. "Look, I'd love to stay and talk with you about this, but my mother is in serious trouble. I need to hurry along—but I would like to continue this conversation. What's your name?"

The woman grabbed her arm and stopped her as Janice tried to shuffle away. The two women looked at each other straight in the eye, the gaze never wavering. "My name's Bertie, but don't ever use it in public. Remember, mum's the word. They'd come after me if they knew I told you."

"You've got my word," Janice said, placing her own hand over the arthritis-gnarled hand of the woman. "I won't say a word."

Janice got to her mother's room to find Dr. Price and two other nurses talking in hushed whispers outside the door. She realized when she approached them that they were all giggling behind their hands.

"Look here, what's going on?" Janice demanded. She was dismayed to see that her mother's door was closed, and, upon opening it, was even more dismayed to see the blue curtain pulled around the bed.

"I thought you were going to save my mother," Janice said accusingly to Dr. Price. "You've left her in there with that man."

The two nurses hurried away, their shoulders visibly shaking with laughter as they walked away. Dr. Price collected his composure before turning to address Janice. "I don't know exactly how to explain this to you, but your mother and Hank are consenting adults, and in this case, they've both consented to having sexual relations."

Janice looked horrified. "You must be kidding. Mother would never in her right mind consent to . . . . to . . . that," she said, gesturing toward the bed, where the curtains were moving slightly from the activity going on within. "Mother, stop that!" Janice called out. The curtains stilled.

"She doesn't know any better," Janice said sadly. "I was afraid this would happen, but I think mother's finally losing all her faculties. And its men like Hank that prey on helpless, unsuspecting women like mother. I want him removed from here." "Janice, it's your mother's prerogative to have sex if she wants to. Personally, I can't tell that she's losing any of her mental capabilities, and until that can be proven, we've got to respect her wishes."

From the corner of her eye, Janice saw the curtains move. "Mother! Would you two please stop for just a moment while we get this straightened out?"

Her mother's voice called from within the curtained area, "But we've only got five more minutes before they let Miss Suzy back in the room!"

"Where's the victim?" a policeman called, running toward the doctor and Janice. "Where is she?"

"She's in there," Janice cried out, suddenly panicked again. "And so is the perp." She turned to Dr. Price and explained, "That's short for 'perpetrator.'" Janice had learned the term 'perp' from the true life crime television shows she watched all the time.

The policeman approached the curtain hesitantly, pulled his gun out of the holster on his hip.

"Wait a minute, I should explain Dr. Price said, approaching the policeman. "I really don't think that's necessary."

"A rapes been reported, sir. You two just stay outside and I'll take care of this."

From outside the room, Janice heard the policeman yell, "I've got you covered. Don't make a move." She then heard the scraping of the metal curtain hooks as the curtain was thrown aside by the overzealous police officer. Janice couldn't make out what they were saying, but after a few moments she heard the officer say, "Oh, my, I'm really sorry." He came back outside, sheepish. He holstered his gun.

"You didn't arrest that man?" Janice asked incredulously. "He has raped my mother, and you haven't arrested him?"

The police officer looked uncomfortable. "Well, ma'am, they both said it was something they'd agreed to. I can't arrest somebody just for having sex, even if it is your mother."

Janice marched back into the room and found her mother and Hank fully clothed. "Well, it's about time."

"Who can be romantic when you've got police officers, nurses, doctors and a lunatic daughter running around?" her mother said angrily. "Now we'll have to wait for another time." Janice noticed with surprise that her mother and Hank were holding hands. In any other situation, the gesture might have been sweet, Janice thought, but this was her mother, and this was a man who was not her father.

Ethyl seemed to read her daughter's mind. "Look, Janice, your father's been gone for several years now. It's not like I'm trying to replace him, I just enjoy Hank's company."

"Mother, you don't know what you're saying," Janice said gently, as though she were talking to a child rather than a woman twenty years her senior.

"Do not patronize me, young lady," Ethyl snapped. "I'll have you know I am more in control of my senses now than I have been in months. And I can thank Hank for that," she said placing her free hand on top of their already clenched hands.

"Won't somebody do something?" Janice cried out, looking toward the open door. The policeman had been joined by two women. "What, have you all come to giggle at my mother's dilemma?" she asked. "Who are these women?"

The policeman cleared his throat before answering. "This here is Ms. Whitehead from the Rape Crisis Center—it's customary for her to be called immediately when a rape is reported. And this," he said, indicating the woman on his other side, "is Ms. Clarke, who is the ombudsman for the nursing home. She has to be contacted whenever incidents of this sort occur." "Well, I'm so glad you could all join us today," Janice said sarcastically. "Mother, would you and that man like to perform a few tricks for the audience?"

"Janice, I will not have you talking like that to me," Ethyl said. "What has gotten into you?"

"My own mother is having sex in a nursing home with some man I've never met before and everyone wants to know what's gotten into me. What's wrong with this picture?"

Ms. Clarke, the ombudsman, approached Janice, placing a hand on her arm. "Janice, we know this must be difficult for you to understand, but your mother is entitled to the same rights as everyone else, including sexual relations."

"But they're not married," Janice said.

"That happens a lot these days," the ombudsman said.

"But they're old," Janice said with a shudder. "How can they possibly . . ."

"What do you want us to do," Ethyl said firmly to her daughter, "sit around and do these stupid crafts you keep bringing me? I'd much rather make whoopie than decoupage."

"Sex is a part of everyday life," Ms. Clarke said. "Around here we deal with it by setting aside certain times when it's convenient for all involved and providing as much privacy as we can. It's their right," she reminded Janice again. "You should be happy that your mother is still enjoying life."

"My mother's acting like a harlot and you all think I'm being the unreasonable one," Janice said, throwing her hands in the air. She turned to the woman from the crisis center. "So, what are you doing about this? Anything? Or have you joined their club, too?" she asked, gesturing toward the policeman, Dr. Price and the ombudsman.

"I'm going to speak with your mother and make sure nothing has happened that she didn't want to happen," the woman said. "I'll know what my next plan of action will be after that. Would you all mind leaving the room so we can conduct this interview?" "That's a great idea," Dr. Price said, signaling for everyone to clear the room. "Then maybe we can get to the bottom of this."

Janice turned back to her mother and saw Hank plant a kiss on her forehead and squeeze her hand. "Will someone please get that man out of here?"

"No assistance necessary," Hank said with a wave of his hand. "I'm going." He turned back to Ethyl. "Goodbye, dear. I'll be in my room if you need me."

"I'll call you after the third degree," Ethyl said with a laugh. "And I'll let you know if the pregnancy test comes back positive." "Mother!" Janice said.

*   *   *

While Ms. Whitehead conducted an interview with her mother, Janice spoke at length with the nurses at the Roost. She first cornered Lucy, the aide who spent the most time with her mother.

"How often does mother . . . you know . . ." Janice trailed off, not sure how to finish the sentence.

"You mean how often does she have sex?" Lucy offered helpfully.

"Yes, that."

"Well, she and Hank have been going at it for the past month now, I suppose," Lucy said. Janice flinched at Lucy's choice of words. "They have been quite an item."

"Has she only been with Hank, or have there been others?" "Just Hank. I guess you could say the two are going steady,"

Lucy said. "I like to see that here. Sort of gives the old folks a second wind."

"How often do they sleep together?"

"Oh, I'd say a couple of times a week. I'm surprised you didn't know about the relationship."

Janice was shocked. Two times a week was more than she and her own husband had sexual relations any more. In a state of shock, she talked to a few of the other nurses before going to the recreation room.

"Dr. Price? I'd like a word with you," Janice said. The recreation room had a television blaring a game show with two residents watching intently from a vinyl covered couch and another snored softly while slumped in a chair also pointed at the television. One wall was lined with well worn books and magazines which had obviously been read over and over.

Two game tables and a backgammon table were set up in the middle of the floor, one of which had a game of checkers under way which Janice interrupted very abruptly.

"I'll be back in a minute, George," Dr. Price said, getting up. "Don't cheat while I'm gone." George nodded his head and grinned. He was aware of the situation and was thoroughly amused by it all. Dr. Price was becoming more and more like a friend instead of a doctor and George was really enjoying the camaraderie.

Once out in the hallway, Janice turned to Dr. Price and let him have it. "You must stop this from happening again," she commanded. "I will not have my mother sleeping with strange men."

"I'm sorry, I can't do that. I told you, the only rime we interfere is if one of the two is declared mentally incompetent or being abused. I don't see any of that going on," he said patiently. "Look, what do you want us to do, issue an order that all women must wear chastity belts and all men must take salt-peter?"

"If necessary . . . what's salt-peter?" Janice asked.

"Oh, it's a blood pressure medication that often causes impotency if it's given in high dosages," the doctor said off-handedly. "Basically, what I'm trying to say is that for your mother's sake, you need to come to grips with this. She's entitled to a normal life as much as you are. If she wants to have sex, be happy for her."

*   *   *

Officer Radburn nodded thoughtfully as he jotted down notes in his notebook. "You've actually seen them dealing drugs here?" he asked the old woman, who nodded quickly.

"Seen it with my own eyes. Even bought some from 'em a couple of times," she said as she kept a vigilant watch glancing up and down the halls to be sure no one was eavesdropping. "Still reeling from the effects. I won't get in trouble for that, will I?"

"Not if you help us break this case wide open," he said. "This sounds like a big ring going on here. Have you told anyone else?"

"Not a soul, I've been afraid for my life," she said melodramatically.

"I can understand that," Officer Radburn said gravely. "We'll look after you from now on," he promised. "In fact, I think I'll put an undercover guy in here for a few days and I'll let you know who he is for your protection."

An hour later, the excitement of the day had settled down somewhat. The interview between the Rape Crisis Center woman and Ethyl had revealed that the sexual act was consensual and not at all uncomfortable or unpleasant for Ethyl. The ombudsman was gone, satisfied that Ethyl would be allowed to continue in her search for sexual pleasure. Janice had also calmed down and returned to her home, unusually agreeable toward her mother. Janice had agreed to come back the next day for a long talk.

The only outsider still at the Roost that afternoon was Officer Radburn, who had arranged a meeting with Patti, Steve and Dr. Price.

"I can't believe what I'm hearing," Patti said. "Members of this staff are dealing drugs? That's just not possible."

"I can only tell you that there is a resident here who has not only seen drugs being dealt, but has actually purchased drugs from members of your staff," the officer said.

Dr. Price and the administrator shook their heads dumbly. "What can we do to find out who's involved?" Steve Tallison asked. "I'll bet Tommy's got something to do with this. I knew we should have never let him come here."

"Now wait a minute, Steve," Dr. Price said. "You don't know that Tommy's involved at all. I think you're being a bit unfair." "That's where we come in," Officer Radburn said. "I'm going to place an undercover policeman here for a few days to watch the staff. I need you all to pass the word that you've got a new resident so that no one thinks anything about it. I would bring in someone as a staff member, but I'm afraid that would make everyone too suspicious."

Everyone in the conference room agreed to help with the officer's plan. They were all concerned, not only for the safety of the residents, but also for the onslaught of media coverage that was likely to follow if a drug bust went down at the Roost. They were just getting the census back up after that scare over the possibility of closing the facility over lack of funding. Beatrice Wellington had shown up just in time.

The next day, a new resident checked into the Roost. He was younger than most of the residents and didn't talk to anyone. That set him up immediately as a topic of conversation.

"I don't care what you say—that man's not old enough to be here," George said when he saw the new resident. "He only looks to be in his late fifties at most. What's he doing here and why isn't he out working in the real world?" he asked Dr. Price, who was currently ahead in the checkers game.

"He has some physical disabilities," he explained. "His family thought he'd be better cared for here."

"He might be in a wheelchair, but he looks like he has plenty of ability to me," George said. "All he's been doing since he got here is wheel up and down all the hallways—like he's some sort of guard or something. And, I think he's wearing a toupee," George said with disgust.

Dr. Price made a mental note to tell Officer Radburn to instruct his undercover agent not to look so obvious. "He's probably just like everyone else who comes here—it'll just take him a while to settle down."

"He looks like someone I know," George said, jumping one of Dr. Price's black checkers with one of his red ones.

That afternoon, Janice returned to the nursing home for a confrontation with her mother. She'd had a long time to think about what she wanted to say and was prepared. The door to her mother's room was open, Janice was relieved to see, and her mother was alone in the room.

"Mother, may I come in?" Janice called into the room.

"Oh, now you ask," her mother replied. "You couldn't have been so polite yesterday, could you? Come on in."

Janice sat across from her mother, on the love seat positioned below the window.

"I suppose you and Hank sit here a lot," Janice said. She couldn't believe she was being such a smart-ass to her mother, but couldn't seem to control her own tongue lately.

"As a matter of fact we do, when we're not in bed," her mother retorted. Both women fell silent.

"Look, mom, I'm really not here to argue with you. I just want you to understand where I'm coming from," Janice said.

"I know where you're coming from. You're coming from the same position I was in when you were a teenager. Remember when I found you and Todd in bed together that time?"

Janice flushed with the memory. She had been eighteen years old at the time, still living at home and going to the local junior college. Janice thought her parents had gone to the beach for the weekend so she invited Todd to spend the night with her. Shortly after midnight on Saturday, her mother tiptoed into Janice's room to tell her that they were home from the beach. It was then that her mother got the surprise of her life.

"Yeah, I remember," Janice said. "And you grounded me for six months. Hey, does that mean I can ground you now?"

"No, that's the point I'm trying to make. You were young then, and as a parent it was my duty to instill some values in you. I, on the other hand, am an adult several times over, and am capable of making my own choices in life without the aid of a parent-like daughter."

"But mom, you're old . . ."

"Being old has nothing to do with this. I just so happen to like Hank and he likes me, and we both enjoy sex. If there ever came a time that Hank said he wasn't inspired to have sex any more, well that would be okay with me, too. I'd just enjoy being with him."

"You like him that much?" Janice asked, surprised.

"Yes, I do," her mother said. "He's different from your father, you know. As wonderful as Bill was, he never excelled in the romance department, but Hank . . ."

"Will I be hearing wedding bells?" Janice interrupted. She had no desire to hear about her mother's sex life with Hank or her late father.

"I've proposed, but he won't accept. He's so silly—says he won't marry me until he controls his high blood pressure. He's had a time with it lately."

Janice got up to leave. "I need to go show a house to some people at four, so I guess I should leave."

"Janice, honey, don't worry about me, I do just fine here. Hank makes me happy."

Janice hugged her mother and left. She immediately began searching for the old woman who had given her the inside scoop on the drug dealers there at the nursing home. She found Bertie sitting alone at a table in the cafeteria, waiting as though a meal was about to be served.

"Hi, Bertie, do you remember me? You told me about the drug dealing that goes on around here."

Bertie looked at Janice with wide eyes and searched the cafeteria to see if anyone had heard what she said. "Shhhh, you're playing with fire. Don't talk so loud, I think they're watching us," she said as she looked over her shoulder.

"I've only got a few minutes, Bertie, but I need you to show me where I can buy some drugs," Janice said. "They're not for me," she added quickly, "I'm just getting them for a friend." "Are you part of the investigation?" Bertie asked suspiciously. Janice nodded eagerly. "Oh, yes. I'm buying drugs and then I'm going to turn them over to the police."

"Okay, then, come on. But you've got to be quiet and you can never tell that I helped you catch them." Janice nodded again and followed Bertie into the main hallway of the Roost, where the twosome sat down in chairs that leaned against the wall. "Now," said Bertie, "we'll just wait here and watch. They should be by at any time."

After a few minutes Bertie exclaimed, "It looks like we struck gold, there they are now!" Janice turned to look and Bertie said, "No, don't look now, we don't want them to get suspicious. Wait a minute and I'll tell you when." Janice waited patiently until Bertie gave the signal. When she turned to see the drug dealer, she saw a nurse she didn't recognize pushing a medicine cart. What a perfect cover-up, Janice thought, who would suspect a nurse with a drug cart? She was excited. She was about to play a part in true life crime—just like on television.

"Are you sure that nurse will sell me drugs?" Janice asked Bertie.

"Sure as I'm standing here. I bought me some last night and I'm still reeling from them," Bertie said.

She approached the nurse quietly and whispered, "I need to make a buy."

"Excuse me?" the nurse said, puzzled.

"It's okay, I know all about what's going down," Janice said. The nurse still appeared puzzled. Apparently, the woman wanted to see some cash up front. That was fine with her. Janice reached into her brassiere and pulled out a twenty dollar bill. "I need Reserpine," she said in a conspiratorial whisper. "I don't know the street name," she said apologetically. She offered the bill to the nurse.

"I'll take that, if you don't mind," a voice said from behind. Janice gasped as the handcuff clicked over her wrist. The other cuff clicked over the wrist of the nurse.

"What are you doing?" Janice demanded.

"I'm arresting the two of you for drug dealing," the undercover officer said as he pulled off the gray moustache and removed the gray wig. "I'm undercover Officer Radburn." He had been unable to convince his superiors that an undercover cop was needed, so he had taken on the assignment himself. Besides, the high drama crime in this small town left a lot to be desired and he wanted to be a part of every minute of this particular case. It had potential.

"Who's dealing drugs?" the nurse asked, genuinely surprised. "I'm a nurse—I give out drugs all the time. Nobody's dealing." "I just saw this woman offer you twenty dollars. If that's not drug dealing, I don't know what is," the undercover man said. He pulled a walkie talkie out of a pouch behind his wheelchair and called the precinct. "Hey, Jay? Yeah, it's me. Send a squad car—I nabbed me a couple of drug dealers here at the Roost." This is great, he thought as he fought an almost uncontrollable urge to say, "Book 'em Dan-O."

"Look, I didn't take her money, did I?" the nurse asked. The officer shook his head. "So then what did I do wrong?" she asked.

"Let's just say I got it from a reliable source that certain staff members are selling drugs here."

"That certain reliable source wouldn't be an old lady, who stands about four feet ten inches and wears a flowered housecoat all the time, would she?" the nurse asked. "Oh, and she's got arthritis in her hands real bad, too. That wouldn't be her, would it?"

"Um, I'm not at liberty to divulge my sources," Officer Radburn said uncomfortably. The nurse's description was right on the nose. "But why do you think it's her?"

"That woman tells everybody who walks in here that there's a drug ring involving the whole staff here. She's the best story teller of anyone I've ever met, but usually people don't fall for her stories," she said, staring at the officer.

Red-faced, Officer Radburn decided to focus his attention elsewhere. "What drug were you trying to buy?" he asked Janice. By this time, several of the residents were out in the hall, including Janice's mother and Hank.

Janice, terrified of the prospect of going to jail, decided to comply with the police from here on out. "Reserpine. I was trying to buy Reserpine," she said between sobs.

The officer turned to the nurse. "What's that?"

"Reserpine? That's high blood pressure medication," the nurse said.

"Why in the world would you want to buy high blood pressure medication?" Officer Radburn asked, clearly confused. "I mean if you're going to do something illegal like buy drugs, you might as well go all the way and buy a drug that has more of a kick than that."

"I think I know the answer to that question," Hank said, stepping out from the crowd.

"You do? Would you care to elaborate?" the officer asked Hank, feeling that old Barney Fife is in control feeling once again.

"Sure, you see, Janice just discovered that her mother and I are dating each other—intimately. And, she's not too pleased about that fact," he said matter of factly. "Coupled with the fact that I have problems with high blood pressure, it only makes sense that she would try to get some Reserpine."

Radburn was still confused. "I'm sorry, I'm not making the connection here. What are you trying to say?"

"Reserpine is high blood pressure medication whose chief side effect is impotency," Hank said. Janice's face turned red.

"Janice . . ." her mother said in dismay, "I can't believe you would do something like that."

"Well, I never actually got that far. I hadn't figured out how I was going to switch the medicine anyway," Janice said, struggling to speak.

"Oh, it's all right, Ethyl," Hank said, to everyone's surprise. "I suppose if my daughter was dating someone I didn't approve of, I'd probably do everything in my power to stop them." He chuckled. "Using Reserpine was actually a pretty clever plan. I'd a never thought of that."

Janice stared open-mouthed at Hank. The old man was actually defending her to her own mother. Even after he knew Janice was trying to render him . . . manless. She suddenly felt silly for the way she'd been treating her mother. "Mom, I'm really sorry," she said.

"I think you owe Hank the biggest apology," Ethyl said. "You're right, I do. Hank, can you ever forgive me?" Janice asked. "I really wasn't thinking clearly."

"Of course. Like I said, I understand. I feel as protective over your mother as you do," he said, looking over and winking at Ethyl.

Janice made a motion to step over and hug her mother, but was restrained by the handcuff

"If you go, I go with you," the nurse said, whose wrist was held tightly in the other handcuff.

"Where is that police officer?" Janice asked. No one had seen him in several minutes.

"So you're saying that they all found out about the drug bust and cleaned up the act?" the officer asked Bertie, writing furiously in his notebook. They were standing outside in the courtyard, away from prying eyes and ears.

"Oh, yes, someone bugged my room last night and I must have talked in my sleep about it," she said. "I heard this morning that they got rid of all the illegal drugs and money and they turned to another line of work."

"And what is that?" the officer asked excitedly.

"Bootleg whiskey," Bertie said. She looked all around the courtyard for spies and saw none. "You remember seeing that water cooler in the lobby? The big glass one?"

The officer nodded that he did remember.

"Well, don't let it fool you. At night, they hook up all these copper coils to it and make corn mash whiskey in it. In the morning, they replace the whiskey with water. Sometimes you can still smell the whiskey when you get a drink of water."

"Are you sure of this?" the officer asked suspiciously. He was still smarting over not being able to make his first drug bust. Maybe this tip would pan out. "Are you absolutely sure about all this?"

"Sure as I'm standing here. Bought some of that bootleg myself last night—and I'm still reeling from it."

CHAPTER 7

PATTI watched closely as Tommy scrubbed around the base of the toilet.

"I thought there are janitors around here to do this kind of work," Tommy groused, tired of leaning over, tired of scrubbing. His hands ached from the bleach and water. He'd been working a full twenty minutes so far.

"We do, but everyone pitches in around inspection time—we never know when it's going to happen, so we start early to be prepared."

"How do you know you're starting early if you don't know when it'll happen," Tommy countered crossly. Patti couldn't argue with his logic. She shrugged.

"We don't know exactly, but it still doesn't hurt to keep the place ship-shape," she said. "The state inspector looks for everything—from dirt on the floor to lint in the patients' bellybut—tons."

"I'm not checking for lint," Tommy said, standing up. He hit his head on the sink as he stood. "Ow, that's it. I quit—I'm going to juvenile detention. Better yet, I'll just report you all for child abuse."

Patti checked Tommy's head quickly to make sure no damage had occurred. "That's enough for today, you can go."

"Thanks, boss woman," Tommy said with a half-salute. "I be's going now." The teenager left the bathroom in a hurry for fear that Patti would change her mind.

Patti sat on the edge of the sink and raised her feet, trying to keep her balance. Her white crepe soled shoes were almost even with her rear-end when she heard the laughter.

"Good Lord, Patti, what in heaven's name are you doing?" Jack said. Jack and Blue, his dog, stood in the doorway to the bathroom.

"Hi, Jack, you were gone so I decided to inspect the room without you," Patti said, easing off of the lip of the sink. "I'm checking to make sure the sink is attached to the wall sufficiently. It is."

"Who's going to be checking for that?" Jack asked.

"The inspector. You haven't been here during an inspection before, but it can be brutal. Once a year the state sends an inspector to make sure we meet all the state requirements in terms of patient care. They check things like whether the sink has been attached properly, and if the residents have been informed of their rights, and if the food is edible . . . things like that," Patti said.

"What happens if you don't pass inspection?" Jack asked.

"That depends on how serious the offenses are. If they're really bad, the state could close us down." Patti looked at Blue. "That reminds me, when the inspector comes, we've got to find somewhere to hide Blue until the inspection is over. The state would really have a field day over that one."

"I'll think of something to do with him," Jack said. "I really appreciate you all letting him stay here," he added.

"Well, if we pull this one off, Blue can be a permanent fixture around here," Patti promised. "If he blows this one for us . . ." she said, trailing off her sentence for effect.

"I understand, and I'll take care of it. How will we know when the inspector is here?" Jack asked. "Do they call first?"

"I wish," Patti said. "No, they like the surprise attack. They try to catch us off guard so we don't have time to prepare. Fortunately, we can usually pinpoint the visit to the right month, since the state has always been a creature of habit, so we try to keep everything spotless during that month's time. And usually, someone is able to spot the inspector when he or she pulls into the parking lot. They usually drive one of those government—looking cars and if it's a man, he looks like a nerd with a pocket protector, and if it's a woman, she looks like an ultra-prudish librarian."

"I'll help keep watch," Jack promised.

Michelle Peterson spotted George making his way down the hall as she was tacking up the notice on the activities bulletin board.

"Come here, George," the activities director called out amiably. "You'll be pleased to see this."

George shuffled over to where Michelle stood and looked up at the notice. His eyes grew bright and a smile played about his face. "A fishing trip! Well, it's about time."

"I know it, George, and I was getting real tired of hearing you gripe about how we never have any male activities' as you call them, so I decided we'd try for a fishing trip."

"Now, Michelle, you know how much I enjoy those Mary Kay makeover parties," George teased, "but there's got to be something more to living than deciding if I'm a Winter, Spring, Fall or Summer."

Michelle laughed. "Well, round your buddies together. We're going to try and do this thing tomorrow."

"Can we keep it 'men only?'" George asked. "Women cramp my style—especially Gladys."

"I thought you liked Gladys," Michelle said. "I thought you two were getting along famously at the funeral."

"She's all right, but she keeps getting under foot. Just this time make this a guy's only event."

"You know we can't do that, that would be against the rights of the residents," Michelle said sternly. "But I doubt if you have to worry, I don't know too many of the women here who would want to go fishing with all you old codgers anyway," Michelle said, laughing as she touched George on his shoulder as he walked away.

Later that afternoon, Gladys is standing in front of her open closet door with a thoughtful expression on her face.

"Now, Mona, what would you wear if you were to go on a fishing trip," she asked.

"You can't be serious. That's the men's trip," Mona said, scolding her friend.

"But I know George is going—he loves to fish—and if George is going, I want to be there," Gladys said decisively. She pulled out a floral polyester pantsuit and held it in front of her. "What about this?"

Mona shook her head.

Gladys replaced the pantsuit and pulled out a tea-length gown with lace across the bottom. "This?"

Mona shook her head.

"Well what in God's creation do people wear when they go fishing?" Gladys asked in desperation. "I know nothing about the sport."

"When my husband Carl used to go, he wore khaki pants, a flannel shirt, boots, and one of those floppy hats with lures stuck in them."

"Then that's what I'll wear," Gladys declared. "I'm going to call my niece to come get me and take me shopping. Care to go along?"

Mona nodded with enthusiasm. She loved to shop.

Steve Tallison, the administrator of Milly's Merry Roost, stood in front of the staff who had gathered in the conference room. He paced back and forth in front, as though he were a sergeant instructing his troops.

"This, as you all know, is the beginning of inspection month," he said, looking at each staff member, trying to impress the importance of inspection month on each one. "We don't know when it'll happen. It could be tomorrow, it could be the last day of the month. I want everyone to pitch in with cleaning and straightening. And, be on the lookout for any infraction. Whoever discovers and corrects the most infractions during this month will receive one free day off—with pay," he said with emphasis. He knew that one way to catch the attention of the staff was either through money or days off.

"What's the code this year?" Lucy asked from the back of the room. Each year, they used a different code to announce that the inspector had been spotted in the parking lot.

"I thought this year we'd go with 'Code Blue in Room 413,'" Tallison said.

Everyone thought about this for a moment. Lucy's hand shot up, "But there's not a Room 413," she said.

"Precisely," the administrator said, "that's how we'll know it's the code for the inspector. "And, I'll offer the same thing—a day off with pay—for the person who spots the inspector first."

The staff began talking excitedly among themselves. Days off were few and far between for nursing home employees.

Early that evening, the sun would still be up for a couple more hours, three men sat in rocking chairs lined up along the porch. One other man sat in a wheelchair beside them. Each of the men had a rod and reel in hand and were taking turns casting their lures out into the front lawn of the nursing home.

"Watch how you sling that thing," George yelled at Jack, ducking his head. "If I didn't know better, I'd guess you'd never been fishing before."

"Damn thing slipped out of my hand," Jack snapped back. The rod was lying about ten feet in front of him on the grass. "Blue, fetch." The pointer jumped off the porch and gingerly took the padded handle of the rod in his mouth. After some difficulty trying to maneuver himself and the rod back on the porch, he finally reached his head up to the level of the porch, opened his mouth, and dropped the rod at Jack's feet.

"You may not be so smart, but your dog's a genius," George said. Jack bent down and picked up the rod.

"I hope the two of you don't talk this much tomorrow," Hank said, casting his lure out into the yard. "The fish'll be too scared to come anywhere near us," he said, cranking his lure back in slowly.

"You'll all shut your mouths when you see the size of the fish I'm gonna be bringing in," George said confidently. His bright yellow tackle box sat beside him, the lid open and three trays of lures, hooks and sinkers stacked on top of each other. George reached for one of the lures, a plastic fish with a moveable tail. "This here Hot Spot will catch any bass that happens to be in that pond."

"Nope, you need a Rattle Trap like the one on my line," Hank said. He'd cranked his line in by now and the lure was dangling from the tip of the rod. He shook the rod lightly. "See? It makes a little tiny noise when it moves through the water—attracts the fish," he said with a nod of his head.

"Scares the fish," George grumped. "Ain't never heard of a noise-making lure."

"Who else is going tomorrow?" Jack asked the man in the wheelchair beside him. The man didn't respond. Jack poked him with the butt of his rod. "Hey, Earl, you sleeping again?"

The man stirred slightly. "Quit poking me. No, hell I ain't sleeping. Just taking a little cat nap. Fishing makes me tired," he said.

"We're only practicing like we're fishing," Hank said in exasperation.

"Well then I'm only practicing like I'm sleeping," Earl said. "Now leave me alone."

The next morning, Michelle stood by the front window, looking out into the parking lot anxiously.

"You looking for that inspector person?" Lucy asked as she passed by the lobby.

"No, I'm looking for the van to come around and pick up everyone for the fishing trip. It was supposed to be here by ten o'clock."

"Good luck if you're counting on one of the vans from the county motor pool," Lucy said with a shake of her head. "They're about as dependable as the weather."

"If anything goes wrong with this trip, those men are going to string me up with their fishing lines," Michelle said worriedly.

"You are not going, and that's that," George said to Gladys.

"It's a free country, George, so I can go if I want to," Gladys said, disappointed with his reaction. Gladys' niece had taken her and Mona shopping at the outdoors store last night and Gladys had invested in fishing attire. She wore khakis, a floral blouse—she didn't agree with the flannel—and wore white tennis shoes. Her big purchase was the floppy fishing hat she wore, already adorned with lures. She'd even gotten a rod and reel, a very simple Zebco with the lure already attached.

"This is a guy thing, Gladys," George said. "You wouldn't understand. It's like when you women get together and do your hair or go clothes shopping—we men like to get together and fish." He turned to the six other men who were gathered behind him waiting for the van. "Right, guys?"

Several of the men grunted their agreement with George's position.

"Look at your rod and reel . . . and that lure! Where did you get that lure? You won't catch anything with that cheap thing, it looks like somebody broke off the bottom of a baby spoon and tied it on your line," George said.

Gladys's face crumpled. She wanted so badly to be with George. She'd thought after the funeral that things were looking up for the two of them, but evidently she'd misread him.

"Fine," Gladys said defiantly, holding her head up and looking each man in the face. "That's just fine. I hope each one of you gets stuck by a hook and gets trichinosis or lockjaw or something." With that, she was gone out of the recreation room, leaving the seven men staring after her in wonder.

"That was a little harsh," Jack said to George.

"I stand by my feelings, and I say this fishing trip is a guy thing. The women need to stay here where they belong." For most of his life women had been a convenience. Besides, his mother had died when he was young, and times got even harder. He and his brothers had to learn real young to make ends meet. That's how he started some of his penny ante burglaries. Women had come and gone, but they were never much use to him. All but one—but that was years ago and it was her fault that she never understood his lifestyle. "To hell with the rest of them," he thought bitterly. "They're nothing but trouble anyhow."

Michelle, still standing by the window, saw Gladys walking slowly down the hall. After taking in Gladys' attire, her slumped shoulders, and the fact that she was walking from the direction of the recreation room, Michelle knew what had happened.

"You know they can't keep you from going on the fishing trip," Michelle said helpfully. "Anyone who wants to can go."

"I don't want to be where no one wants me," Gladys said sadly.

"The way things are looking, we may not be going at all," Michelle said, holding back the curtain to search the parking lot again. "The van still hasn't shown up."

The telephone rang at the receptionist's desk. The receptionist spoke into the phone for a minute before hanging up. "Michelle? The van's broken down on the side of Ebenezer Road. They sent a mechanic out, but it's too serious and they're going to tow it back to the shop. They said they're sorry but they don't have any other vans available."

"You should have let me speak to him," Michelle said. She would have liked to vent some anger on the unsuspecting van rental man.

"I know, but he specifically said he didn't want to talk to you directly. I suppose he knew how mad you'd be," the receptionist said.

"Oh, well, Gladys," Michelle said, turning back to talk to the elderly woman, "looks like you don't have to. Gladys was gone. Michelle shrugged. "I think I'll call a couple more rental places before I give up. If any of the fishermen come looking for me, tell them I'll be back in a minute," she said to the receptionist. "Don't let them know there's a problem . . . yet."

Fifteen minutes later Michelle walked to the recreation room, knowing how poor a reception she was going to get. She hoped they didn't throw things at least. The men had been so looking forward to this fishing trip. But then they could always reschedule. That was little consolation to a woman who had to face a roomful of angry, disappointed old men.

"It's about time," George said, when Michelle appeared in the doorway. "We were beginning to think you'd gone fishing without us. What were you doing, digging for worms?" he laughed.

Michelle didn't laugh. "I've got some bad news for you," she said. "The van is broken down. It looks like we will have to do this another day," she said tensing herself for the onslaught of groans and complaints.

"I should have known . . ." George began.

"Not so fast," Gladys said from behind Michelle. "We're going after all."

"What do you mean?" Michelle asked.

"I have another mode of transportation for us," Gladys said, "that is, as long as I'm allowed to go fishing, too."

Michelle looked quizzically at Gladys and then back at the seven men gathered in front of her. "Well? What will it be? You can stay here and gripe or we can all go fishing with Gladys."

There was silence, save for George's low rumbling mumbles, before Jack piped up. "Oh, come on George, what's it going to hurt if she goes? I just want to go fishing. What, are you scared she's going to catch a bigger fish than you?"

The last comment brought George to life. "Are you kidding? With that cheap rod and reel she's got? Get serious." He clapped his hands together suddenly. "Okay, fishermen," he said, then glanced at Gladys, "and fisherwoman . . . let's get going."

The collection of elderly people, rods, reels, tackle boxes and bait buckets clattered through the Roost and out into the bright sunshine.

"Where's the ride?" George asked Gladys.

"Right there," she said triumphantly, pointing to the limousine.

"Beatrice's limousine?" Jack asked in surprise. "You've got to be kidding. Does she know about this?"

"Of course she knows. I asked her if we could borrow it for the afternoon and she grudgingly agreed, as long as Niles drives us all there and we pay for the gas." Niles appeared from the hallway, as though summoned. He was dressed in his driving clothes and cap, stiff and formal. "It couldn't have been that easy," Jack persisted. "Beatrice doesn't do much of anything out of the goodness of her heart—she must be getting something out of this."

"No, she truly wanted us to use her car," Gladys lied. She didn't want the others to know that she'd just sold her soul to the devil for this particular favor. She'd had to promise to take Niles' place for one whole week while he went to visit his relatives in New York. Gladys would basically be Beatrice's slave for seven days. She shuddered at the thought

"Good enough for me," George said, making his way across the parking lot to where the limousine was double parked.

It took half an hour to load the limousine. They ended up having to tie the rods, reels and tackle boxes on top of the limousine. Earl's wheelchair was placed in the trunk, along with assorted fishing baits and nets. Three men sat in front, Earl, George and Niles, and the others wedged themselves into the back of the limousine. Blue lay on the floorboard of the front seat. Michelle opted to stay behind since Dr. Price was going.

"You know more about fishing than I do," Michelle said to Dr. Price, who had never been fishing a day in his life, but had looked forward to the trip with the rest of the men.

"This would probably be a comfortable ride if there weren't four hundred people going," Earl cracked.

"Is everyone seated and prepared for travel?" Niles asked the group.

"Yes," they chorused.

Just then a blue Chevette with tinted windows screeched into the parking lot, beside the limousine. Tommy jumped out. "Why aren't you in school?" George asked Tommy sternly.

"I cut. I wanted to go with you guys," he said with a grin. "It's all right, I'm actually doing okay in school this quarter," he said. "So, can I go?"

"I don't think we've got any more room in here," Gladys said from the back of the limousine. She was pinned between Jack and Dr. Price. "In fact, I'm quite sure if you get in here, I shall be crushed to death."

"No problem," Tommy said. "Me and Red'll just follow you guys." He slammed the door to the limousine and jumped into the passenger side of the Chevette before anyone could respond.

From the front porch, Patti and Michelle were watching the loaded down limousine leave. "It would be our luck for the inspector to come now, while everyone's gone," Patti said. "But then, we wouldn't have to explain about the dog."

Michelle looked around the lobby as they walked back in. "You know, I knew something's been missing around here today. Where's Ida? I don't think I've ever been in the lobby when Ida wasn't here, greeting people and giving directions."

"Several members of the staff were afraid Ida would be the first one to spot the inspector, since Ida's in the lobby all day every day. The first person to spot the inspector gets a day off with pay . . . Ida's confined to her room," Patti said.

"You're kidding—they can't do that," Michelle said, shocked.

"I'm kidding," Patti said with a smile.

The limousine pulled up to a wooden gate, at which time George got out of the car and swung the gate wide. The sign nailed to the front of the gate read "No Trespassing" but George was undaunted.

"The sign says we're not supposed to go in," Earl said.

"Stop whining, Earl. We've paid the guy who owns the pond so we can use it. Don't get your adult undergarments in a wad," George said.

Niles drove the big limousine slowly around the perimeter of the pond. "Where would you like for me to park?" he asked the others.

"We should fish over on the other side, where all the shade trees are," George said. "There'll be more fish there."

"Who died and made you Fish Master?" Jack asked George.

"I know more about fishing than any of you put together," George said. "It would do you all a world of good to stop jabbering and start taking notice of what I do."

Gladys was more than willing to do just that.

Niles pulled the limousine under an old oak tree. The sun was warm and Niles had no desire to be out in it. He helped the others unload the limousine, wincing each time a rod and reel bounced onto the black lacquer of the limousine.

"Hey, Niles, old chum," George said good naturedly. "Why don't you loosen up and go fishing with us?"

"No, but thank you," Niles said stiffly. He was perfectly content to stand beside the limousine while the others fished.

"I'll let you wear my hat," George said, holding his floppy fisherman's hat in the air, complete with lures of all shapes and sizes.

"That's quite tempting, Mr. George, but I shall stick with my former decision," Niles said. George shrugged and followed the others to the shore.

"Gladys, do you need help?" Jack asked, watching as Gladys tried to untangle the fishing line from around her torso. She had made an unsuccessful attempt at casting her rod—as a result, the lure had circumnavigated her body several times with the line in tow.

"No, thank you Jack. I'm perfectly capable of doing this, I just lost my grip is all," Gladys said, trying to locate the beginning and ending of the line. She finally resorted to biting the line in two.

"Hey, you've still got your teeth?" Earl asked Gladys, amazed.

"Well, of course I do," Gladys retorted. She'd never be caught dead with dentures, or at least she'd never let anyone know she wore them.

"I still have my teeth," Hank said to Earl, flashing him a smile.

"Yeah, and you're still getting some from the old lady, too," Earl said with a scowl.

After the initial hubbub, everyone quieted down to fish.

"What kind of redneck are you if you don't know the rules of fishing?" George asked Tommy.

"Never had a dad to take me fishing," Tommy said brusquely.

George stood off by himself near a stand of trees, daring anyone else to try and share his fishing hole. Jack and Blue stood about twenty yards from George, and the others were bunched together on the shore. Tommy and his friend took their radio and wandered off into the woods to listen to music after George told them they had to stay quiet.

For many of the residents, the afternoon outing was the first time they'd been outdoors for an extended amount of time in months. The day couldn't be any prettier, Jack thought to himself as he watched Blue chew on a stick by the water's edge. Fie used to fish quite a bit with his son and then later with his grandchildren. After they all moved away, he lost interest in fishing and eventually gave away all his tackle. Maybe the next time the kids came to see him he'd take them on a fishing trip. Jack smiled at the thought.

Gladys thought about the sheltered life she'd led as she tilted her head back and enjoyed the warm sun tickling her face. Her mother had firmly believed in the old adage that women belonged in the house, so Gladys had spent her life washing, cleaning, cooking and ironing while her late husband did all the fun things—like fishing. She promised herself that in the future she would try to get outdoors more often and try new things. Maybe she could get Mona interested as well.

Though his eyes were closed and his breathing slow and steady, Earl wasn't sleeping. Sometimes when he closed his eyes and let his mind drift, he'd go back to the days when he wasn't confined to a wheelchair. Though that was over ten years ago, Earl could remember the sensation of walking as though it were only days ago. Before the degenerative disease took his legs, Earl had been active. He walked around the block, puttered in his garden and worked in his tool shed nearly every day since he retired from teaching. Earl smiled before felling sound asleep.

Jack was the first to catch a fish. It was a bream, about six inches long, and its red/orange breast shone in the sunlight. "What a beautiful fish," Gladys said in admiration. "Will you throw it back?"

"I will not," Jack said. "I'm going to take it back and have the cook fry it up for supper." Jack took the fish off the hook with ease. "Hey, where are we going to keep the fish?" he asked George.

"I hadn't thought of that," George said. "We didn't bring a single cooler, ice, nothing . . . Hey, Niles! Doesn't that vehicle have a refrigerator in it?"

"Yes," Niles said, waking from his nap. He hadn't heard why they were looking for a cooling system.

"Can we use it?" George asked.

"Of course, Madame said you all were to enjoy the use of the vehicle today, and I would think that includes the use of the refrigerator." Niles put his head back on the seat to sleep. Once George was sure the Englishman was asleep, he took Jack's fish and placed it in the refrigerator beside the Perrier and the Grey Poupon.

When he got back, he found Hank fussing with Earl.

"Earl, how do you expect to catch anything when you keep falling asleep and dropping your rod and reel?" Hank asked. "Why don't you just give up fishing and work on your nap," he suggested.

"Nope, I'm here to fish," Earl said stubbornly. He took the butt of the rod and stuck it in the side of his wheelchair. Earl wiggled the rod to make sure the rod would stay. It was a good fit. "Now, at least the rod won't go anywhere if I fell asleep," Earl said. "You can quit your worrying, Hank dear."

Across the pond, Bubba Wilkes had just gotten home for lunch. He was vice president of the bank in Stalvey, had been for the past twelve years. Loosening his tie in the kitchen, he glanced out the window that faced the back of the house and the pond. His eyes grew wide. There, on the other side of the lake, was a big black limousine, a smaller blue car, and about eight old people fishing on his property! Actually, the property belonged to him and his two brothers, both of whom were out of town that week on business. They would have told him if anyone had rented the fishing pond. Bubba was sure he had some trespassers on his hands. He tightened his tie, put his suit coat back on, and walked out the back door toward the trespassers.

Just before Bubba reached the side directly across from the elderly fisher people, a twelve pound bass took hold of Earl's lure. Unfortunately, Earl was once again sound asleep with his rod tucked tightly into the side of his wheelchair. More unfortunately, he had neglected to put the brakes on the wheelchair. The fish, realizing his predicament, tugged mightily on the line, pulling the tip of the rod, which pulled Earl's wheelchair down the sloping incline of the shore.

Splash! No one saw what was happening until too late. The wheelchair hit the water and Earl spilled into the pond, asleep until his nose went under water, at which point he woke up sputtering.

"Somebody's trying to drown me!" Earl yelled. By this time George, Jack and Hank had hurried into the water after him. George and Jack each took one of Earl's arms and lifted him up. Hank grabbed the wheelchair, the fishing rod still attached and the tip bobbing wildly. He cranked the line in slowly, the rod bent over from the weight on the other end. Just as Hank got a glimpse of the big fish, the line snapped, sending Hank toppling back into the wheel chair.

"Quit your blabbering," George said to Earl. "The water's not even a foot deep here." He shook his head, "That had to be some kind of fish to pull you in like that. The next time you go fishing, remember to put on your wheel locks," he said to Earl. Everyone started laughing then, not noticing the big man in a suit approaching them at a rapid clip from the other side of the pond.

"What in the world are you all doing fishing on my property?" Bubba yelled as he approached. "Is that man all right?" he asked, more out of concern of a lawsuit than concern for Earl's wellbeing.

"He's fine," Dr. Price said, helping Earl back into his dripping wet wheelchair. "Just a little wet around the ears."

"As for what we're doing here," George chimed in, "we rented the pond for the afternoon. We're from the Roost down the road."

"I don't believe that," Bubba said with his hands on his hips. "I happen to be the primary owner of this property and no one informed me that it was rented."

"What are you going to do, cart us in?" Gladys asked sarcastically. "You should watch out—us old folks can be pretty mean and vicious sometimes."

Tommy and his friend had heard the commotion and came wandering out of the woods and approached the group gathered on the shore.

"Who are these two?" Bubba demanded. "You can't tell me they're from the nursing home."

"They look pretty good for their age, don't they?" George said.

"What were y'all doing in the woods, smoking pot?" Bubba asked the boys accusingly.

Tommy held up the radio for Bubba to see. "No, we were just listening to music and didn't want to bother them fishing."

"Look, we paid to rent out the pond this afternoon and we'd appreciate it if you'd just let us enjoy ourselves," Hank said. "We've really been looking forward to this fishing trip, you know, not everyone has a pond in their yard."

"Well, I'm going to talk to the administrator of the Roost," Bubba said. "I'm going to make sure this doesn't happen again." The burly man began walking back toward his house on the other side of the pond. Halfway across, he turned back toward the others, his hands on his hips. "You all can stay on the shore, but I'd appreciate it if you didn't pull out any more fish until I know for sure you've paid for them. I'd hate to lose all my fish to vagrants."

"Well, I never," Gladys said, still trying to untangle her fishing line.

"Don't worry about it, we're going to keep on fishing until it's time to go back," George said. He walked over and helped her tie the spoon lure back on the end.

"Thank you, George," Gladys said, batting her eyelashes.

"I just want to make sure everyone catches at least twenty fish a piece before we leave here," George said. "If there was a plug at the bottom of this pond I think I'd send Blue down to pull it out."

Lucy began jumping up and down in the lobby with excitement. "I see the inspector, I see the inspector. Happy day—hello day off with pay!" she sang out as she told the receptionist to make the announcement.

"Code Blue in Room 413," the receptionist said into the microphone. All over the Roost staff and residents alike stopped what they were doing and began straightening up and cleaning their respective areas.

Ida, upon hearing the announcement, rushed back to her place in the lobby since the inspector had been spotted.

Patti breezed through the day room, glancing at all the residents gathered in there to watch the daily soap operas. She stopped and stood directly in front of the television, her hand precariously on the on/off button.

"Okay, folks, have you all been apprised of your Rights as Residents?" she asked the group.

"Yes," they said, anxious for Patti to move away from the television. The show was going to reveal who was the real father of the little girl they all thought was the child of the state senator. It was an important day.

Patti still hadn't moved. "Belly button check," she instructed the group. They groaned. "I'm not kidding, this inspector will check for that." Patti watched as each resident exposed their belly buttons and checked for lint.

"All clear?" Patti asked.

"Yes, now leave," said Mae irritably, she was one of the die-hard soap opera fens of the Roost. She had a bet going with the other Garden Club members that the real father was that convict they'd just released from the penitentiary after ten years of hard labor for that child pornography sting.

Next, Patti headed down the hallway to Jack's room to check for any visible signs of Blue. She peeked into his room and was pleased to see that he had cleaned up before going on the fishing trip. On impulse, she walked over to his bed and pulled up the covers away from the floor and peeked underneath. There was a huge collection of dog toys, leashes, bowls and a big stuffed flannel bed all crammed up under the little single bed. "Oh, great," she thought in panic as she hurried to look for a box to put everything in and hide it. Anything on the floor, under the bed was sure disaster.

Out in the parking lot, Bubba got out of his car and straightened his tie. He couldn't have old people traipsing around on his property, rent or no rent, he thought as he headed up the front steps. What kind of liability would be involved if one of them croaked on his land? Just like that old man in the wheelchair almost did right before his eyes? Old people should stay in the nursing home—that's what they're there for.

"Welcome," Ida said, as Bubba walked into the Roost. "May I take your coat, get you a beverage, and get you a shopping cart?" she asked sweetly.

"Huh? Uh, no," Bubba stammered. Lunatics lived here, he thought to himself.

Patti and Steve Tallison, the administrator, breezed by Ida and took turns grasping Bubba's hand. "Were so pleased you're here," Patti said, in her most sincere voice. "We didn't expect you so early, though," she said.

"Glad to have you here," Steve said administratively. "We hope you'll find your visit pleasant, and if we can help you in any way, please be sure and ask."

Bubba was so taken aback by all the fuss and commotion he didn't know what to say. He had come here prepared to chew out someone for letting those old folks run loose on his property, but he hadn't expected the people here to act this way.

"Where would you like to start?" Steve asked. "The residents' rooms?" He took his silence for assent and led him down the hallway, jabbering all the way about the great strides the nursing home had made since Ms.

Wellington came and gave a financial boost. As they walked away, Patti darted down the hall in the other direction to do a quick check of things.

A woman in a floral housecoat stopped them on the way. She grabbed Bubba by the elbow. "You know, they don't sell drugs here anymore," she said conspiratorially. "Its bootleg liquor now," she said with a nod of her head. "They store it in the water cooler."

"We're going to check on that today, Bertie," Steve told her loudly. To Bubba he said quietly, "Don't mind Bertie," guiding Bertie out of the way and Bubba around her. "She's a little confused, but otherwise a delight to be around."

Patti caught up with them and the threesome walked through each wing of the Roost, Patti and Steve manipulating the conversation and Bubba remaining silent. He didn't know what they were up to, but it was probably something no good, Bubba thought. They were probably just trying to keep his mind off of what he came here for.

"Don't you think this is a very clean place?" Patti asked. "As you can tell," she said with a sniff as though smelling the bouquet of a fine wine, "we are doing a good job of odor control. Of course, there's only so much we can do about Mr. Simmons on the Yellow Wing. He just comes unglued when we try to bathe him. Word is, he's been like that all his life. Most of the time we can't even get him to change clothes without calling in the National Guard."

"Well, yes, I suppose it smells good," Bubba said. The nursing home was clean, much cleaner than he remembered it being when he used to come visit his grandmother years ago.

They walked into the day room where the same group of residents were still glued to the television set.

"Do you have any questions for the residents?" Patti prompted Bubba. This was the most prepared group in the Roost and Patti wanted to capitalize on that fact.

Bubba studied the group, then noticed the soap opera they were watching on the television. "Yeah, have they said who the real father is?" he asked.

"Shhh," Mae said, signaling for silence. "It should be in the next five minutes. Sit down and be quiet."

Bubba looked at Patti and the administrator. "Do you mind? Just for a minute?"

"Sure, sure," Patti said, her eyes wide with surprise. She'd never seen an inspector act this way. It must be some kind of test or something.

"We'll be back for you at two-thirty, when the show's over," Steve said, puzzled. Bubba waved that that would be fine and settled onto the couch with the others. No one seemed to even notice he was there.

"Hey, Niles," George yelled up to the limousine. Niles was sitting in the driver's seat, still stiff, still very formal. At least the door was open to let in some air, George thought in exasperation—that man takes his job way too seriously.

"Yes?" Niles said, turning in George's direction.

"Don't you hate working for that old nag?"

Niles looked shocked. "Why, no, I don't. I find my position with Ms. Wellington quite agreeable."

"But you're working for a little old lady who orders you around," George said. "I mean, she tells you to jump and you ask how high—are you going to do that for the rest of your life?" "This is what I have been bred to do," Niles answered simply. "It's what my father did, and his father before that."

"You can't even pass on the heritage because you don't have the time to even meet some woman and have a son," George pointed out.

Niles remained silent for a while before answering. "I still have hopes for that."

"How? You're never out of her sight, Niles. You don't have a life to call your own. You're living her life. Why don't you look for a job where you get to call the shots?"

Niles answered firmly, "I am perfectly satisfied with my current occupational situation, thank you." George took that as a signal for the end of the conversation. He went back to fishing.

"I've got one!" Gladys yelled excitedly, her rod bending and dipping precariously under the weight of whatever was on the other end of the line.

"You've probably just caught a stump," George said, "or a turtle." He set his own rod down and walked over to where Gladys stood clutching her pole. "Relax a minute and let's see what it does, if it doesn't move, it's a stump. Or a body," he said mischievously.

Gladys did as George said and relaxed her grip, at which point the rod jumped forward, nearly out of her hands. George helped her hold onto it.

"I can't hold onto it, George," Gladys said in despair. "Would you please help?"

"Be glad to," George said. Gladys knew that all men loved to be called on for their strength and he was no exception. He tilted his floppy fisherman's hat back at a jaunty angle and grabbed hold of the butt of the rod. "Stand back now, Gladys, you never know what might happen. The line might pop or the fish might come sailing out of the water. Just let me handle this."

George and the fish battled for about ten minutes. The old fisherman was patient with the fish, letting it pull the line out, but not too far to wrap it around a stump. He would then crank the line in a little, and then let it out again, trying to tire out the fish.

"This has got to be huge," George said excitedly. "I've never fought with one this long before."

Gladys was clapping her hands excitedly to the side, watching her man pull in the 'big one.' Hank was standing to the side, ready with a net. Blue was staring at the moving cork, trembling with excitement.

Finally, with a mighty pull, George landed the fish. Everyone gathered around to see it as it flopped around on the ground. "That's the biggest fish I've ever seen," George said in wonder. He took off his floppy hat and wiped his sweaty brow. "It's got to weigh over twenty pounds."

"That's the biggest fish I've ever caught," Gladys said. Actually, it was the only fish she'd ever caught.

"Whoa, wait a minute," George said, putting his hat back on his head. "I think I caught that beauty."

"That's my pole and my little spoon the fish bit," Gladys said righteously.

"That 'little spoon' is a lure," George said in disgust. 'You don't even know what a lure is." The old man and the old woman were standing face to face, inches apart.

Jack clapped his hands suddenly. "Okay, everyone, excitement's over with. We need to head back to the Roost before they send the troops out looking for us."

Hank and Jack carried the big fish to the limousine and deposited it into the refrigerator. They had to take out a couple of bottles of Perrier to make room for the big bass.

"Hey, let's call the newspaper and have them come out and take a picture of the fish," Hank suggested excitedly. "I'll bet this is the biggest fish anyone's ever caught out here."

"That's a good idea," George said. "I'd look mighty handsome posing beside that big fish I caught."

"I caught that fish and I'll be the one posing beside it," Gladys said, wishing she had time to fix her hair.

"Hey, Niles, call the Stalvey Enterprise on your earphone," Jack suggested. "They could be there waiting on us when we got back—before the fish starts smelling bad."

Niles had enjoyed the afternoon outing and was agreeable. He called information, got the number to the little weekly newspaper and handed the telephone to Jack. Jack spoke to someone on the other end for a few minutes before hanging up.

"That's done. They'll have a reporter and a photographer there to meet us by the time we get back. This is big news to them," he said with a laugh. "They're all excited about it."

"Now we've just got to decide who poses with the damn thing," Earl said.

"That would be me," George said, crossing his arms across his chest.

"George, you would have never had the chance to pull that fish in if I hadn't caught it on my line," Gladys said.

"You wouldn't even have a fish to take a picture of if I hadn't pulled it in," George retorted.

"I only asked you to pull it in so you could feel useful," Gladys snapped. Temperatures were rising in the limousine.

"How about some music?" Dr. Price suggested. Everyone stopped talking in surprise—Dr. Price had been so quiet during the afternoon that they had forgotten he was even there. He'd played solitaire in the back seat of the limousine all afternoon except when he went to help beach Earl after his Jacques Cousteau imitation. Niles turned on the radio and the rest of the ride was spent in relative silence.

Patti went back to get the inspector at two-thirty. He was talking excitedly with the residents when she returned to the day room.

"I can't believe it was Jean Paul," Bubba was saying.

Mae nodded her head energetically. "I knew it the whole time—came as no surprise at all."

"Are you ready to continue with the inspection?" Patti asked Bubba.

He looked at her curiously. "Inspection? What inspection?" he asked.

"Aren't you here to inspect the premises?" Patti asked. Now she was confused.

"No, I came here to complain about the old folks fishing around my pond," Bubba said. He suddenly remembered his role as the complainant and stood up, buttoning his jacket and straightening his tie.

"You mean you're not the inspector?" Patti asked.

"No, I'm the guy who owns the pond where about eight of your old people are fishing today," he said. "I was never notified that the pond had been rented and was just curious as to whom you all spoke to about fishing there."

Patti took Bubba to meet Michelle, who had arranged the outing. It turned out that the pond hadn't been rented after all. One of Bubba's brothers had simply given Michelle permission for the Roost to use it that afternoon.

"I'm sorry, but we don't do business that way," Bubba told Michelle. "We'll lose money—after all, it's not free to keep that pond stocked." He explained to her that he was the primary owner of the property and in the future she would need to go through him for permission and rental of the pond.

Michelle apologized for the misunderstanding and offered to pay rent for the afternoon, but Bubba, feeling generous, declined to take the offer. He exited the front door of the Roost just as the limousine pulled up front.

"Well, there's our long lost friend now," George said when he saw Bubba. "We've missed you terribly and thought of you often."

Before Bubba could respond, a tall thin man with a camera pushed past him and reached to shake George's hand.

"I got the call. Who caught the fish?" the photographer asked.

"I did," George said.

"I did," Gladys said, climbing out of the back of the limousine. Jack and Hank followed, carrying the fish.

"Wow, what a huge fish," the photographer said in amazement. The bread and butter of the county newspaper was pictures of the "biggest" whatever—the biggest deer, the biggest rattlesnake, the biggest baby, the biggest fish . . . whatever. Once, Jake, the photographer, had received a call from a woman boasting to have the biggest squash in the state. Unfortunately, by the time she had shown the squash to all her friends and family throughout the county, and left the squash in her car while she worked in the poultry plant, it was rotten. The photographer had used his telephoto lens to take the picture from as far away as he could without having to get near the rancid vegetable.

"Okay, so who's posing with the fish?" Jake asked. George and Gladys stepped forward to claim ownership.

"I'll take that," Bubba said, reaching for the fish out of Hank's hands.

"Did you catch the fish?" Jake asked.

"It was caught on my property and they were fishing there without a permit, so the fish is mine," Bubba said.

Michelle, who had followed Bubba outside, nodded her head somberly at the residents. "It's true. I didn't pay the rental fee."

The others watched as Jake took several photographs of Bubba and the fish.

"I hope he eats the damn thing and gets pinworms," George said disgustedly, walking away.

"Yeah," Gladys said, following George inside. He stopped and waited for her to catch up, a certain kinship having developed between the two after having lost "the big one."

A tiny woman in her forties was standing by the receptionist desk when the group entered the lobby.

"Can I help you?" Patti asked the woman.

"Yes, I need to speak with the administrator," she said primly.

"Sure, may I ask what about? I may be able to help you," Patti said helpfully.

"I just want to go ahead and do the exit interview," the woman said. "My preliminary inspection is complete."

"You're the inspector?" Patti asked, her stomach turning to ice.

"Yes, and I've completed my once over. It looks great around here. The only thing I noticed is that many of the resident's rooms are empty—where do you hide them all?"

CHAPTER 8

NILES leaned back against the wrought iron of the garden bench, puffing contentedly on his cigar. He swirled the bourbon around in the bottom of his tumbler before holding it up to his mouth and taking a small sip. Enjoy, he reminded himself. Four o'clock was his favorite time of day, when Madame Wellington was taking a nap and he had a whole hour for his own leisure. A good cigar and a stiff shot of good bourbon were his vehicles to while away sixty minutes every day. He remembered his father and grandfather spent similar hours on their posts as well.

"A respectable post, a good cigar, and aged bourbon," his father used to tell him, "those are the necessities of life. Everything above and beyond that is gravy."

Niles puffed at the big Cuban cigar, remembering his late father. He'd spent his entire life working for the same family, from the time he was fourteen until his death at 68 years of age. It looked as though Niles was heading in the same direction. He'd been with the Wellingtons for 30 years now, having accepted the post when he turned 21. Niles had been Madame Wellington's personal servant the entire 30 years. His father would be proud that his only son had carried on the tradition of being a man servant so faithfully.

He was brought out of his reverie by the sound of a woman humming. He saw her auburn hair over the tops of the rose bushes as she made her way toward the courtyard. She turned the corner into the bricked in area and abruptly stopped humming, seeing Niles on the bench.

"Oh, my, I didn't know anyone was around," she said, her hand flying to her mouth. "I hope I didn't disturb you."

"That's quite all right," Niles lied to the woman. He savored these times in the afternoon because it was one of the few times he could be completely by himself with no one to wait on, no one to serve, no one to talk to and no one to be talked to. Perhaps she would go away and leave him alone.

The woman took a seat on the far side of the courtyard. "I mean, you look like you're enjoying yourself so much, I hate to barge in, but I like coming here to look at the pretty flowers and that's all I was doing" she said in a rush.

Niles stared at the woman silently. He'd been told before that he had a certain look that chased people away and provided a wide berth around him. He was trying to achieve that now, but saw that his efforts were in vain. The woman was clueless as to her invasion. She looked at Niles expectantly. Her eyes were bright and sparkling-green, he thought they were from this distance—and her smile was broad. She was very attractive, Niles thought, and only a few years younger than himself. But then, she was also bothersome.

"It's quite all right," Niles finally said. He pulled out his pocket watch and saw that he only had a few minutes left before he had to get back to Madame Wellington, anyway, so what was the harm?

"Thanks," she said cheerfully, looking around and taking in the rose gardens. "Aren't they lovely?"

"Pardon?" Niles asked.

"The roses. Aren't they beautiful?"

"Oh, yes, quite," he said, taking another puff of the cigar. He exhaled across the courtyard, as he had done every afternoon since Madame Beatrice was brought here.

"Oooh, isn't that a smelly thing," the woman said, fanning her hand in front of her face. "My late husband used to smoke. Used to, before it killed him," she added.

"How unfortunate," Niles muttered. The woman probably nagged him to death if the truth be known, he thought to himself.

"My name is Mary Grace Tanner," she said, offering a half wave to the stoic man servant who sat across from her.

Niles nodded in greeting. She was beginning to agitate him.

"And you are?"

"Mr. Fenwick," he said, standing up and snapping shut his pocket watch. "Goodbye, Ms. Tanner," he said, heading out the gate.

"Oh, goodbye, Mr. Fenwick," Mary Grace said, obviously disappointed that her new acquaintance was leaving her company. "Perhaps we'll see each other again," she called out just as he reached the side door of Madame Wellington's wing. He paused momentarily before walking inside. Mary Grace was humming again.

A half hour later, Mary Grace found Gladys in the hall talking to George.

"Hi, Gladys," Mary Grace said.

"Hello, Mary Grace—visiting your father again today?'

"Yes, but he's sleeping so soundly I hate to wake him. I've been wandering around in the rose garden again."

"You should join the Garden Club, as much time as you spend in that rose garden."

"I have no desire to join that group of old biddies," Mary Grace said, looking around to make sure she wasn't being overheard. "But there is someone I'd like to get to know better. I saw him in the courtyard just a little while ago." She noticed that George was paying close attention. "Close your ears, George. Or at least turn your hearing aid down."

"It's nothing I want to know about," George grunted, but didn't make a motion to move out of earshot.

"Who is it?" Gladys asked.

"A Mr. Fenwick."

Both Gladys and George looked puzzled. "I don't know any Mr. Fenwick around here," George said. Gladys shook her head, too.

"Well, he looks tall, although I'm not sure because he was sitting down the whole time. He's got black hair with a touch of gray on the sides, and he was smoking a big cigar and drinking from a tumbler in the courtyard just a little while ago."

"Niles," George and Gladys said together.

"Who is Niles?" Mary Grace asked.

"He works for Beatrice Wellington, a resident here," George said. "He's her personal servant or something like that—drives the limousine, waits on her, basically does everything but chew her food up for her."

"I didn't think he was a resident," Mary Grace said thoughtfully.

"If you're thinking about him as a romantic interest, don't," George said. "I don't think all the sex in the world could tempt him away from that woman's side."

"George!" Gladys said, swatting him on the arm. "That was a tasteless thing to say."

"But it's true," George said, attempting to avoid her swing.

"Oh, you mean the two of them are together?" Mary Grace asked in disappointment.

"No, no. He's just very devoted to her and to the job," Gladys explained.

"Does he ever go out with anyone?" Mary asked.

"Not that I've ever seen," Gladys said. "Are you planning on asking him out?"

"I just might do that," Mary said. "He seems a little shy, so I might have to make the first move."

The next afternoon, Niles was making his way to the courtyard when he heard the humming. He had been looking forward to a quiet afternoon in the courtyard—Madame Wellington had been particularly cantankerous today and he desperately needed some time to regroup. He stopped, trying to decide whether or not to join the woman in the courtyard or find another quiet place.

"Oh, Mr. Fenwick!" she called. She'd seen him walk out the door—an event she'd been anxiously waiting for the past half hour.

Niles walked into the courtyard. "Good afternoon, Ms. Tanner. How are you today?"

"Just fine, Mr. Fenwick, but I wish you'd call me Mary Grace—that is my name."

"Very well, Mary Grace," Niles said tightlipped. He was carefully taught not to address anyone by their first names, but this woman seemed not to care about basic formalities.

"May I call you Niles?" she asked with a smile.

Niles cringed inside, but nodded politely.

"Very good then. Niles, I wonder if you would be interested in going out on a date some time with me," Mary Grace said confidently.

Niles was stunned. In less than five minutes time, he had called a woman by her first name, had been addressed by his own first name, and was now being propositioned by the same woman. "Oh, I he stammered. All eloquence went out the window with her question. "I don't . . ." he tried again.

"It's very simple, Niles. Would you like to go out with me?"

"This is very unusual," he began again. He'd dated once or twice years ago, but he'd always been the one to ask the woman out. This turning of the tables was something he wasn't accustomed to, although the idea of going out with Mary Grace was not totally displeasing. "I appreciate the invitation, but I really cannot," he said. "My position with Madame Wellington is such that I have very little time for social outings."

"Are you turning me down?" Mary Grace asked with a pout.

"Yes, Madame, I am regretfully turning you down," Niles said. They spent the remainder of Niles' hour break in silence, Niles smoking his cigar and drinking his bourbon while Mary Grace plotted how to get Niles to accept her offer.

They never knew George had been standing behind the rose bushes with his hearing aid turned on high.

That evening, after Beatrice had gone to bed, leaving Niles alone once again, he had time to reflect on the day, and on Mary Grace. She was not what you'd call handsome, but then again, she was quite pleasing to look at, he thought. At least he enjoyed looking at her. He gathered together his things and prepared to make the journey to his home, only a couple of miles away. Niles liked to walk; it gave him a sense of accomplishment as well as much needed exercise at the end of the day. Walking in the brisk night air, Niles once again turned his thoughts to Mary Grace and the fact that he'd never had a normal social life because of his occupation. Why, some nights, if Madame Wellington was having a fitful rest, he would stay with her and wouldn't go home at all. No wife in her right mind would put up with that kind of behavior, Niles thought. "Wife," he laughed out loud. He had already progressed Mary Grace from a casual encounter in the rose garden to being his wife—they had barely spoken and knew each other only a little. Niles walked up the driveway to his house, pausing briefly to look at the dark, empty house. He had no family, no friends to speak of besides Beatrice, and no lady friend. He didn't even have a pet—a conscious decision he made due to the fact that he was away from home all the time and didn't have anyone to help take care of it. He'd resisted the urge to pet Jack's dog, Blue, simply because he thought it wasn't proper behavior, not because he didn't want to. Madame Wellington, despite her act of kindness in helping Jack get his dog at the nursing home, didn't really care for Blue.

"It's a redneck dog, plain and simple," she had said, when Niles commented on the dog's disposition.

Redneck or not, the truth was, Niles would appreciate the company of any woman or beast right now.

The next morning when Niles arrived at the Roost at 6 a.m., he found George rocking on the front porch with the newspaper in his hand.

"Good morning, Mr. George," Niles said politely. "What causes you to be up at this hour of the morning?"

"Sit down here for a minute, Niles," George invited, indicating the rocking chair beside him.

Niles glanced at his pocket watch in response.

"That's what I'm going to talk to you about, Niles. You worry too much about Beatrice and what she needs. What about what you need? Have you ever considered that?"

"I really must be going to Madame Wellington," Niles stammered. "I'm close to being late."

"Late for what, Niles? Late to tie her shoes, fix her tea, plump her pillow, change the oil on her wheelchair? What does she need that can't wait for five more minutes?" George challenged.

Niles glanced at his watch one more time, snapped shut the lid and sat down. "I suppose a couple of minutes won't hurt." "The other day, I couldn't help but overhear your conversation with Mary Grace— she's quite a looker, huh?—and I want you to know I understand your dilemma and I think I can help you with it."

Niles looked at George suspiciously. "What do you think you understand?"

"The fact that you'd probably go out with this woman if you had the time to go out with her, right? Am I right? I mean, Niles, old buddy, you're a man, I'm a man, we understand these man things. There are certain things that men need, right? And one of them is women."

Niles nodded slightly, loosening up under George's banter. "Yes, I must admit I am intrigued by her, though she's not what I'd call my type."

George hooted. "Your type? Niles, from all I've seen, you've never had a chance to establish what your type is. Mary Grace might be your type and you don't even know it yet. Good grief, I wish I was her type. Maybe you can tell me your secret."

Niles smiled slightly. "Still, I really don't have the time to go out with her or anyone. My job is very demanding on my time."

"That's where I come in," George said, folding back the newspaper he'd been holding on his lap. "Look at what I've done for you." He held out the classified sections, which was riddled with red circles. "I've gone through and circled all the jobs I thought you were qualified for," George said proudly.

"Why?"

"Because you need to get into a new occupation, or else you're never going to have any time for yourself."

"I can't leave Madame Wellington," Niles said defiantly.

"Sure you can. She can replace you," George said simply.

Niles looked shocked. "Replace me? I don't think so. I've been with her for many years." Niles stood up to leave. "And now, I must leave and go to Madame Wellington."

"Think about what I've said, okay?" George called after him. He tucked the newspaper under his arm, sure that Niles would come back in the near future.

Niles entered Beatrice's room, his head swimming with all of George's words. "Good morning, Madame Wellington," he said as he stepped into the room.

"Where on earth have you been, Niles?" Beatrice lamented. "I always have my coffee at 6:30 in the morning, and you weren't here."

"Forgive me, Madame, I was detained," he said, cringing under the demanding tone of her voice.

"Well, you can make it up to me tonight, Niles, because I want you to stay late and make out invitations for a dinner I'm holding at the country club next month."

Niles thought about how nice it would be to spend the evening with Mary Grace instead, but said nothing. "Very well, Madame."

As the day progressed, Niles realized his patience with Beatrice was wearing thin. George's words had opened a window for him, allowing him to see just how much time and attention she demanded of him every day. During his afternoon break, instead of sitting out in the rose garden,

Niles went in search of George, finding him at the chess board in the recreation room.

"Excuse me, Mr. George?" Niles said hesitantly.

"I thought you'd be back," George said, not turning his head from the chess board.

"I'd like to hear your suggestions about possible employment," Niles said.

"Sure, I've won this game anyway," he said, moving his queen in close proximity to his opponent's king. "Checkmate." He turned away from the board and pulled the folded newspaper out from under his chair, handing it to Niles.

Niles took the newspaper and began reading the job advertisements George had circled in red. "Lawn care maintenance? George, I've never worked on lawns," he said scanning through the list. "Short order cook . . . security guard . . . George, these jobs are . . . beneath me," Niles said with a sniff. "I will not lower myself to these jobs."

"Look, Niles, you've got to realize one thing. You have no education and you have no worthwhile experience. There are not too many positions that require applicants to have experience waiting hand and foot on an old rich lady."

"There must be something I can do," Niles said defensively. "I've spent my entire life working for her family—that experience must count for something."

"Maybe you could be a taxi driver," George suggested, "since you drive Beatrice around all the time, but there's not much call for a limousine driver here in the mountains of North Georgia, or a taxi driver for that matter. Everything in this town is within walking distance."

Tommy walked in, having just started work for the afternoon. "Hey, guys—what's up? What's Niles doing here in the recreation room?"

"We're trying to figure out another job for him to do," George said.

"Is he quitting his job with Beatrice?" Tommy asked incredulously.

Niles didn't answer. "He's thinking about it," George said quickly. "The only problem is that we can't think what kind of job he's qualified for."

"What about waiting tables?" Tommy asked. "He serves Beatrice her meals every day."

Niles frowned. "It's different, however, to serve the meals of one respectable person than it is to serve meals to anyone and everyone, regardless of their social stature."

"I'll tell you one thing, you're going to have to get off your high horse if you want to seriously find another occupation. You should have thought about this years ago when you decided to be a butler or whatever it is you consider yourself."

"I prefer to call myself a manservant," Niles said.

"Whatever. You just need to realize that you're not as marketable as you think you are. Does Beatrice know you're looking for other work?"

"No, and besides, I'm not sure I am looking for work, but if I do, I intend to tell her before she finds out from other sources."

Throughout his break, he vacillated back and forth about his situation. "She really can get along without me," he thought, "and I have to admit I have no companions my age. On the other hand, I'm the only one that knows her habits and puts up with her bad side . . ." Before he knew it, his break was over. Niles returned to Beatrice's room. He stood stiffly inside the front door with his hands behind his back and held his breath.

"What is it, Niles?" Beatrice asked. "Aren't you coming in?" "Madame, I have decided to leave your employ and search for other work."

Beatrice inhaled sharply. "Leaving? You can't leave me, Niles. You've been with me for so many years!"

"I have come to the realization that I need more time off of work, to enjoy social activities, and I need a job that will allow me to have that time."

"Have you found a woman, Niles?" Beatrice asked with a sniff as she looked away.

"Yes, as a matter of fact, there is this woman I have some interest in and would like to pursue," Niles said.

"How long before you go?" Beatrice asked almost too quickly. "Oh, some time I'm sure. I haven't even begun interviewing for other jobs yet. I'll be more than happy to help . . . train someone else to take my position." He looked at the floor.

"Yes, I'll need someone right away. Would you mind seeing to it that an advertisement is placed in the newspaper?"

"Yes, ma'am. I take it you approve of my leaving?" he said as though not even believing his own words.

"I'll get used to it. There are a lot of people out there who would like to work for me, I'm sure."

Few words were spoken between the two old friends the rest of the evening. When Niles left for the day, Beatrice finally let down her guard. She was worried and afraid. Niles had been with her for so many years, she wasn't sure she could find anyone else like him. She was much too old and cantankerous—suppose no one wanted the job? And it wasn't so much what Niles did for her than the company he provided. So many changes. Neither she nor Niles were deep in friends or family. Then again, if this is what Niles really wanted, he had been a loyal employee . . . Beatrice slept little that night.

The next morning Niles found George on the front porch once again, newspaper in one hand, red pen in the other. "There are some new positions in the paper today, Niles," George said cheerfully. "Have a seat and see what you think."

Niles looked through the classifieds, carefully reading the description to each red-circled job. "What is a busboy?" he asked.

"That's someone who cleans up tables at a restaurant, after everyone's through eating."

"No," Niles said with distaste. He read on. "Summer camp counselor? Let's be serious, Mr. George, I don't exactly have the charm and charisma necessary for a camp counselor, do I?"

"I threw that one in for a joke—keep reading."

"Substitute school teacher?"

"You don't even have to be certified, you just have to put up with the little kiddies all day until the real teacher comes back." "No, I'm afraid I would physically abuse them."

George laughed. "Okay, how about the one I circled at the bottom? Maitre d' at a swanky restaurant in town? Actually, it's the only swanky restaurant in a hundred mile radius. You'd be over all the other waiters, and you'd be the guy up front who talks to the customers. Usually restaurants look for older, dignified guys for those positions. I think you'd suit it to a 'T.'"

"Do you think so?" Niles seemed to consider this one. "What are the requirements?"

"Previous experience of being a waiter, mature, dependable, blah blah blah. The same old stuff. I think you should go for this job. They're taking interviews all day today, from noon until four in the afternoon."

Beatrice allowed Niles to leave for the afternoon in order to interview for the job. It felt weird to Niles to be out during the day without Beatrice.

Weird, but somehow exciting. "What would he be asked during the interview?" he wondered.

"Why are you leaving a position you've been working in for so many years?" the restaurant manager asked Niles. "Were you unhappy with your job?"

"No, not unhappy, sir," Niles said slowly. "I'm simply ready to try other things."

"If you'll forgive me, you seem a little old to suddenly change your occupation," the manager said, looking at Niles carefully. There had to be a good reason why this man was leaving his job besides a desire to try something else. Not that he was complaining or looking a gift horse in the mouth, because this guy would make a perfect maitre'd.

"No offense taken, sir. I'm simply prepared to try a new position," Niles said. Then he reconsidered his answer. "Actually, sir, that's not entirely true."

"Aha," the manager thought to himself. Here comes the real story."

"The real reason for my seeking another occupation is so that I may have more time off to spend with a particular lady friend. Currently I'm on call all day and most of the evening, which has never been a problem up until now . . ." Niles trailed off. He hadn't meant to burden this complete stranger with his own concerns.

"Now I understand," the manager said, smiling. "That makes a lot of sense. So when can you start?"

The question caught Niles by surprise. He'd thought the interview process would take longer and that he'd still have a few more days before he made up his mind.

"Niles?" the manager said again.

"Oh, I suppose I shall be able to begin immediately. Would that be all right?" There was a gnawing feeling in Niles' stomach as he gave his verbal commitment. Did he want to leave the employ of Madame Wellington? He wasn't entirely sure.

Beatrice wasn't surprised when Niles returned several hours later with the news that he had gotten the job.

"When do you start?" she asked indifferently, as though it didn't matter.

"As soon as possible—tomorrow, if I could," he said apologetically. "But I've worked out a situation. I don't begin work until four in the afternoon, so I thought I could come in the mornings to help you and until you find a new person to take my place."

Beatrice seemed relieved. "Very well, I'll see you in the morning. Take the rest of the evening off."

Niles, surprised, did just that. As soon as he got home he realized he had no one to share the events of the day with. Without allowing himself the opportunity to talk himself out of it, he called Mary Grace and asked her out to dinner. She accepted.

"How on earth did you get off work tonight?" she asked when she answered the door, her eyes smiling brightly. She had taken great pains on short notice to go all out for the date. Her hair was set and styled, and the dress she wore was one she picked up on sale at Mervyn's just hours before.

"I have decided to quit my job and look for other employment that will allow me more time off," Niles said with a slight smile.

Mary Grace smiled back warmly, reached out and tapped his arm. "I'm glad of that," she said. "What will you be doing?"

"I'll be the new maitre d' at the restaurant we will be dining at tonight," he said, carefully searching her face for a response.

She smiled again and clapped her hands together. "Why, that's just wonderful! I shall take all my meals there in the future," she said. Niles smiled back.

The next morning the front porch was empty. George was sleeping in, satisfied that his job search was complete. Niles missed seeing him there, wanting to be persuaded by George into sharing the details of his date with Mary Grace. Niles would have complied willingly. He felt a spring in his step and a smile on his lips. And, his new job would begin tonight. Beatrice seemed or pretended not to notice anything different about Niles.

"Good morning," she said simply, still stewing over the fact that he was leaving. "Did you put that advertisement in the newspaper?"

"Good morning, Madame Wellington," he said brightly. "Yes, the advertisement will run as of this morning until someone has been found to take my position. Incidentally, I shall be leaving this afternoon at three o'clock."

"Fine," Beatrice replied, much to Niles' surprise. He had expected to receive more resistance from Beatrice than this. She was taking the news rather well, he thought with a mixture of relief and sadness. Niles had thought she would be more upset to see his departure after so many years of loyal service.

Beneath Beatrice's stony exterior was a woman shaken to her roots. She got little sleep the night before, worrying about what would happen to her once Niles left. She was not a capable person, she knew. Her whole life she had depended upon others to do things for her—prepare her meals, handle her accounts, drive her around, find things and bring them to her, and even shop for her. Niles had done all these things for her and more. He had gradually become indispensable. And now he was leaving. If no one responded to the job advertisement—seriously, who would want to work in a little hick town in North Georgia for a bitter old woman?—she didn't know what she would do. She'd have to push her own wheelchair, pick up her own food tray from the cafeteria, and ride the bus or the nursing home van if she wanted to go into town. Next month, at her country club dinner party, she would have to arrive in a city bus! Beatrice shuddered at the thought and considered cancelling the entire affair. But most of all, she would miss the comfort of their relationship.

The two old friends spent the rest of the morning and the first part of the afternoon in silence, each lost in their own thoughts. Niles was thinking about which suit he was going to wear for his first night as maitre d' and Beatrice was wondering who was going to hang up her clothes that evening. She'd never done that before in her whole life.

Niles left at three o'clock and walked home quickly. He would have to start driving his old Plymouth from now on if he expected to get anywhere on time, and he was always punctual. When the restaurant manager unlocked the back service door at four o'clock, Niles was there waiting. Although he had never had true experience as a waiter, the manager had been impressed with Niles' appearance and manner of speaking. It never hurt for a maitre d' to have an English accent, either. A foreign accent implied worldliness, which was impressive to the type of clientele that frequented La Chateau. This guy was just too perfect.

"Niles, how are you?" the manager asked.

"Fine, Mr. Jacobs. I'm ready to begin work."

Thomas Jacobs was impressed with Niles' businesslike approach to his position, another reason he had hired him over all the others with much more experience. He explained to Niles his responsibilities and left him to the front desk. "Any questions, just ask," he said, going back to the kitchen.

The evening was a great success as Niles had no difficulty handling the restaurant or its patrons. Mary Grace and three of her friends showed up as well, all tittering and whispering to each other as Niles led them to one of the best tables in the house. Although he was extremely busy all night, Niles still found his thoughts wandering back to Beatrice, wondering if she was being taken care of adequately. Maybe I should give a quick call to be sure everything's okay, he thought.

Beatrice was wondering the same thing. Two job applicants had shown up at the nursing home after Niles left, and Beatrice tried out each one for two hours as a trial run. One was lazy and overweight, more interested in which soap operas were on the television than caring for Beatrice. The other was an elderly woman who fell asleep every time she sat down in a chair, which was often. Beatrice sent the last one away at seven o'clock in the evening and settled down in the quiet of her room. She stared at the television until seven thirty, when there was a knock at her door.

"Beatrice? May I come in?" Gladys was at the door.

"Yes, come in," Beatrice said, glad for the company.

"I came to see if you wanted to go to the bingo party tonight in the recreation room," Gladys said. "I know you don't normally join us in the activities, but since Niles is gone and all . . ." she said, trailing off.

"I'd love to go," Beatrice said quickly. She was more anxious than she thought about getting out of her lonely wing of the Roost. Niles had never been much of a talker, but his presence alone offered a great deal of comfort. She stood up from her chair and reached for the walking cane that rested beside the chair.

"Don't you want your wheelchair?" Gladys asked in surprise. It was seldom that she saw Beatrice walk on her own, usually Niles pushed her wheelchair wherever they went.

"No, I'm not too good at pushing that heavy wheelchair, so I'll just walk this time," Beatrice said, not realizing she had taken her first step toward independence. She and Gladys walked amiably to the recreation room, Gladys waiting occasionally as Beatrice stopped and rested before continuing.

"You should get out and walk more often," Gladys suggested gently. She knew that Beatrice rarely walked anywhere with Niles around.

"I know, and I think I just might start doing that," Beatrice said. "Would you care to join me?" Gladys nodded yes, that she would be happy to accompany her. She knew how important friends were at times like these. After her husband died she thought she was going to die too, but her friends soon forced her to get out and get busy. "That's what Beatrice is going to need," she thought.

At the end of the evening, having won twice in bingo and put her own clothes in the wardrobe, Beatrice felt more comfortable about Niles' absence. Not that she didn't miss him, because she did, but she felt more capable of handling things on her own.

The next morning when Niles came into her room, Beatrice was sipping a cup of coffee from her silver service.

"Madame Wellington, who made coffee for you this morning?"

"I did," she answered, tipping her chin at a determined angle. "I thought it didn't look so hard to make, so I made it myself. Would you like a cup?"

Niles was so shocked that she had made the coffee that he accepted and poured himself a cup. It was extremely strong and bitter. Niles tried to hold down the grimace with a straight face.

"Pretty bad, isn't it?" Beatrice said with a heavy sigh, then grinned.

"Yes, Madame, it is quite awful. If I may, I'd like to show you the correct way to brew coffee," Niles suggested. By this time he, too was smiling. She listened patiently and attentively as he walked her through the steps of making coffee. As he instructed her on measuring the coffee, she reached up and touched his hand lightly.

"I missed you last night, Niles, but I think I'm going to be all right. In fact, I went and played bingo with Gladys."

"Bingo? But Madame, you said that bingo was a game for . . ." Niles protested.

"I know, a game for rednecks, but who knows? Maybe I'm a closet redneck. We had fun."

"I missed you as well, Madame," Niles admitted. "I enjoyed my first night of work, but I don't think it's something I could stomach for very long. The patrons are very demanding and rude. One man even called me 'boy,' and snapped for my attention."

"Oh dear," Beatrice said, her hand flying to her mouth. "How did you stand for that?"

"I didn't. After performing all of my necessary duties for the evening, I gave them my notice. I cannot continue there. And it looks like I've worked myself out of a job around here," he said, sadness in his voice. "I think you've been able to handle yourself quite well all these years and were just letting me do it for you."

"Let's not jump to conclusions, Niles. Just because I played bingo and made coffee doesn't mean I don't need you. It could just be a temporary mental breakdown. Fortunately, I play bingo a lot better than I make coffee. If you're interested, and since you're now unemployed, I would like to offer you your old job back, with a few changes in the job description."

"Yes?" Niles was definitely interested. He was born and bred for this type of work, not for serving boorish people who didn't know a salad fork from a finger bowl. The management part of being a maitre'd had been enjoyable, the fact that all the waiters looked to him for instruction, but the job overall was just too demeaning. There was one thing Niles wasn't willing to give up, and that was his pride. Being a manservant was nothing to be ashamed of. It was a worthy occupation for worthy people.

"What are the job changes?" he asked. After his behavior, he wouldn't be surprised if she wanted him to become a twenty-four hour manservant, which would be the only thing that would keep him from accepting.

"To begin with, since I now know how to make coffee, you don't need to come in to work until nine in the morning," Beatrice began. "And, since I have decided to become a practicing redneck and participate in activities such as bingo and crafts, you may leave each evening at six o'clock, after dinner."

"But Madame," Niles started to say, but was interrupted. "I'm not through. You will also have every weekend off, from Friday at six until Monday morning at nine o'clock, and I don't want to hear from you or see you until then, understood?" Niles nodded dumbly. He couldn't believe what he was hearing.

"And furthermore, you can have four weeks paid vacation per year, and use of the limousine, if you give me notice."

Niles continued to nod. Madame Wellington must have lost her mind overnight, maybe suffered a stroke over his absence. He would have Dr. Price give her a checkup this afternoon.

"And there's one more condition, which is imperative that you follow."

"Yes?" Niles said expectantly.

"You must call me Beatrice. I mean, really, Niles, I've known you longer than I knew my first husband."

Niles nodded again. He was speechless.

"Now, under these conditions, will you take your old job back?"

"Yes, Madame," Niles stammered, "I would dearly like to have my former position."

"Very good, then, shall we go to breakfast?"

"To the cafeteria? You always take your meals in the room," Niles said, surprised once again.

"Yes, but I promised to meet Gladys in the cafeteria this morning. Are you coming or not?" she asked, reaching for her cane. She waved away the wheelchair that Niles pulled out for her to use. "Put that thing away. I'm walking."

"Yes, Beatrice," Niles said, following the determined old woman down the hall.

CHAPTER 9

"**W**ELCOME," Ida said brightly to the elderly couple walking into the lobby of the Roost. "If you need any assistance finding anything, you can ask me or go to the information desk," she said, pointing toward the receptionist desk. The couple looked at Ida with puzzled expressions. "We're looking for Betty Jean Collins' room," the woman said. "She was brought here Saturday."

Ida turned and pointed down one of the hallways that branched out of the lobby. "Aisle three on the left, beside the linens." The couple walked away, occasionally looking back to make sure Ida was real and not a figment of their imagination. Ida watched them all the way down the hall, and as soon as they were out of sight, she sat down on one of the couches against the wall. When she thought no one was looking, she slipped off her shoes, bent down, and rubbed her feet. They'd been hurting a good bit lately, she reflected. She'd have to remember to soak them in Epsom salt water tonight when she went back to her room.

Patti McLeod stepped out of the administrator's office and, glancing into the lobby, was surprised to see Ida sitting down. Ida never sat down during the daytime except to eat her meals. Other than that, you could always find her standing in the lobby, right inside the front door.

"Ida, are you okay?" she asked.

Ida jumped at the sound of Patti's voice. She hadn't heard her approaching. Ida quickly began jamming her feet back in her shoes and stood up. "I'm fine, Patti. Just fine," she lied. In truth, her feet hurt pretty badly stuck in those shoes. They'd gotten quite fat lately and didn't fit in her shoes as well.

"You know, it's okay if you sit down sometimes," Patti said with a laugh, foiling to notice the grimace on Ida's face as she shifted weight on her feet. "We don't expect you to stand up all day."

"No, it's my job to stand here," Ida said defiantly. "You won't catch me sitting down again, Ms. McLeod."

"But it's okay if you sit down, Ida. That's what I'm trying to tell you. This isn't a job, you know. No one's making you stand here."

Ida paid no attention to what Patti said, but instead fidgeted with the plastic name tag pinned on her dress which read: "Hi! I'm Ida!"

Patti laughed to herself as she walked away. Ida had been at the nursing home for nearly five years now, and every morning since she was first admitted Ida would report to the lobby and welcome guests and visitors into the Roost. She would work from eight in the morning until five in the afternoon, after which she would go to dinner in the cafeteria, and then to her room for the rest of the evening. She rarely even spoke to other residents while 'on the job' and seemed as though she felt she had nothing in common with them when she was off the job. It's as though she feels she is the only working resident here and doesn't belong with the others.

Patti knew that Ida worked for one of those big department stores for most of her life as a "welcome lady," but no one knew why she continued to perform those duties—especially when she wasn't getting paid for it. She didn't bother anyone; in fact, people seemed to enjoy the attention Ida bestowed upon them when they walked through the front door. The only problem they'd ever had was one time when a resident's daughter came to visit and, seeing that her mother's plant was doing poorly, decided to take the plant home with her at the end of the visit so that she could nurse it back to health. When the woman tried to leave the Roost with the plant, Ida demanded to see her sales receipt. The woman, familiar with Ida's peculiarities, laughed and tried to explain the situation. To make a long story short, Ida called the police and claimed that the woman had shoplifted the plant from the Garden Center. But even that incident was more amusing than embarrassing. She had developed cordial, friendly relationships with the regulars and took her role as the greeter very seriously. The "Welcome Woman" of the Roost, as she was known, had become a regular fixture at the facility for the past five years.

Later in the afternoon, Lucy approached Patti in the hallway. "Patti, have you noticed how swollen Ida's ankles are? They look like they're about to bust out of her shoes."

Patti didn't remember seeing Ida's feet when she talked to her earlier in the day. "No, I can't say that I noticed. I remember seeing her sitting down, which I thought was strange. Ida never sits down."

"I think you should get Dr. Price to check her feet," Lucy said.

"Thanks," Patti said. She walked up to the lobby to see for herself. Ida was standing in front of the entranceway, prepared to greet visitors, but it was obvious that she was very uncomfortable.

"Hello, Ida," Patti said cheerfully. "How are you this afternoon?"

"Fine, fine," Ida replied with a forced smile.

"That's not what I hear. Someone told me your feet are swollen. Is that true?"

"They're a little fat, but they'll go back down by morning," Ida said confidently. They always do."

"Always?" Patti asked, alarmed. "Have your feet been this way for a long time?"

"Not too long," Ida replied.

"I'm going to send Dr. Price around to check on you, okay?" "You'd better make that appointment after five o'clock. That's when I get off work," Ida said, looking at her watch.

Patti found Dr. Price in the recreation room and told him about Ida's legs. He promised to check them that afternoon. "Tell her to come around to my office on her way home from work," he said with a smile. Ida showed up at the recreation room at five fifteen. Dr. Price could tell from a distance that she was in a great deal of discomfort.

"Sit down, Ida," he said, getting up from his place at the checker board and waving her into the seat.

"I don't know what all the fuss is about," she said with a scornful expression. "It's nothing a little Epsom salts won't take care of."

Bill Price knelt in front of Ida and lifted the hem of her dress, which had dropped over her feet. Underneath, he was amazed to find that her legs, ankles and feet were three times their normal size. "Ida!" he said in surprise. "Why haven't you come to me sooner about this? I can't believe you're still working on your feet all day. You've got a serious case of edema."

"I've just got a case of swollen feet," Ida said, matter of factly. "There's nothing serious about it."

"I'm going to start you on some diuretics," Dr. Price explained. "That's medicine to take the swelling out of your legs and feet. And, I want you to stay off of your feet for the next couple of weeks, all right?"

"I can't do that, Dr. Price," Ida said, looking at him in amazement. "I have to be at work in the morning, and I don't have any sick time."

"I'll write you an excuse," Dr. Price said, playing along with her game. "You've got my permission to stay home for the next two weeks until we see if that swelling gets out of your feet."

"I just can't do that. Do you know I haven't missed a single day of work since BestMart hired me in October of 1945? Not one single day."

Dr. Price was impressed. "How old were you when you first started?"

"Sixteen years old. I was the first welcome lady BestMart ever had," she said, pride showing in her voice. "They decided in 2007 that I needed to come work here—and they were right. This place was in dire need of a welcome lady."

"I see," Dr. Price said. "Now, promise me you will stay off of your feet for the next two weeks. And, you need to prop your feet up, too. Keep them elevated. That'll help."

"I'll take your medicine and I'll prop my feet up when I can, but I can't promise you that I'll stop working, Dr. Price. They just don't have anyone else here to substitute for me."

"We'll see about that," he said as he left the room to put a notation on her chart. Before leaving the Roost for the day, he gave all the nurses and staff instructions to keep Ida out of the lobby for the next two weeks.

George was sitting on the front porch that evening when Tommy found him. "Hey, George, what's up? You want to play some checkers?"

"Nah," George said without interest. He was staring off into space.

"What's wrong with you, old man?" Tommy teased. He wasn't used to seeing George so despondent. "I didn't see you at dinner." "I've got woman trouble," George said.

"Gladys? I thought you two have been getting along pretty well lately."

"We are—that's the whole problem. Her birthday is coming up soon and I don't have a dime to my name," he said.

Tommy pulled a rocking chair up beside George. "She'll understand if you can't get her anything. You know the saying—it's the thought that counts."

"That's not how she counts," George said. "Gladys keeps dropping hints about needing a new watch. I just don't know how to get the money. All those years I spent in jail are catching up with me. I've spent most of the time making license plates." "You could make her something," Tommy suggested. "What, a license plate?" George laughed bitterly. "I'm not very creative or talented except for breaking and entering." "When's her birthday?"

"Next week."

"We'll think of something by then," Tommy assured him. "I'll help you. Hey, I'd loan you the money, but I don't have any either."

"Don't worry about it," George said. "I'll come up with a plan. Go on inside, now and do your work. I've got some thinking to do."

Tommy, unused to being dismissed by his old friend, walked back inside.

George heard people approaching from the parking lot and looked at his watch. It was seven o'clock. Time for the second wave of visitors to come through. Usually people came to visit either right before lunch or right after dinner, he'd noticed.

"I can't believe how much we had to pay to go see that movie last night," the woman lamented to the man who walked beside her. "And it wasn't even that good."

"And by the time we paid for parking and for popcorn and drinks, we'd spent a good twenty dollars," the man agreed. "It's getting too expensive to go out any more."

The couple continued complaining the whole way up the sidewalk and into the front door of the Roost. They nodded at George politely, but he never noticed. George had a plan.

Ida reported for work in the lobby at eight o'clock sharp. Her feet felt better than they did last night, but not a whole lot better, she realized. Patti was the first to notice her.

"Ida, you're not supposed to be here. Dr. Price said you were to stay off of your feet and take it easy for the next two weeks." "I can't do that, Patti. Who's going to tell all the customers where to go around here? It can be quite confusing."

"That's why we have a receptionist," Patti said, pointing toward Margie behind the desk. Margie waved in response.

"I'm not leaving," Ida said firmly.

"At least sit down out here, okay?" Patti said, pulling up a chair to the spot where Ida normally greeted visitors. "Sit here and greet people."

"Fine," Ida said, sitting down in the chair.

"Good. Thank you," Patti said, surprised that Ida sat down without much of a fight.

As soon as Patti walked away Ida stood up and moved the chair back to its original position. She turned to Margie and said, "Don't you tell on me."

"I didn't see nothing," Margie said, going back to filing her nails.

Dr. Price found Ida standing in the lobby at ten o'clock that morning. "Ida, you've got to go back to your room and elevate your feet. All you're doing is making things worse."

"I'm not leaving, Dr. Price. And if you want me to go, you're going to have to call security to remove me, at which time I'll claim physical abuse," she said smartly.

Dr. Price, who knew Ida to be good on her word, left her alone. He went to find Patti.

"Patti, what are we going to do about Ida? She won't stay off of her feet, and she's got a serious case of edema."

"I know, I've already tried to get her to sit down once today but she won't."

"Why in the world does she insist on being the welcome woman around here?" Dr. Price asked, throwing up his hands.

"That's 'welcome lady' to you. That's what she was called at BestMart."

"I know, I know, she told me all about that yesterday. It's too bad we don't pay her to work here, then maybe we could fire her."

"I don't think that would work, either. She'd be back here the next morning, with or without pay." They laughed in agreement.

Dr. Price got serious. "You know, her legs are really swollen. I'm afraid if we can't keep her off her feet, they're going to get much worse. It's not unheard of for gangrene to set in with severe cases of edema—which she's going to have if she doesn't slow down. Does she have any family?"

Patti shook her head. "No family and no friends that I know of. To be a welcome lady, she's quite a loner. The state admitted her here as a Medicaid patient."

"We've got to convince her that she doesn't need to work anymore. How do employers get rid of employees when they get too old or sick?"

"They lay them off," Patti said. "But since we don't even pay her, we can't fire her."

Dr. Price's finger shot into the air. "They retire them."

"I don't get it," Patti said, confused.

"Ida thinks she still works for BestMart, doesn't she?"

"I guess so."

"Then we get somebody from BestMart to come over and tell her she's being retired—maybe give her a gift or something." Patti nodded her head slowly in approval. "You may have something there. I'll go call BestMart's main office and see what they say about it. I mean, after all, Ida did work there for nearly fifty years—I would think they could do something for her."

Patti went back to her office and looked up the number to BestMart. She briefly explained her problem to the secretary who answered the telephone.

"Oh, I remember Ida. I think you need to speak to the personnel director, Richard Wysong," she said. "I'll connect you."

A few minutes later, Wysong came on the line. "So, you're calling from Milly's Merry Roost, where Ms. Lee is a resident." "Yes," Patti said. "We're having sort of a problem with her and I was hoping that perhaps BestMart could help."

"I don't understand," Wysong said.

"She thinks she's still the welcome lady for BestMart. Every morning she gets up and goes into the lobby where she stands for eight to nine hours straight, greeting people and asking them if they need a shopping buggy."

"Now I understand," he said. "We had the same problem with her when we fired her."

"You fired her?" Patti asked, surprised. "I was under the impression that she'd worked for BestMart fifty years. That's a pretty good track record."

"Fifty years, really?" Wysong asked. "Let me pull her file." The line was quiet as Wysong rifled through her file. "You're right, she did work here fifty years. I had no idea she'd been here that long. It was unfortunate what happened at the end. A new president took over in 1989 and decided to cut back on expenses. The welcome ladies were the first to go. He said they were a frivolous expense and fired every single welcome lady in the chain, without so much as a thank you. Ida was one of the first to go."

"So she wasn't retired from BestMart?"

"No," Wysong said, heat rising through his collar. He hadn't looked very closely at Ida's record. "She should have been retired. You know, now that I see her record, she's got quite a distinction. We just gave a celebration for a store manager the other day for having worked forty seven years at the time of his retirement. We thought he had the record of longevity, but it looks as though Ida's topped that one."

"That's why she keeps performing those duties here," Patti exclaimed. "She was never retired, so she thinks she has to keep working because she never understood being fired."

"That explains what happened after she was fired," Wysong said, equally excited.

"What do you mean?"

"She kept showing up for work, even after we fired her. We kept trying to get her to leave when shed show up in the mornings but she refused to leave. She'd take the city bus, walk through the rain, anything to get to work. A couple of times she even hitchhiked to work. We finally had no recourse but to report her case to Social Services. Apparently, when they checked on her, she wasn't eating right, her apartment was a shambles and she was very confused. Since there was no family to help out they had her admitted to your nursing home, if I remember correctly."

"Do you think BestMart would send a store representative to officially retire her?" Patti asked tentatively.

"Of course. I can't believe she fell through the cracks like that—I feel entirely responsible for this. I'll do even better. I'll call the president himself and see if he would come down, give her a gift and make a speech. We'll throw her a big party. After all, she's got the employee record now."

Wysong promised to call Patti the moment he heard from the president of BestMart.

"This might work," she said to herself as she hung up the telephone feeling pleased with herself.

Tipper Wellington pulled into the parking lot of the Roost that afternoon for his weekly meeting with Beatrice. It was, after all, part of the agreement he made with Niles that he would visit his grandmother regularly. Before he could turn off the engine to his Mercedes, there was a tap at the window. Tipper looked up to see the face of an elderly gentleman pressed to the glass. The man was saying something, but Tipper couldn't understand what it was. He rolled down the window.

"Excuse me?"

"I said, how long will you be staying?" George asked politely. "I don't know, a couple of hours I guess. Why?"

"That'll be two dollars," George said, hitching his thumbs over the money belt around his waist.

"When did they start charging to park?"

"Just this week. It's a new policy," George said as he took Tipper's money and zipped it into the leather pouch.

"I'm going to talk to Steve Tallison about this," Tipper said. He stepped out of the car and laced George. "I've never heard of having to pay to park at a nursing home before."

"You tell Tallison and I'll tell your grandmother about that DUI you got the other night—it was in the newspaper, you know." George said with a smile.

Tipper's face turned red. "The breathalyzer was faulty," he sputtered.

"Maybe so, but your grandmother would still be awfully interested to hear about her only relative making a public spectacle of himself."

"You wouldn't," Tipper said, his face turning from red to white.

"Try me. Or, just shut up about the parking fee," George said. Tipper fished around in his wallet and dropped a fifty dollar bill in George's outstretched hand. "I can't take that, Tipper. You've already paid your two dollars for the day. Folks'll say you're giving me hush money."

"Consider that a season pass for parking," Tipper said. He locked the car and hurriedly walked inside.

Richard Wysong called Patti the next morning. "I talked to the president. He doesn't like the idea," he said with a sigh. "I'm really sorry—I thought he'd go for it."

"Did you tell him it's a great human interest story that the media is sure to pick up? Or about Ida being employed by BestMart longer than anyone else? Or that she was the very first 'welcome lady'?"

"I told him all that," Richard said. There was a long pause. "He said it was my fault we missed the boat when she was first let go and that it was too late to rectify the situation. He also said that Ida was fired, not retired, and we can't change our policy for one person. It was my oversight to begin with, so I suppose you have me to blame for this whole mess.

"Can I talk to him?" Patti asked. "Maybe I can explain to him how Ida's been acting lately . . ."

"I don't think that'll do any good," Richard said. "I talked to him until I was blue in the face about how much Ida loved her job and still performs those same duties at the nursing home and he was still unmoved."

"What about her edema? Did you explain to him how serious that is?"

"I told him Ida's legs were black with gangrene and nearly falling off."

"But that's not true," Patti said. "Her ankles are pretty swollen, but . . ."

"I know, I know, but I was going for dramatic effect. I tell you, nothing could melt that ice cube of a president BestMart has."

"I appreciate the effort," Patti said glumly. "I just don't know how to keep her off her feet to allow the swelling to go down besides tying her up. She's back out there in the lobby again today. Hopefully we can figure something out before her legs do become gangrenous. I'd rather she voluntarily sat down than for us to have to force her into immobility."

"I haven't given up yet," Wysong said. "I have a few more avenues to travel, but I should warn you not to get your hopes up too high."

"I won't," Patti said, but kept her fingers crossed behind her back for good luck.

Steve Tallison pulled into the parking lot of the Roost later that afternoon. He was frustrated because he'd just spent the last hour at his car mechanics, trying to convince him how imperative it was he got his car back that afternoon. The mechanic had shrugged, spit out a stream of tobacco juice and said, "So? Yours ain't the only car here." Steve had been forced to rent a car after the mechanic assured him it would take him at least three days before he got to Tallison's alternator problem.

He had been trying to figure out how to release the key from the car's new-fangled ignition lock when the rapid knocks assaulted his window.

"What?" he asked, turning to see who wanted his attention. It was George. George's eyes grew wide as he realized who was driving the car.

"George, what in the world do you want?" Tallison asked as he rolled down the window.

"Uhh, nothing," George said. "I was just sitting on the front porch when you drove up—wanted to talk to you about something."

"Sure, George. What's the problem?"

"Um, I was just wondering," George said, frantically spinning the wheels in his brain in an effort to come up with a problem, "if it was possible for you to speak to the kitchen staff about serving brussels sprouts."

"Brussel sprouts?" Tallison repeated, as though he hadn't heard George correctly.

"Brussel sprouts," George repeated. "They're awful and they smell really bad. I was just wondering if you could ask the cook not to cook brussel sprouts anymore."

"Well, I'll talk to her. Maybe there's something we could do about the smell, all right?" Tallison said.

"Thank you, Steve. I surely do appreciate it," George said. He walked back up to the porch and took a seat in the rocking chair. Tallison shook his head at Georges retreating figure. The old man must finally be losing it, he thought to himself.

Gladys and George were sitting in the courtyard Sunday afternoon. "Don't worry about getting anything for my birthday," she said gently as she squeezed his hand. She knew that George didn't have much money and didn't want him fretting over getting her a birthday present. "Just spend the day with me and that'll be all the present I'll need."

"Don't you worry about what I do for your birthday," George replied. End of subject, no more discussion, was the tone of his voice. Gladys had gotten pretty good at picking up on his mood swings and subtle hints.

Despite his gruff expression, George was inwardly smiling to himself as he thought of his plans for the next day. Michelle Peterson had promised to take him shopping for Gladys' birthday present. He'd made enough money charging for parking at the Roost to put a little over half on the watch he wanted to buy Gladys. The jewelry store had promised that if he came with cash tomorrow, they'd let him take it with him. After that he had thirty days to pay the rest, which didn't concern George too much, especially if everyone followed the example Tipper set in paying for parking fees. Seasonal parking passes might not be such a bad idea, he thought to himself.

George and Michelle Peterson left at nine o'clock Monday morning. They were heading for the towns only jewelry store—the Gold and Diamond Galleria.

"George, are you sure you want to go there?" Michelle asked tactfully. She was aware of his financial difficulties. "Don't you want to go somewhere . . . less expensive?"

"Nope. There's a watch there that Gladys wants and I plan on getting it for her," he said, outlining the wad of dollar bills in his front pocket with his fingers. "They said if I could put half down, I could take it today."

"But how did you get the money?" Michelle asked. "This store is pretty expensive."

"Where I get my money is my business," George snapped. "You just drive me to the jewelry store and back and I'll be out of your hair."

Michelle bit her bottom lip as she drove. She wondered if George knew how much it was going to cost to buy a watch from the Galleria. She didn't want to offend him any more than she already had, but she didn't want him to be embarrassed by the salespeople when he got there, either. "Are you sure?" she asked again.

"Just drive me there," George said. The rest of the drive was spent in silence.

Perhaps George had been doing odd jobs lately to make money, Michelle reasoned with herself. After all, she hadn't seen much of him in the past few days. On more than one occasion, Dr. Price had asked her if she'd seen George because he wanted to play a game of checkers. He seemed to stay outside on the front porch a lot, rocking in that rocking chair. He couldn't make too much money doing that, though, she thought.

When she pulled into the parking lot of the Galleria, George stepped out. "You don't need to go inside," he told her.

"I'd like to go," she said. She was determined to save him from any embarrassment he might encounter by the snooty salespeople who worked there. Once they found out George didn't have enough money, there was no telling what they might say to him that could hurt his feelings. "I'm going with you," she said decisively.

"Suit yourself."

She followed George as he walked into the Galleria, past the security guard and into the showroom. He walked directly to the jewelry case that held all the watches. Michelle looked over George's shoulder as he considered the selection. All of the watches were beautiful . . . and very expensive. She watched as George called a salesperson over.

"May I help you, ma'am?" the salesperson said, looking over George to Michelle.

"No, but you can help me," George said with a snap. "I'd like that watch right there," he said, pointing to a particularly beautiful one displayed in the center. It was gold with tiny diamond chips inset around the dial.

"Sir, you have extremely good taste," the salesperson said in appreciation. Michelle held her breath, seeing the expensive watch in the display case.

"I sure do, and I want it," George smiled back. "I talked to a salesperson on the telephone and he said if I paid half up front in cash I could take it with me and pay the rest later."

"That's true," the salesman said.

"Please wrap that watch up for me."

"Cash or credit card?"

"Cash," George said, pulling a wad of bills out of his pocket. Michelle watched, open mouthed, as George counted out the bills to the salesperson. When he finished counting, he looked up at the salesperson. "Will that do?" he asked with a smile.

"Yes, sir, it will do quite nicely. I'll take it in the back and have it gift wrapped. And may I say, you made a wonderful selection. That's one of our best watches."

"George, where did you get all that money?" Michelle asked open mouthed.

"Don't worry about where I get my money," he groused. "It's none of your business."

Michelle dropped George off at the front of the Roost before parking her car. She thought it was sweet that George was spending all that money on Gladys, but there was no way he had gotten that kind of cash legally.

"Carlos?" she called to the nursing assistant when she saw him in the hallway.

"Yes, ma'am?" he asked.

"I want you to do me a favor today, all right?"

"Sure."

"Do you know George?"

He grinned. "Everybody knows who George is around here. He makes sure of that."

"I want you to follow him around today, without him knowing that you're following him, all right?"

Carlos looked at her curiously. "What for?"

"Just follow him around all day. At the end of the afternoon, you tell me what he did all day, okay?"

"Anything in particular I'm looking for?"

"You'll know when you see it," Michelle said.

George was so excited when he got back from the jewelry store he couldn't stand it anymore. He went to Gladys' room and handed the gift wrapped box to her.

"Even though your birthday is tomorrow, I want to celebrate today," he said with a smile. "Happy birthday, Gladys." He kissed her lightly on the cheek.

"Oh, George, you shouldn't have. What a marvelous surprise!" Gladys took the box from him and looked at it lovingly. "That was so sweet. You really shouldn't have bothered to get me anything. It's the thought that counts."

"Just open it," George said.

Gladys took her time opening the gift, being careful not to tear the paper or the ribbon. The anticipation of her reaction was driving George crazy. "Just open the damn box, Gladys," he said.

She tore the last part of the paper and opened the box. Gladys gasped. "Oh, George. I can't believe it—that's the watch I told you about!"

George nodded and smiled. "I wanted you to have it."

"But it was so expensive," she said worriedly.

"I suppose you're worth it, Gladys," he said.

She put it on her wrist and admired the way it twinkled under the light. "I've got to go show it off—do you want to go with me?"

"No. I'm going to play checkers." Instead, he went back out into the parking lot, intent on making the rest of the payment before the jewelry store came back to reclaim the watch.

Carlos followed George at a distance from Gladys' doorway out into the lobby. Carlos watched from the front window as George began collecting money for the day.

"Excuse me, young man, but may I help you?" Ida asked Carlos. He jumped. He hadn't seen anyone in the lobby when he first walked in.

"No, Ida, I'm just . . ." his voice trailed off as he noticed her feet. "Ida, your feet. What's wrong?"

"They're just swollen," Ida said impatiently. She wished everyone would leave her alone about her feet.

"You should sit down and put your feet up," Carlos said in concern, bending down to take a better look at her puffy, darkening ankles. "I'm going to call Dr. Price."

"He's already seen me," she said firmly.

"What did he tell you to do?"

"Sit down."

"And?"

"I'm not sitting down," Ida said. "My job is to stand right here by this door and take care of customers when they walk in. I can't sit down and do that."

Carlos glanced toward the window to see what George was doing. He didn't see him. "Look, Ida, I've got to go outside . . . um . . . to the Garden Center to check on a few things," he said as he went out the front door in search of George. He'd make sure something was done about Ida when he came back.

"I'm going to have to put her on bed rest," Dr. Price told Patti when she confronted him about Ida's condition that afternoon.

"No, Dr. Price, I'm serious. "What are you going to do? Her feet and ankles are turning black."

"I am serious," he said, turning away from the checker board to face her. "If she won't get off her feet by tomorrow, I'm left with no choice other than to restrain her until the swelling recedes."

"You can't do that," Patti protested, "It's her right to refuse treatment."

"I feel horrible about it, but I will not stand by and watch her feet rot away," Dr. Price said angrily.

"Have you spoken to her today?" Patti asked.

"Yes, I spoke to her early this morning and she all but ignored me. I told her to go back to bed and put her feet up and she told me to mind my own business. I told her she had until tomorrow to cooperate with my treatment, and if not, I would have her physically restrained."

"What did she say to that?"

"She said I was a meddlesome old goat," Dr. Price said with a surprised laugh.

At the end of the afternoon Carlos reported to Michelle's office. "You're not going to believe what that old fool is doing," he said, laughing.

"What?" Michelle asked, alarmed.

"He's making people pay to park here. Sometimes he goes up to the car windows when they pull in and makes them pay, and other times he sits on the front porch and collects money as they go inside."

"You're kidding," Michelle said, amazed.

"Nope. He's got a thriving business going. I might want to start working for him," he teased.

So that explains it, Michelle thought. "Thank you, Carlos. Do me a favor and don't say anything about this to anyone, okay?"

"Sure. And if you ever need another investigator, call me up. This was a whole lot more fun than cleaning bed pans."

Michelle had no choice but to confront George with the information Carlos had given her. She went out to the front porch and found him sitting in a rocking chair. She sat down beside him.

"You need something?" he asked.

"I need to talk to you about something," Michelle said, not sure how to broach the subject.

At that moment, a middle aged man walked up the steps, having just parked his car. "Hi, George. How are you today? Here's the two bucks," he said, offering the two dollars to George.

"What's that for?" George asked, pretending to be confused by the offer. "You don't owe me any money."

"No, that's for parking remember? The new policy? I hope you folks are able to build that new wing you're raising money for." He dropped the two dollars in George's lap and continued inside.

"The new wing?" Michelle asked. "That's exactly what I want to talk to you about. You've been making visitors pay to park here, haven't you?"

George looked away and didn't answer.

"George, is that the money you used to buy that watch?" "Why don't you go somewhere and plan some activities," George said grouchily. "Aren't there some spring hats that need to be made?"

"George, I'm going to have to tell Steve about this, you know." George turned to her. "Now you don't need to go and do that. I'm still on probation. They could turn this whole thing into stealing and have me slammed back into jail so quick it'll make your head spin."

"Then we have to come up with another plan."

"I'm not hurting anyone. A dollar here, a dollar there, these folks don't mind paying to park," George said in defense of himself.

"But it's wrong and I can't let you continue this. Next, somebody will be taking up money to let people in the front door."

"I already tried that one, it doesn't work," George said.

"We've got to return the watch and get that money back, George," Michelle said gently.

"No! We can't do that. It'll kill Gladys," George said. Gladys had shown the watch to everyone in the nursing home by now. He was sure of it. He'd be the laughing stock of the Roost if he took it back.

"We handle it this way or I let Steve Tallison handle it however he wants to," Michelle said.

"You play hardball," George said. "What'll you do with the money?"

"Well, it'll be too hard to give it all back to people you've charged to park. And besides, if we give it back, somebody might raise a stink about what you did. I'd like to keep this as quiet as possible. Why don't we take the money and make an anonymous contribution to the building fund? Then you haven't been lying to everyone about the new wing."

"Boy, do I feel cleansed," George said sourly.

"I'll take the watch back to the jewelry store for you," Michelle offered.

"I suppose I'll have to go talk to Gladys," George said, standing. He thought he should go ahead and do that before too much damage was done.

"Gladys?" George said, poking his head in her room. There were two other women sitting in her room.

"Hello, George. The girls were just admiring the beautiful watch you gave me. Would you like for me to tell you the time?" Gladys said, beaming. The other women beamed at him as well. This was going to be tough, he realized.

"Gladys, can I talk to you alone for a minute?"

"Sure, George. Run along, girls, while George and I talk, okay?"

George closed the door behind the women as they left. "You're not going to like what I have to say, so I'm going to apologize up front."

"What is it, George?" Gladys asked worriedly. "Is something wrong? Have I done something wrong?"

"No, but I have. The watch I gave you—I got it through ill gotten gains."

"What do you mean?"

"I mean, I sort of stole the money I used to buy it," George said, looking at the floor. He couldn't look at her in the eyes. "I'm going to have to set things right by taking the watch back from you."

"Oh, George," Gladys said, pressing her right hand over the watch on her left wrist. "Take it back?"

"I have to, Gladys. I sure don't want to, but it's the only way. Otherwise I'm going to get into a whole lot of trouble."

A tear slipped down Gladys face as she unfastened the clasp on the watch. She handed it to him.

"I'm sorry, Gladys." He was sorry. He really was.

"It's okay, George. It's the thought that counts," she said, the sentiment sounding flat and empty as she said it.

"If you don't want to see me anymore, I'll understand," George said, walking out of her room. Gladys didn't respond.

The next morning Dr. Price was waiting in the lobby when Ida arrived at eight o'clock. He watched from his vantage point as she walked painfully down the hallway into the lobby. She didn't see him until she reached into the lobby to flip on the overhead lights.

"Why, Dr. Price what are you doing here this early?"

He was sitting on one of the patched vinyl couches beside the front door, sipping coffee from a styrofoam cup. "I've come to ask you the sixty-thousand-dollar question," he said. "Are you or are you not going to stay in bed so the swelling in your feet can go down?"

"Dr. Price, I just can't stay in bed. I have a job to do."

"Okay, then," he said, slapping his leg. "You've left me with no choice." He left the lobby and returned a few moments later with Carlos and Jake, two nursing assistants.

"Take her away, boys," Dr. Price said, as though his instructions pained him. They looked at Ida and then back at Dr. Price.

"Just carry her?" Carlos asked uncertainly. Ida probably weighed no more than ninety pounds.

Hesitating, Dr. Price finally nodded in approval.

The orderlies stood on either side of Ida and lifted her by the elbows.

"Whoa," Ida said, running in place in the air. "Set me down. Set me down right now."

"Take her to her room and put her on bed rest," Dr. Price instructed the orderlies. "I'll be in there to check on her directly. And tell her if she doesn't keep her feet up on some pillows, I'll play checkers in her room all day with George and we will be loud."

Richard Wysong sat in the back of the airport taxi with the president of BestMart, Wallace Taggert. He was grinning from ear to ear. Wysong had gotten a telephone call just yesterday from the big boss saying that he'd changed his mind about holding that retirement party for the little old woman in the nursing home. BestMart had run into some problems over the weekend with the media because their main line of children's clothes turned out to be highly flammable. BestMart needed some good media right now.

"This is going to be such a wonderful surprise for Ida," Wysong said. "And what a great idea you had to turn it into a surprise party."

Taggert smiled faintly. "Did you call the media?"

"Yes, but unfortunately there's not a whole lot of media in Stalvey, Georgia. Of course the local newspaper will be there as well as BestMart's own PR department. I called the Associated Press, but they didn't seem particularly interested."

"I'm not surprised," Taggert said. "What about the party preparations?"

"Everything's in order. I've hired a caterer to provide hors d'oeurves, a florist to provide decorations, and I called a bunch of BestMart employees that Ida used to work with. We're meeting up with the rest of the crowd, plus any interested media, once we're in Stalvey and then we'll all storm the nursing home and retire Ida," Wysong said excitedly. He didn't care if the party was being given under false pretenses, Ida would still appreciate the effort. He hoped the plan worked to keep her off of her feet, he added seriously, remembering the original reason for the party. "Did you bring the gift?" Wysong asked Taggert.

"Of course," Taggert said, tapping his breast pocket.

"Ida should be in the lobby of the Roost—right inside the front door," Wysong said. "The nurse there says she's there at eight o'clock every morning until five in the afternoon. She considers herself the 'welcome lady of the nursing home." Taggert smiled at the story. "We should get great publicity from this one."

The caravan of four vans and a taxi weaved its way down the winding road to Milly's Merry Roost sending billows of dust into the adjacent cow pasture in its wake.

George was on the front porch when the vehicles arrived. If only he'd been busted a little later, he thought to himself bitterly, he'd have collected a good amount from the folks that just pulled into the parking lot. He was still stinging over having to surrender Gladys' watch to Michelle yesterday. Gladys had been, as always, a lady about the whole thing, which only made George feel worse about what he'd done. Was it worse to have given her something and yank it back than not to have given her anything at all? He wasn't sure.

He watched as the odd assortment of people tumbled out of the vans and cars in the parking lot, some carrying flowers, some balloons, some food. Two important-looking men in business suits stepped out of a taxi and led the way up the front steps of the Roost. The local newspaper photographer dropped beside them, his camera raised high and ready.

"Good morning," the friendlier looking of the two businessmen said to George.

"Morning," George responded, wondering what all the fuss was about.

Richard Wysong pushed open the front door with a flourish and then stood aside. "Surprise," he yelled as Taggert and the photographer walked into the lobby. Wysong dropped in behind him.

"There's no one here," Taggert said. The photographer had dropped into a crouch, ready to catch Ida's surprised reaction, but there was no one to focus on. His eye to the back of the camera, he swung the camera back and forth, searching for a subject

Wysong looked around. Sure enough, the lobby was empty, except for the receptionist.

"Can I help you?" the receptionist asked.

"Yes," Wysong said, taking control of the situation. "Where is Ida this morning?"

"I don't know—she's here every morning. But I haven't seen her so far. You might want to check her room."

"All right," Wysong said. He directed the caterer and florist to the dining room, along with all the BestMart employees. He and Taggert and the photographer followed the receptionist's directions down the hall toward Ida's room.

Dr. Price had seen all the commotion as he passed by the dining room and stopped to quiz the receptionist about it on his way to the Green Wing.

"Oh, they're people from BestMart looking for Ida," she said. "Something about a surprise retirement party."

Dr. Price's face turned white. "Where are the representatives from BestMart?"

"I sent them to Ida's room. They were looking for her here in the lobby but couldn't find her."

"Oh my," Dr. Price said, taking off in the direction of Ida's room. He hoped that they got side-tracked or lost or something on the way there and wouldn't walk in and see her with pillows surrounding her to keep her from getting out of bed—that wouldn't look too good for the guest of honor to be restrained.

"What's the hurry?" Patti asked as Dr. Price trotted by her in the hallway. Too breathless to speak, he motioned for her to follow.

"Best . . . Mart . . . folks . . . here," he said in between breaths. "Here? Today?" Patti asked, confused. "Why?" "Re . . . tire . . . ment . . . party . . . for . . . Ida." he said. They were now approaching the Green Wing. He didn't see any sign of business suits as they turned the comer.

"They've come to give Ida a retirement party?" Patti exclaimed. She was having no trouble at all keeping up with the old doctor's gait. "That's wonderful!"

"No . . ." he gasped. "Ida . . . pillows . . . bed."

Patti's eyes grew wide with understanding. "I'll try and head them off at the pass," she said, breaking into a trot. She caught up with the three men just before they got to Ida's room.

"Hi!" she called out, still halfway down the hall. "Wait up just a minute." They waited for her to catch up.

"You must be Patti," Richard Wysong said, offering his hand. "We were just heading to Ida's room."

"That's why I stopped you," Patti said, breathless. "She's not in her room."

"Where is she?" Taggert asked impatiently glancing at his watch. He had to catch a plane in a couple of hours and wanted to make this short and sweet.

"In the dining room, probably. I'll take you there." On the way down the hall, Dr. Price passed by. "Just a minute," Patti told the men as she walked over and whispered to Dr. Price.

"Take Ida out of the bed and bring her to the dining room as fast as you can," she instructed.

Dr. Price nodded.

The dining room had been decorated beautifully with flowers and balloons and banners proclaiming Ida's retirement. Former and present BestMart employees lined the walls, waiting for Ida's appearance.

"Where's Ida?" Wysong asked. He was beginning to wonder if there was an Ida.

"She's on her way," Patti explained. Dr. Price and Ida showed up a few minutes later, Ida angrily rubbing red marks on her shoulders. She was wearing a different outfit than the one she'd had on earlier.

"I ought to report you," she said to Dr. Price, "except my feet feel a whole lot better."

"Surprise!!" everyone in the dining room yelled as Ida turned around. Her eyes went wide as she scanned the room, recognizing many of the people from her days with BestMart.

"Oh, my!" she squealed happily. "What's everyone doing here? Why, that's Ben from the hardware department—Hi, Ben."

"Hi, Ida. You're looking great."

"Oh, Ben, you flirt," Ida shot back. Everyone laughed. She looked around at the others. "And there's Jake from menswear, Norma from household, and Nancy from lingerie."

Everyone stepped forward to say hello and wish her well.

"Um, Ida," Nancy said, leaning over to whisper in her ear, "did you know your dress is on backward?" Ida looked down at her dress and laughed. She was over being angry now that all her old friends were there.

Wysong stepped forward to grasp her hand. "I'm so happy to see you here. We were beginning to think you didn't really exist." Ida opened her mouth to respond just as feedback from the microphone interrupted the conversations and everyone turned to see who was about to speak. Taggert stepped forward to the microphone that had been set up in the middle of the room and cleared his throat. Everyone stopped and turned toward him.

"I'd like to say a few words to Ida. We've recently discovered that you are BestMart's Best Employee of all time. You worked for us for fifty years—three years longer than the employee we thought was the longest employed with BestMart."

He stopped talking to allow for the applause that followed. "In appreciation of all the years you've spent with BestMart, we'd like to honor you with a well-deserved retirement party. As of today, you are a woman of leisure. You can sleep late, go to bed whenever you want, and never have to worry about being a welcome lady again. In other words, Ida, you are retired. In honor of that, we'd like to give you this token of our appreciation." Ida stepped forward to receive the box he proffered. Taggert turned so that the photographer could get a clear shot of him handing the box to Ida.

"I don't know what to say," Ida said, all flustered.

"Just open the box," George yelled out. He hadn't spoken to Gladys since he took the watch back, but noticed she had just stepped beside him and placed her hand in his. He squeezed it gently. "Thank you," he said to her. She smiled back.

Everyone crowded around Ida as she opened the box and exclaimed happily as she held it aloft.

"Look, George, it's the exact same watch you gave me," Gladys exclaimed.

"I'm sorry you couldn't keep it, Gladys. I promise I'll do something real special for you."

"Legal?" she teased.

"Legal," he said.

She squeezed his hand tightly. "I don't care. It really is the thought that counts," she said, this time meaning what she said. "And besides, I'll bet Ida will let me borrow that watch for special occasions."

Ida woke up early the next morning and followed her regular routine. She put on her makeup, her dress and pulled her flats over swollen feet. The final touch, the name tag, went on last. She'd slept in the watch, and looked at it to be sure it was still really there. She arrived in the lobby, ready to start the day. Patti was sitting on one of the couches, as though she expected to see Ida there that morning.

"Ida, what are you doing here?" she asked kindly.

"I'm going to work," Ida said as though it was a silly question.

"But Ida, you're retired now," Patti said.

Ida looked at her, puzzled. "But . . ."

"No buts. You're retired—a woman of leisure. Look at that watch on your arm. When you accepted that gift from BestMart you were accepting your retirement."

Ida looked at her arm and smiled. "I suppose you're right. But what do I do with my time now?"

"That's the best part about retirement, you can do anything you want. In fact, there's a big sing-along about to start in the recreation room. Would you care to join me?"

Ida looked one last time at the lobby with fondness in her eyes. "Yes, I would care to join you." She took Patti by the arm and walked with her to the recreation room, happy to begin her retirement.

CHAPTER 10

PATTI carried the old wooden box to her desk and set it down with a thud. An overzealous resident had, years ago, taken a wood burning kit and had scrawled ROOMMATE REQUESTS in wavy letters on all six sides of the box.

"Ouch," Patti said, pulling out a couple of splinters that had lodged into her hand. She hated the old box with its crudely burned-in letters almost as much as she hated the nursing home's cantankerous old van. Both were symbolic of the Roosts financial despair. Maybe she could talk to one of the residents or visitors and see if they couldn't get another box made. It was such an eyesore in the recreation room.

She opened the top right drawer of her desk and pulled out the tiny key from its hiding place, taped onto the bottom side of the drawer. When she first came to the Roost seven years ago, she had laughed at the sturdy lock on the wooden box.

"What, do you think someone's going to break in and steal the roommate requests?" she had laughingly asked the departing Director of Nursing.

"Don't laugh," had been her response, "when it comes to roommates, nothing's sacred around here. 'You'd be amazed at some of the things the residents will do in order to get or avoid a particular roommate."

During the past years, Patti had found the old Director's advice very prudent and had, in fact, upgraded the lock to one with a higher grade of steel. The last one had been beaten with a metal cane until the lock sprung open. The abuser had heard that his name was being dropped into the box as a roommate request and he was violently opposed to the idea. After he sprung the lock, he had fished out the particular request and eaten it without blinking. "I wouldn't room with that old codger if he was the last person on earth," had been his reply.

Patti inserted the key into the lock and twisted until the hasp sprung open. The hinges complained loudly as Patti swung the lid off of the old box. She glanced inside and sighed as she fished out the requests. Patti despised dealing with roommate problems. There was nothing that ever happened in the Roost that could stir up as many emotions as roommates could. Sometimes she felt like she was running a family counseling center. He said, she said . . . he took my . . . she took my . . . the room's too hot . . . the room's too cold. It never seemed to end.

"Okay, request number one," Patti said to herself as she pulled the first one out. It was from Hank and Ethyl. They'd been dropping in requests for the past several months. Unfortunately, under federal law, residents of opposite sex couldn't live in the same room together unless they were married, and Ethyl and Hank weren't married. Patti placed the request to the side—she'd go talk to them first.

The second request was from Johnnie. It read: "Get that old biddy out of my room before I kill her. Johnnie." Patti balled up the note and threw it into the trash. Johnnie was one of those residents who could never be happy rooming with anyone. She was a bitter old woman who caused more trouble than any of the other residents put together. Patti had tried her with every single female resident in the Roost; in fact, the one Johnnie was complaining about this time—Earlene—was the very last available resident for her to be roommates with. If this one didn't work out, Patti would either have to start the matching process over again or simply ignore Johnnie's complaints. The latter had a better chance at success.

The next request was from Johnnie as well, it read: "Earlene snores too much and she drools in her sleep and makes me sick. Get her out of my room. Johnnie." Patti threw the piece of paper in with the other at the bottom of the trash can. The next three requests were also from Johnnie: "I can't get any peace and quiet with Earlene in my room, she hollers too much. I want another roommate. Johnnie." Then there was "If you don't remove her, I will. Johnnie." Finally, "I'm serious. Johnnie."

Patti laughed as she threw the last request into the trash can. The only entertaining part about going through the request box was reading Johnnie's requests.

"Well Johnnie, you've gotten creative," Patti said as she read the last note. The request was from Earlene, and read: "I do not want to room with Johnnie anymore." Patti fished one of Johnnie's crumpled notes from the trash and compared it to the one signed by Earlene. They were both done in the same handwriting. "Pretty smooth, Johnnie, but I've got you figured out," she laughed. She closed the box and went to talk to Hank and Ethyl.

"If we're both consenting adults, why can't we do whatever the hell we want?" Hank asked angrily. He was holding Ethyl's hand tightly in his own.

"It's the law, Hank," Patti explained. "I can't do anything about it except make sure it's carried out. We cannot allow the two of you to live together unless you get married. Why don't you just get married? If you love each other it makes good sense."

Hank and Ethyl exchanged quick glances. "Hank doesn't want to," Ethyl said.

"Why not?" Patti asked. Ever since the two of them met they'd acted like newlyweds—taking every single conjugal visit they were allowed to have—and then some, Patti suspected.

"Hank thinks he's still got some wild oats to sow before he settles down," Ethyl said.

Patti's mouth fell open. "Is that true, Hank?" He had to be at least in his mid-eighties.

Hank nodded. "I'm just not ready to get tied down yet."

Patti bit her lip in an effort not to smile. "Well, then, until you're ready to make a legal commitment to Ethyl, the two of you can't live together."

"That's a stupid rule," Hank groused.

"Maybe, but we're stuck with it," Patti said. She looked at Ethyl. "Do you mind if I talk to Hank alone for a moment?"

"Oh, sure," Ethyl said, leaving the room.

Patti turned to Hank and lowered her voice. "You know, Hank, if you're concerned about sowing your wild oats and not being tied down, then moving in with Ethyl should be the last thing you'd want," she said knowingly.

"Why is that?"

"What if some single woman moved in to the Roost—I mean, a really good looking single woman? She wouldn't look at you twice because you were living with Ethyl. You wouldn't be considered a swinging single any more, you know what I mean?"

Hank scratched his chin. "You know, you've got a point there. I never thought about it that way. Not that I don't love Ethyl, because I do. But sometimes a man just has to leave his windows open."

"I understand completely," Patti said with a wink. "From now on, I wouldn't push this roommate issue any more."

Hank agreed.

After her chat with Hank, Patti returned to her office, pleased that she'd been able to handle the request box so quickly. Generally there were at least three real requests in addition to Johnnie's repetitive pleas.

She pulled her lunch bag out of her oversized purse and arranged the tupperware bowls on her desk.

"Having an early lunch?" Michelle Peterson asked from her doorway.

"Yes, I thought I'd take advantage of a job well done and have an early, extended lunch," Patti replied.

"Then I won't bother you except for a minute. Northeast College School of Law contacted me to ask if they could send out a couple of students for a Law Day. They'll go over wills, living wills, advance directives, or any legal issues the residents may have."

"Good—when are they coming?"

"How's Monday sound? Too soon?"

"No, Monday's fine. We'll need posters and flyers put up to advertise and let everyone know. Last year one of the residents slept through Law Day and was fit to be tied when she found out she'd missed her chance to file a free law suit."

"I remember," Michelle said with a laugh. "I'll get the Garden Club and the Blue Bird Singers involved—they all love to make posters."

The next day Johnnie approached Patti in the cafeteria. "Why haven't you come talk to me about my roommate problems?" she asked with a pout. I saw you in Ethyl's room yesterday talking to her and Hank."

"What are you doing, following me around?" Patti asked.

"No, I just want to make sure I get treated fairly is all," Johnnie said. "You never did come to talk to me about it last month either."

"That's because I'm getting tired of all your complaints. You can't get along with anyone I've matched you with yet, and I've run you through the gamut. I put you in with Rosie and you said she talked too much. I put you in with Jessie and you said she hollered too much. I put you in with Madge and you said she watched the television too loud. I put you in with Beth and you said she wouldn't let you watch television. Then I put you in with Camilla and you said she just irritated you."

"She did irritate me," Johnnie said defensively.

"Johnnie, how can Camilla irritate you? She's been in a coma for nearly six years now," Patti said, throwing her hands up in exasperation.

"She stared at me all the time."

"Now you're in with Earlene and if you can't make it with her, I've got to start you all over again from the beginning, which is going to be hard to do considering you've worn out your welcome with everyone else."

"I don't care what you do, just get me out of Earlene's room," Johnnie begged.

"Why? What is she doing?"

"Everything."

"Such as . . . ?"

"I can't put my finger on any one thing because there's so many things she does wrong," Johnnie said.

"I'm sorry, Johnnie. But I'm at the end of my rope. You've got to make an effort this time to get along with your roommate. You know you don't have the money for a private room and we can't just give you one out of the kindness of our hearts—we're in enough financial trouble as it is, you know."

Johnnie walked away in a huff. A brightly colored poster caught her eye as she walked down the hallway toward her bedroom:

LAW DAY!!

Monday, 9 a.m.-5 p.m.

Local law students will offer free advice on wills,
living wills, advance directives, and more!!

Sign below for an appointment.

"Now there's someone who will help me," she said. Johnnie signed her name in the first available slot on the appointment list.

Two law students from the local college arrived Monday morning and set their brand new brief cases on the cafeteria tables.

"I hate nursing homes," Scott Durant said. "I used to have to visit my great-grandmother years ago and I always begged not to have to go. The smell, the atmosphere, everything was horrible. I'll never put my parents in one of these."

Lynn Stanton, one of his classmates, nodded her head. "I know what you mean, but so far, I really haven't smelled anything bad. It's actually sort of nice here," she said.

"A nursing home is a nursing home," Scott said. "Let's just get this over with fast. If anyone drools on me or calls me Sonny Boy, I'm splitting. I think I'm geri-phobic or something—grossed out by old people."

"Shut up, here comes the first one," Lynn hissed at Scott. George sat down in the chair across the table from her. "Hello, sir. How are you today?" she asked cheerfully. "How can I help you?

"I need a will," George said.

"Do you already have a will?" Lynn asked.

"Yes, but I want to change the benefactor."

"You mean the beneficiary?"

"Whoever gets all my stuff when I croak—that's what I want to change."

Lynn pulled out the form for a will and began filling in the blanks, asking George various questions: name, social security number, and marital status. "Now, who do you want to name as your beneficiary?"

"Gladys Mumford."

"Is she related to you?"

"No. Just a friend," George muttered.

"Okay, and what do you want to leave her?"

"Everything."

"I know, sir. But I need you to be a little more specific if you don't mind. For example, what about money or savings accounts?"

"Don't have any," George said.

"Stocks and bonds?"

"Don't have any."

"Jewelry?"

"Nope."

"What about possessions like a house, a car, or a boat?" "Nope, nope and nope."

"Don't you own or possess anything?" Lynn asked incredulously.

"Three pairs of pants, four shirts, some boxers and a couple pair of shoes," George said, as if by memory.

"Okay . . . ." Lynn said slowly. "And would you like to leave those items for Ms. Mumford?"

"Don't be stupid—she won't have any use for those things." "What do you have to leave her?" Lynn asked, her patience ebbing away.

"Nothing, I guess, but it doesn't hurt to be prepared in case I ever get something," George said.

Lynn finished filling out the form, leaving many blanks open. "I'll send this will back to you after I type it all up, all right Mr. Anderson?"

"Good enough," George said.

Scott had been watching and listening to the entire exchange between Lynn and George. Once George left the room he hooted, "See? What did I tell you? They're all kooks!"

"Scott, be nice. I thought that was really sweet."

Johnnie walked in next. She stood in front of the table and looked back and forth between Lynn and Scott. She finally sat in front of Scott's brief case.

"No offense, honey. He just looks meaner," Johnnie said to Lynn.

"No offense taken," Lynn said with a laugh.

"Damn," Scott said under his breath. He really didn't want to work with these old folks. He'd lost a bet with another guy at school who was supposed to be here instead.

"Excuse me young man, what did you say?" Johnnie asked. "Um, I said 'ma'am,'" Scott said quickly. "What can I do for you, ma'am? A standard will or a living will?"

"Neither one. I need some real lawyering done for me."

"Okay," Scott said, turning to wink at Lynn. "What kind of lawyering do you need?"

Johnnie leaned in close to Scott's face and whispered, "I'm being abused by my roommate."

"Really?" Scott said, intrigued. He'd thought today was going to be nothing more than filling out forms—something he detested. "Physical, verbal or emotional abuse?"

"All of 'em," Johnnie said with a nod of her head. "Hmmm," Scott said, pulling out a legal pad. This little jaunt out to the nursing home could potentially net him a big case if all this were true.

"Okay, let's start with the physical abuse," he said, businesslike. "What has your roommate done to physically harm you?" "Well," Johnnie said excitedly, "one night I woke up in the middle of the night to find her standing over me with a pillow—like she was getting ready to smother me."

"Really?" Scott asked. "What did you do?"

"I fought her off, but that didn't stop her from trying other things. Another time I woke up to find her stuffing a wash cloth in my mouth."

"What was she doing that for?"

"She said I was snoring."

"Another time she kept me tied up in a wheelchair all day because I didn't want to watch her favorite soap opera."

"That's plenty for now. How about the verbal abuse?" Scott asked excitedly. The woman seemed to be telling the truth. This could be his big break into the legal community.

"I can't repeat the names she calls me when the nurses aren't around," Johnnie said, looking down at her feet. "And she tells me I'm a useless bag of bones and good for nothing and that I'm one step away from the grave all the time."

"That's horrible," Lynn piped in, listening in horror to the old woman's account.

"Ain't it, though?" Johnnie said.

"This one's mine, Lynn. Butt out," Scott snapped. "And mental abuse?" Scott asked Johnnie.

"She's forever playing tricks on me, like hiding my things from me and then saying that I lost them. One day she brought Jack's dog, Blue, in and told me Jack had given him to me for a present. I was so excited! That afternoon she took him back and said Jack changed his mind."

Scott was shaking his head in righteous anger. "So I suppose you want to press charges against your roommate—what is her name?"

"Earlene. No, I don't want her to go to jail. I just want a new roommate," Johnnie said simply.

"Wait a minute, let me get this straight," Scott said, holding up his hand. "This woman has physically, mentally and verbally abused you over a period of time and all you want to do is change roommates?" His visions of legal grandeur were fading quickly.

"Yes," Johnnie said sweetly. "I don't want to cause anyone any trouble. I just want to get a new roommate, but the nursing home won't let me change roommates."

"They have to allow you to change roommates," Scott said, excited again. Suing the nursing home could be a big civil suit. "It's your legal right."

"I know that, but they ignore me whenever I tell them I'd like to move out. I try not to cause any trouble," she said with the look of a saint on her face.

Scott was so moved by Johnnie's story that he placed his hand on top of hers, forgetting his rule to never ever touch a client, no matter what.

"So, you want to take a lawsuit out against the nursing home for violation of civil rights?" Scott asked, his hopes soaring.

"No, I just want you to scare them real good," Johnnie said. "Write 'em a letter or something and tell 'em that if they don't get me out of Earlene's room, then we'll sue."

Although deflated, Scott agreed. He continued interviewing Johnnie for fifteen more minutes, gathering information. He'd decided to approach the administrator that afternoon.

"There's no reason for you to continue living in that kind of hell," he said gently to Johnnie. "I'm going to personally see to it that you're out of there by the end of this week."

"Thank you so much," Johnnie said, wiping an imaginary tear from the corner of her eye. "You just don't know how awful this has been."

That afternoon Scott knocked on Steve Tallison's door, puffed up with his mission of mercy. Steve waved him inside.

"Aren't you one of the law students?"

"Yes, sir."

"Thank you so much for your help. You've no idea how helpful you are to our residents," Steve said warmly.

"Thank you, but that's not why I'm here," Scott said matter-of-factly. "I'm here on behalf of one of your residents—Johnnie." "Yes?" Steve said. "Whatever for?"

"It seems as though Ms. Humphrey has been subjected to mental, emotional and verbal abuse by her present roommate for some time now."

Steve looked at the young law student in surprise. "Really? She's rooming with Earlene. Earlene can be somewhat of a pain sometimes, but she's simply not capable of doing those things. What has Johnnie said to you? Wait a minute, let me pull out Johnnie's file first." He walked into the room next door and came back with a file folder six inches thick

Scott looked at his notes and cleared his throat. "She says that she awoke one night to find her roommate standing over her with a pillow, as if to smother her. Also, she said that she has often caught Earlene trying to spike her drinking water with sleeping pills that she's cheeked over a long period of time. Also . . ."

"Wait, wait a minute . . ." Steve said, interrupting. He was flipping through the file folder rapidly. "And did she also mention the time when she was tied up in the wheelchair because she wouldn't watch the same soap opera?"

"So you know about these instances and you're not doing anything about it?" Scott asked, openmouthed.

"No, son. You've been duped by the best. I know about those things because that's what Johnnie has been doing to her roommates ever since she was admitted here. Feel free to look through her file—oh, don't worry, it's not her personal file. This is just the file we keep on her containing all the complaints that have been lodged against her."

Scott took the folder from Steve's hands, nearly dropping the heavy bundle of documents on the desk. "All of these are complaints against Johnnie?"

"Afraid so. Johnnie's one of our more . . . active residents, I should say. She's also one of the more entertaining ones—she keeps the place rocking."

"Then I'm sorry I've taken your time," Scott said, his face red with embarrassment. It wasn't often the wool was pulled over his eyes by an eighty-year-old woman.

"Don't worry about it," Steve said with a wave of his hand. "Tell me this—what kind of action did she want you to take?" "Quite simple, really. She just wants a new roommate," Scott said.

"And there are some people who want ice water in hell," Steve said with a laugh.

Scott laughed along with him, in spite of himself.

A few minutes later Patti looked into Steve Tallison's office. "You rang?" she asked, holding her pager up in the air.

"Yes, I just had an interesting visit from one of those law students. It seems as though Johnnie retained him to fight for her civil rights over having a new roommate."

Patti rolled her eyes. "I opened the request box last week and most of them were from Johnnie. I've run out of roommates for her, so I just decided to ignore it this time."

"I sympathize with your situation, really I do, but we need to try again. If she's really miserable there with Earlene we should try her somewhere else."

"But where? She has honestly roomed with every single female in this nursing home."

Steve took a file folder off of his desk and held it up in the air. "I know, but guess what? We've got a new female resident joining us tomorrow. Want to try her?"

"She'll run out of the Roost screaming, but I guess we can try," Patti said. "I'll make the arrangements."

Marianne Langston arrived at the Roost the next day and was immediately placed in a room with Johnnie. Patti took care of the introductions.

"Marianne, this is Johnnie; Johnnie, Marianne. 'You'll be roommates,'" she said, smiling at both of them. She had her fingers crossed behind her back for good luck. Hopefully there would be at least a week's respite before the fireworks began.

"I'm pleased to meet you," Marianne said, smiling warmly at Johnnie.

"I don't like her," Johnnie said to Patti, turning away from her new roommate.

"Johnnie's not very . . . social," Patti explained to Marianne. "That's quite all right. I'm not very social myself," Marianne said, smiling broadly. "I'm sure we'll get along quite well." "Hah!" Johnnie said, her back still turned.

Against her better judgment, Patti left the two of them alone in the room. It took only two days before the grape vine started up concerning Johnnie and her new roommate.

"The woman has the patience of Job," Gladys said with a nod of her head. Patti knew that of everyone in the Roost, Gladys was the Waffle House of the information highway. She cornered her in the cafeteria one day and plagued her with questions about Johnnie and Marianne. She herself hadn't heard a word from either one of them since the coupling, but then again, she wasn't due to open the roommate request box for another three weeks.

"On Tuesday night—Marianne's first night—I heard that Johnnie took all the sheets off of her bed and told her she was supposed to bring her own from home. Marianne slept without any sheets, blankets or pillows for the first two days before anyone noticed," Gladys said, shaking her head sadly.

"Why didn't Marianne come to me?" Patti wondered aloud. "I tell you, the woman's a saint," Gladys said. "All she does is smile and say how happy she is around here. I asked her one time if Johnnie didn't drive her crazy and she just smiled and said Johnnie was a wonderful roommate."

"Has Johnnie done anything else to her?" Patti asked.

"Of course. On her second day, Johnnie went through all her clothes and took out everything that was red, telling Marianne that no one was allowed to wear red at the Roost because of a federal law. Marianne let her take her red clothes and watched her throw them away without so much as stopping her."

"I'm scared to ask if anything else has happened, but go ahead and tell me."

"Well, there was the incident with the adult undergarments . . ." Gladys started to say.

"Oh, that's an old one of Johnnie's tricks. What else?" "Tying her up in the wheelchair?"

"Yep, heard it. What else?"

"One day she picked all the prize roses from the Garden Club's rose garden, put them in a vase and gave them to Marianne." "Well that was pretty nice," Patti ventured.

"No, then she went and told the Garden Club that Marianne had picked the roses for herself, so now all the club members have a warrant out for Marianne's hide."

"Okay, that's all I want to hear. I think I need to go talk to Marianne herself," Patti said. When she got to the room she found Marianne knitting quietly in the corner and Johnnie cheating at solitaire on one of the TV trays.

"How are you two getting along?" Patti asked. Both women looked up, Johnnies expression was surly while Marianne's was cherubic.

"Wonderfully," Marianne said, pausing in her knitting to answer. "Would you like to sit down?"

"Yes, as a matter of fact I would," Patti said, taking a seat on the edge of Marianne's bed. "Johnnie, would you mind if I spoke to Marianne alone for a moment?"

"Why, so you can talk about me?" Johnnie asked. "Sure. Knock yourself out."

Once Johnnie left the room Patti turned to Marianne and said, "I've been hearing some horror stories about some of the things Johnnie has been doing to you. Are you all right?" Marianne's expression was one of confusion. "Why, I don't know to what you're referring to. Johnnie has been nothing but nice to me since I've been here. She's a little rough around the edges, but it's nothing a little love, tolerance and compassion won't take care of in time," she said with a smile befitting the face of a nun.

"Are you sure?" Patti asked.

"Quite. I'm happy here."

When Patti walked out into the hall she found Johnnie eavesdropping beside the open doorway. "What are you listening for?" Patti asked.

"Nothing," Johnnie said, jumping back from the doorway. "Just wanted to make sure the old biddy wasn't making up stories about me."

"She really likes you, Johnnie. I'm surprised. How do you like having her for a roommate?" Patti asked.

"Check the request box and see for yourself," Johnnie replied sourly. "She's stupid."

"Why do you say that? She seems like a very intelligent woman to me."

"All she does is sit around and smile and knit."

"Maybe she's just a happy person."

"Maybe she just gets on my nerves," Johnnie said.

"Not again, Johnnie. I'm serious this time. You have got to make this one work," Patti warned. "I'll be checking back frequently." Halfway down the hallway she turned back around and called to Johnnie. "Oh, by the way. Please tell Marianne I got a telephone call from her family today and they're coming to visit at five o'clock this afternoon. She'll probably want to make sure she's in her room around that time."

"I'll make sure to tell her," Johnnie said with a grin.

Johnnie walked back into the room.

"Tell me what?" Marianne asked pleasantly.

"Oh, Patti told me to tell you there's an opening at the beauty parlor for five o'clock if you'd like to go. The beautician here gives really good rinses."

"How sweet. I'd love to go. Five o'clock you say?"

"On the dot," Johnnie replied.

At five o'clock Marianne's son, his wife and children walked into the room bearing gifts and flowers. Johnnie was sitting on one bed, her face in her hands. The other bed was completely stripped—no sheets, no pillows, no blankets. All of Marianne's personal belongings had disappeared as well.

"Where's mother?" the son asked. "Did she change rooms?" He distinctly remembered bringing her to this room. Her name was on the door outside along with Johnnie's name, so he was sure he had the right room.

Johnnie looked up, her eyes red from having rubbed them repeatedly for the past fifteen minutes. No tears, though. "Oh, my you haven't heard," Johnnie said, her words a lament.

"Heard what?" the son asked, suddenly worried. His mother hadn't been sick a day in her life.

"Your mother . . . . she's . . . she's . . . ." Johnnie was unable to complete her sentence.

"She's what?" the son demanded.

"Gone on to a better place," Johnnie said, wiping her eyes with a handkerchief.

The son braced himself on the corner of Johnnie's chest of drawers. "Mother . . . she died?"

Johnnie didn't answer, but broke out into a loud wail instead.

Marianne's son was joined by his wife and two children, who rushed to his side for support. Johnnie stood and joined the grieving group as well, throwing her arms around the two children as she mourned the loss of her friend.

"What in the world is going on?" Marianne asked, witnessing the group hug from the doorway. "What happened? What are you doing here, Craig?"

The room grew silent as the family turned around to face what they thought must surely be an apparition.

"Mother?" Craig said in disbelief. "You're alive?"

"Of course I'm alive, son. You didn't even notice my hair—isn't it beautiful? Johnnie, you were right about that beautician," she said, "she's just the greatest." Johnnie had crept away from the family and was trying to hide behind the drapes. "Johnnie? Where are you going?" she asked, puzzled.

Craig went over to his mother and wrapped her in a big bear hug. "Your roommate said you . . . passed away . . ." he said.

"Now, no I didn't really say that," Johnny said defensively, her hands on her hips. "I just said she'd gone to a better place. The beauty parlor is a really nice place—much nicer than this room."

"Passed away? Of course not—how silly. I just went to the beauty parlor."

Everyone suddenly turned and looked at Johnnie. "How could you?" Craig's wife asked in disbelief. "How cruel."

"How could you do something like that?" Craig asked incredulously.

"Now, I'm sure Johnnie didn't mean anything by what she said. You probably just misunderstood her," Marianne said in defense of her roommate. She looked around the room, suddenly confused. "Johnnie—where are all my things?"

Johnnie pointed to the closet. "In there." She stepped over to the closet and opened the door, jumping out of the way before she was hit with an avalanche of Marianne's belongings that had been piled up high behind the door.

"That's it," Craig said decisively. "Mother, you're coming with us. You're not going to stay here another minute."

"But I like it here, son," Marianne said. "Johnnie didn't mean anything . . ."

"Your roommate led us to believe you had died," Craig said, trying to keep his voice under control. "That's the crudest trick I've ever heard of before. We made a mistake by bringing you here in the first place. Come on. We'll send for your things later."

The entire family swept up Marianne in their emotion and took her out the door without so much as a goodbye to Johnnie. Johnnie sat on the edge of Marianne's bed, chewing her nails nervously. She'd really done it this time, she realized. Thirty minutes later Patti walked into her room.

"I can't believe what you did," Patti said, her voice raised to a shrill level. "Of all the low . . . despicable . . . heartless things to do . . ."

"I know," Johnnie said.

"What?" Patti asked in surprise.

"I said I know. I'm sorry," Johnnie said, her face a mask of remorse.

"Are you putting me on this time?" Patti said, the question of a woman who'd been had too many times by Johnnie.

Johnnie shook her head sadly.

"Well, then," Patti said, "let that be a good lesson to you. Your new roommate will be here as soon as we get her paperwork finished."

Johnnie looked up in fear. "Who?"

"You'll see. You're in no position to be picky right now," Patti said as she walked out the door.

Late that night the telephone rang in Johnnie's room. Johnnie picked it up on the first ring, too wired to sleep.

"Johnnie?"

"Yes?"

"It's Marianne. I just wanted to see how you were doing."

"Fine," Johnnie said coolly. "There's a lot more room in here now."

'Yes, I suppose there is," Marianne sighed. "Well, I just wanted to say goodbye since I didn't get a chance to tell you that earlier. I'm not happy here—the kids don't need me as a burden."

"Oh, okay. Well, 'bye," Johnny said quickly, hanging up the telephone. "I'm sorry," she said, looking at the telephone.

For the next several days Johnnie went on a cross-nursing home crime spree, preying on the old and innocent residents of the Roost. By the end of the week Patti was at her wits end. She had even called Johnnies family and asked for their help in calming her down. They refused, questioning Patti as to whether they had missed a payment or something. They had not, she assured them, but added that their mother might be asked to leave soon if she continued with her behavior.

The following Monday, Craig came through the front doors of the Roost, holding his mother by the elbow. He spoke quietly to the receptionist and a few moments later Patti arrived. Craig and Patti left Marianne in the lobby while they went into Para's office.

"I'm at the end of my rope," Craig said to Patti. The man was obviously in the throes of some sort of emotional crisis. "I've never seen mother like this. Ever since we brought her home she's been going downhill. She's lost control of her bladder—something she never did before—and she's constantly babbling."

"Babbling?" Patti asked.

"Yeah, you know, she mixes up people's names and things like that. And she acts like she never said anything wrong in the first place when we ask her about it. She accuses us of putting words in her mouth. The incontinence would be no big deal if she'd let us put those adult undergarments on her, but she takes them off as soon as we're out of sight. We don't have enough hours in the day to sit with her around the clock," he said to Patti, as though looking for absolution.

"We want to put her back in the nursing home," he said finally, the pain showing in his expression. "Is there still an opening here?"

"Unfortunately, the only opening we have is for a roommate for Johnnie," Patti said. "I'm sure you don't want that for your mother, and I understand completely. The woman at the top of the waiting list still has some final paperwork to be approved by the state. We just can't break up roommates who are already together—it wouldn't be . . ."

"No, you don't understand," Craig said, interrupting. "Mother wants to be in Johnnie's room." He saw the look on Patti's face. "I know, I don't understand it either, but she says she really enjoys Johnnie's company and wants to go back. But then again, she's been acting so strange lately I'm not sure what to believe from her any more. She's really talking out of her head. I wish there was another way, but we just can't take it anymore." "What about Johnnie's pranks?"

"I've thought about that. The next time something like that happens, I'll just be more prepared—especially if it's coming from Johnnie."

"We'll be glad to take her back, but I'll need to reassess her condition, especially since you say she's changed so radically lately."

"Of course."

Craig and Patti went outside to the lobby and sat beside Marianne on the couch. Patti stood up quickly, realizing too late that Marianne had wet the couch.

"Sorry," Marianne said, grinning widely. Her face was sunken in.

"Mother, where are your dentures?" Craig asked.

"Took them out," she said, "because I wet myself."

"That doesn't make sense, Mother," Craig said. "Why would you take out your dentures after wetting yourself?"

"Because no one else would," she said, still smiling.

Craig looked at Patti and mouthed the words, "See what I mean?"

"We'll page Dr. Price to check her out as soon as possible. Your mother may have suffered a stroke," Patty said worriedly. "She's exhibiting some of the symptoms of a stroke victim." Craig nodded worriedly. "I didn't think about that, but it does make sense."

"Let's take her back to her room for now. I'll have one of the nurses come in and clean her up." They walked down to Johnnie's room and knocked on the door. "Johnnie? We've got a new roommate for you," Patti said brightly.

"Don't want one," Johnnie said. "I like it better by myself." "Then I'll just take Marianne down to someone else's room," Patti said, turning away.

"Wait!" Johnnie called out. "Marianne's out there?"

"Yes, she is, and we were going to put her back in your room, but if you don't want her . . ." She left Craig and Marianne out in the hall and approached Johnnie. "Before you answer, I think you need to know that Marianne has . . . changed since the last time you saw her. She's had some sort of stroke or something—she's lost the control of her bladder and she's saying strange things."

"Really?" Johnnie said, concern showing in her eyes. "That's terrible. Bring her in here."

Craig brought his mother in and sat her down on her old bed. Johnnie watched her curiously as the nurse came and cleaned up the mess Marianne had made. Marianne babbled to Craig and Patti for about thirty minutes after that, not making one bit of sense. Finally, Craig stood up to go home.

"Well, I guess I'll leave mother with you. I left her suitcase in your office."

"We'll get it for you later. And don't worry, Craig. We'll take good care of your mother, and I'll check in on her all the time to make sure Johnnie doesn't terrorize her," she said glaring in Johnnie's direction.

"I really appreciate your help," he said gratefully.

Patti turned to Marianne and spoke loud and slow: "I'm going to the office to get your suitcase and I'll be right back. Okay, Marianne?"

Marianne stared at Patti vacantly and smiled, her face a deep cavern without her dentures. Patti left.

Johnnie stared at Marianne a few moments longer before speaking. "There's not a damn thing wrong with you, is there?" she said suddenly.

Marianne turned in her direction and smiled again.

"Where's your teeth?" Johnnie asked.

Marianne put her hand down the front of her blouse and pulled her dentures out of her brassiere. "Right here they are," she said, popping them back in.

"Why in the world did you go to so much trouble for them to bring you back here?" Johnnie asked.

"I was bored at home. This was the only way I could think of to make them bring me back here. It's time for me to be with people my own age. Young people have their own lives to lead. Anyway, you're much more fun than my family."

"Hmmph," was all Johnnie could say in response, but her smile gave away her true sentiment.

CHAPTER 11

TOMMY gingerly opened the soft peanut shell, plucked out one of the three red peanuts nestled inside and tossed it in his mouth. The corners of his lips turned up with distaste. With dramatic effort he chewed the salty boiled peanut.

"That's gross," he exclaimed. "Why do you eat those things?" "Boiled peanuts are good for you and help you, too," George said, pulling a handful of peanuts out of the bag and placing them on top of his rounded belly. "Now shut up and eat 'em. You know some folks eat the shell, too."

"Well I guess some people are just plain stupid," Tommy said with a laugh. George laughed along with him. He had stopped at one of those roadside stands with the huge cauldron of boiled peanuts on the way over to the Roost that afternoon. He'd heard George talk about how much he loved boiled peanuts and thought he'd surprise his old friend with a two-pound bag straight from the kettle. Tommy didn't care for the soft salty mush in his mouth and searched around for a place to spit it off of the front porch.

"You spit that out and I'll box your ears," George said calmly, still rocking and chewing. The doubled brown bag of peanuts were placed between his legs and a larger 'graveyard' bag was by his side for the peanut carcasses. George bypassed the graveyard and pitched the shells directly into the yard. "You don't know what's good for you. How long have you been a Southerner?"

"All my life," Tommy said defensively, pride swelling his chest. What his family lacked in education they more than made up for in terms of patriotism.

"Then you ought to like boiled peanuts," George retorted. "I guess you don't care much for grits, collard greens or fat back neither."

"Nope," Tommy said, shaking his head. "Mama has tried to make me eat that stuff all my life but I won't."

"You don't do what your mama says?"

"Not when she's wrong," Tommy said, leaning back on his hands. He was sitting on the edge of the front porch of the Roost, in front of George. Every once in a while a peanut shell would fly past his head and into yard. The Garden Club was going to have a fit when they found all those shells in their flower garden, Tommy thought, but didn't share his thought with George. The old man would only laugh and probably make an ever greater point of strategically placing the shells to cause the greatest upset for the Club.

"There's one thing you've got to learn, Tommy—your mother is never wrong—at least not until you're old enough to think for yourself," George said, chewing thoughtfully. "Which you're not."

"She's wrong lots of times," Tommy said. "I'm just smart enough to know better."

"Hmph," George said, pitching another shell past Tommy's ear. "What are you going to do when you finish serving your time here at the Roost?"

"Go back to hanging with my buddies," Tommy said, although he really hadn't missed any of them too much since he had been sentenced to work afternoons and weekends at the nursing home. The old folks here weren't all that bad, he thought. Especially George. George was all right—except when he started lecturing him.

"No, I mean after that, hard head. What are you going to do with your life after high school, presuming that you make it out of high school."

"Hey, I've been doing all right this quarter," Tommy said defensively. He had. Ever since George started tutoring him in math and science his grades had picked up a good bit. He might even clear a 'B' this time on his report card. And, providing he didn't screw up royally between now and the next two months, he was going to graduate with the rest of his class. Not in the top percentile, mind you, but at least he'd graduate. That was a pretty big accomplishment coming from his family.

"But what are you going to do after graduation?" George persisted.

Tommy shrugged. "I can always go work on my uncle's dairy farm."

"You? Work on a dairy farm?" George hooted. "You'll have to get up at three in the morning to milk the cows and go to bed around seven o'clock every night. I can't see you doing that."

"I can do anything I set my mind to," Tommy said, lying back against the cool concrete of the porch. His legs swung gently back and forth off of the end.

"Then do something a little more challenging than pulling the teats of a cow."

"Like what?" Tommy asked.

"I think you ought to think about going to medical school," George said seriously.

Tommy sat up quickly and turned around to face his friend. "Medical school? You've got to be kidding. Me—a doctor? Get real, George." Tommy laughed loudly.

"Why the hell not?" George asked gruffly. He disliked being the object of laughter.

"Because I've got better things to do than be a doctor," Tommy said, leaning back against the porch again.

"Yeah, like playing with cows," George responded. He threw a peanut shell and hit Tommy square in the middle of his forehead.

"It's nice to know you're working so hard while the rest of us are goofing off," Patti said sarcastically as she walked out onto the porch. She floated a bright yellow memo down on Tommy's face. She'd been skeptical of Tommy's purpose around here ever since the juvenile court system sent him to the Roost to work off his community service sentence. He was a fair worker, but tended to slack off whenever George was around.

"He's keeping me company," George said.

"What's this?" Tommy asked, caking the memo off of his face and holding it far enough away from his eyes to read it clearly. "CPR classes? No way."

"Way," Patti said. "From now on, every single employee at the Roost will be trained in CPR."

"I'm not an employee, remember?" Tommy said.

"You prove that to me every day," Patti said. "But you're still here, so you're going to have to be trained. No ifs, ands or buts. Or we could send you to juvy. I'm sure they'd love to have you there." She saw the look on Tommy's face and knew she'd won the battle. "See you tomorrow afternoon at three in the activity room for CPR training."

"I don't want to do CPR training," Tommy said after Patti left the front porch.

"Why not? That's a great first step to take if you plan on being a doctor," George said.

"I'm not going to be a stupid doctor," Tommy said firmly, standing up and brushing off his jeans.

"Then be a smart one," George said. He crumpled the empty peanut bag and handed it to Tommy. "Or you could always be a garbage collector— the city dump's always looking for a few good men."

"So, how did it go?" George asked Tommy late the next afternoon.

"What?" Tommy asked.

"The CPR class."

"Okay I guess."

"Did you pass?"

"Yeah."

"What was your score?"

"I did pretty good," Tommy answered non-committally. "How good is 'pretty good?'"

"98." He pulled the certificate from where he'd folded it up in his back pocket and showed it to George.

"That's pretty damn good, I'd say," George said, clapping Tommy on the back. "You're on the way to medical school."

"It was easy. I think the Resuscitate-Annie doll fell for me," Tommy answered with a grin. "But being able to press on someone's chest and breathe in someone's mouth doesn't mean I'd make a good doctor."

"No, but it might help you on your next date" George said with a smile. "No, seriously, Tommy. You've gotta start somewhere and CPR's as good as any. You want to play a game of chess?"

"You think you can beat me again?" Tommy asked. "Sure, I'm game."

Dr. Bill Price grabbed the worn handles of his black medical bag and clipped the pager on his belt, ready to head home for the evening. No wife, no kids, no dog to greet him when he got there, but he enjoyed going home all the same. He liked to putter around in the vegetable garden. He laughed to himself at his use of 'putter.' When you're younger and you're walking around slowly or aimlessly, it's called strolling. When you're old like he was, it was referred to as 'puttering.'

He lifted the bag off of the examination table and turned toward the door leading to the hallway. The snap of pain that shot through his left arm left him breathless and weak. The bag dropped back onto the table with lots of clinks and clanks from the medical instruments inside.

"Damn it," he said out loud. He placed two fingers on his carotid artery and tried to take his pulse before the next bolt of pain hit him, leaving him breathless. No time to treat himself, he realized in a panic. Time to get some help. Dr. Price stumbled out into the hallway, holding onto the railing as he made his way to the next room—the recreation room. Someone needs to heal the healer, Bill Price thought grimly to himself.

George and Tommy were so intent on their chess game that they never even heard Dr. Prices stuttering steps in the hallway. They did, however, hear the crash as Dr. Price lost consciousness and fell into the room.

"What the . . ." George said, getting up from his chair. "Bill!" he yelled, looking at Tommy. "It's Bill!" He knelt beside the doctor, turning from his side onto his back. His old friend's color looked particularly bad. George put his hand up to Bill's mouth and nose, then dropped and put his head onto Bill's chest.

"He's not breathing!" George yelled at Tommy. "Do something!"

Tommy looked stricken. "Me? I can't do nothing."

"You just learned CPR a couple of hours ago—you've got a certificate . . . do something."

"Did he have a heart attack?"

George looked at him in exasperation. "No, I think it's just a bad case of hangnail . . . of course he's had a heart attack, now do something."

Tommy was frightened. This was the first time he'd seen anyone go into cardiac arrest, and, perhaps even more upsetting to him was the fact that George was teary-eyed, something else Tommy had never seen before. He rushed to Dr. Price's side, frantically trying to recall what he'd learned in class that afternoon.

"Annie, Annie, can you speak?" Tommy yelled, grabbing Dr. Price's shoulders and shaking them gently.

"Who the hell is Annie?" George asked, "and stop shaking Bill like that."

"That's what they taught us to do," Tommy explained. What was next? he wondered. He wished he had that CPR book with the color pictures beside him right now.

"Hurry!" George yelled at him. "Bill's getting blue."

"Okay, okay." Think, think, think, Tommy told himself. He loosened Dr. Price's tie and placed his hand behind his neck, pulling up and tilting his head back slightly. Then he pinched Dr. Price's nose and looked into his mouth, sweeping his finger inside for any kind of obstruction. There was none.

Now, did he breathe or pump his chest first? Tommy wondered. He couldn't remember. Breathe first, he decided. Keeping his hand under Dr. Price's neck, he pinched his nose with the other hand and wished with all his might that he had those alcohol wipes they were using in class to clean the spittle around Dr. Price's mouth before he began resuscitation before placing his mouth tightly on the doctor's and blowing two strong breaths.

That done, he moved down and placed his hands at the appropriate position on Dr. Price's sternum and began pumping.

"Atta boy," George said encouragingly, as he turned to the door to call for help.

"One one thousand . . . two one thousand . . . go ahead one thousand . . ." Tommy said, sweat popping out on his forehead from the exertion. Resuscitate-Annie was a whole lot easier to pump than Dr. Price. Her lips were a whole lot cleaner and softer, too.

"What's going on?" Gladys asked from the doorway. She'd been looking for George to play shuffleboard with her.

"Bill's had a heart attack," George said quickly, "and Tommy's doing CPR on him. We need help in here!"

Soon, the room was full of onlookers—everyone except a trained health professional, Tommy noted. He'd dearly like a break, and plus, he wasn't exactly sure he was doing this the right way.

"You're doing great, Tommy," Jack said admiringly. Blue walked over and licked Dr. Price on the lips as Tommy pumped his chest.

Great, Tommy thought. Now I've got to put my mouth on dog spit as well. "Some-one-please-get-help," he said, keeping rhythm with the compressions. "He's-not-coming-a-round."

"You're doing fine, dear," Gladys said. "Dr. Price doesn't look real good, though," she said, clucking her tongue.

Dr. Price didn't look good at all, Tommy noted as he passed from the sternum back to the lips. It had all become mechanical until Gladys said that. He panicked again, realizing that a living, breathing . . . well, he wasn't living or breathing right now, Tommy told himself.

"Come on, boy," George commanded. "You're doing great—keep it up. Come on everybody, back up . . . give him room," George yelled to the others.

Suddenly, as if on cue, everyone began clapping in rhythm to the compressions, softly at first, then more loudly in strong unison. Tommy, spurred on by the cheering, continued doggedly trying to revive Dr. Price. Where is the help, Tommy wondered to himself.

Two miles away the White County ambulance made its way to the Roost, in no particular hurry.

"You want to stop and get something to drink on the way?" Ray suggested to his partner. "The drink machine out there at the Roost only has Chek cola in it."

"Nah, I guess we'd better head on out there," Hugh said with a yawn, reaching to flip on the siren and lights to the ambulance.

"You know it's going to be Johnnie—she's tried to commit suicide or something again."

"If she'd go ahead and get it right, we wouldn't have to drive out here all the time," Hugh said, pressing the gas pedal harder. He liked going last down the gravel drive to the nursing home—if you hit the brakes and gas just right, sometimes the rear end to the ambulance would fish tail back and forth the whole way-down to the Roost, leaving a cloud of dust in its wake.

"What do you think she's done this time?" Ray asked.

"I dunno. Probably has the Garden Club held hostage in the cafeteria or something," Hugh answered with a laugh. "I wouldn't be surprised at anything she did anymore."

Hugh drove the ambulance to the front door of the Roost. No one stopped them as they ran straight to Johnnie's room and knocked on her door.

"Yes?" Johnnie called out.

"It's Ray and Hugh," Ray shouted. "Somebody called for us."

"Oh, really?" Johnnie answered in surprise. She opened the door for the paramedics. "I'll get my bags."

Ray and Hugh helped Johnnie onto the stretcher and buckled her on tight.

"So what's wrong?" Ray asked her politely.

"With me? Nothing," Johnnie said. "I thought you boys had decided something was wrong with me."

"You're not the reason we're here?" Hugh asked in surprise.

"Not that I know of. But it probably wouldn't hurt to ride along with you two for a check-up."

Ray and Hugh looked at each other with concern and all but dumped Johnnie out of the stretcher onto the floor. "Sorry, Johnnie," Ray called out. "There must be somebody else here that needs us."

Patti was running down the hall toward the recreation room when she saw the paramedics in Johnnie's room. "This way," she yelled. "Somebody just told me Dr. Price had a heart attack in the rec room."

"How long ago?" Hugh asked as they wheeled the stretcher after her.

"Several minutes, I think I don't know why I wasn't notified."

"Shit," Ray said. "If it happened ten minutes ago, he's a goner by now."

Patti and the two paramedics burst into the recreation and encountered a bizarre scene. There were approximately twelve residents forming a wide circle, clapping and chanting in rhythm, while Tommy performed CPR on Dr. Price inside the circle.

"Let us through," Hugh said, once he found his voice. The circle broke open, allowing passage for the paramedics and the chanting ceased. Tommy was pushed aside as Ray and Hugh took over the CPR. Within three minutes they had placed Dr. Price on the stretcher and had him wheeled out to the ambulance, continuing CPR the entire time. Nearly all the residents and staff members of the Roost stood on the front porch watched as the ambulance sped away to the hospital, ten miles away.

George stood beside Tommy, his hand resting on Tommy's shoulder. "You did all you could, son," he said reassuringly. Tommy didn't answer. They'd told him in class that the sooner you started compressions and breathing after the initial heart attack the better chance the patient had of living. Well, he'd started almost immediately and Dr. Price never came to. What if he died? He probably did it wrong.

Forty-five minutes later Patti announced over the loudspeaker that Dr. Price had pulled through and was resting comfortably at the hospital. She then delivered a message to Tommy in person.

"Tommy, the paramedics said that it was all because of you that Dr. Price is still around," she said. "You kept his heart and lungs pumping that whole time until the paramedics arrived. They couldn't do any more than you did—they brought him around with those shock paddles at the emergency room. So it looks like you're a hero," she said, squeezing both of his shoulders.

"He's going to be a doctor, you know," George said to Patti. Tommy was a little too dazed to speak in response to her good news.

Patti searched Tommy's face closely. She'd never thought of Tommy as anyone with any ambition in terms of a career. In fact, he didn't seem very bright at all. "Really, Tommy? A doctor?"

Tommy shook his head in reply.

Patti nodded her head. That's what she thought.

Steve Tallison, the administrator, called Patti into his office the next morning. "Well, the word from the hospital is that Bill is resting comfortably and should have a fairly successful recovery. Unfortunately, he's going to be out for some time before his doctor will allow him to come back to work. We're going to have to find a replacement until he gets back."

"Why?" Patti asked sarcastically. "We've been doing without one all along."

"Now Patti, be nice. I know you don't care for Dr. Price that much, but we have to have a resident doctor here. What exactly is it that bothers you about him?"

"All he does is sit around and play checkers or chess in the recreation room all day with George," she said. "Whenever any of the residents need something I have to go find him."

"He's a good doctor, Patti. He may not be overly attentive, but he's still a good doctor."

"He doesn't follow detail—he doesn't do what he's supposed to do around here."

"And what exactly is he supposed to be doing?"

"Caring for the residents!" Patti exclaimed. "He just doesn't do his job very well."

"Who has he neglected?" Steve challenged. "He does his rounds every single day without fail—I know that for a fact." "Sure, he does. But he spends the whole time talking to the residents about stuff like . . . How's your family? . . . How's your shuffleboard game coming along? . . . When's the last time you won at Bingo? He asks things like that instead of medical questions."

"Patti, sometimes those other things are more important to the residents than the medical questions," Steve said patiently. "The residents really like Dr. Price."

"Yeah, well I guarantee that no one's going to even notice he's gone, except maybe George, and that's only because he's going to need a new chess partner now."

"That's cold, Patti," Steve said. He knew better than to waste his breath with Patti about certain topics—Dr. Price being one of them. "We'll j just see what happens, but I will have a temporary replacement in here by tomorrow."

"Oh, when you're looking for a replacement, make sure he knows how to play chess and checkers. Other than that, I can't think of any particular requirements."

Dr. Rodgers showed up for work at the Roost the next day, at seven in the morning. He was waiting for Patti in her office when she arrived at eight o'clock. He stood, introduced himself, and shook her hand loosely before sitting back down, making sure to straighten the pleats in his trousers as he sat.

"I've taken the liberty of going through all the patients' files this morning to familiarize myself with each one," he said without smiling. This was obviously a very serious business for him.

"That's fine," Patti answered, pleased. His thoroughness meant she didn't have to look over his shoulder as he went through each one. He was already exhibiting more care about the residents than Dr. Price ever had. She'd be surprised if Bill had ever cracked open any of the residents' files except to make a notation.

"There are seventy-four patients here, am I correct?" he asked.

"Dr. Rodgers, we like to refer to them as residents instead of patients," Patti said.

"But they are patients," he said without emotion.

"Yes, but it creates a more comfortable atmosphere to think of them as residents instead of patients."

"I shall refer to them as patients," he said matter-of-factly.

"Fine," Patti said. This man was obviously all business. Good—perhaps Steve would hire him on full time instead of waiting for that useless Dr. Price to recuperate.

He stood. "And now I shall go about my rounds," he said, turning to leave.

"Let me know if you need anything," Patti offered, but he had already left the office. She smiled to herself. Now the Roost was going to get a taste of what it was like to have a real doctor around here.

Tommy stopped by Patti's office later that afternoon, as soon as he arrived from school. He wanted to talk, he told her, about becoming a doctor.

"I've done a lot of thinking the past two days and I think I want to be a doctor," he said shyly.

Despite Patti's doubts, she thought it was important to encourage young people into taking on challenging occupations. She was amazed how he handled the situation yesterday with Dr. Price. "How can I help you, Tommy?"

"George told me that sometimes the Roost has helped finance an employee who goes back to school."

"You told me the other day you weren't an employee," she said.

"Yeah well, anyway, I was just wondering about it and stuff," he said, standing up to leave.

Patti felt guilty. She didn't need to pick on Tommy. "I'm sorry, Tommy. Please sit down. Why have you decided to become a doctor?"

"George has been talking to me about it, you know, what I want to do when I get out of high school, and I guess I never thought much about it. I sort of thought I'd go work at my uncle's dairy farm."

"So you're torn between being a dairy farmer and a doctor," Patti said, trying to control her laughter. How ludicrous!

"Yeah," Tommy said with a shrug.

"Before we start talking about financial aid, I want you to try something," Patti said. She had an idea. "Why don't you follow that new doctor around for a couple of days? Dr. Rodgers just started with us this morning. He's going to take Dr. Prices place until he can come back. To tell you the truth, you'll learn a lot more by following Dr. Rodgers around than you ever will with Dr. Price."

"I like Dr. Price," Tommy said, surprised at Patti's comments. "He's a nice guy and I truly am sorry he had that heart attack, but you've seen him—he likes playing chess a whole lot more than he likes tending to the residents."

Tommy shrugged. "Okay, I'll follow Dr. Rodgers around." "If you hurry, you can accompany him on his afternoon rounds," Patti said. "He should be on the Green Wing by now." Tommy found Dr. Rodgers in George's room, about to begin his assessment.

"Hey, Tommy," George said. He cocked his head toward Dr. Rodgers. "See if you can loosen this guy up some. He's way too serious about all this."

"Who are you?" Dr. Rodgers asked Tommy.

"Tommy Melton. Patti said it would be okay if I followed you around this afternoon because I might want to be a doctor. Said I might learn something."

"You might at that," Dr. Rodgers said seriously. "Your first lesson should be in keeping charts. These charts are like a grocery list," he said sourly. Dr. Rodgers leafed through George's chart. "Any complaints?" he asked, pen poised and ready.

"Yeah, I lost my chess partner," George said. "Do you play chess, Doc?"

"Not with patients and certainly not during the working hours," came the firm reply.

"Well excuse the hell out of me," George said, taking offense at the doctor's tone. "I'd truly hate for you to stoop so low as to play a game of chess with me." He crossed his arms and refused to cooperate as the doctor continued his assessment.

Dr. Rodgers gave up, finally writing down: "Patient uncooperative" on George's chart.

Tommy didn't say a word as he observed the doctor at work. He certainly wasn't impressed with Dr. Rodgers bedside manner. He shrugged helplessly at George as he left the room.

About the same time George was being offended by Dr. Rodgers, Patti was approached by several residents who wanted to visit Dr. Price at the hospital.

"We just want to use the van to take some of us out to go see Dr. Price," Jack said. "Niles said he'd drive us there. If we can't use the van, Beatrice said we could use the limousine and we'll just take a few people at a time."

"I miss him already," Gladys said. "That other doctor came in this morning and was cold as a fish. Asked me a bunch of questions about how I felt and the medicines I'm taking, but didn't even ask my name. At least Dr. Price acts like he cares about us."

"Yeah, and he used to always pick up lottery tickets for me on Fridays," lamented Mona. "Who's going to buy them for me now?"

"Save your money," said George, walking up from behind, "the lottery's a crock any way." George turned to look at Patti. "I just had my first encounter with Dr. Rodgers and I'm here to say I don't give a flip about him."

"Me neither," Johnnie said. "He wanted to put me in a harness and tether 'cause he heard I was a threat to myself. Can you imagine?"

"Well, you are," Patti said lightly. "You're all going to have to get used to Dr. Rodgers because he's here to stay until Dr. Price comes back. Dr. Rodgers just happens to be very professional, which is a nice quality to have and something you'll enjoy getting used to. He's just doing his job. Now, as for visiting Dr. Price, I don't see any harm in letting a few of you go at a time as long as an aide accompanies you. The latest word from the hospital is that he's doing fine and should be out of the hospital in a few days and have to recuperate at home for a few weeks. Don't worry so much."

During the rest of the week, Dr. Rodgers waited for Patti every morning in her office. Sometimes she came in to find him working at her desk, which really unnerved her.

"Why don't you work at Bill's desk?" she had asked him.

"It's too messy," was his reply. "You at least keep yours in a somewhat orderly fashion."

By the next Friday, Patti was sick of Dr. Rodgers. He was thorough, that was true, but to the point of overkill. He made all the nurses sign anything and everything they took out of the medical supply room besides the medicine, which they already had to sign out for. Dr. Rodgers also harped on the nurses constantly, instructing them on how he thought they should be doing their jobs. Patti was up to her ears in complaints from her staff and the residents. None of them disputed the opinion that he was a good doctor, it was just his bedside manner—or lack thereof. Now she found herself wishing Dr. Price would hurry up and recuperate so they could send Dr. Rodgers back from whence he came. Everything seemed to run much smoother when Dr. Price was there—even when he was in the recreation room playing chess.

She made a mental note to tell him all these things as soon as he got back to the Roost.

"No, I will not wait until then," she chastised herself and began gathering together her things to leave for the day. She told everyone goodbye and drove to Dr. Price's house.

The small farmhouse sat well off the long dirt road. If Patti hadn't gotten directions from George first, she'd never have been able to find the place on her own. Turning into the long driveway, she tapped her horn twice to let him know he was getting a pop-call. The gardens around his house were breathtaking—ones that even the Garden Club members would drool over. She wondered if they knew about them.

A nurse answered the door when she knocked. "Is Dr. Price in?" she asked, realizing too late what a stupid question that was. Where else would Bill Price be after having a heart attack? The nurse led her through the house toward the back bedroom. Patti thought the little house was simple but charming. Bill had obviously put a great deal of time and effort in selecting the various pieces of furniture and decorations that spotted the beautiful hardwood floors. They walked down the hall to the back bedroom where Dr. Price was resting in bed, propped up with several pillows.

"Patti!" he exclaimed happily. "What a nice surprise. It gets so lonely around here these days . . ." he started to say, then stopped awkwardly in mid-sentence.

" . . . that it's even nice to see me," Patti finished for him. "Now, I wasn't going to say that," Bill said lamely. "You and I have never exactly gotten along very well."

"It's okay, Bill. Since you've been gone I've done a lot of thinking and I think I've done you a great disservice by passing judgment on you."

Dr. Price looked at her curiously. "And how is that?"

"It's been my opinion that you were well . . . let's just say, not as medically astute as I think you should have been, and besides, you spent too much time playing chess and shooting the breeze with the residents," she said in a rush of words. There, she thought, feeling immensely better, I've come clean.

"And your opinion now?" he asked.

"You're a good doctor, and what's more important, you know how to make the staff and the residents feel special. This new guy—Dr. Rodgers—he treats everyone just like they're expendable crew members or something. You know what I mean? He's afraid to get close to them or talk to them on a level deeper than their medical conditions. I always thought you were just wasting time by doing all that talking at work. Now I realize how important it is."

Dr. Price smiled shyly at her, not used to receiving compliments, especially from Patti.

"I hope you come back soon," she said, meaning it. She grabbed his hand and squeezed it gently. "If there's anything I can do, I want you to let me know."

"There is one thing . . ." he said.

"Anything, you name it."

"Do you play chess?" he asked with a smile.

"Sure do. Where's your chess board?"

"Under the bed."

Patti pulled out the chessboard and set it on a TV tray beside his bed. She pulled up a chair and set up both sides. "I'm a little rusty, so go easy on me, okay?" she said with a smile as she moved her pawn forward.

George and Tommy were back on the front porch Saturday evening. Tommy was staying later than usual these days—well past the hour he normally went home.

"How did Dr. Price look?" Tommy asked. He knew that the nursing home van took a load of people to the doctor's house for a short visit early that afternoon.

"A bit under the weather, but good otherwise," George said. "Actually, I was surprised at how good he looked. Maybe he just wanted a vacation and didn't have a heart attack at all. Poor guy—everybody's bugging him about him hurrying up and getting better so he can come back soon."

"George, I can't be a doctor," Tommy blurted out.

"Why not?"

"After following the new doctor around for the past couple of days, I realize it's not what I thought it'd be. I mean, I used to watch Dr. Price a lot and he seemed to really enjoy his job. The people around here like him so much and he likes everyone else a bunch, but this guy's another story. Patti says he's what a doctor ought to be; that his way is the correct way to be a doctor. Well, I'm here to tell ya that if his way is the right way, I don't want to be a doctor."

"Now, Tommy. Just because Patti says . . ."

"No, I've made up my mind. Besides, Dr. Price seemed like home folk to me, but this guy is so smart and uppity, I don't think I can do anything like that."

"Dr. Rodgers is a jerk, plain and simple," George retorted. "That's not the way a doctor should act and I think if you asked Patti in private, she'd even agree with that. Dr. Price is the role model you want. He takes care of everybody without overdoing it and he manages to enjoy himself at the same time."

"I just don't think I want to be a doctor," Tommy said quietly. "Don't make up your mind just yet," George said.

"Why not?"

George thought last. "Because we've got to play a game of chess for it. You win, you don't have to be a doctor; if I win, you've got to give it a chance."

"Why do you care what I do?"

"Just shut up and tell me if you want to lose at chess or not," George snapped.

"But I always lose," Tommy said.

"All the more reason for you to take the game seriously," George said, getting up from his rocking chair. "Let's go to the recreation room.".

The twosome walked down the empty halls of the nursing home to the recreation room. It was ten o'clock, well past the time most of the residents went to sleep. George flipped on the fluorescent lights as they stepped in, allowing his eyes to fall on the spot where his good friend Dr. Price had lain near death weeks before. One good friend had saved the other, he thought, throwing his arm around Tommy's thin shoulders as they made their way to the chess board.

George was surprised at how protective he was over the kid. He'd never really taken to children before—he didn't have any of his own—but Tommy was different. Tommy needed some guidance and a firm hand from a father figure, not from his mother who sprang tears at the drop of a hat and overreacted to everything Tommy did or didn't do. He wanted something good to come of the boy, he thought as he took a seat on the folding metal chair across from Tommy. He wanted Tommy to go to medical school if for no other reason than to prove to himself that he could do it. Self esteem and pride seemed to be two characteristics that ran flat and shallow in Tommy's patchwork family.

George watched as Tommy pulled out the game pieces from the drawer of the table and opened the cardboard playing board. Although the challenge had been made in relative jest, George was determined to win so he'd have even a little bit of leverage in getting Tommy to go to medical school—or any other kind of post high school educational institution for that matter. George interlocked his fingers, palms facing out, and cracked his knuckles loudly. "You ready to lose, boy?"

"Not hardly, old man," Tommy retorted. He'd taken enough of the man's beatings, lectures and opinions lately to last him a lifetime. Even Tommy's own father . . . . he stopped his own thought process. His own father hadn't been around for years, and even when he was he didn't act like a father. He let Tommy get away with anything and everything as long as he didn't steal his beer and didn't walk in front of the television when his dad was watching it—which was most of the time.

Tommy smiled back at George. "I gave you the white men, so you can go first. Age before beauty, you know."

"Then you'll never get a turn because you're ugly as hell," George said, picking up one of his pawns and moving it two spaces forward. The two played silently for a moment, each making basic conservative moves about the checkered board. When they finally looked up, each had the same number of prisoners stacked on their respective sides of the board. George had four of Tommy's pawns, a bishop, and both of his knights. Tommy, in turn, had captured three of George's pawns, a rook, and a bishop. Tommy was so intent on the game that he never noticed as George moved his arm beside Tommy's prisoners, plucked up the rook and dropped it into the loose sleeve of his shirt. George then dropped his arm. The rook fell out of the sleeve and into his hand.

"Was that the janitor that just walked by?" George asked, looking at the open door.

"I dunno," Tommy said. "Why?"

"Because I need to ask him something. Would you mind going after him? My legs aren't what they used to be."

"Sure," Tommy said, pushing his chair away from the table and heading toward the door. George dropped the rook back on his own side and settled back in his chair before Tommy turned back around after sticking his head out of the door into the hallway. "I don't see anyone," he said.

"My mistake—I must be seeing things," George said apologetically.

"Did you go yet?" Tommy asked.

"No, I was waiting for you," George said, reaching for the ill-gotten rook and capturing Tommy's remaining bishop.

"Wait . . . I thought . . ." Tommy began in confusion.

"Speak up, son," George said. "I can't make out what you're saying."

"Nothing," Tommy said sadly as George placed his bishop along with his other prisoners.

The game went on for over an hour, each player using a tedious amount of energy in selecting which man they wanted to move and in which direction.

"Checkmate," Tommy said triumphantly at a quarter to midnight.

"Damn," George said, staring at the board in disbelief. He hadn't even seen Tommy's queen sneaking up on his king.

"I guess you don't have to be a doctor after all," George said, standing quickly and spilling over the table and chess pieces. "Sorry," he said. He left Tommy to clean up the mess. Tommy found him back on the front porch.

"George?"

"Yes?" George responded.

"What's wrong? What's the big deal over losing a chess game? I saw you losing to Dr. Price a bunch of times."

"It's not the game, it's the wager," George said quietly.

"You mean about the medical school thing?" Tommy asked incredulously. "Why are you so concerned about my going to medical school? Do you want free prescriptions or something?"

"No, I guess I've just gotten sort of fond of you and want to see you do well," George said. "I hate to think of you going through life settling for the easy way out. You've got too good of a head for that, despite your stupidity."

"Why George, I didn't know you cared," Tommy said in mock surprise.

"Oh, shut up," George said. "I don't care—go on and play with cows for the rest of your life." Tommy was holding out a piece of paper in the darkness. "What's that?" George asked.

"Go on and look at it," Tommy said.

"I can't read it in the dark," George said, pulling out his glasses and setting them on his nose.

Tommy pulled a cigarette lighter out of his pocket, spun the wheel and held the flame close to the paper.

"What are you doing with a lighter?" George asked gruffly as he read the paper. "Why, it's an application for college," he said in surprise.

"Yep. I was just stringing you along," Tommy said with a grin. He released the wheel of the lighter, returning the porch to darkness. "I've already talked to Patti about it and she's going to help me get some kind of grant or financial aid to go to college. And, if I make it through there, who knows? I may go on to medical school."

"Boy, you're a pain in my side sometimes," George said. "You were just going to let me blabber on and on about that, weren't you?"

"For as long as you would," Tommy said, smiling in the darkness.

CHAPTER 12

"**T**HIS salmon mousse is exquisite," Pearl purred as she slipped the mousse-covered wafer into her mouth. The expression on her face was one of pure ecstasy. "Mmmmm," she said for effect. "Who made this one?"

"Is that the Heavenly Mousse?" Virginia asked. "I believe Madeleine came up with that little masterpiece, didn't you Maddy?"

Maddy smiled with feigned modesty. "Oh, it's just something I threw together for the cook book," she said, not mentioning the fact that she lifted the recipe off of the chef at the Four Seasons the last time she was in New York. He'd been hesitant at first, as all chefs are about giving out their recipes, but she had wheedled and coaxed him with as much Southern charm as she could muster without looking incredibly foolish. The chef had finally given in, anxious to rid his kitchen of her overbearing presence.

Pearl stepped back and admired the tables laden with many of the recipes that would be included in this year's cook book The Junior League, for as far back as she could remember, had put together a cook book every year for fundraising purposes. This year's cause was illiteracy.

"Ladies, ladies," Maddy called out from the lectern that was set in the back of the room, opposite from the food tables. "We have a small amount of business to take care of before we have lunch, so if everyone will take a seat we'll begin." The fifteen women pulled away reluctantly from the tables and took their seats facing the lectern.

"Okay, now where's Peggy?" Maddy asked. Peggy raised her hand. "Would you read the minutes from the last meeting?"

Peggy stood up and began reading from a notebook that she held out in front of her. "The last meeting was held at Francine's adorable little house over on Elm Street a month ago. Maddy called the meeting to order at eleven thirty in the morning," Peggy said, turning to smile at Maddy at the mention of her name. Maddy smiled back.

"The meeting began with everyone reading and describing the recipes they'd collected for the upcoming cook book. Things went smoothly until one of the members, whose name I won't mention here in these minutes, suggested one of the dishes that was a big hit in last year's cook book. Maddy told the offender that she had stolen the recipe from last year's book and that it couldn't be used again. The offender claimed the recipe to be her own and said she saw nothing wrong in using the recipe again. Maddy told the offender that she needed to use some creativity and come up with something original. Well, then the offender got offended and told Maddy she'd heard that Maddy's son hadn't been accepted at Harvard and then . . . ."

"That's quite enough," Maddy said, interrupting Peggy's report. "I really don't think we need to hear any more about that particular meeting," she said, clearing her throat. "We don't really have time, anyway. This week, we need to decide what particular angle we'll take with the cook book. For those new members, what we usually do is pick a theme to carry throughout the book For example, last year the theme was 'The Best Places to Shop in North Georgia'—a big hit among the members— and in between each food section we would have a page dedicated to a particular clothing store. The year before, the theme was 'Ivy League Schools and Our Kids Who Go There,' which highlighted the son or daughter of Junior Leaguers who attended Ivy League schools. That, as well, was a big hit." She stopped to smile at all the members. She wondered if they'd even noticed the brand new Laura Ashley outfit she had on today.

"This year, I think we should focus more on the community, since this is the one-hundredth anniversary of Stalvey. In honor of that, I think the theme should be of a historical flavor. Any suggestions?"

Several hands shot up. "Yes?" Maddy called out, pointing to one of the upraised hands.

"I think the theme should be 'Relatives of the Junior Leaguers,' and each page should focus on any of our relatives who lived in this area a hundred years ago."

"Next," Maddy said, pointing to another.

"Where Settler Women Shopped a Hundred Years Ago?" suggested another.

"Next."

"Life before the Junior League?"

"Let's not even think about that one," Maddy shuddered. She pointed to another hand.

"Historical Places in Stalvey," said a woman in the back of the room.

Maddy considered the suggestion and nodded. "I like that. Yes, I think I like that a lot. Of course, it would swing attention away from the Junior League, but in light of the special circumstances this year I think it's only fitting. Do I see a show of hands in support of having a cook book with 'Historical Places in Stalvey' as its theme?" Over half of the women gathered in the room raised their hands in support.

"The majority has approved the theme, so be it," Maddy said with a crack of her gavel. "Now, the next question is, who will write the historical accounts?" No one raised their hand. "Now girls, someone has to write these stories. Why is it such a tedious effort each year to get volunteers to write the articles?" Still no one raised their hand. "Okay, I shall be forced to appoint a reporter," Maddy said. She looked around the room slowly. Everyone avoided eye contact with her and instead studied their nails or hem lines. "Suzy," Maddy said. One small pinched face from the back of the room looked up as the others released their breaths in a rush of wind.

"Me?" Suzy said meekly. Hers was a relatively new face in the crowd but she already knew enough to know not to volunteer for anything.

"Yes, I think since you're new to the group you should take on the responsibility of writing these articles."

"But, I really don't write well and my time is pretty limited," Suzy said.

Maddy placed her index finger on her chin as though deep in thought. "You know, now that I think about it, I don't think we ever voted on your admission into the Junior League yet, have we?" she asked, staring at Suzy.

Suzy withered in Maddy's gaze. She wanted to be a member of the Junior League more than anything. Also, her husband had been transferred here and promoted to vice president of the local bank, so it was very important for her to be involved in particular social circles such as the Junior League.

"I'll volunteer," Suzy said.

"How sweet of you," Maddy gushed happily, as though she hadn't just fixed Suzy with one of her 'you'd better do as I wish or else I'll have you and your entire family blackballed' looks that made her famous as well as president of the Junior League.

"What do I write about and where do I get my material? Me and my husband j just moved back here after being away for nearly 25 years," Suzy said helplessly. "I don't know anything about Stalvey anymore."

"The library," said one woman.

"The newspaper," another chimed in.

"The nursing home," Pearl said from the back.

"The nursing home?" Maddy asked.

"Of course," Pearl said. "Milly's Merry Roost. What better resource for historical stories about Stalvey than to talk to the people who lived it?" Pearl said, obviously pleased with her own suggestion.

"That's a great idea," Maddy said. "Suzy, I think you should go out to the Roost and talk to the residents there in order to get your stories."

"The nursing home?" Suzy asked doubtfully. She'd always avoided nursing homes whenever possible. The last time she had to visit one was years ago when her grandmother was doing so poorly and she hadn't gotten over that particular visit yet. The smell of urine, the sounds of people screaming in the hallways, the indifference of the staff toward the patients . . . she didn't think she could do it again.

"I think the library would be a better . . ." she started to say.

"No, I think Pearl's right on this one. In fact, I remember reading about Kensington Place, that wonderful old Civil War era house outside of town, being sold because the woman who'd lived there all her life had checked into the Roost. Beatrice something or other. Your first story can be about her and Kensington—what it was like 'way back when and all that."

Suzy hesitated.

"You know, Suzy, I think you'd be a real asset to the Junior League," Maddy said in warning.

"Okay," Suzy relented.

"We need the stories by the next meeting—okay? Write four or five total stories about whatever subjects you choose besides Kensington."

"Okay."

Two days later Suzy was driving up the long driveway toward the Roost. She glanced at her watch and made a mental note to keep track of time. Not wanting to upset her mother by telling her she was going out to the nursing home, Suzy had said she was going to visit a friend for a couple of hours. Suzy's mother had moved in with her and her husband years ago after Suzy's father had died. As the years progressed she got to be more and more of a handful to take care of, but she'd promised her father on his deathbed that she would never put her mom in a nursing home. Her mother had heard the promise and brought it up to her on a fairly regular basis. Suzy knew her mother had the same memories of grandmother in a nursing home as Suzy had and just didn't want to ever wind up in a place like that.

Suzy had called the Roost yesterday and talked with Steve Tallison about her project. He had agreed that it was a wonderful idea and encouraged her to come out any time.

"These folks have a wealth of fascinating information," he'd assured her and began to name off several of them. He obviously knows all about the people that live there, she thought to herself.

When she arrived at the Roost she asked to speak to Beatrice Wellington and was shown to the recreation room to wait for her. There were eight other residents in the room, five watching soap operas on the television and the other three gathered around a checker table. No one paid Suzy any attention as she walked in and took a seat on the far side of the room where a small table and two chairs had been placed. Within fifteen minutes Beatrice arrived, accompanied by Niles' steadying hand.

"What can I do for you, dear?" Beatrice asked, puzzled. "We're not related or anything are we?"

"Oh, no ma'am. My name is Suzy and I'm writing some articles for the new Junior League cookbook and wanted to get some information from you."

"I don't cook dear, I leave that to others in my employ," Beatrice said kindly. The young woman obviously didn't know who she was.

"I'm sorry, I haven't explained myself well," Suzy said. "The theme of our cook book is 'Historical Stalvey' and I'm here to talk to you about some of the town's history—primarily Kensington."

Aha, so the young woman *did* know who she was, since she was familiar with Kensington. Hearing the name of Kensington sent a warm wave of emotion over Beatrice. She'd spent her entire life, save for the past few months, there at the grand old house. "What can I tell you?"

Gladys, who was watching soap operas with four other women across the room, reached for the remote control and turned the volume down so she could hear what Suzy and Beatrice were saying.

"Why'd you turn that down?" Johnnie demanded. "I want to know if it's his baby or not and I can't hear as well as the rest of you," she complained.

"Shhh," Gladys said, placing a finger in front of her lips. "I want to hear what they're talking about." The others quieted down so they could hear as well.

"Tell me about Kensington, like when it was built, what it was like, and about growing up there," Suzy said. "Everyone considers Kensington the most beautiful home in the area." "And so it is," Beatrice said with a wistful look in her eyes, "but it's so much more than a home. During its splendor Kensington employed over a hundred people to work in the house and grounds alone, not including those that worked the farms or tended the cattle and horses. To answer one of your questions, it was built in the late 1800's as a gift from an English nobleman to his wife. The story is quite tragic because the wife died on the day she moved into Kensington—fell down a flight of stairs and broke her neck."

"That's horrible," Suzy exclaimed, caught up in the story. "Quite. As the story goes, the Englishman was so distraught over his wife's death that he closed the house down and moved back to England, where he committed suicide months later. The house was caught up in legal technicalities and so was left empty for twenty years. My father's family owned the 200 acres adjacent to the Kensington estate and had been raising cattle and farming it since the mid 1800s. My father acquired Kensington in 1910 and I was born there shortly thereafter, the first child to be born there," she added proudly.

Suzy smiled warmly. She liked this genteel woman very much. "That's a fascinating story. Do you have any more? Maybe about the history of the town of Stalvey or some interesting things that might have happened there when you were a child."

The women in the TV area had completely stopped watching television and turned the set off in order to hear the stories Beatrice was telling.

"To tell you the truth, Kensington was such a city within a city that I never got into Stalvey that often. There was no reason to because everything we needed was brought to us at Kensington," Beatrice said, pride in her voice. "I don't know too much about the town itself."

"Oh," Suzy said, dejected. She'd found such a gold mine with Beatrice and the Kensington story, she'd hoped her luck would continue.

The other women were practically falling over themselves in the TV area to offer information.

"I know a good deal about Stalvey," Gladys said, raising her voice to get Suzy's attention.

"Not hardly as much as I do," Johnnie countered. "After all, you moved here when you were five while I've lived here all my life."

"Neither one of you know as much as I do because my daddy was the sheriff," Mona said. "The only two people who know everything that goes on in a town is the sheriff and the pastor," she said with a nod of her head, "and my daddy was best friends with the pastor, too."

Suzy looked over at the old women clamoring for attention and smiled. "I think I'll need to speak with each one of you, if you don't mind."

"I guess I don't mind so much," Gladys said, acting as though she wasn't as anxious to share her stories as she had been a moment ago.

"What story can you tell me about Stalvey back when you were growing up?" Suzy asked.

"I remember when they brought the railroad through the town," Gladys said, thinking back. "Everyone was so excited about it because they could travel to Athens and Atlanta by train instead of horse and buggy. The whole thing took a long time to build. First, they came through and cut down all the trees and then they laid down the rail. Me and my brother used to watch the big strong men on the chain gangs lay down the rail, driving in the spikes to hold it all in place. It was quite exciting. The day the first train came through was a day I'll never forget because for most of us, we'd never even seen a train before except in pictures or sketches. We saw the smoke and heard the whistle long before we saw the train pull into the station, and by that time I'd already gotten it into my head that it was going to be ten times bigger than it was and look like some kind of roaring monster. My little brother ran away in fright before it got there." Suzy's eyes were shining. "That's a wonderful story." She'd been writing furiously on her note pad the whole time Gladys was recounting the story. "Could you describe the train and the station and maybe the people who lived there then?" she asked. Gladys was more than happy to oblige. She pulled up a chair beside Beatrice and began describing all the sights and sounds of the first train that visited Stalvey, Georgia. When she was finished, Suzy sat back with a satisfied smile. "That's two stories for the book," she said. "Only two or three more and I'm through." She turned to Mona. "Mona, since your father was sheriff, do you know any stories about crime back then?"

"To tell you the truth, there wasn't a whole lot of crime then, just occasional lynching's and a little bit of cattle rustling. Back then the hobos even knocked on folks' doors for handouts and ate on the back porch. Nobody ever thought about being afraid of hobos. Other than that it was pretty boring." She paused. "Wait a minute. There was this one time, back in the '30s, that there was a rash of burglaries that no one could ever solve." "Really?" Suzy asked, picking up her pen again.

"I remember it because it used to frustrate my dad so bad because he couldn't solve the crimes. The funny thing about the burglar was that he always committed his crimes during the day and never at night."

Something was nagging at Suzy, something about the burglaries . . . "Wait—I think my mother was here then! She told me she was working as a cashier at Bob's Ready-To-Wear when they were robbed during broad daylight by some guy with a handkerchief tied just under his eyes . . ."

"You're right!" Mona exclaimed. "Dad said he *did* have a handkerchief tied over his face."

"He was never captured?" Suzy asked, writing furiously. She thought the girls at the Junior League would love to read about an unsolved mystery in small-town Stalvey back in the '30s. They probably think she's going to come back with run-of-the-mill historical stories like when the town was founded and the population then compared to the current population. Well, she'd show them. She'd bring back true accounts of the first train, an unsolved mystery, and a tragic romance story involving Kensington, not to mention whatever else she'd uncover in the next day or so.

Suzy stood up and recapped her pen.

"You're not leaving," Gladys said, disappointed.

"I really have to," she said, "I told my mother I'd be back in a couple of hours and I've already been here two and a half hours." She had an idea. "Would you all mind if I come back tomorrow to finish up and brought my mother with me? I know she'd love to talk to you all."

"Of course," they said, pleased at the prospect of her return. On the way home, Suzy thought about how she was going to get her mother to accompany her to the nursing home. She thought her mother would really enjoy the company of Gladys, Beatrice, Mona and the others. All her mother did any more was sit around and watch television. She never even visited her friends or received visits because of a stroke she'd had a few months ago which caused the right side of her face to droop.

"I don't want anyone to see me this way," she'd told Suzy after it happened. Suzy was faced with two problems—getting her mother out of the house and getting her to visit at the nursing home. Ruth was as adamant about not leaving the house as she was about visiting nursing homes.

"They're too depressing," Ruth always said whenever Suzy suggested they go visit one of her old friends in a nursing home. "And besides, you might leave me there," she'd throw in for good measure.

"Where have you been all this time?" Ruth called out as Suzy walked into the kitchen. Her mother was preparing dinner for the three of them.

"I was visiting some people," Suzy said, which wasn't a lie at all.

"Who were you visiting all that time?" she asked, stirring a pot of spaghetti sauce on the stove. The aroma was delicious.

"Some women out at Milly's Merry Roost," she said, catching her breath.

Ruth turned around. "The Roost? What were you doing out at that nursing home?" Suzy briefly explained her assignment for the Junior League and repeated some of the stories some of the women had shared with her, especially the one about the unsolved robberies.

"Really?" Ruth said, turning to face her daughter. "I remember that like it was yesterday—the man with the red handkerchief tied around his face. I remember his eyes."

"Mother, would you like to go with me when I go back to the Roost tomorrow? I think you'd really enjoy talking to those women and hearing their stories . . . and telling some of your own."

To her surprise, Ruth didn't respond immediately. "Sure, I'll go with you."

"Great," Suzy said.

The next afternoon Ruth put on one of her church dresses for the visit to the nursing home—one of the dresses she wore when she *used* to go to church. Ruth was as anxious to get out of the house as her daughter was to get her out. Her reasoning as to why she chose Milly's Merry Roost as the site of her first outing since the Bell's palsy was a mystery to her daughter, she was sure, since nursing homes were places that Ruth generally steered clear of even without the palsy. "I've got my reasons," she said to herself as she dressed for the visit, although her reasons weren't ones she was particularly proud of. It had been many years since she had lived in Stalvey. She had completely lost touch with her old group of friends and it was unlikely anyone would remember her. Since the palsy, she was too embarrassed about her face to let her good friends back home see her; however, she was tired of being indoors. So . . . she figured that the women at the nursing home wouldn't have any reason to be appalled at her appearance because they were all probably three steps from death's door themselves. She could spend a leisurely afternoon outside of the house without being under scrutiny. "Ruth, you're awful," she said to the mirror as she applied makeup. She didn't share her reasoning with Suzy because for some reason her daughter was quite taken with the old women.

They arrived at the Roost around three in the afternoon and went back to the recreation room. The same women were sitting in the TV area, but the television was turned off. They were chatting among themselves so boisterously that they didn't hear Suzy and Ruth approach.

"Hello, ladies," Suzy said. She introduced the group to her mother.

"Hello, Suzy," Gladys said. "You've stirred up a lot of rusty memories around here. We're all comparing stories. Turns out, ours are much better than those stupid soap operas," she said, gesturing toward the television.

Suzy pulled a small black tape recorder out of her purse. "I hope you don't mind if I record everything today," she said. "I want to be able to enjoy the conversation instead of worrying about writing everything down."

The group of women arranged their chairs in a circle, with the tape recorder on a chair in the middle. "Now, I want you all to tell stories about Stalvey in the 'old days,' just like you did yesterday." Johnnie began talking first this time, telling the group about how she used to work at the factory while all the men folk were serving in the war. Her job, she said, was to make bullets at a factory that used to stand where the new country club was located. One by one the women took turns, each slowly weaving their stories from memories that hadn't been tested in years. Even so, each face in turn lit up with the memories of their experiences as though it were yesterday. Even the smallest details of the past did not seem to be forgotten. It seemed that the years were shed from their faces as they talked animatedly about "do you remember when?"

Suzy fed tapes into the recorder as the stories went around the circle several times. Her mother even joined in occasionally and seemed to enjoy both telling stories and listening to them. No one ever mentioned her mother's sagging face and, to her mother's surprise, none of the women were "three feet from the grave" like she thought they'd be.

"Why in the world would women like that want to be in a nursing home?" Ruth had said to Suzy during a bathroom break. "It's not like they're crippled or anything."

"You don't have to be crippled to go to a nursing home, mom," Suzy said. "This is a nice nursing home. I think they all really like it here. I mean, look at all the friends they have."

"It's not like I remember," Ruth said as they went back to the recreation room and took their seats. Suzy turned on the tape recorder and began the story-telling process again, listening with fascination to all the details of early-1900s in Stalvey.

"We're going to play a game of chess if it won't bother you ladies," George said, walking into the recreation room. Tommy followed along behind him and they both took their seats at the chess table, Tommy with his back to the circle of story-tellers and George facing them.

"Go right ahead," Suzy said. "Feel free to join us if you'd like to share some stories about historical Stalvey."

"Nah," George said, dismissing them. He started setting up his pieces on the chess board.

"Who is that?" Ruth asked her daughter softly, nodding toward George.

"Why, mom? Are you interested?" Suzy asked, a smile playing on her lips. It would be too much to think she could get her mother out of the house, to a nursing home, and find her a boyfriend all in the same day.

Johnnie was sitting beside Ruth and heard her comment. "Watch out, Ruth. That man belongs to Gladys and she wouldn't take too kindly to your interest in him," she warned good—naturedly.

"No, no," Ruth said, shaking her head. "I think I know him from somewhere."

"That's George Anderson," Johnnie offered. "He's been here for about a year now. New kid on the block."

"Where did he come from?" Ruth asked.

"I have no idea about that. You might want to ask Gladys." "I've seen him somewhere before . . ." she said. She turned back to hear the story Gladys was telling about the one room school house in Stalvey. Occasionally she would sneak glances at George, trying to figure out why he looked so familiar. Gladys had noticed Ruth's interest in George and was getting a little unnerved by her attentions. Johnnie watched all three of them and enjoyed herself immensely.

"Ahh, ahh," George said, reaching for his handkerchief to catch the sneeze that was coming. Ruth watched as he pulled the handkerchief from his back pocket to his face, covering his nose and mouth.

"Oh, my," Ruth said, standing and pointing at George. George looked up at her in surprise. "What? Didn't I get it all off my face?" He mopped over his face again with the red gingham handkerchief.

"You're the one," she said, still pointing at him.

"He's already taken," Gladys said, standing up and crossing her arms over her chest.

"What the hell are you all talking about?" George asked, confused.

"Fifty some years ago you robbed the store where I worked—Rob's Ready-To-Wear. It was you. I only saw your eyes because you had that red handkerchief tied around your face, but I'd recognize those eyes anywhere."

Everyone had gotten silent. George's face turned ashy white as he stared at the woman as though he'd seen an apparition. "You must be mistaken," he said, not very convincingly.

Ruth started walking toward him. "No, I'm positive. I'm quite certain you were the one."

Mona stood up and walked to Ruth's side. "*You* mean the one my daddy could never catch? The same burglar?" Ruth nodded.

"Leave George alone," Gladys said, rushing to his side. "He couldn't hurt a fly, could you, George?" George looked at Gladys blankly, too shocked to speak. Of all the things that might happen to him. When he got out of jail, he never expected to come face to face with that sixteen year old cashier from Bob's Ready-To-Wear. This would get him back in jail for sure, he thought in a panic. He was still on probation, and if this witness put him in jail, he'd never see the light of day from the outside world again.

"Please," George said to Ruth, his eyes pleading along with his words. "I've already served so much time."

"Served time?" Gladys said, staring at George. "Whatever are you talking about?"

Suzy took her mother by the arm and led her back to her chair. They were both shaking. "Mom, are you sure?" she asked.

"I'm positive," she said.

"But it was fifty some years ago."

"I'm positive," she said, staring at George.

"Call the police," Suzy said to the people in the room. "I'm going to turn him in."

"Wait a minute, okay, honey?" Ruth said. "Just take me home right this minute and we'll decide what to do later." Ruth followed her daughter as she led her out of the nursing home.

Everyone in the recreation room was staring at George in silence. Even Gladys had been immobilized. She stood with her arms hanging down limply by her side, not sure what to do.

"I think I need to tell my 'historical' account now," George said, nodding at the group gathered in the recreation room. "I may not get another chance if that woman goes to the police because what she says is true."

"George," Gladys said, her hands fluttering nervously to her mouth.

"Hush, Gladys," George said gently. "I need to tell you all some things. I'm just sorry it had to happen this way. I came here to the Roost last year straight from the state penitentiary where I served thirty years for a couple of burglaries I committed back in the sixties. The irony of the whole thing is that while I have committed my share of penny-ante burglaries, I never did the major operation I got arrested and sent away for. I was completely innocent of that particular crime. However, I *did* commit the crime that woman is accusing me of, but I sure don't want to go back to jail. I just spent 30 years of my life serving a whole bunch of time for something I didn't do, so I guess I feel like the two break even."

No one spoke.

"I guess we'll find out soon enough," George said with a sigh. "I'm just too old to go back there."

Suzy helped her mother to a kitchen chair and brought her a glass of water when they got back home. "Can I get you anything, mom?" she asked worriedly. Recognizing George had been quite a shock for her mother. Suzy had heard the robbery story over and over again as a child, often asking her mother to repeat the exciting story in front of Suzy's friends. She had been both fascinated and terrified by her mother's account of the masked bandit.

"What are you going to do?" Suzy asked.

"I don't know."

Later that evening, several residents of the Roost gathered in the dining room, without George.

"What can we do to help George, Gladys?" Jack asked. He'd heard through the nursing home grapevine about the afternoon's incident. He thought his old friend might have a shady past, but nothing had prepared him for *that* shady. Still, he wanted to help him out if he could.

"I don't know. I had no idea . . ." she said lamely.

"None of us did," Jack said. "But that's beside the point. How can we keep this woman from going to the police?"

"We could call her," Johnnie suggested.

"Do we have their number?"

"No, I don't even know their last names," Gladys said glumly. "Never thought to ask and I don't think they ever said."

"We'll just have to wait until they get in touch with us, I suppose. Hopefully they haven't gone to the police already."

"The funny thing about the whole robbery was that the guy was really nice," Ruth said to her daughter. "He told me he had a gun, but I really don't believe he did. He had his hand in the pocket of his coat like he had a gun in there, but I think it was his finger he was pointing underneath that heavy material. Oh, and when he went behind the counter to the cash register he knocked over a stack of shirts I'd just ironed," Ruth started laughing. "I want you to know he was so apologetic about that, he stopped what he was doing to pick up all the shirts off of the floor and stacked them back on the counter top. He must have asked me twelve times if I was all right." Suzy's mother had a faraway look in her eyes. "In fact, I used to think about him a lot after that, because from what I could see, he was quite handsome. And still is," she added with a laugh.

"Watch out or Gladys will come after you," Suzy warned. "Does this mean you're not going to press charges?"

"I don't think I can, honey. Did you see the look on the poor man's face when I recognized him? He looked scared to death. No, I don't think I could live with myself if I did that now. I mean, it's been over fifty years."

"But mom, what he did was wrong, not to mention illegal. Remember how scared you were then? A long time ago when you told that story you'd get this look of fear in your eyes and I'd dream that I'd find the man one day and get him back for you. Now's my chance."

"He's old, Suzy, and not likely to do any more harm. Why in the world would you want to do that to him?"

"Because of what he did to you years ago," Suzy said, her eyes blazing in anger.

"But I'm okay now. I got over it and no harm was really done except Bob's Ready-To-Wear lost a little bit of money—Bob's been dead for years now anyway."

Suzy stared at her mother. "I don't care what you do, but I'm not going to stand around and let him get away with this. Besides, the police could arrest us for withholding evidence if we don't report that man."

"I hardly think the police are going to care about a case that old," Ruth said.

"You do what you want to, but I'm going to the police tomorrow."

Ruth sighed. She knew her daughter well enough not to argue with her any more. "You do what you feel is necessary, but I wish you'd go out there and talk to that man again before you have him carted off to jail."

Suzy didn't respond to her mother. She was too busy thinking about all the headlines in the local newspaper when she solved a fifty year old burglary case for the police. The Junior League would *beg* her to be a part of their group once they saw how famous she'd become. Her husband would be so disappointed if she wasn't asked to join the group. He'd worked so hard to finally get to be vice-president and she knew how important her role in society would be now. She'd be the best member the Junior League had ever seen, she vowed to herself. Not only would she report an escapee of justice, she'd also write the historical articles they needed for the cook book. Speaking of . . . where in the world was that tape recorder?

"Mom, have you seen my tape recorder?" she called out to Ruth.

"I think you left it at the nursing home, dear. We left in such a hurry today . . ."

"Oh, great. They're probably breaking it to bits right now just to get back at us about this robbery thing."

"Those were nice old people," Ruth said. "They wouldn't do anything like that."

"Should we break it to pieces or just steal the tapes?" Johnnie asked Gladys when they realized Suzy had left her tape recorder in the recreation room.

"Just take the tapes right now and hide them," Gladys said thoughtfully. "I have an idea."

"I'll hide them in my brassiere," Johnnie said, dropping the mini cassettes into her cleavage. "No one'll think to look there."

The next morning Suzy saw George sitting on the front porch of the Roost, where he'd been rocking for most of the night. George looked up, surprised to see her.

"What are you doing here?" he asked gruffly. "I figured you made a beeline for the police department."

"As a matter of fact, I'm on my way there now," Suzy said, hurrying past him. "I just stopped by to pick up my tape recorder."

"Miss?" George asked. Suzy stopped, but didn't turn to look at him. "I just want you to know that what I did was foolish and I don't blame you one bit for being angry. But I never hurt your mother and I never would . . . anyway, you go on ahead and do what your conscience tells you to do. If I have to go back to jail, well, I brought it on myself." George started rocking again, looking out into the parking lot. Suzy hurried inside to the recreation room.

The tape recorder was sitting on the chair where she'd left it, but none of the tapes were there. They'd gone through at least four of those mini cassettes yesterday, she was sure of that.

"You looking for your tapes?" Johnnie asked from behind. Suzy turned around to see Johnnie leaning in the doorway looking smug.

"Yes, do you have them?" Suzy asked pleasantly.

"That depends on you."

"What do you mean?"

"It means," Johnnie said dramatically—she was enjoying her role, "if you tell the cops about George, you don't get your tapes back."

"That's silly. Anyway, I think I have enough from the other day to write my articles," Suzy said.

"You can't use our stories without our permission," Johnnie said, "and if you report George, you don't get our permission, you can't write the articles, and you can't join the Junior League."

Suzy stared at Johnnie, a smile frozen on her face. "You must be kidding."

"Try me," Johnnie said.

Suzy thought quickly. If she turned him in, she'd be sending an eighty-year-old man to jail for the rest of his life and probably alienating her mother. Ruth really seemed to enjoy talking with all the women at the Roost, too. If she turned the man in, they'd keep her cassettes and she'd have to start all over getting new stories, and, she'd have to explain to the Junior League why she couldn't get stories from the nursing home like they all wanted.

"Who cares about a fifty-year-old burglary?" she said out loud, throwing up her hands in defeat.

"No one I know of," Johnnie said, reaching into her cleavage and pulling out the cassettes. She handed them back to Suzy with a smile. "I'll go tell George he's a free man."

Suzy was unanimously voted into the Junior League at the group's next meeting, not only because her articles would help to make the cook book a financial success, but also because a publishing company had seen a copy of the cook book and contracted with the Junior League to write an entire book on the history of Stalvey—through the eyes of the people who were there.

CHAPTER 13

MORRIS Tanner took off his old fishing cap as he entered Steve Tallison's office and rotated it between his hands. "Hmph," he said, clearing his throat politely. Steve looked up from his desk where he'd been going through receivables.

"Morris, how are you?" Steve asked, genuinely concerned. He liked the Roost's maintenance man not only because he knew how to fix anything and everything, but also because he was a nice, down-home sort of fellow who had worked for the Roost as long as Steve could remember. "How's the wife and kids?" "Thank you for asking, Mr. Tallison," Morris said, smoothing the thin hair on top of his head with the palm of his hand. "Becky and the children are fine." Morris and his wife had five children, all polite as their father.

"What can I do for you, Morris?" Steve asked. He generally didn't see the maintenance man unless there was a big problem that needed his authorization.

"It's the chiller for the air conditioning system again, Mr. Tallison," Morris said, almost apologetically

"Yes, it's been acting up again, I know. Can you fix it?"

"No, Mr. Tallison, I can't," Morris said seriously. Steve looked at Morris questioningly. This was the first time he'd ever heard Morris say he couldn't fix something.

"You can't fix it?"

"No, sir. Not anymore. Over the past few years I've used everything but bubble gum and my wife's hair spray to fix that air conditioner. I've run out of ideas and it's running out of steam."

Steve sighed heavily. "Okay, so where do we go from here?" "You need a new central heat and air system real bad," Morris said.

"Could you install it?" Steve asked hopefully. That would save the nursing home a lot of money right there if Morris could do all the installation.

"No, sir. That system you've got right now's about thirty years old. That's the kind of system I was trained on, but if you get a brand new one, well, they're too new-fangled for me."

Steve ran his hand through his hair in frustration. He'd just been going over the Roost's financial statements when Morris had walked in and the future didn't look any too bright. "How much is a new system?"

Morris wiped the sweat off of his forehead. "I don't know for sure, but for a place this size I'd bet on at least a hundred thousand dollars."

Steve whistled in amazement. "I was afraid of that. Look, do you think you can get the air conditioning system to run just a little longer? I'll buy you some bubble gum and hair spray if that'll help. I just need to buy a little time before I approach the board of directors with a request this big."

"I'll do my best, but I can't promise you anything," Morris said. He nodded to Steve in parting.

Steve sat back in his chair and exhaled loudly. This was all he needed to hear right now, he thought glumly. He'd just been crunching numbers trying to come up with fifteen thousand dollars to repave the parking lot, which was full of pot holes and cracks. Now he needed about ten times that amount. He turned to his computer and quickly typed a letter to the board of directors that notified them of a meeting in two weeks. That should give them time to work the meeting into their busy schedules, Steve thought sarcastically. Lately, it seemed as though whenever there were any problems at the Roost, the board had more pressing matters at hand.

"Excuse me, Mr. Tallison?" Steve looked up to see the county fire marshal, Judd Rankin.

"Hi, Judd. How are you?" Steve said, grateful for the distraction. He disliked writing letters to Board members because he had a feeling they cringed whenever they got their mail, sorted through it, and spotted the Roosts return address. "No news is good news" according to the six members that comprised the board of directors for the nursing home.

"Fine, but I've got some bad news for you," Judd said. He, too, looked guilty and apologetic.

"Is there a problem?" Steve asked, genuinely surprised. Judd came out every year and gave the Roost a clean bill of health each time. All the fire door exits were cleared from obstruction and Steve made sure they only had as many patients as the fire marshal thought appropriate for the size of the building.

"Steve, I think you know that every year I come out here, I close my eyes and walk through," Judd said. "I can't do it anymore."

"What are you talking about?"

"The Roost just doesn't meet the new fire codes anymore," Judd said. "It hasn't in some time, but I just kept my mouth shut and didn't tell you about them because major repairs will have to be done."

"How new are these fire codes?" Steve asked.

"'Bout ten years new," Judd said, "but the superiors haven't really pushed us to enforce any of them as long as the structure is sound. This year, they're making us enforce all of the codes. Nobody slips through the cracks this year, and to make sure, they're sending another inspector in after me."

"What codes are we violating?" Steve asked with a sinking feeling in his gut. The building itself was fifty years old, so there was no telling how many violations had been cited.

"The hallways are too narrow, all doors need to be widened, you need to have exit doors and exit signs installed, a sprinkler system . . ."

"Whoa, whoa," Steve said, shaking his head. "All that has to be done, or what?"

"I'll have to shut you down if it's not done soon," Judd said, averting his eyes from Steve's. "It's nothing I want to do, but this time my hands are tied. I've been turning a blind eye to this place for years now and they just won't let me do it anymore. Besides, it really is a fire hazard. Think of what could happen if the Roost caught on fire and all the residents couldn't evacuate properly." "I know," Steve said, "but I just don't know where the money's going to come from. You're talking about a complete renovation job. That could cost a million bucks."

"I know that," Judd said before leaving. "I'm real sorry about it, too."

Steve turned back to his computer and hit the backspace button, erasing the time frame of two weeks and replacing it with Monday, three days away. The Board would have to meet immediately whether they wanted to or not. Some decisions needed to be made. He grabbed his coat and headed to the bank.

Steve adjusted his tie as he walked into Bubba Wilkes' office. "How are you doing, Bubba?" he said as jovially as he could.

"Just fine, Steve. How's the Roost doing these days?" he asked. They'd mistaken Bubba for the nursing home surveyor one day and had given him the royal treatment. He still came back to visit occasionally to watch soap operas with some of the residents.

"Not so good, actually. That's why I'm here. The Roost needs a loan—a big loan."

"How big?" Bubba asked cautiously.

"In the neighborhood of about a million dollars," Steve said. "You need to go to another neighborhood before I can help you," Bubba said, shaking his head. "I can't give you a loan like that." He took out a file on the Roost and glanced through it before continuing. "The building's old and it's really not pulling in that much money. I just don't see how you'd be able to pay it back. Can't do it."

"Isn't there something we can do?" Steve asked. Bubba shrugged and looked down at the papers. Steve placed both hands on the arm rests of his chair and pushed himself up. "Then I guess we'll be closing down pretty soon. All I need now is the Board's seal of approval, which should take all of about five minutes—they're all biting at the bit to dump the place."

"My hands are tied, Steve, or else I'd be glad to help you," Bubba said. "You know how much I've come to enjoy the company of the residents there."

"I know but we don't have any other recourse. Keep this quiet, will you? I'll tell them all after the Board meeting on Monday if it comes to that. I wouldn't want them to hear it from anyone else."

While Steve and his wife usually spent Friday evenings at the local country club dance, this night they stayed at home, sipping wine on the back porch, and discussing alternatives to closing the nursing home. Both Steve and Joyce came up empty.

"The Board's just going to rubber stamp the whole closing thing once they hear how much money we need to stay open," Steve said, swirling the deep red wine in his glass in front of his face. He fished a drowned gnat out of the glass with the tip of his finger before taking a sip. "The only board member that might side with me would be Reverend Monroe, and that's only because his mother-in-law is at the Roost and he'd all but die if she had to move back home with him and his wife."

"Talk to him, then," Joyce suggested. "Maybe you can persuade him and then he can persuade the others."

"It would take a lot more than Reverend Monroe to change the other guys' minds," Steve said. "It would take the actual hand of God rather than one of his messengers. No, what we need to do is come up with the money before the board meeting. That's the only way they'll even listen to anything I have to say; otherwise, they'll all just pull out a pen and fight over who gets to sign the dotted line first."

"Where are you going to find a million dollars over the weekend—the lottery?"

"It could happen," Steve joked back. "If only I knew someone who could just hand me the money, no strings attached." He sat up quickly. "Wait a minute, I do know someone like that. Beatrice Wellington!"

"But you can't approach one of your residents and ask her for a million dollars," Joyce said. "There's something ethically wrong about that."

"I know, but there's no harm in her pastor asking for the favor, is there?" Steve picked up the cordless telephone beside him and punched in the number. "Reverend Monroe? You and I need to talk—mind if I buzz on over? Great. See you in a minute." He kissed his wife quickly on the way out the door. "Keep your fingers crossed for some divine intervention."

Reverend Monroe lived on the outskirts of town, only five miles from Steve's own home. About sixty years old, he and his father had been the spiritual leaders for the First Presbyterian Church of Stalvey for as long as Steve could remember. The senior Reverend Monroe had passed away several years ago, leaving his son to man the pulpit alone. The gray-bearded man who answered the door wore loose cotton pajama bottoms and a white tee shirt.

"I'm sorry it's so late, Reverend, but if it wasn't such an important issue I wouldn't bother you on a Friday night," Steve said apologetically.

"Come on in," Reverend Monroe said with a smile, waving him inside. He was munching a handful of popcorn as he spoke. "You can join the wife and me in the den. We're watching Lawrence Welk, and then Hee Haw comes on after that." "That's tempting, but I'd rather talk to you alone if you don't mind," Steve said.

"My wife and I don't keep secrets from each other, Steve," the Reverend said in friendly warning. "That's the secret of a successful marriage, you know."

Steve lowered his voice. "This is about your mother-in-law." "I stand corrected," The Reverend said, the smile leaving his face. He flung his arm toward the back of the house. "Shall we go to the back porch and chat?"

"So what has my dear mother-in-law done this time?" the Reverend asked with a sigh as they walked onto the porch. He fished a lighter out of his pocket and lit a citronella candle beside a wooden bench. "The mosquitoes are fairly unforgiving out here. Please, have a seat." His whole demeanor had changed at the mention of his mother-in-law's name, Steve noticed. He wasn't quite as relaxed as when he'd first opened the door, as though a low level of voltage had been applied underneath his skin. "Nothing at all. She's been quite cordial lately," Steve said. "Liar," the Reverend laughed. "Agnes is anything but cordial." Agnes Broomfield had been at the nursing home only a year and had done nothing but gripe and complain since she got there. She was one of the residents that Steve would categorize as "doesn't play well with others." "She hasn't killed anyone lately," Steve added lightly. His attempt at levity had no effect on this troubled man of God, so he turned serious. "It looks like the Roost might have to close down."

"What? I can't believe that," Reverend Monroe said in surprise. Steve explained the Roost's financial dilemma to the Reverend. "That's too bad. That nursing home has been a part of the community for so long."

"Have you thought about what that means to you personally?" Steve asked.

"What do you mean?"

"The only other nursing home in this area is at least forty-five minutes away and you know your wife isn't going to allow her mother to be placed that far away from her. Besides, I hear they have a long waiting list."

"Oh my, you're right," Reverend Monroe said as the shock registered on his face. "That means she'll be moving back in here. I just got my sanity and my den back a year ago, I'm not ready to part with either one of them again," he said without humor. "She can't live here. She just can't."

"If we can't come up with the money, there's no way to stop it," Steve said. He threw his hands up in the air to emphasize the hopelessness of the situation.

"Steve, do you have any idea how crazy she drives me?" the Reverend said, his voice shaking.

"I know the two of you don't get along all that well, but no, I didn't realize it was that serious," Steve said. He was more than a little surprised at the Reverend's response.

"Do you remember a little over a year ago when the church had its annual retreat and I didn't go?"

"Yes," Steve said slowly, thinking back. It had been odd for an entire congregation to go on a week-long retreat and for its pastor not to go along as well. Some scrawny kid straight out of divinity school had led them for the entire weekend. "Where were you? I heard it was a family emergency."

"I had a nervous breakdown—drooling, babbling, the whole bit—thanks to Agnes. I went on a self-prescribed vacation for nearly a month to collect myself. That's when I finally convinced my wife that her mother had to go into the nursing home, or else I did. The jury was out for a while on that one."

Steve was staring openmouthed. "I had no idea. I'm sorry." "Do you know she used to correct and grade my sermons after I'd write them? Or that she would sit in the congregation and make gestures, like 'talk louder' or 'enunciate?' Afterward, when we went home, she'd tell me everything I did wrong and how to correct it the next time."

"No wonder you had a breakdown," Steve said sympathetically.

"She means well with her 'helpfulness,' I think, but it tries my patience. She used to steal my robe, you know the one I preach in? She'd take it and alter it."

"How would she alter it?" Steve asked.

"Well, I never knew what she was going to do week to week. One time she lowered the hem so that I tripped on it on the way up to the pulpit; another time she raised the hemline so that it was over my knees. Both times she said I needed to keep up with the fashion styles. One Sunday I put on my robe and discovered she'd sewn a fly in the front! She told me she couldn't bear the thought of my having to pull off my robe every time I had to go to the bathroom, so she sewed a fly in. I tried to explain to her that I only wore the robe an hour or two each week and I could very well control my bladder for two hours, but it didn't make any difference."

Steve shook his head in amazement. "I'm sorry, Reverend Monroe. I had no idea . . ."

"I'm not through. When I first got my toupee I was having trouble keeping it on my head, so she got the bright idea to put this super adhesive glue on it in place of the regular stuff—you know the kind of glue that can hold a multi-ton tractor trailer attached to a suspended steel bar indefinitely. I had to douse my head in gasoline to get it off of my head. So when I say she's caused me to lose my hair, I mean that literally. Agnes honestly has good intentions when she does things, but they almost always turn out wrong and I'm almost always the one who suffers from her efforts." He took a deep breath. "That woman cannot come back here. I'll do whatever it takes to make sure the remainder of my own years are spent relatively peacefully."

"There is one possibility . . ." Steve began thoughtfully, " . . . nah, we shouldn't do that."

"What?" Reverend Monroe asked eagerly. "Tell me what the other possibility is and I promise to help however I can, short of committing one of the seven deadly sins."

"We have someone in common—for you, a parishioner and for me a resident—who has large sums of money at her disposal. If she were approached in the right way . . ."

"Beatrice Wellington? Why, of course," Reverend Monroe said excitedly, pacing back and forth across the porch. "How can we get her to part with that much of her money?"

"We need to rephrase that to say, 'How can *you* get her to part with that much of her money,'" Steve said. "As administrator of the Roost, I can't exactly beg for money from one of my own residents. But *you* can," he added.

"I'm a board member of the Roost."

"Doesn't matter, you were her pastor first, and you'll be asking her as a pastor, not as a board member."

"If Agnes wasn't involved, I wouldn't even think of approaching Beatrice with a request like this," Reverend Monroe said. "But these are special circumstances. We're talking about my sanity and well-being now. I'll call her tomorrow. Actually, I'll do better than that. I'll take her to church with us on Sunday."

"God loves a cheerful giver," Reverend Monroe boomed from his pulpit. He glanced at Beatrice, pleased to note that she was paying close attention from the front pew where he had personally seated her. Beatrice had been smiling throughout the entire service, pleased with the attention the preacher had unexpectedly lavished upon her.

"Give with a cheerful heart and your rewards in Heaven will be great. God will smile upon you and your good deeds," he continued. Then, in a more somber tone, he addressed the congregation of the First Presbyterian Church of Stalvey. "Tell me, what good is money if you can't bring about some good with it?"

"Amen," replied someone from behind Beatrice. She didn't turn around to look and see who it was, but would have been surprised to know it was Steve Tallison who spoke out, especially since she knew that he was Baptist. Steve and his wife were there both for support and out of plain curiosity. They sat a couple of rows directly behind Beatrice.

"If you can't part with your money in order to help someone or something who dearly needs it, then you don't need money to begin with, right, brothers and sisters?" Reverend Monroe boomed out again, challenging his flock. More people mumbled their support, encouraging the preacher's emotion-driven sermon.

"Amen."

"Hallelujah."

"Right on, Brother Monroe," Beatrice said happily, caught up in the spiritual tidal wave. Her thin, reedy voice echoed throughout the tiny church. From behind Beatrice, Steve caught the Reverend's eye and exchanged pleased glances with him. Steve later watched in amazement as Beatrice dumped the entire contents of her purse in the offering plate as it was passed by her.

"You know, Beatrice," Reverend Monroe said later to Beatrice at the country club where he'd taken her out to lunch, "I've always considered you one of my most devout members of the congregation. It always pleases me to see you in church on Sundays."

"Well, thank you, Reverend Monroe," Beatrice beamed back at him. "You're definitely my favorite minister, but then again, the only ministers I've ever heard are you and of course your late father. I was quite fond of your father, you know. He performed my wedding service when you were just a little tyke."

"I know that, and he used to tell me that yours was the most beautiful service he ever performed," Reverend Monroe said, mentally ducking lightning bolts from Heaven. He hoped his father wasn't paying close attention to earthly goings-on right at this moment or else he'd be sorely disappointed in his son. He turned the topic of conversation to avoid any more trouble. "Beatrice, may I ask you how you like living at Milly's Merry Roost?"

"Well, at first I wasn't any too pleased with Tipper or his idea that I should live there. I found the place offensive and oppressive for the longest time and made sure everyone knew how unhappy I was there."

"Oh, then never mind . . ." the Reverend said in disappointment.

"Wait a minute, I'm not through," Beatrice said quickly. "Now, I'm happy there. The people and staff there are delightful and I have even made a couple of friends, which, as you know, isn't that easy a task for me. Yes, I rather enjoy it there."

The Reverend breathed a sigh of relief. "So you'd be sad if you had to leave?"

Beatrice looked at him in shock. "Leave? Why on earth would I have to leave the Roost?"

"Because it's run out of money and can't operate any longer." "Oh, my," Beatrice said. "Oh, my. Where will I go now?" "You may not have to go anywhere."

"What do you mean?"

"I mean, if a certain wealthy benefactor found it in her heart to donate the money necessary to keep the Roost alive, then it could remain in operation," Reverend Monroe suggested.

"Why of course!" Beatrice exclaimed, much to the Reverend's relief. "Why didn't I think of that?" she said. "But where could we find someone like that?"

"Beatrice, I'm talking about you," he said firmly.

"Oh, my, yes, I suppose you are," she said excitedly. "I have lots of money and I could save the nursing home," she said, as though she'd just thought of the idea herself.

"That's a wonderful idea, Beatrice," Reverend Monroe exclaimed. "What a generous and kind woman you are."

Beatrice took her checkbook out of her clutch and pressed it open on the table. "How much money do you need?"

The Reverend cleared his throat. "A million or so dollars," he said. He watched dejectedly as Beatrice snapped her checkbook closed.

"I will notify my accountant in the morning that I want to make a donation of a million dollars to the Roost. Will that help?"

"Yes, absolutely," the Reverend said, overcome with gratitude. "Beatrice, with this kind of ultimate offering you're making, you can consider yourself paid up for the rest of your life. Oh, the Board of Directors meets in the morning at ten o'clock. Do you suppose it could be arranged by then?"

"I don't see why not," Beatrice answered.

"I think, in light of the situation, you should be the guest of honor at the board meeting tomorrow," the Reverend said. "Would you please come?"

"I'd be delighted."

Steve Tallison woke up early the next morning, excited to see the expressions on the surly bunch of board members when he told them they had a financial crisis, but that it had worked itself out without them having to lift a finger. Then, the remodeling could begin and everything would go back to the way it was before all these fire codes and air conditioning problems had come to light.

"Beatrice, how wonderful of you to do this!" Steve said in greeting. He'd been waiting anxiously for Beatrice and Reverend Monroe to arrive for the past half hour. It was almost ten o'clock and the other members of the board were already seated inside.

"I'm sorry we're late, but I was trying to get in touch with my accountant this morning," Beatrice said. "He seems to be occupied, so I had to just leave a message with his secretary."

"So everything is still okay?" Steve asked anxiously.

"Of course," Beatrice said, ruffling with self-importance, "I don't need his permission to spend my own money, I simply need his advice on the best way to proceed."

"Shall we go inside?" Steve said, beaming broadly at Reverend Monroe and Beatrice. He took Beatrice's elbow and guided her toward the door.

"Beatrice! Wait a minute, please," the receptionist for the Roost said, rushing to Beatrice's side. "You've got a telephone call—he said it was extremely urgent and I should contact you immediately. He said to tell you it's your accountant."

"Wonderful," Beatrice said. "I'll just be a moment while I wrap up this little matter with my accountant." She followed the receptionist to a telephone in the adjacent office. Fifteen minutes later she returned to the boardroom, visibly shaken. Steve and Reverend Monroe had already taken their seats at the table along with the other five board members.

"For those of you who have never met this wonderful, magnanimous woman, this is Beatrice Wellington," Steve said, helping Beatrice into her chair.

"Steve, I . . ." she said, then seemed to lose her voice.

"What is it, Beatrice?" Steve asked.

"I've got some news . . ." she started to say when Steve cut her off.

"Not now, Beatrice, I want to save that until later, okay? Then we'll tell everyone your wonderful news."

"What in tarnation is so important that we have to meet with only a week's notice?" Turk Prichard asked in irritation. He was a local hog farmer who didn't like to be separated too long from his brood. "Time is money—can we make this quick?" Prichard had been on the Board for the past five years and had griped during every meeting they'd had since then. All Board members were voluntary, since the Roost itself was a non-profit organization, but none of them seemed to appreciate or recognize the community status they were assured would accompany the positions.

"No," Steve said in apology. "I'm sorry to have to drag everyone out today, but we've got some serious problems. The Roost is in serious financial trouble."

"It's never been in great shape to begin with," Gillooly said, who ran Gillooly and Sons Funeral Home. Rumor had it he was trying to bribe someone to take his place on the Roost's board. Although none of the members were legally bound to stay on the board, the county pressure was great for community leaders to hold those seats.

"It's worse now. We need to come up with roughly one million dollars in order to stay in operation," Steve said as calmly as possible. The table got deathly quiet as each Board member stopped complaining long enough to stare open-mouthed at Tallison. He briefly described the conversations that he'd had with Morris and Judd, and then passed around quotes from local construction and air conditioning companies.

"You'll find all the figures on these sheets," Steve said.

"You must be crazy if you think we're going to be able to come up with one million dollars," Dooley, the town barber, said.

"It's been taken care of," Steve said quietly. All the board members turned to look at him in amazement.

"Taken care of?" Dooley said.

"Beatrice Wellington has reached deep into her heart—and pockets—to provide us with the funds to stay in operation," Steve said grandly. Everyone turned to look at Beatrice, obviously uncomfortable in all the attention.

"That certainly was generous," Dooley said in surprise. "The world needs more people like you."

"Yes, she's quite literally a God-send," Reverend Monroe added with pride.

Beatrice's face had lost all color and her expression was one of extreme distress. "I don't have any money," she blurted out in a burst of tears. "My accountant just told me that my grandson has frittered it all away."

"All of it?" Steve asked in dismay.

"I've enough to live comfortably the rest of my days," Beatrice said, sniffling. "But not enough to help out the nursing home. I'm sorry." Steve, although he felt as though someone had just stepped on his stomach, rushed to her side while the rest of the board members sat in stunned silence.

"It's all right, Beatrice. At least you tried and were willing to help the Roost out of its dilemma—that's more than anybody else did. Are you okay? That's quite a shock to find out."

"I'm fine, but I think I'll leave now, if you don't mind," she said, dabbing at her eyes with a piece of twisted tissue paper.

"I'll go with her," Reverend Monroe said. "She doesn't need to be alone right now, and besides, I can't bear to see the rest of this meeting—I think I know what's going to happen." He led the sobbing Beatrice out of the meeting room.

"What's in the building fund right now?"

"Two hundred and forty nine dollars," Steve said.

"That's not even enough money to paint the place," Dooley said, disgusted. "The bank's not going to loan us that much money, and no one in their right mind would co-sign for this place. It's not a good bet."

"Dooley's got a point," Gillooly said. "The place is already fifty years old and it makes barely enough to keep operational, much less have any left over for major repairs or renovations. And, this area is not as popular as it used to be years ago. Little by little the old folks are dying off—which helps our business—but the young folks are moving to bigger places like Atlanta and Athens. Nope, the heyday of Stalvey is coming to a close," he said with a shake of his head. "Soon even my job isn't going to be secure anymore."

Turk Prichard slapped the dining room table with the palm of his hand. "I vote we close the place down. No other choice, the way I see it."

"I hate to, but I agree," Gillooly said and was joined by Dooley. The other two members of the Board nodded their heads solemnly. The only member holding out was Reverend Monroe, plagued by visions of his mother-in-law in the house. He finally nodded as well.

Steves face turned white. "Wait a minute, do you all realize what you're saying?"

"Yes, were saying it's in the best interest of the Roost to close down," Dooley said. "I mean, it's fairly simple. We don't have any money and the only person who could have loaned us money is now out of money, so we can either shut down or get closed down by the fire marshal or the sheriff once residents start dying of heat stroke."

"What about the residents?" Steve asked. "Some of these people have lived in Stalvey their entire lives. What do we do with them? Farm them out to other nursing homes across the state?"

"There's no better solution," Gillooly said gently. "Our hands are tied on this one. I would love nothing better than to be a board member of a financially successful nursing home, but as facts stand, the Roost is going down quickly. I'm ready to jump ship before I get sucked under, too." He stood up and looked around the table. "So, if were agreed . . ."

"Wait a minute," Steve said in a panic, "we are not through yet. Do any of you have an idea about what goes on around here? How much good we do here at the Roost?" he demanded of the table. Turk reached over and patted Steve on the back.

"Now, Steve, if you're worried about finding another job, I'm sure you won't have any trouble at all . . ."

"That's not what I'm worried about," Steve said, meaning it. "There are so many residents who have benefitted by coming here. Look at Johnnie. When she first got here, she was suicidal and depressed. Now she's happy and relatively well-adjusted." He thought it best not to mention the roommate dilemma of weeks ago, or the fact that Johnnie was still tormenting the Garden Club. "Or what about George? He was sent here from the federal penitentiary after serving about twenty-five years. He's had a productive life here, which goes to show you that criminals can be rehabilitated." Steve realized he was talking quickly now, so none of the board members would have a chance to interrupt his flow. "Then there's Ida, who was sent here by the state because she doesn't have any family. She was having trouble with severe edema but now heads up the welcoming committee here at the Roost. And then there's Gladys, who is helping a local writer compile historical accounts of the area for a book . . . there's just so much going on around here. Not to mention the friendships and relationships that might possibly be destroyed in the transition from our nursing home to others," Steve finished, looking around to see if he'd hit home with any of the Board members. They all stared at him impassively, unmoved by his emotional speech.

"I appreciate your genuine concern," Prichard said, "but I think the only recourse is to shut down. Or wait until the Fire Marshall closes us down or until the air conditioner goes completely out," Prichard said. "This summer's supposed to be a real scorcher."

"So if we're in agreement . . ." Gillooly said. The motion passed swiftly, without a hitch.

Steve cradled his face in his hands.

The next move Steve had to make was to notify everyone about the nursing home's closing before they heard it elsewhere. The Board members wouldn't waste any time spreading the word. Steve walked to the receptionist's desk in the lobby and pressed the loud-speaker button. "Would all available staff members, residents and their visitors please report to the dining room in half an hour for a group meeting please? See me if there's a problem with staffing during the meeting or if residents need special assistance."

All across the Roost, residents and staff members alike looked at each other in confusion for some type of explanation. This sort of meeting had never occurred before, with residents and staff together. They all began working their way to the dining room.

"What's going on, Steve?" Patti asked as she walked into the dining room and joined the others.

"I'll tell you all at once," he said. He looked at the people gathered in the dining room—a mixture of staff, residents and their friends. Bubba Wilkes was there; he'd been watching soap operas with his pals in the recreation room when the announcement was made over the loudspeaker. Suzy and two other Junior Leaguers were present. They'd been interviewing several residents about the introduction of automobiles to Stalvey years ago.

They all watched as Steve stepped up heavily to the microphone and said, "Please, will everyone be seated?" Once the sound of scraping chairs and conversation had subsided, he began: "I've got some rather unpleasant news and know no other way than to just tell you all and go from there. The Roost is going to have to close down." He waited for the expected outburst. There was none. Instead, a deep silence pervaded as though everyone was having trouble digesting his words. Steve stumbled ahead. "Um, we've got some insurmountable financial problems. I've tried all my resources and just can't find a way to save the Roost. I'm sorry," he added as an apology.

Bubba watched sadly as the meaning of Steve's words sunk into the staff and residents. Some looked at each other, open mouthed while others began whispering to each other frantically. He turned away, not wanting to be a voyeur of such a painful moment.

"The Roost can't close," George called out from the back. "How much money do you need?"

"About a million dollars, George," Steve said with a weak smile. "You can't park enough cars in your lifetime to raise that kind of money."

"Where will we all go?" Gladys asked worriedly. "Will it be to the same place?"

"Michelle Peterson will be helping out in terms of placement," Steve said, glancing at Michelle. She looked as stunned as the rest of them. Perhaps he should have told her before he broke the news to everyone else. "It's very unlikely that everyone will go to the same nursing home. We'll probably have to spread you all out around the area, wherever there are vacancies. As for the staff, I'll be more than happy to give glowing recommendations for whatever job you seek in the future."

Suzy clutched Gladys' hand as they heard the news. Gladys was having difficulty speaking, her throat had a lump and her eyes were filling with tears. "What if George and I can't go to the same place?" she said, anguished over the thought. "What if we're separated?" Suzy tried to console her, at the same time wondering if there was anything anyone could do to help save the Roost.

"How long before the Roost closes?" someone called out from the back.

"Until the Fire Marshall kicks us out or the air conditioning breaks," Steve answered. "Whichever comes first." He gave a brief description of the problems brought to his attention by Morris and Judd.

"How much money could we get and still be able to stay open?" George asked.

Steve rubbed his chin. "I don't know, that's a good question. Bubba, do you know the answer to that?"

"I'll have to check, but I suppose if you can scrounge up half of it, we'll help you get the rest," he said.

"Then we need about six hundred thousand dollars," Steve said. The room was quiet. Everyone was trying to digest all the zeroes in the amount of money they needed. Most had never seen that kind of money before and the prospect of having to raise it seemed insurmountable.

"So were just going to give up?" George challenged those gathered in the dining hall. No one responded.

CHAPTER 14

"**W**ANT to buy a square?" George asked Patti when she came into the recreation room. Instead of the usual checkerboard, George had set up a money box and a cardboard cutout of a football field with squares placed on various areas of the field.

"What's it for?" she asked. Lately anyone and everyone at the Roost had their own money-making scheme. Woe to the visitors and staff alike who had to walk through the building, constantly accosted by money-grubbing old people.

"Don't ask," Jack called out from across the room.

"It's a cow plop," George said.

"What's a cow plop?" Patti asked.

"Don't ask," Jack yelled.

"Why not?" Patti said, totally confused, turning back and forth between George and Jack.

"This cardboard represents the local high school football field," George said, indicating the cardboard football field. "For five dollars you can buy any one of these squares on the field. Once I sell all these squares we're going to let a cow loose on the football field. Whichever square the cow plops on is the winner."

Patti stared at him open mouthed. "You have got to be kidding."

"Nope, and it's all biodegradable," George said, smiling at her. "You better buy one now before they all get gone."

"I'll take my chances," Patti said, walking away.

"For a dollar I'll guess your weight," Gladys called out from a recliner in the television area. Patti laughed.

"No, thanks, Gladys. I've put on a few pounds lately and I would rather you not announce that fact to everyone here." "Then for five dollars I won't guess your weight," Gladys said, an evil smile playing about her lips.

Patti threw her hands up in the air as she left the recreation room. "You people are too much. There's such a thing as carrying something a little too far and I think you've all reached and surpassed that boundary." She bumped into Steve Tallison on her way out the door and grabbed him by the shoulders. "Don't go in there," she warned, "they've all turned into mercenaries." Steve laughed as he passed by her.

The past couple of weeks had been wearing on everyone. Bubba Wilkes had somehow sparked the community into coming to the Roost's aid. Various groups, like the Junior League and the Kiwanis, were hosting fundraisers all across the county. He wasn't sure how much money the community had raised so far, but the circus tricks developed by the residents had failed to do anything but scare off visitors. Every visitor was accosted by at least six residents who desperately wanted their money. In addition to George and Gladys' "get rich quick" schemes, Johnnie had dressed as a homeless woman and spent an afternoon at an intersection in town before Steve caught her. She had messed up her hair, wore a baggy dress and a sign that read "Will Not Work for Food. Please Give Money." By the time Steve caught up with her, she'd raised nearly seventy dollars. Though tempted, his conscience wouldn't allow him to leave her there for the rest of the day; however, she'd been the biggest money maker so far.

Tommy and his friends had organized a car wash out in the parking lot of the Roost which didn't last very long because the cars would get washed and then become caked in muddy silt by the time they reached the end of the dirt driveway. George sold as many Cow Plop tickets as people he had offended, which was around twenty. Niles had Beatrice's permission to organize an evening limousine service where he would drive people to restaurants, parties, or wherever they wanted to go for a hefty fee. Gladys had successfully not guessed the weight of several hefty visitors in the past week and Michelle Peterson had organized a couple of all night Bingo games in which the community was invited to participate. Everyone was certainly trying, but the cash kitty was still a long way from half a million dollars. He didn't see the money-raising plan as a viable alternative and had begun sending resumes to a variety of places in the area.

"Not even close," Bubba said as he completed tallying the money in the Save the Roost fund. While individuals and groups around the county had tried their best at fundraising, the total amount—while admirable for any normal fundraising event—was even less than a drop in the bucket of the nursing home's debts.

"It was a valiant effort," Travis told Bubba consolingly as they sat in Bubba's office. "You shouldn't feel bad about it at all." Travis didn't want to be the negative one of the group, but he'd spent the past couple of weeks watching his wife and his best friend knock themselves out over a rundown nursing home. "Let the place die in peace."

"You just don't understand," Bubba said. "You should go visit out there with your wife and mother-in-law sometime. I hope the place is around for a long time because if I ever have to go to one . . . I want it to be the Roost." He liked Travis, but sometimes his attitude was poor. "I wish I could loan them the money."

Travis laughed. "You do and this bank will be the next building to close down. The community will be holding benefits to keep us open."

"Don't flatter yourself," Bubba said, "I don't think we rank as high as the nursing home in terms of community favor." He looked thoughtful for a moment. "I can't even find anyone who would co-sign for them to get a loan."

"Who's got that much money in the bank to insure the Roost makes good on their payments?" Travis asked. "No one in Stalvey, that's for sure."

"I know," Bubba said despondently. Although it suddenly came to him—an article he'd read in the newspaper not too long ago. It was worth a try. "Gimme some room," he said, picking up the telephone.

"What have you got up your sleeve, boss?" Travis asked but Bubba didn't respond. That was his cue to leave, he thought as he tiptoed out of the office. He hated seeing his friend all wrapped up this situation—it was like using a teaspoon to bail out a sinking yacht.

Michelle Peterson was at her wits' end and ready to pull all the hair out of her head. Since Steve's announcement she'd been bombarded with questions and requests regarding future placement. She didn't blame them; she'd be concerned as to where she would end up if she were in their shoes. Hank and Ethyl had been the first to approach her.

"Is there any way to guarantee that we'll be able to go together?" Ethyl asked worriedly.

"I can't guarantee anything," Michelle said, "because it's going to be hard enough to find seventy four vacancies at nursing homes in Georgia—do you realize how few nursing homes there are in relation to how many people want to get in them?"

Hank wasn't interested in Michelle's trivia. "Can we go together?"

"The only way you can make sure of that is for the two of you to get married. The state won't separate a married couple, but they'll bust up anyone else if they have to. We're not going to have the luxury of being able to pick and choose."

Ethyl eyed Hank warily. "Hank doesn't want to get married," she said.

"I'll do it if it means we'll be able to stay together," Hank said grumpily.

"What a romantic you are," Michelle told Hank. "You should get married because you love Ethyl, not for any other reason."

"Well, if it'll make her happy I'll go along with it," Hank said.

"Was that a proposal?" Ethyl asked Michelle. She was confused.

"I think so, Ethyl. Your suitor is quite the eloquent one," Michelle said.

Ethyl turned to look at Hank. "If that was a proposal, then I accept," she said.

"Okay, then it was a proposal," Hank responded.

Jack was the next to visit Michelle.

"Do you think I'll be able to find a place that'll take Blue, too?" he asked. Jack scratched the old dog's ears fondly as Blue sat between his legs.

"It's highly unlikely," Michelle said truthfully. "You had a very unusual situation here, you know."

"I know." Jack went away unhappy.

Michelle assured each resident that she would do her absolute best to keep roommates, boyfriends and girlfriends, and men and their dogs together. The burden was overwhelming. There were waiting lists all over the state of people waiting to get into nursing homes. How could she be expected to find placement for seventy-four people? Some families would be able to take their loved ones into their homes for a time, but most were at the Roost because they needed to be there. It was on Michelle's shoulders to worry about what would happen to each resident after the Roost was closed down.

As the end of the thirty days neared, subtle changes were taking place at the Roost. Little by little, personal belongings were being packed away, relationships were cooling down as the reality of separation set in, and the uncertainty of the moving date had everyone sitting on pins and needles.

Bubba's call came on Friday, a full week before the end of the thirty days. His great idea on how to save the Roost had only met with brick walls at every turn. He, too, was throwing in the towel.

"We want to throw a party for everyone out at the Roost," he told Steve.

"A party? I don't think anyone around here is in the mood for a party," Steve said. He sure wasn't in the mood for festivities, especially since he hadn't been able to find a job anywhere. The mortgage on his house wasn't cheap and what was he going to tell his children? Sorry, kids, but you'll have to move back home and I'll send you back to college whenever we can afford to send you again. "Don't you think a party's in poor taste?"

"I know, it sounds like it but hear me out. These folks here have been busting their collective butt to raise money to keep the Roost open. They've only scratched the surface of the debt, but it's not for lack of trying. Instead of making everyone feel useless for not being able to save the nursing home, why don't we have a big party, announce how much money everyone did raise and just have a big celebration? I think it would help both the community and the residents come to terms with the whole idea. We can come up with a creative idea as to what we're going to do with all the money that was raised."

Steve thought about it for a moment. "You know, that's really not a bad idea. Who knows? A party might help the wound heal faster. Sure, let's have a party and blow it out. We don't have to worry about the landlord kicking us out because we've got to go anyway." They agreed to hold the party Wednesday night, two days before the first possible day of eviction.

Folks started drifting into the nursing home late Wednesday afternoon, dressed to the nines. Many brought cameras and took pictures for posterity, posing beside the front yard sign that read—ironically— "Milly's Merry Roost, Where Everyone is Welcome and the Doors are Always Open." Now the doors would be closed indefinitely until the building was scrapped or until it was purchased by someone else. The likelihood of selling the old place was about as likely as seeing Hailey's comet twice during the same year. If it was sold cheap enough, some local farmer might buy the land and use the building to store hay bales out of the weather.

"How would they like it if we all went to their house and had our pictures taken on their fronts steps?" George said irritably.

"Now, George, it's sort of a historic occasion," Gladys said soothingly. They still didn't know if they were going to be able to go to the same place once the Roost closed, which had driven a slight wedge between them. The uncertainty was maddening. "People just want to be able to remember the place later on." "Then they can do what I do and remember it in their head; I don't need a silly picture of a sign to remind me of this place. I don't remember needing to take a photo of the penitentiary when they let me out after thirty years."

"That's a bit different," Gladys said.

"Depends on how you look at it," George snapped back. "I just don't like all these folks traipsing around like tourists." "Then act like a native and charge them five bucks if they want to have their picture taken with you," Gladys retorted.

"Or I could tear up pieces of the linoleum floor and sell them for two bucks a piece."

"Johnnie's already beaten you to it," Gladys said with a heavy sigh. "There's no need for you to take your anger out on me, George Anderson."

"You're right," George said. "I'm sorry. I just hate not knowing where I might be next week or next month. It reminds me of when they'd transfer us from prison to prison when they thought we were getting too comfortable in the one we were in. I'd get there, settle in and make some friends and then they'd send me to another place where I didn't know anyone." He shook his head suddenly and stared into her eyes. "No, Gladys, what I'm really trying to say is that I really care about you and I don't want to spend the rest of my miserable days without you."

Gladys leaned forward and kissed him gently on the lips. "I do believe that's the sweetest thing you've ever said to me, George. I promise I won't let on to anyone what a softie you really are."

"Thanks," he said, grinning. "If it got back to the boys in the pokey, I'd be ruined forever."

The dining room was so well-decorated that many of the residents had to look twice to make sure they were in the same old dining room where they ate three meals a day every day. Hay bales were stacked in one corner of the room, complete with a pitchfork and scarecrow. A makeshift split rail fence surrounded the bales and a life-size horse was tethered to one of the fence posts. Red, white and blue streamers seemed to bounce along the ceiling from one end to the other and swirled their way down the support poles in the middle of the room. One ton of saw dust had been spread across the floor for square dancing and clogging, the area's two favorite pastimes and the refreshment tables were lined along one side of the dining room, balanced on each end by a big tub of apple cider.

Ida, who had since been given the title of Special Events Greeter, was at the front door of the dining room, welcoming everyone inside. Her feet had healed quickly from the edema once she agreed to stay off of her feet for a couple of weeks and now she was able to get around much better.

"Howdy, Pardners," she said as people walked by. "Welcome to the Ranch."

"Isn't this magical?" Beatrice asked as she and Niles and Mary Grace Tanner made their way into the dining room. The invitations encouraged everyone to dress with a country/western theme in mind. Beatrice wore a cowgirl hat decorated with an assortment of rhinestone studs while Niles wore cowboy chaps over his dress trousers. Mary Grace sported a blue flowered prairie dress and hung tight to Niles' arm. They'd been dating steadily for the past several weeks.

"Yes, indeed it is, Beatrice," Niles said with a smile. He squeezed Mary Grace's hand affectionately.

Gladys wore a red gingham dress, one of the dresses she used to wear to her square dance classes, and George wore the same old blue jeans he always wore, but with a big silver belt buckle and a vest. "Isn't this wonderful?" she asked George.

"No, and I feel stupid," he replied. "Yee hah, yippee-kiy-ay—cow daddy and all that stuff."

"Be-have," Gladys instructed. "If you think we look silly, take a gander at Hank and Ethyl." George hooted. They were dressed—collectively—as a horse. Although they were in complete costume, it was easy to tell who they were by their shoes—Ethyl always wore white skipper shoes with yarn tassels and Hank had on the same blue bedroom slippers he wore every day. The blue slippers were in back while the skipper shoes assumed the head role of the beast.

"Thank you, Gladys, for not making a horse's ass out of me," George said with a laugh. His sour humor was beginning to lift.

"Hey, Annie Oakley, you got a permit for those guns?" Officer Radburn asked Johnnie as he approached her with his hands in the air. He was dressed appropriately as a sheriff from the old west, complete with a five star silver badge bearing the name SHERIFF He was accompanied by the two paramedics, both of whom were dressed as Indians.

"These are all the permit I'll be needing," Johnnie said, attempting to twirl the guns around the joints of her arthritis gnarled fingers.

"Johnnie, I don't know what we're going to do around here anymore what with you leaving," one of the paramedics said. "You kept us jumping all the time."

"I suppose the county'll just have to let one of you go," Johnnie quipped.

"I guess I'll just have to go back to part time," Officer Radburn said with a laugh. "The town won't be any fun anymore, that's for sure. You old folks sure are imaginative when it comes to breaking the law."

"You be respectful when you're talking to your elders," Johnnie said. "Especially when the elder in question is a pistol—packing mama like myself."

"Good point," Radburn said, continuing to mill about the dining room.

"What will you do now that the Roost is closing?" Gladys asked Ruth as they stood beside one of the tubs of apple cider and watched the members of the Junior League put on a country/western dance performance. They were quite good, with the entire club dressed in matching frilly blue and red gingham dresses, tiny white cowboy hats and white shoes.

"Oh, I'll just continue staying at Suzy's," Ruth said, sipping her apple juice from a tin coffee cup—another country/western prop. "The only reason I was going to move here was because you all seem to have so much fun and get along so well. Sometimes I get so lonely at Suzy's house. I need some folks my own age to amuse me."

"I know. It's sort of like having another family," Gladys agreed. "I wouldn't trade any of them for the world, but I guess I'll have to now. My own family has offered for me to come back home and live, but I just don't want to. I love my grandchildren dearly, but I'd rather not live with them, the little monsters. And, I hate to say it, but my daughter can be quite a pain herself."

"It's funny because most people think that old people live in a nursing home because their family doesn't want them anymore. They don't sec that many of you would rather not live at home," Ruth said with a laugh.

"I know I've learned a lot from all of you. Tell me, though, what's going to happen to patients like Camilla now? I mean, she's been in a coma for years. Will there be someone to look after her and make sure she gets into a nice home and settles in and everything?" Ruth asked with concern. "They obviously can't fend for themselves."

"Patti said they take particular care with those patients," Gladys answered. "I asked her that same question the other day. She said if anything, they'll get more preferential treatment than the rest of us for that very reason."

"Anybody need a doctor?" a voice boomed from the doorway. Everyone turned to see Dr. Bill Price, thinner than before, but looking healthy and tanned.

"Yeah, you know where we can find one?" George called out. Everyone crowded around Dr. Price to find out when he'd be back to work.

"You know, when I first had my heart attack, I thought it was a sign telling me to stop working, that it was time to rest," Dr. Price said. He glanced at everyone standing around him and noticed with satisfaction that his replacement, Dr. Rodgers, wasn't present. "The longer I stayed home, the more I realized how much I missed everyone here and knew I couldn't stay away. So, if you'll have me back," he said, sneaking a glance at Patti and Steve, "I'd love to be your doctor again—for at least as long as the Roost stays open."

"We'd love to have you back," Steve said, "for as long as were open."

"Back by popular demand," Patti said with a smile. "Even I'm glad to see you if you can believe that. But there's one problem with this picture," she said, staring at him closely.

"What?" Dr. Price asked.

"You're not dressed appropriately," she said, taking off her own over-sized cowboy hat and placing it on his head. "There, now you're an authentic cowpoke."

"Excuse me, folks, but we're ready to start the program," Bubba Wilkes said. He was dressed in blue jeans, dusty cowboy boots, a western shirt and bolo tie and looked every bit the part of a cowboy.

"Isn't he dashing?" Gladys whispered to the other women who stood near her. They all agreed enthusiastically.

"The reason we're all here tonight is to celebrate Milly's Merry Roost," he told the crowd that had gathered in front of his podium. "Now I know the Roost has to close, but we can still celebrate the occasion that brought us all together. In the past month I've witnessed a new life in Stalvey. People I haven't seen budge in years were out pounding the pavement trying to raise money to save this wonderful nursing home. From what Steve Tallison says," he said, indicating Steve in the comer of the room, "the residents even busted their tails raising money. Unfortunately, it wasn't enough, but that's not what counts tonight. What counts is that fact that everyone tried their best. I'm going to give everyone the opportunity to tell how much money they raised and at the end, we'll tally it all up and take a vote as to where the money should go. Is that all right? Without any real objections, let's get started."

"The street dance and barbecue sponsored by the fire, rescue and police departments was a great success. How much did you raise, boys?" Bubba asked.

"Seven thousand dollars," Officer Radburn called out. There was a great "whoop" from the paramedics followed by deafening applause and cheers.

"Great work," Bubba called out happily. The darkness of the mood began lifting as everyone got into the spirit of the evening.

"Law students!" Bubba called out. "Where are you?" Four guys dressed in wrangler gear stepped forward. "Now it says here," Bubba said, reading from an index card, "that you guys sponsored a Law Week where you wrote wills and gave legal advice for a nominal fee, of course," he added with a smile. "How much did you raise?"

"Fifteen hundred dollars," they all called out, raising their hats high. The crowd erupted into cheers. Bubba continued with the system, calling out the names of individuals and clubs gathered in the dining room. They, in turn, responded with the amount of money raised.

The Junior League had turned over the most amount of money so far, Bubba noted. Not only had they unanimously decided to turn over all the profits of the cook book to the Roost, the stories written by Suzy were such a success that the book was picked up by a small Atlanta publisher and marketed throughout the south. The result, including sales and the initial purchase of the book, totaled nearly twenty thousand dollars. The Kiwanis sponsored a turkey shoot and brought in every hunter in a hundred mile radius—a considerable amount considering the sparse population of the area. That particular venture brought in a couple of thousand dollars.

"Now for the Roosters," Bubba said, calling the residents by their nickname. "I think everybody has heard about the great Cow Plop idea of George's." A loud murmuring went up throughout the crowd. "How much money did you make, George?" Bubba asked.

George stepped forward, looking sheepish. "None."

"None?" Bubba said, surprised. "Last I heard you'd sold about twenty squares."

"I had to give all the money back," George said sourly. "The cow was constipated." Everyone started laughing uproariously. George stepped back into the crowd, his face red with embarrassment.

At the end of the roll call, Bubba asked the town accountant for the grand total of all the fundraising efforts by community members and residents alike.

"Thirty-two thousand, four hundred twelve dollars and thirteen cents," the rotund accountant called out. He'd been adding the amounts on his calculator as they were called out. The applause was more sparse this time.

"Not anywhere close," Jack said sadly, pulling Blue close beside him. Blue wore a red bandanna for the occasion.

"Only time 'close' matters is with hand grenades and horse shoes," George said with a nod.

"Or cow plops," Jack said, needling his friend.

"Everyone should be proud of themselves for raising this much money," Bubba said encouragingly. "Now we need to decide what we're going to do with the money we've got here. It's quite a substantial amount."

"Put it toward Tommy's medical school," George suggested. Tommy stared at his old friend in surprise.

"No, now you guys can't give me all that money . . ." Tommy said, embarrassed by everyone's attention on him.

"I think that's a great idea," Patti called out. "It won't cover the whole thing, but at least it's a start."

"I second the motion," Steve said, squeezing his wife's hand. Despite the sadness of the occasion, it had turned into a "feel good" kind of evening.

"Any objections?" Bubba asked the crowd. No one spoke out. "Then it's settled. The money will be put into an account—at my bank—to be used for Tommy's medical school bills."

"Make us proud, Tommy," Dr. Price said as he slapped him on the back.

"I'll never be as good a doctor as you are, Dr. Price," Tommy said.

"I know that, Tommy, but try anyway," Dr. Price said with a grin. Tommy was choked with emotion. No one had ever given him anything in his life before, much less thirty thousand dollars.

"I don't know what to say," he floundered awkwardly.

"Just do your best, son," George said kindly. "That's all anyone can ask of you. And we'll beat your tail if you drop out."

Bubba stepped back up to the microphone. "I guess that's all for our program," he said looking at the residents spread out across the room. "We just wanted to let you all know how special you are and how much we'll miss you and the Roost." Tears sprang to Bubba's eyes as he tried to figure out a way to close the evening. It all seemed so sad, so final. As he looked around, searching for words, he saw a commotion at the front door of the dining room. Several men had walked in, all dressed in business suits.

"Wait a minute," one of the men called out as he threaded his way through the crowd. "Nobody leave, please." It was Richard Wysong, the representative from BestMart, followed by the store president and several reporters and photographers. Richard cleared the way for his boss and then allowed him passage to the podium. The photographers began pulling out their flashes and jockeying for position around the microphone. Wallace Taggert swaggered up to the microphone and turned it up to meet his mouth. The feedback squeal was loud and piercing, enough to cause even the hard-of-hearing residents to cover their ears.

"Sorry," Taggert said. He pulled a piece of paper out of the breast pocket of his suit jacket and began reading. "The reason we're here tonight is to bring renewed hope to the residents of the Roost and to the town of Stalvey. In this world of big business and booming corporations, we at BestMart want you all to know that you're not alone and you're certainly not . . ." he trailed off as he flipped over to the second index card . . ."forgotten." He looked up and attempted to fake a genuine smile. "In order to prove this to the rest of the country, BestMart has decided to use the Roost as an example of our humanitarianism. We're going to donate $250,000 to the Save the Roost Fund, and, in addition, were going to co-sign for the rest of the loan." He held out a check written for $250,000 and posed for the cameras that were aimed at his face. Steve Tallison was shocked. Someone behind him gave him a push forward to accept the check from Taggert.

"Could you step back just a minute until they're finished with this photo-op?" Taggert asked Steve. Steve stepped backed obligingly. When the flash bulbs finished popping, he stepped forward again and received the check.

"I don't know how to thank you," Steve told him.

"You don't have to," Taggert said. "You scratch my back, I scratch yours."

"I don't understand," Steve said. "What can we do for you?" "You've already done it—this is fantastic public relations for us," he said, smiling at the cameras again. He spoke in a low voice as the two of them posed together so that no one else would hear. "The welcome lady thing a few months ago put our chain of stores at the top. This'll send us through the roof."

"Does that mean the Roost stays open?" George called out skeptically.

"It sure does," Wysong replied. "It means you all get to stay and the Roost will be like new after all the renovations are complete."

A cheer went up throughout the dining room and out into the hallway where others were standing. Residents and community members hugged each other in celebration.

Bubba sidled up to Richard Wysong. "I thought you said the answer was no."

"It *was* no," Wysong said with a grin. He, unlike his boss, was truly enjoying the exuberance of the evening. Taggert was ready to leave now that the photo opportunity was over with. "I went about it the wrong way the first time," he explained. "I tried to tell Taggert what a charitable gesture it would be for BestMart to save the Roost, which he didn't care for in the least. Then, this morning I decided to switch gears and told him about how great it would be for public relations, especially since we're presently getting slammed for running small businesses out of communities. This time we're actually saving a small business instead of squelching it. I tried to call you and let you know of our decision, but you must have already left for the day."

"Hey, I don't care how it happened, I'm just glad you guys were able to help out. Maybe BestMart could start a new business—running nursing homes."

Taggert heard his comment. "You know, that's not a bad idea," he said thoughtfully.

"I guess the two of you don't have to rush into marriage after all," Michelle Peterson said to Hank and Ethyl. They had removed the horse costume, having gotten too hot in the crowded dining room, and stood side by side in front of an open window.

"No rush, but we're going through with it anyway," Hank said.

"You are?" Michelle asked in surprise.

"Yes, he just proposed to me," Ethyl said. She was thrilled that her marriage was no longer a shot-gun wedding. "We're going to be married as soon as the renovations are complete. He's decided he's sown enough wild oats after all."

"Now your daughter will be pleased that her mother's not 'living in sin,'" Michelle said. "And you can both live in the same room—what could be better?"

Hank looked at his watch. "I'll tell you what could be better. We've got just enough time to squeeze in a conjugal visit before midnight," he said. He took Ethyl by the hand and led her out of the dining room.

George stood off to the side with one arm around Gladys and the other around Tommy. The three were silent as they watched the others in the dining room congratulating each other and slapping each other on the back. They laughed as Niles awkwardly hugged Beatrice and vice versa; the two obviously had little experience in physical affection.

"Looks like we're going to be around for a while yet," George said.

"You sound surprised," Gladys said.

"Who, me? No, I was never worried."

"We really are a family, aren't we?" Tommy said slowly.

"Well, of course we are," Gladys said, placing her arm around his thin shoulder.

"No, I mean all of us," Tommy said.

"Of course we are."

About the Authors

Neil Shulman M.D., a.k.a. the "real" Doc Hollywood, is Associate Professor of Internal Medicine at Emory University School of Medicine. He's often referred to as a "Renaissance Man." He is the founder of the Global Health & Humanitarian Summit. He is the author of over 25 novels, children's tales and consumer health books. He was co-producer of the movie "Doc Hollywood," starring Michael J. Fox, which was based on one of his books. He has also written and/or produced for CBS, CNN and Disney. He was, at one time, a researcher in cardiovascular disease, receiving over 8 million dollars in grants and co-authoring over 50 scientific papers. Now he is traipsing around the world speaking on serious health issues and performing comedy for kids, general audiences and seniors. The spectrum of his performances range from events for Rosalyn Carter, the UN, Disney, programs for cancer patients, Alzheimer's patients and kids with disabilities, to fundraisers with Jane Fonda and Miss America. He has also served as Chairman of the Board for the real Patch Adam's non-profit organization, Gesundheit! Institute. For more information on Neil Shulman books and projects, see www. neilshulman.com.

P.K. Beville is Founder and CEO of the nonprofit Second Wind Dreams. She is also author and inventor of the Virtual Dementia Tour®, a sensitivity training program about dementia used throughout the world. She has been serving geriatrics since 1983. Her mission is to change the perception of aging and she continues to do this through the programs and services at Second Wind Dreams®. Since 1997, Second Wind Dreams has made thousands of dreams come true from the simple to the sublime.

Dreams of swinging in a porch swing again or being a police officer for a day renews the spirit for everyone involved. Be a part of the movement by going to www.secondwind.org. Watch real time dreams coming true on their facebook page. P.K. has been featured in media world-wide about both Second Wind Dreams and the Virtual Dementia Tour.

Robin Voss is a former newspaper editor, current guitar player and future successful writer.

Books By Neil Shulman

Fiction—adult

The Asolo Accords
The Corporate Kid
The Puberty Prevention Club
Spotless
The Nurse Curse
Your Body Doesn't Have Spare Parts
101 Ways to Know If You're a Medical Services Professional
101 Ways to Know if You're in Retail Real Estate
101 Ways to Know if You're a Medical Records Specialist
101 Ways to Know if You're a CNA
101 Ways to Know if You're a Nurse
Second Wind
The Backyard Tribe
Finally . . . I'm a Doctor
What? Dead . . . Again? (Doc Hollywood)

Fiction—children

Drive Safe, Stop Safe Posterbook (featuring Michael Jordan)
How to Have a Habit Posterbook
Don't Be Afraid of the Dentist
The Germ Patrol: All About Shots for Tots . . . and Big Kids, Too!
Under the Backyard Sky
What's in a Doctor's Bag?

Non-Fiction

The Real Truth About Aging
The Black Man's Guide to Good Health
Your Body's Red Light Warning Signals
Get Between the Covers: Leaving a Legacy by Writing a Book
Better Health Care for Less

High Blood Pressure
Let's Play Doctor
Understanding Growth Hormone
Your Body, Your Health
Healthy Transitions. A Women's Guide to Pre-menopause . . .
    Menopause and Beyond

www.NeilShulman.com
nshulma@bellsouth.net